LOVE MEANT SO MANY THINGS
IN A WORLD AFLAME WITH HATE

For Ilse, love meant her stolen moments of ecstasy with a man haunted by guilt toward his wife, and hunted by the dread Gestapo . . . for Susan, love meant her marriage to her childhood sweetheart being undermined by her affair with a refugee Frenchman . . . for Gina, love meant what men whispered to get you into bed, and what you tried not to feel for the one man you wanted to surrender to . . . for Diane, love was a plunge into unspeakable degradation that happened again and again and again . . .

For each of them, love meant so much in a world where it seemed to mean so little. . . .

THOSE WHO STAYED BEHIND

THOSE WHO STAYED BEHIND

Eleanor Hyde

A SIGNET BOOK
NEW AMERICAN LIBRARY
TIMES MIRROR
PUBLISHED BY
THE NEW AMERICAN LIBRARY
OF CANADA LIMITED

PUBLISHER'S NOTE

This novel is a work of fiction. Names, characters, places, and incidents are either the product of the author's imagination or are used fictitiously, and any resemblance to actual persons, living or dead, events, or locales is entirely coincidental.

NAL BOOKS ARE AVAILABLE AT QUANTITY DISCOUNTS WHEN USED TO PROMOTE PRODUCTS OR SERVICES. FOR INFORMATION PLEASE WRITE TO PREMIUM MARKETING DIVISION, THE NEW AMERICAN LIBRARY, INC., 1633 BROADWAY, NEW YORK, NEW YORK 10019.

FIRST PRINTING, NOVEMBER, 1981

2 3 4 5 6 7 8 9

SIGNET TRADEMARK REG. U.S. PAT. OFF. AND FOREIGN COUNTRIES
REGISTERED TRADEMARK—MARCA REGISTRADA
HECHO EN WINNIPEG, CANADA

SIGNET, SIGNET CLASSICS, MENTOR, PLUME, MERIDIAN and NAL BOOKS are published in Canada by The New American Library of Canada, Limited, Scarborough, Ontario

PRINTED IN CANADA

COVER PRINTED IN U.S.A.

To Art

I

1939

1. *Ilse*

Berlin

They lay on the narrow couch in her dressing room. He made love nervously. Sound carried easily in the immensity of the silent theater. It was after midnight, supposedly every one else had left, but there was no way of being sure. He admired her body as if it were the first time he'd seen her naked, whispering exclamations over wonders she hadn't thought wondrous, such as the long line of her back that he called something French.

Later she grabbed him around the neck as if she would strangle him, and screamed out. And later he cried. He always cried afterward. Not from the beautiful lovemaking, as she'd once thought, but from guilt. He only hurt her, he said. He hurt everyone around him. He was hurting her, his children, his wife. "She's out now. Better. Not living so much in her fantasy world, but if she hears about us, it could send her right back to the hospital," he said. "Oh, God, this is awful. Ilse, I love you. Tell me the situation isn't hopeless."

She didn't know if the situation was hopeless or just Hans.

She got dressed and feeling heartless at the sight of his tears, kissed him as she might a child.

"Wait until I see to things, and I'll take you home," he said. He'd sent the stage doorman on his way with a promise to lock up, half from compassion because the stage doorman's child was sick and half from desperation to be alone with Ilse.

"I'm walking home," she said. "I like to walk."

"That's dangerous. Young girls shouldn't be out on the street alone so late at night."

"Nothing's happened so far."

"So far you've been lucky. What if one of your admirers is still hanging around out there? What if he's the wrong sort? I won't have it."

"And I won't have you ordering me around. Onstage is one thing, offstage another."

"Ilse, *liebchen*, please. Is it ordering you around to see you home? At least let me put you in a cab."

"No," she said, and hurried down the hall and out the side

entrance. There was no one around. Hans's car, an old Minerva, sat high and mighty, dominating the empty street like an aged duchess. Then she saw the two Nazi soldiers patrolling the street, bootsteps muffled by snow. She went in the opposite direction, although it was out of her way. She knew she was being foolish. Ilse Lach, actress, daughter of Fritz Lachermann, baker, had nothing to fear. Her papers were in order, the soldiers weren't just friendly but admiring. Even so, she hated them and their bullying ways.

The snow floated down softly, blurring the night. High up in the theater it drifted into niches and draped eaves. Higher up yet was the moon, poised on a distant church spire. Ilse, too, floated along, snow frosting her eyelashes and the fur trim on her coat and hat. She hummed a sad tune about fickle love. She didn't know why she picked such a sad song. She was exhilarated by the moon, the snow, the applause that still rang in her ears. Perhaps she hummed a sad song because of the pointless lovemaking. The only way to break things off with Hans was for her to go to another theater. Anyway, she was tired of idiotic comedies. She wanted to be Hedvig in *The Wild Duck* or Nora in *A Doll's House*, but Hans said it was better to do light stuff than risk trouble with Dr. Goebbels and his watchdogs, who might pounce on something serious, saying it was either the wrong play or the wrong playwright. Sometimes she wished she'd gone to Hamburg, where her Aunt Greta was an actress, instead of going to Berlin and getting involved with Hans. But poor, sweet Aunt Greta was dead; no reason to go there now. All the big opportunities were in Berlin.

A car came speeding down the street, wheels spraying slush. She jumped back to avoid getting splashed, and glimpsed a sudden movement behind her, but when she turned, she saw only red taillights disappearing into the snowy night. She was sure she'd seen someone. It couldn't be the Nazi patrol; she'd lost them a long time ago. Anyway, why would they play hide and seek with her? She walked on, then turned abruptly. A dark figure ducked into a doorway. Was that Hans following her, out of a misguided regard for her safety? Or, more likely, jealousy? "Hans, is that you? Answer me. Don't scare me like that." Silence. Maybe his dire predictions made her imagine things, maybe it was some poor starving dog who'd been mistreated and didn't trust people.

Another car came creeping up from behind. This time she was sure it was Hans trailing her in his decrepit Minerva. Headlights shone on untrammeled snow and a window display of male mannequins in evening dress with a sign, "TUXEDOS FOR RENT." Then, suddenly, the car zoomed ahead. The driver's face was shadowed by a visored cap. She barely glimpsed the pale face in the backseat, but she recognized the car. The von Frisches's blue Mercedes. Although it wasn't a cold night, scarcely below freezing, she shivered. She'd been unable to tell if that pale face in back was Freddie's or Ursula's. They were twins and looked alike, with black curly hair and black eyes, except Ursula looked like the brother and Freddie the sister. She'd told Ursula quite clearly over a week ago she couldn't go to their party this evening. Nevertheless, tonight, right after the last curtain call, she'd returned to her dressing room to find their driver at the door saying he was there to take her to the party. She'd been afraid to say no again and told him she had a bad cold and was going straight home. Now, at least, it didn't look like a lie.

It frightened her the way the von Frisches pursued her, one of them going so far as to leave the party to check up. She suspected they'd promised their guests she'd be there, dangling her before their noses like some prize. Their parties were always attended by the party elite and Freddie's SS-officer friends. She hated them, in their tunics and high boots. They reminded her of sadistic circus ringmasters. Once a fat, red-faced officer with a dueling scar had paraded her around the ballroom in drunken solemnity, proclaiming her a prime example of racial purity, true Aryan beauty, calling attention to her blondness of hair, blueness of eye, whiteness of skin, her this-ness and that-ness, which had nothing to do with anything. Curious that the very people who most admired these qualities were so often like caricatures of the people they scorned.

The von Frisches were said to come from a line of aristocracy as old as Germany itself. They were also said to practice every known perversion. Of course, rumors were rife, but even if one-third were true, they were people to beware of. Did aristocracy lead to degeneracy? They were tall and bony and looked bloodless rather than blue-blooded. Was it inbreeding that had produced such a strange pair? And how was she to avoid getting mixed up with them, when they pursued her so relentlessly?

She was walking along a street of small shops when she heard the shouts and breaking glass. A few minutes later some soldiers rounded the corner, leaping into snowdrifts and laughing. When they saw her, there was a sudden alert pause, like animals catching a sexual scent. They no longer seemed like soldiers of her country, who would protect her, but enemy soldiers, whom destruction had sexually excited.

Someone grabbed her arm. "Just keep walking. Pretend you're with me."

Slowly the soldiers approached, then surrounded them, their eyes rodent-bright. And all of a sudden they scattered, sprinting off into different directions.

"You're in luck I came along when I did," the man at her side said, but one look at him and she wondered if she wouldn't have been safer with the soldiers. He was also a soldier, skinny and wiry. Although his forehead was low, giving him a look of stupidity, his eyes had a sly cunning. To make his forehead appear higher, he'd brushed his hair up. Thick with pomade, it stood in separate strands like a greasy porcupine's. But it wasn't any of this that scared her, it was the smile slitting his face like a scar. She was sure, too, that she'd seen him somewhere, although she couldn't remember where, despite the fact his face wasn't the type anyone would be likely to forget.

His fingers pinched her arm with a grip she felt through her coat sleeve as he steered her down the street and around the corner from which the soldiers had made their sudden appearance. In the moonlight, glass splinters diamond-sparkled the snow, littered with tiny coils of brass and silver springs and bits of other inner workings, along with watch faces in arabic and roman numerals. A sign hung crookedly by a broken hinge: "HERMAN NEUMANN, EXPERT WATCH REPAIR." Snow blew through a broken, jagged glass window onto a floor strewn with more shattered glass. On the counter stood a cash register, drawer open, empty.

Ilse thought of Herman Neumann sleeping peacefully unaware of his ravaged shop. She wanted to scoop everything up and put it in place before he arrived in the morning. A watch ticked faintly away in the snow like a heart about to give out. She bent and picked it up. "Give it to me," the soldier said. Then, "It's a man's watch, you don't want it." He strapped the watch on his wrist. "Beautiful, isn't it?" he said, kicking a blunt-toed boot at the sparkling slivers of glass. "Destruction is always beautiful. Just like *Krystall nacht*. Remember how pretty the sky was, all lit up by those fires? Everyone in a happy, holiday mood. Like those soldiers. Put them in good spirits. Maybe a little too good," he said, the smile scarring his face again.

Was he crazy? The soldiers crazy? Germany crazy? Or she? She should be used to it. It had been going on ever since

1933, when she was thirteen. She'd seen terrible things. Once a bomb had exploded right in the face of a Jewish shopowner. And what had happened to her dressmaker, Frau Steiner, a sweet-natured woman who'd harmed no one and worked nonstop so that Ilse could have her dress in a hurry? Had she left voluntarily, or had the Gestapo put their dirty hands on her? People pretended not to see, or said it was for the good of Germany. "It's ugly," she said. "Hate is always ugly."

He sneered. "Don't tell me you don't hate."

Only people like you, she didn't say. "Not someone I don't know, and not for long."

"Die and let die, I say." He chuckled. "Everyone's rotten. I know, I've seen it all. I grew up in a whorehouse in Hamburg," he said, as if that were a mark of distinction. "I could tell you some interesting things."

"Don't bother."

"No, you like rose petals and angels strumming harps and everlasting love."

"You wouldn't know what I like."

"I know a lot about you, Ilse Lach."

"How do you know who I am?"

He laughed. "You never noticed me? Third row, center aisle?"

Of course, that's where she'd seen him. Ordinarily the audience was a shapeless, faceless mass, but she'd become aware of him because he was the only person who laughed in the sad parts. He'd been there almost every night in the past weeks. Suddenly she remembered Hans's warning about being followed by an admirer, although the soldier could scarcely be classified as admiring. "You followed me tonight."

He said nothing, just smiled that ugly smile, his face a frightening combination of stupidity and cunning. The snow fell silently around them. She shivered, this time from cold as well as fear, her feet freezing from the melted snow that trickled down inside her galoshes. It was like standing in ice puddles. He gripped her arm so hard it hurt. "Get moving," he said, pushing her forward.

"Where are you taking me?"

"You'll see soon enough."

What if she screamed? Would he strangle her? It wasn't worth the risk, since there was no one around to hear. It was as if the world were dead and they the only two who remained. Snow. Silence. An ice-white moon. And then, suddenly, hope ahead. At the end of the street a sign: "BRUNO'S

RATSKELLER." If she could get away and run into the bar. But he held on to her.

"We'll go in there and have a schnapps," he said. She was in luck. That wasn't very clever of him. The first person she saw, she'd ask for help. She didn't think he carried a weapon. If he did, he'd have threatened her with it by now.

Her hope dwindled as they drew closer and she saw the tattered posters on a scummy window below the red neon sign bloodying the snow. He shoved her down the steps, following on her heels. What was it he wanted of her? If it were sex, why take her to a public place?

Again he shoved her. This time through the swinging door into a noisy room. There were men in flashy, shiny suits and women in showy tight dresses. The women's hair, dyed red or yellow, was as dead as doll's hair. Sweat, dust, smoke, cheap perfume. At one end of a long bar, steaming urns. Eyes glittering in drink-sodden faces.

"Nice, isn't it?" he said.

She shuddered and saw with despair that she wouldn't get help here. Just the opposite. They eyed her up and down from the tip of her fur-trimmed hat to the toe of her fur-trimmed galoshes, as if trying to decide if she were worth more alive on the hoof or dead. Obviously this was no honest working-class bar, but a hangout for prostitutes and petty criminals.

He steered her to a shadowy booth lit by a low-watt bulb in a greasy wraparound lampshade. "Two schnapps," he yelled out to a passing waiter. While they waited, eyes darted in her direction like rats watching from corners. The soldier ran his fingers through his hair. The pomade smelled both sweet and rancid. The waiter, in a dirty apron, splashed the schnapps down on the splintered wooden table and left. The soldier raised his glass. "Here's to Ilse Lachermann."

"What do you mean, Lachermann?" she asked, pretending not to understand. Only Hans knew her real last name in Berlin, and he wouldn't be likely to mention it.

He laughed. "I told you, I know all. I know the name of that hick town you come from on the Rhine. I know where you go every day. Monday, voice lessons; Tuesday, dance lessons; Wednesday, the hairdresser's. Afterward you always stop off for Viennese coffee with *Schlag*. You're crazy about whipped cream. And apricot torte. Got a real sweet tooth."

It upset her to think of such a slimy person spying on her, the type who'd peer through windows into her bedroom or bathroom at the most intimate moments. Lucky she lived eight floors up.

"I fail to see what's so fascinating about me that you follow me around."

"Oh, it's not just for your lovely self. I wanted to be well informed before I made my business proposition. You don't know what trouble and expense I've gone to. All that money I spent on flowers sent up onstage with notes you never read."

"I give the flowers to hospitals."

"At first I figured you didn't like my notes."

"I don't like flowers around. They remind me of funerals. What did you say in your notes you thought I wouldn't like?"

He didn't bother to answer. "Is that why you didn't go to your mother's funeral?"

"I didn't go because she isn't dead. I'm the one who's dead to her." To her whole family. They'd said to never come back after she left. She was always an embarrassment to them. She'd arrived late in her parents' life, and they were disappointed she wasn't a boy. They already had three girls. Only lately had she figured all this out. When she was little she'd thought they'd treated her with contempt because she was contemptible. "My mother always hated me."

"She was crazy about you. Any little item she saw in the papers about some play you were in, she'd cut out and show Mom."

Ilse looked at him hopefully, wishing she could believe this, then laughed. "She disapproved of my being an actress."

"She talked about you to Mom all the time," he insisted. "They started out in the same house together and were great friends. My mom was a whore in Hamburg. That's how I came to grow up in a whorehouse."

"My mother is the most respectable housewife in Einberg."

"She said the theater was in your blood, like your father's."

"My father is a baker. He disapproves of my being on stage even more than my mother, if possible. You've got your facts mixed. Right name, wrong girl. "Thank you and good night." She started to get up.

His hand clamped around her wrist. "Not so fast, we've still got business to attend to." He fingered her fur collar. "That coat must have cost money. Or was it a gift? Did you find one man with a lot of deutsche marks, or a lot with one, as the joke goes?"

"Take your dirty hands off me, I pay for things myself."

"What's wrong? What're you so defensive about?" he

asked, widening his eyes to imply innocence, but with his knowing eyes it didn't work. He fished out a cigarette from a pack of Turkish cigarettes, the kind Ursula von Frisch smoked. Ilse knew they cost more than a private in the Army could afford. As an afterthought he offered her a cigarette. She refused. "I wouldn't take one even if I smoked."

He smiled, lit a wooden match with a yellow thumbnail, touched it to the cigarette, and tossed the match on the floor. "What I need is a lighter. The Army doesn't pay enough. I was doing okay in Hamburg. Brought in girls for Mom and ran things. She's too easy on them. Women need a man to manage them. Not doing half as well since I left. Or so she says. I don't know, maybe the old bitch is lying. Holding out on me."

The steaming urns made the drunken brutish faces waver before her eyes. What was he up to? Blackmail? But what for? Having an affair with a married man? That was over, there were only occasional sexual lapses. Would he say he was going to tell Hans's wife? But why come to her, why not go to Hans?

He finished his schnapps, told her to drink hers, and ordered two more. After they were served, he took up where he'd left off. "I tried making some money gambling, but lost it all. Borrowed, lost that, got in debt. They get pretty tough, those guys, you don't pay up. I'm not going to end up a corpse on a slab. So now we get down to business. Your mom isn't Frau Lachermann from Einberg, but Fräulein Greta Ritter from Hamburg."

He was eyeing her for her reaction, but he didn't get the kind he wanted. She giggled from relief. So that was why he'd followed her, dragged her in here? He'd intended to blackmail her, claiming she was a bastard. As if she'd believe anything he said. As if anyone would. Probably he'd met poor Aunt Greta in Hamburg, and her aunt—such a sweet, friendly person—would have chattered away about her little niece, the actress, in the big Berlin Theater. Her aunt was proud of her. Was? Had been. Poor Aunt Greta, so alive, now dead.

"I'll never forgive myself for not going to her funeral," she said. "I didn't even know she was sick. She just wrote saying she wasn't feeling well and wanted me to come see her." Ilse had been in rehearsal then, and Hans had said they'd have to postpone the opening, and asked if she couldn't leave later. But later turned out to be too late. And then, suddenly, in a flash, Ilse knew the soldier was telling the truth. Her aunt was her mother. It all made sense. Maybe subconsciously she'd known all along. Things fell into place: why she'd been her aunt's favorite, the extravagant gifts, the money passed to her mother during her visits, the kisses and tears upon her arrival and departure. The more she thought of it, the more she liked it. How much nicer to have that beautiful loving woman for her mother than that spiteful one who despised her. "Was she really my mother?" she asked eagerly. "Did she tell you that? She was so good, so beautiful, so full of life."

"She told Mom, not me," the soldier said sulkily, obviously put out that she was so pleased. "She wasn't a bad old girl. I'm not saying she had a heart of gold like whores are supposed to, but she'd tip big when I ran errands for her when I was a kid."

"You're as bad as my family, equating acting with prostitution. I never saw Aunt Greta act, but I know she was good. And I know the name of her theater, the Théâtre Jardin."

"Fancy name for that dump. Oh, yeah, sure, she might have kicked up her legs now and then in the chorus line. Good for business. Your dad was always happy enough to put her to work. Of course, he got his money's worth—that kind always do."

"My father wouldn't be caught dead in a theater."

"I'm not talking about that fat little baker, Fritz Lachermann. He didn't put you in Greta's oven, kid, that was the guy who ran that crummy dump and did his lousy vaudeville skits there."

"Skits! He did skits!" Now she completely believed him. Like father, like daughter. She'd been in a *Thingspiel* skit when Hans had discovered her. The *Thingspiel* was put on by the Nazis in small towns, and although she hated the Nazis, she'd have been in something sponsored by the devil just to get a chance to act. It always drew noisy drunken crowds who called out rude and lewd remarks, but they quieted down when she was onstage. Hans said later that she had a special kind of magic that only the great performers had. Little wonder she'd loved him. Back then, he'd sent up a card engraved with the words "Theater Berlin," and on it an ink-written note saying to look him up if she ever got to Berlin. That was all she'd needed. She'd scraped up the money and left immediately at age sixteen. And she'd never seen her parents in the three years since, but maybe they weren't her parents.

"What was he like, my so-called father?" she asked the soldier, no longer hating him, almost liking him for the good news he brought.

That ugly smile again. "If the SS knew he was your father, believe me, they wouldn't be parading you around ballrooms as a typical Aryan beauty."

She trembled. How did he know that? He'd never be invited to the von Frisches'. And what exactly did he mean? "What exactly do you mean?" she asked.

"Your dad's name is Max Kramer. Sounds like any other decent German name, doesn't it? It isn't. If they catch him, his name will be Isaac and he'll be sporting a yellow star on his sleeve instead of a white carnation in his lapel. He's smart, I'll give him that. He's got himself a new name and a phony I.D. So far, he's got away with it. Doesn't look like a Jew, any more than you do. But you know what that makes you."

"If I'm half one thing and half the other, I'd rather be a Jew, after what I've seen the gentiles do."

"I wouldn't say that so loud. I wouldn't say it at all."

"Anyway, you're lying."

He reached into his pocket and took out a cheap leather case, poked a finger into a compartment, and brought out a letter. "Read that," he said, smirking. "It's dated October 16, 1919, exactly one week before you were born. Not in Einberg, but Munich, where no one knew your family. I suppose Frau Lachermann stuffed pillows in her drawers, but maybe not—she's such a fat old sow, she wouldn't have to."

"I'm not reading something you made up to back up your lies."

"Afraid?"

"I don't have anything to be afraid of," she said, trying to hide her shaky hand as she picked up the letter. There were ink blots, splotches, flourishes, and misspellings.

> Dearest darling Greta,
>
> Liebchen, how happy I am and how sad. It breaks my heart to think I might never see our beautiful child, our love child. Think twice. I know your arguments—a child given a name would be better off. But would it? I don't want our child handed over to anyone, even your sister. Believe me, all will go well. We'll get a place. I'll come over every day. We'll all three be so happy together. I'm not rich, but I'll see our child is as well taken care of as those who bear my name.
>
> Please write and tell me you've changed your mind. I wait pacing the theater as I would the hos-

pital. When our child arrives, send me a telegram first thing. Don't send it to my home. She opens everything. Send it to the theater. Be brave, I love you and our baby-to-be.

Yours forever,
Max

P.S. Excuse the splashes from beer and tears, I am writing this in a café.

Ilse's tears burned behind her eyes, threatening to join those on the nineteen-year-old letter. But she couldn't let the soldier see, couldn't let him know she believed—wanted to believe—that this sweet, loving man was her father rather than that cold fish she'd called *Vati* all her life. She tightened her hold on the letter. The soldier misunderstood, thinking perhaps that she was about to tear it up, and grabbed the letter back.

"I want the money by Friday," he said, and named an amount that sent her reeling. "That's three days from now. Bring it here. Friday night. I give you the letter, and we call it quits."

"That's crazy! Where would I get that kind of money even if I believed any of this?"

"I don't care where you get it, just get it."

"You must take me for a fool. How do I know you didn't make that letter up? That you wouldn't make up others? Or that the letter writer was my father?"

"It's the only one he wrote to her. There aren't any others. He's not a writing man. You can see he can barely spell."

"How's your spelling?"

"Not as bad as that. Believe me, I'd have written a better letter than that one."

"It's a beautiful letter. Anyone can misspell a few words, I got my worst grades in spelling." She realized too late that in defending the letter she'd trapped herself. "There's nothing in that letter to indicate whether he's Jewish or not."

"Call the Théâtre Jardin and ask. They'll tell you. But they won't know where he is. I'm the only one who knows that."

"Tell me where he is and let me talk to him, and if he's my father, I'll pay," she said. If he told her, she could find her father and warn him. She also desperately wanted to see her father, this man who'd loved her aunt—mother—and who'd loved her even before she was born.

"He's working in a mine near Essen. Thinks that'll save him, since we need miners and his papers won't be checked too close. But no matter how much coal dirt he covers himself with, he can't cover up his dirty soul."

She resisted the impulse to splash her schnapps in his face. That wouldn't help her father. "Which mine? There are a lot of mines around there."

"That's all I'm saying. I'm not worried. You'll pay."

"Or you'll give that letter to the Gestapo? Go ahead. See how much money you get from them."

But her bluff didn't work. His voice became flat, dangerous. "I'm not giving it to anyone. I'm selling it, see? Your friends the von Frisches are rich. They'd pay a lot for this letter. All I want is money, but they want fun."

The trembling set in again. Ilse remembered Ursula's greedy eyes on her body. She knew there were women who made love to women, and that never bothered her, since the women never bothered her, but Ursula liked only women who liked men. Not for her the easy conquest. Her favorite sport was making the spirited grovel, breaking the wills of the willful. Freddie, she sometimes felt sorry for. She'd seen the books in his library: *A Prisoner of Torture Castle, Secrets of a Slave Boy, Whipping Boy,* and others. Freddie didn't want to hurt, but to be hurt. He was, however, all too willing to please his SS friends so they would love him. She was afraid he'd hand her over as willingly as he'd handed over the glossy little fox he'd shot that one of his officer friends had admired.

Ilse stood up. Her legs were shaky and she had to lean against the table for support, but she tried to hide her panic. "Go ahead and offer them the letter."

Again her bluff didn't work. "Don't worry, I will if you don't pay up by Friday. And something else. It's not just you who'll be in trouble, but your dad, too."

This time he didn't try to hold her back. As soon as she could get her feet to move, she pushed through the noisy drunken crowd and out into the night. It was still snowing and the air lovely and pure after that inside. She walked as aimlessly as the falling snow, going first in one direction and then the other. She couldn't think straight, only in phrases: money . . . Friday . . . the von Frisches . . . Max Kramer.

She ended up standing before the watch-repair shop, although at first she didn't know where she was. The snow had already buried all signs of destruction. It was only the jagged window glass, the snow piled up inside, and the open cash-register drawer that made her recognize her surroundings. The sign, "HERMAN NEUMANN, EXPERT WATCH REPAIR," hung from the broken hinge. And Max Kramer, her father, could disappear like Frau Steiner, her dressmaker. So could she, Ilse Lachermann, disappear. Head spinning, she fled from the repair shop.

The money, get the money, that was the important thing! But how did she put her hands on such a huge amount? She'd been saving for a car, a small one to drive about in. She had almost half what she needed to buy one, but it wasn't a third of what he asked. She couldn't go to Hans for help, he had a family to support. Then it dawned on her where she'd get the money. The von Frisches. Beat the soldier at his own game, get the money from those who might otherwise give it to him. The fact that it gave them control over her counted little by comparison to how much they'd have if they got their hands on that letter. It was dangerous, but any other way was even more so.

2. *Susan*

Stillcreek County, Ohio

Sleet hit against the window. Susan shivered, partly from the chilliness of the room and partly from excitement.

Tonight was a big night.

As usual when it was cold, she took her basin bath near the stovepipe. The pipe came up through a hole in the living-room ceiling to her bedroom, bringing heat from the potbellied stove and the grave voice of Lowell Thomas on the radio. Her father had talked of installing a furnace and bathroom, but that was before her mother had died two years ago. Since then he paid little attention to the house, staying away as much as possible, as if he couldn't bear it without her mother. When he was home, he listened to the news on the radio and looked gloomy. He kept saying someone should put a stop to Hitler.

Susan dipped the washcloth into the soapy water in the blue-and-white speckled enamel basin and avoided looking at herself as she bathed. She was unhappy with her body, but wasn't sure whether she wanted to be slick-chested as before or big-breasted like her best friend, Penny Detweiler. What was so intolerable was to be neither. Her breasts were like crab apples and hurt if they got the slightest poke. Her legs were long and would be okay if they weren't so skinny.

On the floor lay her discarded clothes: her brother Eddy's old plaid shirt and tan pants. Penny had said that if she were going to get anywhere with boys in general and Richard Lund in particular she'd have to start looking like a girl instead of a field hand. Susan put on her new plaid pleated skirt and white sweater. She looked in the mirror, expecting to see a miraculous change. There was none. She still looked pale, gangly, and flat. To remedy the situation, she cut a Kotex in half with fingernail scissors and poked the pieces into her brassiere. Next she put on the five-and-ten makeup she'd so far only experimented with. She became a raving beauty with bright red lips and long black beady lashes. She thought of the ad, "She's Lovely, She's Engaged, She Uses Pond's," and determined to buy Pond's at the first opportunity, to guarantee her future.

But she didn't stay a raving beauty long. Her father made her take the makeup off. She cried and said she wouldn't go. Her father ignored her tears. He'd lost both his glasses and his speech. She had to find them for him. She wished he'd lost his glasses before he'd seen the makeup, but she was lucky he didn't notice her padded sweater. Maybe he did, but was too embarrassed to mention it. Or maybe he didn't, since he was preoccupied with the speech he was giving tonight for the fieldhouse dedication ceremonies. It was January, and he'd been working on it since August. He was taking nearly that long to get ready.

"We'll be late," she complained, but he took his own good time. Unable to stay in the house a minute longer, she put on her camel's hair coat and headscarf and ran out the back door and through the sleet to the Plymouth. Eddy had left over an hour ago. He was in the school band and had to be at the fieldhouse early. She started the car and impatiently honked the horn.

"Now, you just scoot over," her father said when he came out to the car. "I'm driving."

"Let me drive, please. I know how. Eddy taught me."

"You have to wait two years until you're sixteen, and besides, the road's too slippery," he said. As if to prove his point, the car skidded downhill toward the ice-sheeted river. On one side of the river were willows and black-elbowed trees; on the other side, acres and acres of farmland with no neighbor in sight. Spanning the river was a covered bridge that reminded her of a Conestoga wagon.

"Honey, there's something I've been meaning to say to

you," her father said, turning his attention from the road to her.

He was going to mention her stuffed brassiere. "Oh, God."

"Now, don't take that attitude, just listen, please. I don't want you wrestling with boys anymore."

"I don't wrestle with anyone but Richard."

"That's what I mean."

She blushed. He'd guessed. Lately, she found wrestling with Richard Lund more exciting than challenging. She'd even pretended to lose her balance and fall on him a couple of times. Richard hadn't noticed. He'd said she was the wiriest girl he knew. She'd been in love with him ever since he'd helped her nurse her Hereford calf, Clementine, through pinkeye. Clementine had gone on to win a blue ribbon at the county fair, but she got credit for that. Or discredit. Some old fuddy-duddies claimed she should have entered a cake, like other girls, instead of a calf, like a boy.

"Another thing," her father said, "you don't have to help Bobby with the farmwork. He gets paid for that."

Bobby was Penny's brother. He was twenty years old and retarded but looked scholarly in his glasses.

"If you want to help," her father went on, "you can help Mrs. Hinks around the house." Mrs. Hinks came three times a week to cook and clean.

"I'd rather drive a tractor than mop a dumb floor."

Her father sighed. She knew he was wishing her mother were here to handle things. Since her death he'd become active in community affairs. Besides being president of the board of education, he headed the Farmers' Co-op and the Community Chest. Eddy, too, had changed. Unlike Susan, who'd lost her religion after her mother died, he'd found his. He'd joined the Salvation Army, and every Friday night, except during basketball season, he played his trumpet on street corners with the Salvation Army Band. He also worked after school at the IGA grocery store. Susan said that stood for I Gyp Anybody. Eddy said that wasn't funny.

When they arrived at the fieldhouse, the school band was playing "The Star-Spangled Banner," and they had to wait in the doorway. The new gym floor smelled of varnish. A tarpaulin had been spread under the folding chairs where the band sat to protect the floor from scratches. Richard and Eddy sat together, playing trumpets, both in green school sweaters with white S's. Richard's eyes were nearly as green as his sweater. He was blond and slim and spoke softly.

When the band stopped playing, he smiled over at Susan. Her heart did a tap dance.

Richard and Eddy headed for the locker room to change for the big playoff game between Stillcreek and Brookville. Eddy called out "Hi, squirt," as he passed by. This embarrassed her, since she was far from a squirt. She was five-seven.

Someone kept yelling, "Testing, one, two, three," into a microphone, turning it up to a piercing whistle. Her father left to join the other board members in the front row under a flag suspended from the rafters. Susan went to join Penny, who was jumping up and down in the bleachers screaming her name, jiggling as she jumped. She looked on fire with her red hair. As usual she was surrounded by boys. Everyone had to move over so that Susan could squeeze in beside Penny. From the row above, the other girls in the freshman class looked down on them in prim-mouthed disapproval, and immediately began whispering. Had they noticed her stuffed sweater? They kept warning Susan she'd get a bad reputation running around with Penny, who they said was fast and would do anything with boys. Susan knew it was pure jealousy.

"Guess who's taking me home tonight," Penny whispered.

"Eddy?" Susan asked. She suspected that one of the reasons Penny was so friendly to her was that she was so crazy about Eddy.

"Guess again."

Susan guessed all the attractive boys they knew, which weren't many, then said, "I give up."

"Richard! He's crazy about me!" Penny said triumphantly.

Susan felt as if she'd been punched in the stomach with a giant fist. "But he's *my* boyfriend. You know I like him," she said, too shy to use the word "love." "You like Eddy," she reminded Penny.

"Eddy's a twerp," Penny said loud enough for all to hear, "and if Richard likes me better than you, I can't help that."

Down on the gym floor, Mr. Ashbaugh, the principal, clapped his hands for silence and called for prayer. While he thanked God for the new fieldhouse, Susan prayed to God to strike Penny dead. Even though she knew there was no God, she could still hope.

After the prayer, Mr. Ashbaugh introduced her father, saying he needed no introduction. Susan scarcely listened. Her mind was on Penny and Richard. How did Penny know he was crazy about her? Had he said so, or had Penny made it up? Slowly she became aware that her classmates were poking each other in the ribs and snickering. All over the fieldhouse people whispered and squirmed on the benches. Someone laughed outright. In the middle of the floor, her father stood frail and intense in his good brown suit, talking to himself. No one else could hear. The microphone had gone dead. Susan cringed in an agony of embarrassment. Her father was too intent on what he was saying to notice. The school band might hear, they sat nearby, but they acted as if they didn't, fingering instruments and fiddling with sheet music.

"Hey, we can't hear," someone yelled, but her father didn't hear either. After what seemed like forever, Mr. Ashbaugh walked out and whispered the bad news into her father's ear.

The school band struck up the school song. The Stillcreek Scotties came trotting out, led by the school mascot, the principal's five-year-old son. He pulled a toy Scottie on wheels and wore the same green-and-white uniform as the team. The Brookville Beavers ran out in their purple-and-gold outfits. The game began.

It looked bad for the Scotties from the start. Richard, the best player on the team, had the ball swiped from him repeatedly. Eddy, who was tall and lanky and could almost hand the ball into the net, somehow always missed, so that it rolled around the rim and out. Stillcreek groaned. Coach Moody looked grim. Susan, ordinarily a staunch supporter, was glad. It served them right. At intermission, Penny Detweiler, Wilma Merklin, and DeeDee Aspinall got out on the floor and did their stuff:

Team! Team! Watch that score!
Team! Team! We want more!

Penny twirled, twitched her behind, and jumped high to show a lot of leg and green pants under short white flared skirt. Susan watched in envy and disgust, then went to the supply room, where she put on a hated long white canvas apron with deep pockets for carrying change. Miss Rice handed her the change, a candy-filled box, and a sympathetic smile—for the microphone failure, Susan guessed. She didn't want sympathy. All she wanted was to crawl into a hole. But she had to sell candy, she had no choice. It was traditional at Stillcreek for the freshmen to handle the food concession to pay for such things as field trips to the Ohio state penitentiary or the state insane asylum.

She took her candy over to the Brookville side, not wanting to have anything to do with those who'd snickered at her father. Of course, they'd snickered on the Brookville side, too, but they hadn't known he was related to her.

"Hey, what you selling?" a boy called from several rows up.

She named every candy bar in the box before catching on that she was supposed to give a cute answer, not a detailed one.

"What kind do you like?" he asked.

"None, they all have rat poison in them."

At this, he grabbed his throat, gasped, and rolled his eyes toward the rafters, pretending to die a horrible death by poison. His friends thought this was hilarious. The buzzer sounded. Susan returned to the home-team side.

By the end of the second quarter the Scotties were trailing. Susan returned to the Brookville side. The candy-buying boy bought a Baby Ruth, Mars Bar, Bit O'Honey, and Mr. Goodbar. Not all at once, but each time she passed by.

"Hey, why don't you sit here on the winning side?" he asked.

Susan considered this. It just might be the jolt Richard needed to see her with another boy. She joined him and his friends. While they cheered for their side, she cheered for hers, still secretly hoping Stillcreek would lose. They didn't. Richard was back in top form. Eddy, too. They played as if they were the only two on the team. Eddy sank the winning ball into the net. Stillcreek went wild across the way.

"Hey, can I take you home?" the Brookville boy asked.

"I don't even know you."

"I'm Kenny Braines, but I've got looks, too."

He did have rather nice brown eyes behind glasses, and she was sure he must be at least a junior. When Richard saw her walk out with someone almost his own age, he'd realize she wasn't just Eddy's kid sister. "I have to check first," she said, omitting to mention with whom.

She found her father in the lobby surrounded by friends. It didn't seem fair. Penny was popular with boys, Eddy with girls, and her father with everyone. Small consolation that she was liked by cows, pigs, and guinea hens. "Daddy, can I go to Leyton for a Coke with Penny? Bobby's driving." She'd deliberately picked Penny, knowing her father couldn't refuse without making it look as if he considered his child too good to associate with someone from a poor family with a drunkard father.

After a moment's hesitation her father said she could go. "But I want you home in an hour," he called.

Susan took a long time returning the candy she hadn't sold and the money for what she had, then worried that Kenny Braines might give up and leave. But he was waiting where she'd left him in the bleachers. "It's okay," she said. He didn't seem overwhelmed by happiness. "Oh, yeah, uh, good, let's go," he said. He looked slightly dejected hunched up in his purple school jacket.

They made their way to the lobby. Luckily her father had left, but unluckily, so had her classmates, who wouldn't see her leaving with a boy. Neither would Richard, who was probably still in the locker room. She considered stalling, until it dawned on her that if Richard saw her with Kenny, so would Eddy, since they were always together, and if Eddy told their father, she'd be in serious trouble.

It had stopped sleeting. The night was clear and cold, and even the stars seemed to shiver. Kenny, so talkative earlier, was now silent. They scrunched across the gravel past the few remaining cars to a big shiny red Packard that Susan would have given Clementine's blue ribbon for Richard—and Penny—to see her get into. Kenny opened the back door. Back door? Did that mean she'd sit in the back seat while he sat in front driving? He got in beside her. "Chump's driving," he said. "We have to wait for him."

"Who's Chump?"

"Everyone calls him Champ, but to me he's a chump."

"Is this his car?"

"It's his dad's. Brand-new."

The fieldhouse door opened. Out came Eddy and Wilma and Richard and Penny. Penny was smiling up, Richard was smiling down. Susan wasn't sure which hurt most, those smiles or Penny's perfidy. All four walked to Eddy's third-hand coupé that he'd bought with his IGA earnings. Richard held out his hand to help Penny climb into the rumble seat. Susan could only hope they'd both die of pneumonia sitting in an open backseat in January.

"Wonder what's keeping those guys," Kenny said.

"Guys?" she asked. "What guys?"

"Champ and the others."

"Others? What others?"

Kenny offered her a Lucky Strike. He took a long time to light it and a longer time to answer. "Some of the guys on the team."

"Any girls?"

"Uh, no."

"How many boys?"

"Uh, not the whole team. Just a few."

But it looked like the whole team coming toward them. Kenny nervously lit another cigarette, forgetting he hadn't finished the other one. She wondered if she should just open the car door and get out. But how would she get home? She lived seven miles away. Her father had left. So had Eddy. So had everyone. Kenny stuffed his old cigarette into a clogged ashtray. It smoldered and gave off a sickening smell. He put out the new cigarette. His nervousness made her nervous. He sat tense and tight-mouthed, and in him she recognized herself. Like her, he was an outsider, only perhaps slightly more liked—or less disliked—because he tried harder.

The Brookville team, in purple jackets over gold sweaters with purple B's, peered in at her. "Who's that?" one asked.

"A girl," Kenny said.

"Where'd she come from?" another boy asked. Although he was good-looking with blond wavy hair, she didn't like the smart-aleck look he gave her as he cracked his gum. Then he tossed his sports bag in back and got in the driver's seat. Champ, of course.

"Hey, hey, whataya know, Kenny's got a girl," a fat boy said. Shoving Kenny over, he squeezed in next to her. A pimply-faced boy sat on her other side. Two more got in front with Champ and tossed their sports bags in back, one landing on her saddle shoe. The radio was turned on to the Grand Ol' Opry. A man with a nasal twang sang about being jilted by his ladylove.

"Tell him I want to go home first," she whispered to Kenny.

"Uh, she wants to go home first," Kenny said.

"Where's she live?" Champ asked.

The car skidded on gravel as he made a quick left turn to the highway.

"I dunno," Kenny said, "near here. Not far."

"Tell him just off Route 26 on the other side of Leyton," she whispered to Kenny across the fat boy, who smelled of Dentyne. Since they didn't speak directly to her, it seemed wrong to speak directly to them. Kenny repeated her directions.

"Hell, that's miles from here."

"Hell, I got to get home. Take us, then her."

"Shit, I'm not taking you guys all that distance, then turning around and coming back."

"Watch your language, there's a lady present," Kenny said.

The pimply boy laughed. "She from Stillcreek?"

"Yeah," Kenny said.

"Boy, they play the dirtiest, lousiest, shittiest game I ever saw."

"Yeah, it's not I mind losing if it's a fair game, but that son-a-bitch number fifteen, he kept tripping me, and that son-a-bitch referee, he kept pretending he didn't see," Champ said.

She'd love to tell him that number fifteen was her brother, Eddy, who didn't have to play dirty to beat a lousy team like theirs, but she could see they were in an ugly mood. She was just glad they'd turned their attention from her to the game. Now they were hooting and hollering about what a joke that old man was who'd been talking for so long, too dumb to catch on that no one could hear. Susan felt like a traitor for not coming to the defense of her father and brother. Once she was home safe, she'd tell them all off. But Champ was going in the wrong direction.

They passed a White Tower hamburger stand, an automobile graveyard. an all-night diner, and a succession of shacks dwindling off to a lonely road.

"Hey, Porky, what you doing back there?" a front-seater asked.

"Me? I'm not doing nothing. Hey, honey, how you doing?" the fat boy asked, placing a hand on her thigh.

"Keep your hands to yourself," she said, returning his hand to his leg.

"Oh, hey, guess where Kenny's girl put her hand, oh, oh, oh."

"Hey, girl, you want to watch that."

"What she look like? She cute?"

"Not bad on a dark night."

"This is a dark night."

"She got anything up there?"

Susan clutched her coat to her chest to prevent anyone from grabbing at her. Almost as bad as being grabbed would be for them to find out it wasn't her they grabbed.

"What's it matter she doesn't have anything up there if she's got something down below?"

"Oh, nothin' could be finah than to be in your vagina in the mo-or-or-ning," someone sang.

"Hey, you guys," Kenny said, "cut it out." But he could scarcely be heard, he spoke so faintly.

"Yeah, cut it out," Champ echoed, louder. "If you guys don't know how to act around a girl, it's time you learned."

She was surprised and grateful that Champ came to her defense. He hadn't seemed the type. They became quiet. In the silence, the radio man said, ". . . and we bring you, live from New York, Tommy Dorsey and his orchestra."

Champ drove into Leyton. He stopped the car by the Revolutionary War monument, a general on horseback, in the center of the square. "Okay," he said. "Everyone out. You guys can find your own way back. I'm taking this young lady home."

They protested but got out. That is, everyone but Kenny.

"I'll just come along to see she gets home okay," Kenny said.

"The hell you will," Champ said. "You couldn't see a flea home safe. Get out."

"Don't you want me along?" Kenny asked her. Champ had turned around and was smiling at her. A nice smile. He was really a nice person, not spineless like Kenny. She didn't answer Kenny, didn't look at him. He got out of the car, and she saw him walk off behind the others, who wouldn't have anything to do with him.

"Come on and sit in front," Champ said. "No use your sitting in back."

She got in front.

"I got rid of those guys," he said, grinning over. "We don't need them along, do we?"

"They're a rotten bunch."

"Nah, they're okay. Kenny shouldn't have asked you along. I mean, one girl, a lot of guys, they get the wrong idea. Lots of girls who look nice turn out to be tramps. Debutantes even. I heard about some guy messing around with this rich girl and getting the clap."

"What's the clap?"

"It's something guys catch from girls who play around."

She didn't say anything, deciding it might be better to keep off the subject of sex. His eyes were on her more than the road. She had the distinct feeling that the hand that lay so innocently on the seat between them would find its way to her leg. It did.

"Where do you live?" he asked.

"Just off Route 26 . . . and take your hand away, please."

"A guy never knows until he tries."

She supposed that was true, but all the same stayed alert and over by the door. They drove along a back road, the car lights dividing the black night, occasionally illuminating a barn or a barbed-wire fence.

"Of course," he said, "if a girl goes steady with a guy and she does it with him, that's okay. Later they might even get married."

"Miss Rice says a marriage certificate is just a piece of paper," she said. And had nearly got fired after some kids reported the remark to their parents. There'd been a big uproar, and the school board had met with the parents who said Miss Rice should be dismissed. Susan told her father that if Miss Rice went, she went. She'd transfer to Leyton High School. She didn't know what her father said at the meeting, but Miss Rice stayed on.

"Who's Miss Rice?"

"The best teacher there is. And honest."

"You believe that about a marriage certificate?"

"Sure, just having some minister say a few words doesn't mean anything, it only means what people want it to mean," she said, again quoting Miss Rice.

"Most girls won't let a guy do it until they get a ring on their finger."

She thought maybe they should get off the subject of sex, but it was such a fascinating subject. "They just say that to get married, that's all."

"I really like you. You don't pretend to be one of those goody-goody girls."

"What do you mean, goody-goody girls?"

"You know, girls who won't let a guy near them," he said, moving nearer.

Tommy Dorsey was playing "I'm Getting Sentimental Over You," and Champ was looking at her as if that might be happening to him. He put his arm around her shoulders and pulled her closer. She didn't protest, since she didn't want him to think she was a goody-goody girl, but she worried when he slipped his hand under her coat. The girls at school said a boy didn't respect a girl who let him go too far. And what if he found out she was padded? Her cheeks burned while her heart beat fast. The car bumped across the railroad tracks. A quarter of a mile ahead, the covered bridge loomed up. With his hand so near her breast, she could scarcely breathe. They approached the bridge. A sign said: "Warning, bridge unsafe for heavy loads. Proceed at your own risk." Proceed at your own risk, she warned herself, and felt a thrill as the car rattled across the loose wooden planks of the bridge. A board was missing on the side, and she glimpsed the moonlight on the rippled water. On the other side of the bridge he slowed down. The road divided into two. "Which way?" he asked.

"Turn right," she said regretfully. "That's our house up there."

It sat tall and lonely on the hill under the moon.

He turned left.

"You were supposed to turn right."

"I thought you meant 'right' like 'right now,' " he said.

Like fun he did. But she didn't want to go home, she wanted to stay with him.

"It's still early," he said. "We can just talk and stuff and listen to the music."

He drove along the road following the river and went straight to Lovers' Lane, a dirt path between thick trees.

His finger moved up and down her neck under her hair, tingling her skin, but she knew what he meant by "stuff." "We'd better go back," she said.

"Don't be so nervous. We can just sit here for a while and enjoy the scenery."

He switched off the ignition and pulled back on the handbrake. They were on a hill sloping down to the river.

"You know, a guy takes a girl out and shows her a good time, he expects a good time, too."

She became confused. He hadn't taken her out. She'd had a horrible time. And what did he mean by having a good time, too? But he was smiling down into her eyes the way Richard had smiled down into Penny's, and when he bent his head to kiss her, she didn't stop him. Then she couldn't stop him. It was her first kiss, something precious to be remembered forever, but she didn't like it. She hated it. It lasted so long she couldn't get her breath, and he was pushing her down so that she was soon on her back pinned under him. He breathed harshly. His face looked funny, lopsided, as if he had a dislocated jaw.

"Let me up," she said, but his weight came down on her, heavier. Her head was jammed against the door beneath the handle, her shoulders hunched up to her ears. "Please," she begged.

"Come on, don't give me a rough time. You said yourself marriage was a lot of crap. If you do it with others, you can do it with me."

"I don't," she said. "Stop," she screamed.

His hand clamped over her mouth. She struggled under him, but he held her tighter and moved with her struggles as if she meant to have fun. When she got a hand free, she scratched his face.

"Don't give me any trouble or you'll be sorry," he said.

Her coat was twisted under her. He pulled her skirt up and her underpants down. Something hard and sticky pressed against her, was pushing up into her. With the strength of terror she brought her foot up, kneed him in the stomach, then kicked with all her might. He let out a groan. She kicked again, aiming at where you weren't supposed to kick a man. She'd never wrestled like this with Richard, but she knew the tricks. He was not only groaning but moaning. He jumped from the car and bent over double clutching himself. While he hopped about and moaned, she turned on the ignition, released the handbrake, and pointed the car at the deepest part of the river, pressing down on the accelerator. As it gained speed, she jumped out the other side.

When he noticed what was happening, he looked first at her, then the car, as if he couldn't decide which to go after. She got ready to run, but he was already lunging after the car, grabbing at the bumper as if he could hold it back. The car went faster. It looked like a gigantic red beetle shining in the moonlight as it rolled toward the water. He was running, head bent, so that he appeared to be butting the car into the river. Suddenly there was a big splash and the car stood upended, its front buried in water.

"Oh, God! Oh, Jesus, what'll Daddy say?" he wailed, and stood on the bank, his wails turning to sobs. When he jumped into the river, she thought for a second he was going to commit suicide. He splashed around, water up to the waist of his jacket that glistened black in the night. He pushed the car from the front, groaning with the exertion. As if he could get it out by himself. The only way to get it out was to get help, and the nearest help was the Detweilers, who lived three miles away and couldn't be seen from here, so that he wouldn't even know where to go. He certainly wouldn't be able to show his face at her place.

"Call a tow truck," she yelled, then turned and ran through the crisp frozen leaves, tasting tears and triumph. She ran past trees, over stones under the bridge, past her house, where the porch light shone for her return. She ran in high leaps, her feet scarcely touching the earth, no longer knowing where she was running except away from those who humiliated and betrayed. A train whistled in the night. The Chicago-to-New York train. New York, that city of cities Miss Rice talked about. Someday she would go there, to the Metropolitan Opera and the Metropolitan Museum, to Times Square and El Morocco and the Latin Quarter, to Chinatown, Little Italy, and Greenwich Village, where the artists hung out in coffeehouses and talked about life. The minute she was old enough, she'd leave.

3. *Gina*

New York

It was only four in the afternoon but already dark. And bitter cold. On the corner of Broome and Thompson streets, men in shabby clothes held their hands out to a fire blazing in an oil drum, the flames illuminating defeated faces. Around them schoolboys played a rough game of tag, shoving one another dangerously close to the leaping flames. Their shouts echoed in the narrow street walled by gloomy tenements. Housewives in shapeless coats dragged small children past the various markets, where they bought sparingly if at all.

Gina Sabatini stood shivering in the doorway of Sabatini's Fruit and Vegetable Market. The cold crept up through her thin-soled shoes and under her skirt to bare thighs above her cotton-stocking tops. At fifteen she was already a beauty. Short black hair curled around a perfect oval face, and childishly long lashes shadowed large olive-black eyes.

Two teenage boys passed by. "Hey, Gina, *bella* Gina, Russo loves you," one called. "He loves your great big be-yoo-ti-ful eyes," he said, curving his hands over his chest to depict gigantic breasts. The other boy, Russo, blushed to the roots of his red hair, slammed his friend on the back, and ran off. Gina haughtily ignored them. She was watching a hairy, hunch-shouldered man. Tuillo. Once a week Tuillo made his rounds from store to store, collecting protection money for Don Guidetti. If the storekeeper didn't pay off, there was a sudden outbreak in vandalism—broken windows, fire, theft—and a sudden drop-off in customers. No one had to be told to shop elsewhere. People saw trouble and steered clear. The storekeeper either paid off with interest or landed in the hospital. If he didn't pay, he was quickly put out of business and had to sell his store cheap. That was how Gina's father had acquired the fruit-and-vegetable market.

Her father had bought the market with a loan plus the compensation money he'd received when his leg had been smashed at the dockyard. Five years ago. And for five years, every Wednesday, Tuillo stopped by to collect. But for some funny reason, he'd stayed away for a month. Gina's father, who knew enough to have the money on hand, didn't know how to hang on to it, and Gina was scared Tuillo would stop by today. She suspected he had a reason for passing them by, and that worried her. She knew it wasn't from benevolence or forgetfulness.

Gina was also keeping an eye on Mrs. Calabro, who, after feeling a small eggplant, skillfully thrust it up her coat sleeve. Gina said nothing, biding her time. Mrs. Calabro would make Houdini look like a rank amateur. Last summer she'd made off with a watermelon. What infuriated Gina was that Mrs. Calabro could afford to pay. Her husband was a shoe repairman, and they didn't have any children. People felt sorry for the Calabros because they were childless. Not Gina. She considered them lucky. Better no kids than too many, as in her family.

Gina fingered the five one-dollar bills and change among the lint in her sweater jacket pocket. The money was from old Mr. Samuels, who had got his job back as a cutter on Seventh Avenue and had paid his bill. She'd torn up the slips of paper listing what he'd charged and hoped her father would be too drunk to notice they were missing. She didn't want him accusing Mr. Samuels of not paying, but she didn't want a beating, either. She planned to buy her brother Giuliano a Brownie camera with the money. Tomorrow was his thirteenth birthday. Giuliano had TB and spent most of his time in bed coughing up blood. Sometimes when he wasn't feeling so bad and it was a nice sunny day, he'd sit on a bench in Tompkins Square Park. His big dark eyes in his thin face greedily watched everything that went on. He told Gina what he'd take pictures of if he had a camera. Gina would rather paint. She'd wanted to ever since finger painting in the first grade. She was always drawing on any piece of paper she could find. She'd love to have oil paints, but she couldn't get both paints and a camera. A camera would make Giuliano so happy. She loved him, he was so gentle. He always cried worse than she did when her father beat her up.

"These tomatoes, they no good," Mrs. Calabro said. "Enrico he got better."

"So go to Enrico's," Gina said.

"I do that, Miss Smarty. At least Enrico he talk nice to his customers. Wait till I tell your papa how you talk to me."

"Okay," Gina said, "just put back the eggplant and grapefruit."

"Eggplant? Grapefruit? What you talking about? You crazy? You accusing me of stealing, you little slut?"

"The eggplant's in your coat sleeve and the grapefruit in your apron pocket. Pay up or I get a cop."

"Listen," Mrs. Calabro said, shelling out the money. "I just put them there because my hands got too cold to carry them."

"Yeah, sure," Gina said, and dropped the money in her sweater pocket to join Mr. Samuels' money. Mrs. Calabro huffed off. Gina heard a hoarse chuckle behind her and turned to see Tuillo, short and thick-necked with long arms and hairy wrists. "Hey, caught her red-handed, huh?" he said.

"Yeah, but she steals honestly."

Tuillo stopped laughing. "Watch your mouth, kid, you wouldn't look good messed up."

He broke off choice grapes with hairy-knuckled fingers. She could see him just as easily breaking necks. What did she do when he asked for the protection money?

"Where's your papa?" he said.

"Johnny's Bar." No point in lying, he'd find out.

Tuillo smiled a yellow-toothed smile and lunged off, long arms swinging.

Ten minutes later Gina's father came hobbling down the street. She wasn't surprised to see him. Probably he intended taking every cent from the cash register and giving it to Tuillo, who was waiting for him in Johnny's Bar, where it was warm. There wouldn't be nearly enough money. Gina considered handing over Giuliano's Brownie-camera money, saying she'd forgotten to put it in the cash register. But she knew her father wouldn't believe her, and the money wouldn't make that much difference. Her father bumped along on the artificial leg, which occasionally skidded on icy patches on the sidewalk. His leg had been crushed by a crate falling from a crane. As he drew near, she saw that his dark curly hair was sweat-plastered to his forehead from his effort to hurry. For a moment she felt sorry for him and almost forgave him for making her work at the market while her older brothers got to fool around.

"Okay, I take over," he said. "Comb your hair and fix up. You want to look nice."

"Why?"

"Don't ask questions. I'm your father. Do as I say. I say you go, you go. Is big honor."

"What is a big honor? Where am I going?"

"Shut up. Tuillo he come along soon in Don Guidetti's car. He drive you there."

"To Don Guidetti's?" She looked at her father, but he wouldn't look at her. His mouth was tight. Suddenly she felt sick with fear and loathing. Don Guidetti was in his sixties, fat and bald, with lidless eyes and heavy jowls. He looked like Benito Mussolini. In the summer he always wore a white suit with white tie and diamond stickpin. She didn't know what he wore in the winter. He never went out then. She'd heard about him and young girls. She wasn't sure what happened when they visited him, but she'd seen them later. After just a few visits they looked dirty and worn. When he grew tired of them, the lucky ones were married off to some boy whose father owed him money. The unlucky ones became prostitutes and gave him part of their earnings.

But her father wouldn't hand her over to Don Guidetti. He was so proud, so strict. He wouldn't even let her be alone with a boy. Her dishonor would be his, the whole family's.

"Papa."

"Shut up."

"Don't make me go," she said softly.

He gave her a charming, coaxing smile, the kind that always made his women customers buy more than they intended. "Listen, you see him once, twice like a good girl, okay? Tuillo, he say Don Guidetti take good care of us. Never mind what I owe, it's forgot. He look after your brothers and sisters. Giuliano, he get sent to a sanatorium somewhere. Don't you want to see your little brother healthy? You get pretty clothes, spending money. You don't have to work here no more."

"Then I work the streets, huh?"

"Shut up that talk," he said, and slapped her face. Not too hard. He didn't want to leave marks before she visited Don Guidetti. The tears in her eyes weren't from the slap.

"You throw away money on whiskey and Mrs. Riordin and I pay."

His fingers pinched her arm. "Where you get that Mrs. Riordin, you little snoop?"

She backed away from him. Laughed. "I know all about you and her. Mary Donovan lives upstairs. She sees you going there. I'm telling Mama. Everything. She won't make me go see Don Guidetti," Gina yelled.

He grabbed her as she headed for the door, nearly yanking her arm from the socket, and flung her down into the lettuce bin. She lay there sobbing.

"Shut up that crying, you hear? Look what it does to your face, all red and ugly, and Tuillo comes here any minute."

Mrs. Gabrelli, fingering the zucchini outside, looked in. Gina's father put on a martyred smile. "Won't listen to her papa. Kids today, they spoiled. They don't know how soft they got it," he said in a hurt voice.

"You're telling me," Mrs. Gabrelli said. "Not like we had."

Gina waited her chance. As soon as her father's back was turned weighing the zucchini on the outside scale, she grabbed her coat from the hook in back of the store, edged forward, and sidled out the door.

She might have gotten away if Tuillo hadn't just that minute driven up in Don Guidetti's cream-colored LaSalle. He spied her, yelled, and jumped out. She ran into the path of an oncoming car, heard screeching brakes, smelled rubber, and ran on, while her father called out, "Stop her."

Tuillo didn't need to be told. Gina neared Pepino's Bakery and momentarily thought of going in for help, but old Mr. Pepino was no match for Tuillo or her father. Besides, he wouldn't interfere between father and daughter. The father was always right. It would be the same regardless of where or to whom she ran for help, friend or relative. She passed the oil drum, where the fire now burned low. One of the vagrants reached out to nab her, but she dodged his scarecrow arms.

The streets were nearly empty. Everyone was home for supper. Gina rounded a corner and ducked into a doorway. She stood there, heart pounding, trying to catch her breath. Tuillo dashed by, followed by her father. Already Tuillo's steps were slowing as he looked around.

When her father got far enough away, Gina slipped out of the doorway and retraced her footsteps, running past the market and down the street to MacDougal. As she ran, she tried to figure out where to go. Home was just a few blocks away, but she couldn't go there. Despite her threats to her father to tell her mother, she knew her mother wouldn't defy him. She thought of running into church for Father Bonino's help, but he'd believe her father, not her. Her father would make up some lie about her running wild with boys and say he was only trying to catch her and teach her a lesson.

She heard Tuillo's footsteps behind. He was gaining. She could even hear the distant dragging of her father's foot. Suddenly she was stopped short by a delivery truck backed up on the sidewalk. There was just room enough to squeeze by. But the truck blocked her from view. She paused for a second for breath and noticed the dark alley behind a tall wire fence. She could hide in there. The fence, though, was too high to climb. She spied the opening below and dropped down onto the sidewalk. Turning her face sideways, she wriggled under. A little over halfway through she became stuck, the wires digging into her behind. She'd never make it. She'd be held helpless for Tuillo to come and grab her. Hearing his steps on the other side of the truck, she wriggled frantically. There was a sickening sound of her coat being ripped, but she scrambled through.

It wasn't an alley after all. Just a blank wall lined with overflowing garbage cans. She crouched behind a can and nearly screamed out when a giant rat leaped from the can and scurried away. She could hear other rats rustling in the garbage, but she'd rather be with four-legged rats than a two-legged rat like Don Guidetti.

Peering over the garbage can, she glimpsed Tuillo looking the fence up and down, apparently trying to decide if she could get through. A bit of torn cloth from her coat waved in the wind, but he must have thought it was a rag and the fence too high to climb over or too low to crawl under, for he moved on.

Her father came thumping around the front of the truck to join Tuillo. They stood with their backs to her, discussing where she might have disappeared to. Tuillo's guess was that she'd gone into one of the stores that were still open. "You go after her, I'll wait," he said. Her father went like an obedient dog.

Each time he came out of a store, he raised his palms up to indicate he'd had no luck. Tuillo swore, stamped his feet from cold or fury, lit a cigarette, and blew out smoke and frosted breath.

The wind swept through her coat as if it were made of tissue paper. Her thighs above the stocking tops were raw and goose-pimpled. When her father came out of a candy store, Tuillo loped forward to meet him. They were too far away for her to hear what was said. After a few minutes of consultation they headed back toward Thompson Street, and not long after that she saw the cream-colored LaSalle go by. She breathed a great sigh of relief before wriggling back under the fence.

But they wouldn't give up so easily; she knew that. She stood on the sidewalk slapping her arms for warmth and tried to think whom to turn to. She decided on the Donovans. Mary Donovan was her best friend. Mary's parents might let her stay the night if she could think up some good excuse to give them for not going home. She was too ashamed to tell the Donovans, even Mary, the real reason. The Donovans considered Italians a lower form of life. Once she'd overheard Mrs. Donovan telling Mr. Donovan that Italians couldn't be Catholics, the way they acted.

Hurrying down the street, Gina told herself that things would be better tomorrow. Her father would realize how wrong it was to send her to Don Guidetti. He'd think of the shame it would bring to the family and borrow money to pay off Don Guidetti. Of course, he'd beat her, but that would be on principle, because she'd disobeyed him. It couldn't be as bad as the time he'd knocked her unconscious when her brother Vince had told about her going to a movie with a boy.

She saw the Donovans' apartment building up ahead and walked faster. The building was the same liver color as the one she lived in. It had the same narrow windows and front fire escapes. Even the inside was similar, with steep wooden stairs and the smell of pee from hall toilets. The only difference was the food smell. Here it smelled of cabbage instead of garlic. Gina went up the four flights, passing Mrs. Riordin's place on the third floor. Mrs. Riordin was a big blond with bad teeth. She had a lot of boyfriends besides Gina's father. Gina wished she'd told her father that. Before knocking at the Donovans' door, she finger-combed her hair and straightened her stockings.

"Why, Gina," Mrs. Donovan said, raising her voice to sound glad to see her; but it fell flat. Mrs. Donovan stressed gentility and good manners, and Gina knew it wasn't manners to visit during suppertime. Mrs. Donovan wore a green cardigan sweater over a housedress. She was a thin, plain woman with pale blue eyes. Behind her around a table sat four thin, plain, pale-eyed children—Mary, her two little sisters, and five-year-old Donnie. Mr. Donovan had a ruddy face and a receding hairline.

Gina found their stares disconcerting. And she'd forgotten to think up a good excuse for staying the night. "Some men were chasing me, and I ran here since it was close," she whispered to Mrs. Donovan, not mentioning that one was her father. "Italians," she added. Mrs. Donovan was ready to believe the worst about Italians, but not fathers.

"Don't mention this in front of the little ones," Mrs. Donovan whispered back, alarmed. She patted Gina comfortingly on the shoulder and led her in. "Your friend came to visit you," she told Mary, as if Mary couldn't see that for herself.

"Gina, look, your coat is torn," Mary cried.

Her mother shot her a look, and Mary said no more.

"Sit down and have some supper," Mr. Donovan said politely.

Gina hurriedly sat down and poured thick gravy over boiled potatoes while stuffing bread in her mouth. There was no meat. Mary kept asking questions with her eyes. She looked scared. Maybe she'd overheard. Mary was afraid of her own shadow and admired Gina, whom she considered brave.

The Donovans had finished eating. They watched Gina, who became self-conscious and forced herself to slow down and eat daintily, sticking out her little finger in a genteel way that Mrs. Donovan would approve of.

"Why's your face dirty?" Donnie asked.

Mrs. Donovan said children should be seen and not heard.

Mr. Donovan said he'd better be off. and got up from the table. He worked in a garage at nights, repairing trolleys. Mrs. Donovan went over and whispered to him as she handed him his black metal lunch pail. He put on a sheepskin-lined jacket and a cap with ear tabs. "Come along, Gina, I'll walk you partway home," he said.

Gina knew Mrs. Donovan had put him up to saying that. "Oh, that's okay, I'll go home later, after I help with the dishes," she said. She jumped up and began clearing off the table.

"Won't your parents worry if you're not home soon?" Mrs. Donovan asked.

"There's so many of us, they lose count."

Mrs. Donovan looked shocked but gratified, as if this could only be expected.

After hesitating, Mr. Donovan left.

Mary and Gina did the dishes. Gina insisted on washing. She disliked washing more than drying, but she hoped to get on Mary and her mother's good side. Little Donnie kept hanging around. "Gina, will you marry me when I grow up?" he asked.

Everyone laughed, and Gina stooped and hugged him. "I thought you'd never ask," she said.

"Gina can marry anyone she pleases, she's so beautiful," Mary said.

Gina looked at herself in the cracked looking glass over

the tin sink. She wiped a dirt smudge from her forehead. Other than the smudge, there was no sign of what she'd been through. Her cheeks were rosy, her eyes sparkly. Her black hair curled crisply around her face. Beautiful? Maybe. Only, she'd just as soon be plain like Mary if beautiful meant running from men like that gangster Don Guidetti the rest of her life.

By the time they'd finished the dishes, Mrs. Donovan had patched Gina's coat. She handed it to Gina in an obvious hurry to get rid of her. "My, that coat hardly seems warm enough for this weather," she said. Gina, embarrassed by the coat's thinness, said she never felt the cold.

Mary, her mother, and the three little Donovans watched as Gina started to button up. Besides patching the coat, Mrs. Donovan had tightened all the buttons. Gina fumbled with the buttons, stalling. Even if the streets hadn't meant cold, darkness, and danger, she'd be reluctant to leave this neat, warm home, so quiet by comparison to hers, where everyone squabbled and screamed. She could no longer delay with the buttons. She twisted the final one and thought of her father and Tuillo driving up and down the streets looking for her, and suddenly began to cry.

"Why, Gina, honey, what is it?" Mrs. Donovan said.

"Can I stay here tonight? I'm scared."

"But your mother will worry."

"She'll think I'm over at Aunt Teresa's."

Mary put her arm around Gina. "Mother, please. Let her stay."

"Mommy, let Gina stay," Donnie begged, looking close to tears, too.

Gina wondered what happened in the years between to change the sweetness of little boys to the meanness of grown men.

"Oh, goodness, I don't know what to say," Mary's mother said.

"Come on, we'll do our homework," Mary said. Taking advantage of her mother's moment of indecision, she yanked off Gina's coat and pulled her down on a chair, so that Gina was settled in by the time Mary's mother said, well, she supposed it would be all right.

Under the table, Mary squeezed Gina's hand. Gina was glad she'd bloodied Maria Gabrelli's nose when she'd said Mary Donovan was nothing but shanty Irish and didn't fool anyone putting on airs. The penalty of having to miss recess for three days was well worth it.

Mrs. Donovan hurried the smaller children to bed while Mary and Gina worked on their algebra. Gina, who normally had a hard time with algebra, was even more bewildered tonight. Mary was good at math and patiently explained things while impatiently whispering, "What happened?" Gina said she'd tell her later. She wanted to share her misery with Mary but was too ashamed to admit that her father would do such a thing.

Mrs. Donovan sent Mary into the other room on the pretext of checking to see if the children were asleep, and began questioning Gina. "Did any of those men touch you?" she asked. Gina shook her head. "Was it someone you know?" Gina avoided her eyes. "Who?" Gina wouldn't say. She started crying again. Mrs. Donovan, looking distressed, had to give up, since Mary was back.

Gina and Mary worked a little longer on the algebra; then Mrs. Donovan said they'd better get some sleep.

Mary's bed was in the front room. She slept with Donnie in a bed that folded up into the wall during the day, when the front room became the good room. The younger girls slept on a davenport. Gina undressed self-consciously in the light of an orange-tasseled floor lamp. She was embarrassed by her slip, gray and shrunken from so many washings. Mary wore clean pink knee-length snuggies and vest. Under the vest Mary's breasts looked like pimples.

The room was cold. Gina jumped under the covers and draped her coat on top of the blankets. Just before Mary turned off the floor lamp, Gina noticed the small statue of the Madonna on the mantel. The Madonna wore a pale blue robe. She looked exactly like the one in Gina's home. There was also a picture of Christ, as at Gina's, but this Christ had blond hair and blue eyes, while theirs had dark hair and dark eyes.

Both Gina and Mary hugged Donnie, who lay between them, Mary proclaiming him warm as toast. Then, "What happened?" she asked, and kept asking until Gina told her. By the time Gina finished, she was sobbing again. Mary was absolutely silent. "I don't believe you," she said finally. "You're lying. Fathers don't do such things."

Gina regretted telling her. Mary was one of those people who couldn't take the truth, and resented hearing it. She should have known.

"My daddy would never, never do such a thing," Mary said primly.

"You don't know what men will do."

"I know what my daddy *wouldn't* do," Mary insisted. Then, softly, as if God might hear, she said, "Sometimes I think no men are good except Daddy. On Saturday nights, right here in this building, you can hear. It's awful. They come home drunk and cursing at the top of their lungs, and their wives and children start screaming and crying. On Sunday, when we're on our way to mass, there they are, the same men, crowded into the candy store downing Alka-Seltzer to get rid of hangovers before going to church. I'm not marrying anyone who beats and bullies me. Only, maybe I won't have a choice. I'm not beautiful like you. I'm not even pretty. Maybe I'll have to settle for the first man who asks. If anyone asks."

Gina assured her that she was pretty and that the older she got, the prettier she'd get. "Besides, what's it matter if you get married, unless it's someone rich? I'm not doing like Mama and marrying someone who thinks he's God's gift to women and having a lot of kids and spoiling my shape."

"You have to have children. Sister Elizabeth says it's a woman's duty."

"Oh, sure, she can say that, she's a nun."

"If you're married and a man wants to do it, you do it."

"The hell, I'll tell him to go fuck himself."

There was a shocked silence followed by a giggle. "Gina, you're awful. Would you honestly and truly say that?"

"Sure."

"Girls," Mary's mother called, "aren't you asleep yet?"

Mary poked Gina, and they both giggled into their pillows. They whispered a little longer, then Mary fell asleep. Gina was weary, but this afternoon she'd set foot into a new country where sleep was impossible. She lay, eyes open, listening to the soft breathing of the innocent and looking at the light cast on the ceiling from a slit where the curtains didn't meet, a thin yellow bar cutting blackness in two. There were always paintings of people or fruit in bowls, but no paintings of what you see most, she thought, like light on a ceiling at night or a smudge on the wall. If she were a painter, she'd show people what they looked at but never noticed. Thinking of painting reminded her of poor Giuliano, who wouldn't get his Brownie camera for his birthday.

The wind rattling the window became fainter, the yellow stripe blurred into sleep gray.

"Gina, what are you going to do tomorrow?" Mary whispered.

"I don't know."

"Maybe your father will have second thoughts. Maybe he'll realize what a bad, evil thing he's doing. Maybe if you prayed."

"Praying won't do any good. I've tried."

"You have to pray for the right thing. I'll pray for you, too."

There was a long silence during which Mary must have been praying for her.

"Or maybe if you went to the police," Mary said afterward.

"Don Guidetti has the police in the palm of his hand," Gina said, quoting her older brother Vince, who, however, had said it admiringly. Vince's ambition was to become a big-time crook like Don Guidetti. "Maybe I can just stay here with you."

"Gee, I wish you could," Mary said, but sounded doubtful.

"I'll kill myself before I go visit that ugly old man."

"Maybe if you told my parents, my father would speak to yours."

"Don't you dare breathe a word. If you do, I'll never forgive you. Never."

"If you told your mother, she wouldn't let your father do it."

"Yes, she would. She's scared of him."

"We'll think of something," Mary promised, but must have fallen asleep before she did, for it was quiet again. Gina dozed a little, but the sound of her heart wouldn't let her sleep, its thumping becoming louder and louder until she realized that she'd actually been asleep and the thumping wasn't her heart but something slower and more deliberate. She sat up. Her father! He was coming up the stairs to get her. He'd remembered her saying Mary had seen him visit Mrs. Riordin and guessed she was here. No, it was Mrs. Riordin he'd come to see. Only it now seemed that the dragging foot on the stairs had passed Mrs. Riordin's floor.

She didn't wait to make sure. "Mary, he's here! He's here!" she said, shaking Mary's shoulders, then jumped out of bed and started dressing.

"Huh?" Mary said sleepily. "Huh?"

"Tell your mother not to let him in."

Gina stood for a moment undecided about how to get away, her heart beating fast counterpoint to the slow footsteps on the stairs. Then she remembered the front fire escape. She grabbed up her coat from the bed and ran to the window. It was difficult to pry the window up, even a few inches.

Her father was now pounding at the door.

"Go tell her not to let him in," Gina said in a whispered cry to Mary. Mrs. Donovan was drowsily calling, "Who is it?"

Mustering all her strength, Gina got the window up far enough to squeeze through out onto the fire escape. She shut the window behind her and foot-felt her way down the iron steps.

Below, the LaSalle was parked across the street. Tuillo must be waiting in the car. She hadn't heard him on the stairs. She reached the second floor, only to find the fire-escape ladder pulled up. Her fingers nearly froze to the metal as she tried to budge the ladder. If Tuillo were in the car, he'd hear the ladder when she pushed it down—provided she could push it down. If she jumped, she might break a leg and just lie there until Tuillo and her father found her and dragged her to the car.

But she couldn't waste time standing here trying to figure out what to do. She climbed over the railing, gripped the ice-cold iron slats, and lowered herself. Her feet dangled far above the pavement.

Let go! She had to let go! Her father might come out the door any minute. Tuillo might spot her, if he hadn't already. She cast one last look at the pavement below, released her hold, and landed awkwardly on the sidewalk, wincing at a sudden sharp pain in her foot. She stood up slowly, afraid to put her full weight down, and risked a glance at the car. Tuillo sat slumped behind the steering wheel, head on folded arms. Either drunk or asleep.

She took a tentative step. Her foot hurt, but nothing seemed to be broken. She could walk, but running was agony. She ran, nevertheless, keeping close to the flat-fronted buildings, using what little shadow they gave for cover and avoiding the yellow circles of streetlights. Her steps sounded terrifyingly loud in the cold empty street, but when she tried to run on her toes, it hurt too much.

At the end of the block she turned just in time to see her father leave the building. She was almost positive he was looking her way. She made a split-second decision and went west instead of east. East was the river. It would cut off her escape.

When she heard a car coming up from behind, she ran into a doorway. The cream-colored LaSalle streaked by. They weren't going to give up. They were going to hunt her down if it took all night. She felt the money in her sweater pocket and wondered if it were enough for a hotel room. But it would look suspicious for a schoolgirl to arrive in the middle of the night without so much as a suitcase. Maybe it would be better to spend the night on the subway. At least she'd be warm.

She hurriedly hobbled down the street. With her bad foot, it looked as if she were imitating her father. She'd gone west for what seemed miles before spying the two lighted posts at the subway entrance. As she reached the steps leading down, she heard a car behind her. Without wasting time to look, she plunged down the stairs.

Luckily she had a nickel for the turnstile slot. Unluckily, it was a long wait. There were only a few people, three staring men, two lovers, and an old bum huddled up on a bench.

Gina walked to the far end of the platform and stood behind a post. She kept one eye on the train tracks and another on the turnstile, where her father or Tuillo might come through. Finally she saw a glint of light on the tracks. The light grew brighter. A train roared in. She kept hidden behind the post until the very last minute and made a dash for it just as the doors were closing, squeezing on.

Seated on a stained yellow straw seat, she tried to look like any other ordinary passenger. But it was late for a lone girl to be on the subway, and no matter which way she looked, she received a wink, a stare, or a leer. She couldn't ride the subway all night after all. She wouldn't be given a minute's peace. She had boarded a local. The train stopped at Fourteenth, Eighteenth, Twenty-third, and Twenty-eighth streets. At Thirty-fourth she considered getting off and going to Penn Station, where it was warm and wouldn't look strange for a young girl to be at this hour. Also, if she sat opposite some sharp-eyed old lady, she'd be less likely to be pestered by men. But a train or bus station was just where her father and Tuillo would look.

She rode to Times Square and got off.

At her first sight of Broadway, Gina forgot fear and pain. To think that such a fairyland existed just a short subway ride away! It was bright as daylight in the cold, brisk air. Neon signs flashed on and off and ran in circles. There were women in fur coats with glittery evening bags clutched in gloved fingers. Men wore white silk scarves tucked into overcoats with velvet lapels. Gina stared. She'd never seen a rich person up close, only in movies or magazines. She suddenly yearned for a fur coat, glittery handbag, and a rich adoring man to smile down at her. The street under the lights actually looked gold, like her father had said he'd been told they were before coming to America—and had added, they weren't paved with gold but sweat and shit.

She shivered, pulled her thin coat closer, walked on, pausing to look through the glass doors of a penny arcade, where men played pinball machines or looked at what were probably dirty movies. She'd have gone in if there'd been some women. High up over the street, a billboard man blew perfect smoke rings, scattered by the wind.

She marveled at the contents in a jewelry-store display window, at the rhinestone necklaces, heart-shaped lockets, charm bracelets, ankle bracelets, cameos, rings, and wristwatches. Nearby, separated by a flight of stairs, were photographs of beautiful women behind a glass panel. They wore flowers in their pompadours. Their eyes were sultry, smiles bright, shoulders voluptuous, breasts sumptuous. The most glamorous of the lot was in a full-length photograph. She had a Ginger Rogers hairdo and wore a long clingy dress with a thigh-high slit displaying a shapely leg in a spike-heeled sandal.

Gina believed they were all actresses until she saw the sign above the glass panel. It said "DANCE CASINO—GIRLS! GIRLS! GIRLS!" An arrow pointed up the steps, underneath another sign: "One Flight Up to Heaven! Only a Dime a Dance!"

Imagine getting paid for dancing! And think how much fun it would be. And if she couldn't return home, she'd have to get a job somewhere to support herself. But she could never get a job here. She hadn't really danced except with Mary and other girlfriends at school. But they all said she caught on quickly. And people said she was beautiful. Even if Don Guidetti's choosing her had turned her day into a nightmare, it meant she was the prettiest girl around, because these were the only ones he was interested in. Of course, they soon looked shopworn. It was as if Don Guidetti, old and ugly, wanted everyone else to look like him.

It wouldn't hurt to go up and ask for a job. The worst that could happen was she'd be thrown out, and if by some miracle she was hired, she'd find a cheap room somewhere and rest up to be ready to dance tomorrow night. She dug into her coat pocket for the Tangee lipstick she put on after leaving home and wiped off before returning. Using the glass panel as a mirror, she applied the lipstick and finger-combed her hair. After straightening her stockings, she started up the stairs, praying it would be too dim to see the mess she must look.

At the top of the stairs there was a small barred window with a roll of tickets inside. A sign said, "One Dollar, Ten Dances." Luckily no one was behind the window, and it was also dark. The only light came from a big revolving ball suspended from the ceiling, splashing rainbow colors on table sitters and dancers as it slowly turned. A Negro band played a tango. There were more people in the band than on the dance floor. Girls sat together at tables. A bad sign. They wouldn't need more girls. Or maybe tonight was so slow because of the cold and the lateness of the hour. Maybe the men had all gone home to their wives.

Even in the faint light of the revolving ball, she saw that the girls weren't half as pretty as in the pictures downstairs. In fact, they didn't look like the same girls. It gave her hope until she saw the beautiful woman at the bar. Her head was half-turned so that Gina saw only her profile. It was the woman with the Ginger Rogers pageboy. She was tall. Even leaning over the bar she looked tall. Her hair draped her shoulders and she wore the same dress as in the photograph, with the thigh-high slit. Gina couldn't tell the color of her hair or the dress, since they changed colors with the changing lights.

The man seated on the barstool beside her didn't look worthy of such a beautiful woman. From the back at least. He was fat, thick-necked, and bald. The tall woman, who had noticed her, whispered something to the man, who turned to look her way.

Gina's heart froze. Her knees turned to ice water. Don Guidetti! How had he known she was coming here? Had Tuillo and her father been following her around all this time, and seeing what direction she was headed in, phoned Don Guidetti? The room revolved with the revolving ball, tilting and whirling at high speed as Don Guidetti and the tall beautiful woman came toward her. She stepped backward and slipped down into darkness.

4. *Diane*

Columbus, Georgia

It was down to forty degrees, colder than anyone could remember. Diane lay on her stomach before the fireplace eating potato chips, drinking Dr Pepper, and reading. Her hair spilled over her face, some blond strands obstructing her view of the printed page smeared by potato-chip thumbprints. She pushed back her hair and dreamily watched the leaping yellow flames behind the fire screen. Appropriate background for the destruction of the South, she thought. She was reading *Gone with the Wind*. For the third time.

Her father came tightrope-walking into the room. She knew the drink in his hand wasn't his first. He smelled of good bourbon, good tobacco, and after-shave lotion. He wore his dark dress suit and looked wonderfully handsome, with a silvery blond swoop of hair over his forehead. She wished, though, that her parents would stay home once in a while. Settle down and have a baby. Of course, she'd have preferred a brother or sister near her age, but a baby would be company, too. It got so lonely with her parents always party-going. Daddy didn't make it to his office until late, and sometimes not at all. He said he left it to Uncle Clayton to run the family businesses. "I don't have a head for such things, I just get in the way," he'd said, sounding proud of it.

There was a lot for Uncle Clayton to tend to. When Diane was very little and just learning to write her name, she'd been amazed to see it everywhere—Colquitt Paper Mill, Colquitt Meat Packing, Colquitt Chemicals, and Colquitt Soft Drink Works. Daddy said he hoped Uncle Clayton didn't get things mixed up and put the chemicals in the soft drinks. Daddy was always joking. Uncle Clayton was always serious. Maybe because he had so many things on his mind running the business besides being a lawyer and getting people out of scrapes. Daddy was three years older than Uncle Clayton but looked and acted younger.

"You still reading that book?" he asked now.

"Un-huh," she said, glad he didn't know it was for the third time.

He went over to the Chinese cabinet used for a bar and added bourbon to his glass. "Just killing time till your mama's ready," he said, a little defensively.

"It takes time to be beautiful."

He looked at her closely. Maybe that sounded as if she were jealous. " 'Course, I could spend all day on myself and not look half as good," she amended.

"Just stay as sweet as you are, pumpkin."

"Sweet and pudgy."

"That's baby fat, you'll grow out of it."

At Miss Mayhew's they called her Piggy. It was such an ugly name, it made her cry. Once when she was lying on the sickroom cot with cramps from the curse, she'd overheard Miss Bibb and Miss Emerson discussing her in the next room, the teachers' room, where they went to smoke. Miss Emerson said what cruel little beasts children were, poking fun at each other and calling Diane Colquitt that stupid name. Miss Bibb said, well, it was a pity Diane didn't have her father's charm or her mother's looks. Up until then Diane had liked Miss Bibb.

"Oh, don't worry about that any," Miss Emerson said. "She'll blossom. She's like that 'Summertime' song, her pa is rich and her ma good-looking. Add to that a granddaddy who was a U.S. senator and an uncle who will be."

Miss Bibb, who was years younger than Miss Emerson, said she did wish Clayton Colquitt would look her way. "He doesn't look anyone's way but Meredith Bradford Colquitt's," Miss Emerson said. "Don't you know that? She jilted Clayton and married his big brother, and Clayton's just never recovered."

Diane hadn't known that either. Poor Uncle Clayton. Was that why he'd never married? Because he still loved Mama? But Mama didn't like him. She'd overheard Mama tell Daddy that Uncle Clayton was mean and conniving. "And you're too sweet and innocent to catch on," she'd said. "He's just like your daddy." Mama meant Grandpa Colquitt, who'd been a senator and died in the Spanish-flu epidemic. So had Grandma Colquitt. Both of Mama's parents had died, too, before Diane was born. She didn't know what of. The only living relative she had was Uncle Clayton. It didn't seem fair, no brothers or sisters, no grandparents, and only one uncle. Right here in Georgia where everyone had more relatives than you could shake a stick at.

Diane smelled Joy and looked up to see her mother posing

in the doorway. Her mother always wore Joy—that most expensive of perfumes—and always made an entrance. Her honey-colored hair was coiled around her head, exposing a swan's neck and one luminous shoulder. A jade brooch clapsed her white Grecian gown over the other shoulder. "Look okay?" her mother asked, pivoting on a dainty silver sandal.

"Like a Botticelli," Diane's father said. "Like Venus emerging from a half-shell."

"That's oysters in half-shells," Diane said.

"Your mother is my oyster."

"Oh, my, we've been hitting the bourbon again," Mama said with her Tinkerbell laugh, which was why people called her Merry—in addition to its being short for "Meredith."

"He only had a drink because you took so long getting ready," Diane said.

"And what's your excuse for that Dr Pepper and those potato chips?" her mother asked. "So soon after supper."

Diane's face grew warm. "Hungry," she mumbled.

"I swear you'll be as big as a barn if you keep that up," Mama said. Diane hated her, wished she were dead. She watched as her father approached her mother. For an embarrassing moment it looked like he'd clutch her in an amorous embrace. Instead he said, "May I have this dance?" and humming a waltz, swept her around the room like Rhett Butler with Scarlett O'Hara. They took exaggerated dips and mock fancy steps on the blond parquet floor, but there was no mockery in their eyes as they looked at one another. Diane told herself she was hateful, that she was the luckiest girl alive to have such beautiful parents who loved each other so much, but just watching them increased her misery. Why hadn't Daddy asked her to dance? He'd be dancing with Mama all night.

They danced out into the hall, Diane following, mesmerized.

"You can wear this finally, it's cold enough tonight," Daddy said, draping a white chinchilla cape over her mother's shoulders. He'd given it to her last Christmas. Diane's father stood back and looked at Mama. "My goodness, aren't you devastating?" he said. Then he noticed her. "Don't despair, one of these days you'll give your mama a run for her money."

But looking in the mirror, all Diane saw was her pudgy self bulging out behind her mother, so slim and graceful.

Mama must have felt sorry for her. "Since it's Friday night, you can stay up until we get home, and I'll tell you everything that happened," she promised.

As soon as they were out the door, Diane ran to the window and watched as her father ceremoniously helped her mother into the yellow roadster. Then he got in and went speeding out the driveway like a maniac, turning on two wheels into the street. He never looked in either direction, as if being a Colquitt gave him the right-of-way on the road as it did in life. What if someone didn't yield, though? What if they got hit head-on? A shiver ran up her spine.

Diane wandered aimlessly around downstairs. There wasn't much room to wander in. It was a small house, built a hundred years ago. People who didn't know might think they didn't have much money, but those in the know would notice the curly pine paneling and the Savonnerie rug hand-woven in Vienna. But Mama spent so much time running around she didn't care how the house looked. Sometimes Diane thought it would be fun living at Colquitt Hall, but they scarcely ever even visited there. It looked just like something out of *Gone with the Wind*, with its white pillars and oaks dripping Spanish moss. It rightfully belonged to Daddy, but Mama wouldn't live there. She said it was too isolated and anyway gave her the creeps. "If your brother wants to play plantation owner and have all that fuss and bother of servants and repairs, let him," she said. Daddy didn't argue. He always let Mama have her way.

Out in the kitchen, Diane got some banana cream pie, chocolate cupcakes, ambrosia cake, more potato chips, and another Dr Pepper. While she made her selection, she listened to Bing Crosby crooning away in Jewel's room down the hall. Mama said Jewel was a real jewel and the last of her kind. Jewel had taken care of Mama when she was a little girl.

Diane put everything on a tray and got her book in by the fireplace. Daddy had been too taken up with Mama to put the fire out before he left. What if a spark caught fire and the whole place burned down like Tara? Jewel would escape, since she was downstairs. She'd burn up. Serve you right, too, fatty, she told herself as she went up the steps with the tray.

After she finished eating, she put down her book, brushed the crumbs off the bed, and washed her hands before rearranging her doll collection in the antique glass cabinet. Uncle Clayton had brought back dolls for her from his European trip. Diane's favorites were the flamenco dancers that she called Carmen and Don José. Carmen had miniature castanets that actually clicked. Don José wore a red velvet bolero embroidered with gold threads. Mama said he looked like a waiter. Uncle Clayton had looked hurt. If Mama had jilted him, couldn't she be kinder?

Diane put on her nightgown and brushed her teeth. Standing before the medicine-closet mirror, she coiled her hair high up like Mama's. Suddenly she felt hope. She did look like Mama. At least from the neck up. And hadn't Daddy said she'd slim down? But he was being tactful. She felt fat and bloated and deeply ashamed of herself for being such a pig. Never again. Tomorrow she'd turn over a new leaf and go on a diet. Only she'd told herself that far too often to believe it.

She got back into bed and lay watching the fish swimming around the aquarium. The glass sides were getting mossy. She'd have to clean it again. The snails were supposed to eat the moss and extra fish food, but they didn't keep up. She overfed the fish as well as herself. Through half-closed eyes she watched the angelfish and neon tetras float in the dreamy green darkness, lovely and serene. I *will* go on a diet tomorrow, she vowed. And I will think only nice thoughts. She lay awake waiting for Mama and Daddy to return, then floated off into green darkness, too.

It was ringing and ringing. She opened her eyes to the lighted aquarium and wondered who'd phone at this hour. The ringing went on as if the phone wouldn't give up until answered. She got out of bed and was halfway down the stairs when she saw Jewel shuffle by below in bedroom slippers and a cast-off robe of Mama's. Jewel picked up the phone from the hall table and sleepily said, "Huh?" She kept saying "huh" as if she didn't understand, and all of a sudden gave a sharp short yelp of pain. "Oh, sweet Jesus," she said. She said it over and over, like a chant. Then, "Yes, ma'am, I'll do like you say, let Mistah Clayton take care of it when he get back."

Diane was sure it was about Jewel's son Willy. He'd done something terrible again. Got drunk and went after someone with a knife. Uncle Clayton was always getting him out of jail.

After she hung up, Jewel sat there small and huddled. Maybe this time Willy had killed someone or gotten himself killed. Diane ran down the rest of the steps and threw her arms around Jewel. "What's wrong? Did something awful happen?"

Jewel came to with a start and looked up at Diane, her dark face showing horror and pity. But why pity? "It's nothing, lamb. Come on, you and me'll go upstairs and I'll tuck you in bed."

"Fourteen's too old for that," Diane said. But big tears were rolling down Jewel's face, so that she knew it would comfort Jewel to put her to bed and take her mind off her troubles. "Is it something personal, something you can't talk about?"

Jewel moaned.

"Uncle Clayton will take care of things, don't you worry," she said, giving Jewel a consoling hug as Jewel had so often consoled her.

"Climb into bed, lamb," Jewel said. She pulled the covers up under Diane's chin. The bedroom was chilly but not cold. Jewel sat there beside her, holding her hand, tears streaming down a face as lined and cracked as old linoleum. She kept moaning "sweet Jesus" until the phone rang again and she shuffled down to answer it. The phone rang off and on all night. Poor Jewel, Diane thought sleepily, and wondered what awful mess Willy had gotten himself into this time. He wasn't really bad except when he got what Jewel called "demon likker" in him.

The morning light was strong and bright filtering through the flowered curtains. Diane jumped out of bed, surprised at how cold the floor was when her feet touched. She looked at the alarm clock. Nine-twenty. She'd slept right through her parents' return and hadn't heard about the dance. She pattered down the hall barefoot and in her nightgown to her parents' bedroom. The door was still closed. Probably Daddy was sleeping off a hangover. But Mama never had hangovers. She might be in the kitchen right now having breakfast.

Diane went downstairs and into the dining room. She stopped short when she heard Willy in the kitchen. He was talking fast, excitedly, and Jewel was sobbing. Defending his behavior, most likely. At least he was alive and not in jail, so he hadn't killed anyone, or vice versa. She knew she shouldn't eavesdrop, but she wanted to hear. And she couldn't go out into the kitchen in her nightgown with Willy there. Jewel said she was too old now to run around in her nightgown in front of grown men.

Jewel was talking. Half-talking and half-crying. "Miz Stewart, she so broken up she don't make sense at first. I couldn't half make out what she was talking about. She kept telling me don't say nothing, don't say nothing, Mistah Clayton he been notified and he driving back from Atlanta right away and he tell her. So I takes her up to bed and tucks her in and don't say nothing. She think it you. She think you got into trouble again and say to me, 'Don't you worry none, Jewel, Uncle Clayton he take care of it.' Poor child."

"Hell, I wasn't drinking. I was behind the bar serving drinks. It was Duncan Colquitt doing the drinking. Course, he always do. They nearly last to go. Everyone else done gone except the Stewarts and Judge and Miz Pierce. Not four, five minutes after they left, we hears this big loud explosion sounding like the end of the world.

"Everyone runs out to see what's happening, and there's this great big ol' truck shooting flames sky-high and that yellow car of Mistah Duncan's rammed right smack into its rear end. Miz Meredith, she running. Her hair on fire and blood all down the front of that white dress and white chinchilly coat. The truck driver, he okay. Not a scratch on him. He done jumped out of the cab. He keep saying it wasn't none of it his fault, that that car done turned right outta the lane and come whizzing straight at him. He say he stepped on the accelerator and prayed. Time we get Mistah Duncan outta the car, he black as us, crumpled up like burnt paper."

Diane felt a coldness come over her, a chill that went straight to her bones and hurt her teeth. She let out a cry, and the floor came up.

A damp cloth was pressed to her forehead. Uncle Clayton was talking, sounding angry. "I don't know what damn fool thing you were thinking of, Jewel." And Jewel said, "I swear to God, Mistah Clayton, Willy and me, we talking, we didn't have no idea she was listening, and Willy he say what happened out to the country club, and—"

"Hush. Now, you just hush, hear? You've said enough. Go upstairs and pack this child's clothes. She's coming with me."

Jewel's steps lumbered out of the room. A gentle hand touched her shoulder. "Honey, you awake?"

She opened her eyes and looked up into Uncle Clayton's.

"My poor little girl," he said, "my poor little Diane."

She clung to him, feeling the soft material of his suit and smelling his pipe tobacco. His voice was as gentle as his touch. "Now, honey, you run along upstairs and get dressed. You're coming home with me. You'll have to be brave. We'll both have to be brave and look after each other. We're all we've got."

Diane nodded and reluctantly let go of him. She went up to her room. Jewel dressed her as if she were a baby. She said how it was the most terrible thing she'd ever heard of. "Your mama and daddy, so happy and full of life, and then this. You don't know when you born what the good Lord has in store for you," Jewel said. "But I seen something bad coming. I seen it coming. Many's the time I say to myself, look out there, Miss Meredith, watch your step, Mistah Duncan, you born under a lucky star, but your bad times coming like they come to everyone. The good Lord, he don't like it when folks get so high and mighty. The Bible say the Lord God, he a jealous God, and he wreak his vengeance. Here, honey lamb, you put on your coat, it cold out there."

It was her good navy-blue princess coat with the white lace collar. She held her arms out stiffly. Jewel put her coat on her.

Downstairs Jewel handed her suitcase to Uncle Clayton. The last she saw of Jewel was her face outside the car window streaming tears.

Diane didn't cry. She couldn't. She felt a great remoteness. From Jewel. From herself. Everything looked so strange.

The big black Lincoln glided silently through the streets. Some people recognized the car. They took sidelong glances. She shrank back, trying to blend in with the upholstery.

"Cold?" Uncle Clayton asked. After turning on the heater, he put his hand over hers. Diane was grateful for his hand. His silence. For not talking on and on like Jewel. For not looking at her like Jewel. Who had guessed. Who had known she'd wished her parents dead, and the good Lord had wreaked his vengeance and punished her. No, that was crazy, preacher talk Jewel heard in her Holy Roller church. Anyway, her parents weren't dead. They'd staged the whole thing. It was a joke. Wasn't Mama always saying how boring it was here, how she wished they lived in Atlanta? She bet anything that's where they were right now.

Uncle Clayton was talking, his voice soothing. She didn't listen to what he said, but she liked hearing his voice and the way his hand held hers.

They were outside the city limits now, driving along a country road. Uncle Clayton said, "Chester can put the tank in the pickup truck and bring them to Colquitt Hall."

He was talking about her fish. It was a relief to discuss something so ordinary. She told him how the ride would be too rough for the angelfish, who'd lose their stripes and go into a shimmy from shock. Maybe never come out of it. "They have to be put in some kind of small container so they won't get too much of a jolt," she said.

"All right, honey, we'll tend to that. Delia's bound to have some jars in the kitchen. Maybe tomorrow if you feel up to it, we'll pick up the fish and anything else you want. Your doll collection. You can choose any bedroom you like in the house, including mine," Uncle Clayton said, smiling kindly. He squeezed her hand. He looked just like Daddy, with the same silvery blond hair. When she closed her eyes, it was like having Daddy next to her, hearing the exact same voice.

The car turned up the lane, and they drove through a tunnel of oaks. Gray oaks with thick trunks and branches trailing gray moss. Where had the sun gone? It was like twilight everywhere. The house couldn't be seen for the trees until the Lincoln pulled up into the driveway before the wide curving steps leading up to the veranda. When the motor cut off, a deep silence set in. She wasn't sure, but she thought she saw a face peering out from an upstairs window, but the windows themselves seemed to be peering at her with hostile eyes. She remembered Mama's saying the place gave her the creeps. Suddenly she was scared. She wanted Mama, with her Tinkerbell laugh; Daddy, with his jokes. That was a mean trick of theirs, going to Atlanta, especially after promising they'd be back to tell her all about the dance.

Uncle Clayton got out with her suitcase. His gray suit blended with the gray oaks. "Come along, sweetheart," he said.

She got out and went up the steps behind him. He held the door open, letting her go in first. She went into the entrance hall, empty except for the crystal chandelier suspended from a high ceiling. On either side of the hall, curving stairways led to an upstairs balcony. She felt dwarfed by the vastness.

"Come along, honey, we'll pick you out a bedroom," Uncle Clayton said.

Bedroom? She was confused. "Am I going to stay here?"

"Of course you're staying here, you're living right here with me." He took her hand and led her up the stairs. When they reached the balcony, he set her suitcase down and put his arm around her. "There's just the two of us now, honey, we'll have to look out for each other, won't we?" She nodded, and he kissed her. Full on the lips. No one had kissed her full on the lips before. It was like sealing some sacred vow.

"Now, come along, we'll find you a room," he said.

5. *Gina*

A man's voice. Whispers. Gina opened her eyes and sat up, feeling panic. She remembered instantly Don Guidetti coming toward her from the bar. But where was he now? Was he whispering behind that door? And where was she? She looked around for clues. Autographed photographs of movie stars on the wall. Were they friends of Don Guidetti's? A photograph of President Roosevelt. Him, too?

She'd been sleeping on a davenport. Her sweater, skirt, and coat were neatly folded on a nearby chair. She was in her slip. She must get dressed and get away. But the moment she put her right foot down on the floor, pain shot up to her head. Her ankle was as thick as her calf, swollen and shapeless, her toes fat and purple. How could she escape when she couldn't bear to put her weight on her foot?

She strained her ears to hear the whispering.

"Now, lie back on the floor," a man was saying. "Without bending your knees, lean forward and touch your toes, keeping your arms out straight. Okay, ready? Let's go. Ten times to the count of ten. Uh-one-uh, uh-two-uh, uh-three-uh . . ." The voice was accompanied by music. After the count to ten, the music swelled, then softened. "This is Smilin' Dan, your exercise man. Don't forget to tune in tomorrow, same time, same station. Keep in touch. And keep in shape."

The sound clicked off, and a soft husky woman's voice began to sing "Over the Rainbow," asking if birds could fly over a rainbow why she couldn't too.

The singing came closer. The door opened. A woman peered in. She had pink pageboy hair and wore a white wrapper with bedraggled neck feathers. "Feeling better?" she called cheerfully. It was the beautiful woman with Don Guidetti at the bar last night. Only, in the daylight she didn't look so beautiful.

"Brought you some orange juice. Straight from the orange cow I keep in the backyard, ha-ha," the woman said. She pranced across the room in spike-heeled mules with flea-bitten fluff around the ankles and worn spots on the satin toes.

"Drink up," she ordered, handing Gina the glass and watching to see that she did. Gina sipped slowly, wondering when she'd feel the effects of the knockout drops.

"What's your name, kid?"

Don Guidetti hadn't told her? "Gina. Gina Sabatini."

"That's a funny name," the woman said. She preened herself above the bedraggled feathers. "*I* am Georgette Divine. You've heard of me, of course? People call me Simply Divine for short, ha-ha. Nah, it's Georgette Divine Dinsmore. That's Harry Dinsmore there," she said, tapping a long red fingernail on the groom in a wedding picture. It was a silver heart-shaped frame on a nearby table. The bride wore a tight-fitting bridal gown with a sweetheart neckline. The groom, like her pageboy, came just to her shoulders. He had black bangs and a toothbrush mustache and looked like Hitler.

"Handsome Harry. Don't you think he's handsome?"

Gina nodded, not wanting to irritate her captor. She was sure she wasn't at Don Guidetti's and that Georgette was keeping her here until he came for her.

"Yeah, handsome Harry. Known as Amazin' Harry. A magician. He's a magician, all-righty-right. After our wedding night he took my savings and did a disappearing act."

"That was a dirty trick," Gina said.

"Yeah, a dirty magician's trick, ha-ha. Well, honey, you live and learn. Win a few, lose a few. Some people do you dirt, others a kindness. That's the world we live in. Whaddya want for breakfast? Bacon and eggs okay? I'll getcha some. Your ankle looks like hell. You must've taken a bad fall. How'd it happen? Want some milk? A growing girl needs calcium for her bones, me mither used to say."

She left the room, but this time kept the door open. The better to keep an eye on her. But the knockout drops hadn't worked yet. At the far end of the davenport was a window. Gina scooted down, hoping to find that they were on the ground floor, where she could open a window, tumble out, and crawl for help. What she saw was a thin river far below between thick trees. Alongside ran a ribbon of highway with tiny cars. Gina's spirits slumped, but the delicious smell of bacon and coffee revived her, as if hunger were more important than safety.

Georgette pranced in with a tray holding the food and a flower in a water glass. Gina wasn't sure what kind of flower. She didn't know much about flowers. It was pink, but not a rose. She nearly cried. How could Georgette be so kind as to give her a flower and so cruel as to keep her captive for Don Guidetti? She did cry. A tear sneaked down her cheek. Before she could wipe it away, Georgette saw. "Aw, don't cry, honey. I know, it's a rotten world."

Realizing that tears had a softening effect on Georgette, as they'd had on Mrs. Donovan, Gina cried harder. Maybe if she got Georgette's sympathy, Georgette wouldn't hand her over. "Please help me get away from him. He's so old and ugly."

"Huh? Who you talking about?" Georgette asked, pretending innocence.

"Don Guidetti. When's he coming for me?"

"Jeeze, are you nuts, or me? I don't know any Guidetti guy. You come up with the funniest names."

"That man at the bar last night."

"That's Papa."

"He's not your papa, you can't fool me."

"He's not my . . . Oh, I see what you mean." Georgette let out a laugh. "Papa is short for Papadopolous."

Papadopolous? And she thought Guidetti was a funny name?

"I always tell him he's Greek to me, ha-ha. Nah, he's not a bad guy. He's the boss man. Runs the Dance Casino."

Gina felt tremendous relief, then mounting suspicion. Was Georgette lying? He'd looked just like Don Guidetti—bald, fat, thick-lipped. Except, in her upset condition she'd seen those she was scared of everywhere she went last night.

"Why's this Guidetti guy coming to get you? You done something wrong? You gave us a real scare, kiddo, passing out cold. Naturally, I was the one who got stuck. I always get stuck. That's the story of my life, Georgette Sucker Divine. All the other girls, they said they didn't have no extra room.

"You didn't look sick enough for a hospital, and no one wanted to call the cops, for their own reasons. But I couldn't see dumping you in the middle of Times Square, so I told Papa if he paid for the cab fare, I'd take you home."

Gina felt weak with relief. She couldn't stop smiling. "Thank you," she said.

"You're welcome, I guess," Georgette said. She took a sip of coffee, holding out her little finger as daintily as Mrs. Donovan, but Mrs. Donovan wouldn't have left a lipstick smear on the rim. "If you're not going to drink this, I am. You haven't even drunk your milk. Now, listen, kid—Gina, whatever the hell your name is—I'm not nosy and I don't give unsolicited advice, but if you was to ask what to do, I'd say go home. There's a lot of dirty skunks around ready to prey on young innocent girls. I know. I ran away, too."

"You did? Why?"

"Listen, kiddo, there's nothing no one's done I haven't done—in spades. And if you grew up in a one-horse town like me, you'd see why. Dead as a graveyard. The one big event was the circus coming to town once a year. When I was fifteen, I left with it. Anyways, I always felt like a freak out there in the corn growers' state, so I fit in fine."

While Georgette talked, Gina planned. Although it was a gloomy day, the room was bright and cheerful, with flowered chintz curtains at the windows and all those movie stars on the wall. Georgette must have a bedroom to herself, since she'd slept somewhere else last night. That meant room enough for two. Her seven dollars wouldn't last long, even if she got a room dirt cheap. And she needed a job. Maybe if she got on the good side of Georgette, she'd put in a word with that Papa person and Gina could dance at the Dance Casino.

"You know, you look just like Ginger Rogers," Gina said.

"That's funny, you'd be surprised how many people say that."

"No, I wouldn't. I noticed last night. You could be twins."

"I like you, Gina."

"I like you, too," Gina said. That was true. She'd never met anyone so nice, but she wasn't going to let her feelings get in the way; she wanted to live here and work at the Dance Casino. "And you've got a swell place, fixed up so nice. Anyone can tell you've got good taste."

Georgette beamed. Even her bedraggled feathers perked up. "You'd be surprised how many people tell me that," she said.

"You live here alone?"

"Ever since Amazin' Harry did his disappearing act. With my money. The thing is, I still love that goddamn little sneak," Georgette said, looked glum, and lapsed into silence.

Gina tried again. "What did you do in the circus?"

"Ha, what didn't I do? I did everyone better, that's what. I learned how to ride a unicycle. That's a one-wheeled bicycle. On a tightrope. I got a terrific sense of balance. They gave me top billing. Georgette Divine on Her Flying Machine. 'Course, that don't rhyme if you say it out loud, but I guess no one did. Everything was coming up roses until someone sawed at the rope and I fell. I know who. It was that bitch Tanya the Tattooed Lady. I'm sure of it, since she was jealous of me and Leopold the Strong Man.

"No broken bones, there was a net below, but believe you me I was shaken up. I just couldn't climb back on that unicycle. So I quit the circus and did some other things. No need to ask what. You make do with what you got, is my motto. But I always kept my sights high, no matter how low I sank. I took dancing lessons, tap and ballroom, and hung out at burlesque houses until I got the knack. No one was hiring tap dancers, so I went one better. I tapped and balloon-danced at the same time. There's this picture I got of me tapping and bouncing balloons on my boobs I'll show you sometime. I'm wearing this real cute skimpy little costume."

"I bet you're a real good dancer."

"Yeah, I'm pretty good."

"I bet it's fun dancing at Dance Casino."

"It's a living."

"Do you suppose I could get a job there?"

"Listen, kid, like I told you, take my advice and go home. It's more spills then thrills in the world out there."

"I can't."

"Sure you can, you just think you can't. Your folks will welcome you with open arms."

"Yeah, Papa would, all right. He tried to use me to pay off his debts. That's why I ran away. He was going to hand me over to this fat old guy, Don Guidetti."

"You lying?"

"God's truth. That's why I went to the Dance Casino last night, to see if I could get a job and support myself."

At first Georgette didn't believe her, any more than Mary Donovan had; then her solutions were the same as Mary's, except she didn't recommend prayer. Gina held out for the Dance Casino.

"It's no life for a little kid,"Georgette said.

"It beats streetwalking," Gina said.

"Yeah, but not much." Georgette's feathers looked bedraggled again. She picked at them, trying to perk them up. "Listen, kid, tell you what. You can stay here and get a job somewheres. Maybe clerking in the five-and-dime. I got an extra room. It's filled with my unicycle and mementos and stuff, but I'll clear it out. Don't worry about rent none. When you start working, you can start paying. And I'll charge just for your room, seeing as how the apartment's mine."

"Gee, thanks, I really appreciate that."

"Yeah, okay, I know what it is to be down and out."

But Gina didn't want to clerk at any five-and-dime. "The thing is," she said, "if I get a job at Woolworth's, I can't go to school. I'll be working in a five-and-ten the rest of my life. But if I got a job at the Dance Casino, then I could go to school during the day and get an education, and later a good job like a secretary."

Georgette nodded. "I see what you mean. You're a smart kid, Gina. My one big regret is I don't have no education. All I got is my body, and bodies wear out. It don't matter I exercise to keep in trim. The body goes. Men don't look you over, they look over you."

"Not you, you're the most beautiful girl at the Dance Casino."

"That's not saying much, you see that bunch in daylight. Yeah, I guess I'll pass in soft lights and fixed up some. Okay, kid, I'll teach you dancing and put in a word to Papa. All you gotta know is the basic two-step grind."

"Grind?"

"Yeah, someone gets fresh, you grind your heel in their foot. Listen, they're entitled to a dance for their dime, but no free feel. And if they try to get off by pushing up against you, give 'em a knee in the groin. Anyway, dancing, that's not where the money's at. It's drinking. You get a commish, see?"

"Commish?"

"Commission. Extra money. You drink with them, only you're drinking tea and they're paying for whiskey. All you do is smile and listen. You'd be surprised how many guys just want to talk while you make goo-goo eyes and say how wonderful they are. It's not so bad if you steer clear of the slimy ones. Trouble is, they're almost all slimy."

It took nearly a week for Gina's ankle to get better. She lay around the apartment reading Georgette's magazines: movie, fan, *True Confession*, and *Saturday Evening Post*. Georgette said she read the *Saturday Evening Post* to improve her mind. Before taking Gina to see Papa Papadopolous for the job, Georgette took her shopping for the right outfit. "You're the exotic type," she told Gina, and selected an orange dress with red poppies.

Papa hired her immediately. Georgette said he was a nice family man and wouldn't give her any trouble, but he looked so much like Don Guidetti that Gina couldn't like him. Still, the resemblance helped. Every time Gina had to dance with some slimy creep, she'd look at Papa and think how things could be worse.

After paying off Georgette, Gina bought a coat with a squirrel collar to replace her old coat, shiny and threadbare. She was crazy about her coat and loved pulling the collar up to feel the soft fur caress her cheek. She'd had to dance her feet off to pay for it, but it was worth every cent.

With Georgette's advice, Gina soon learned how to handle the men who tried to crawl all over her. It was the other girls at the dance hall who gave her the trouble. They resented her popularity. In a small back room each girl had a stool at a long bench facing a stagelit mirror for putting on makeup, just as if they were actresses. Often when Gina took her place she found her powder spilled, lipstick broken off, and "WHORE" written in lipstick across the mirror. She pretended not to notice, sure that they'd give up after a while. One night when Gina went into the back room to freshen up during the band break, she saw her coat had fallen off the hook. When she went over to get it, she saw that it hadn't fallen. Someone had ripped the squirrel collar and flung it down. She held the coat in her lap as if it were a child and sobbed.

Georgette came in. "Papa wants to know what the hell happened to you," she said.

Gina mutely held up her coat.

"Why, those bitches, goddamn their eyes. That's okay, honey, don't you worry, I'll take care of things."

When the dance hall had closed for the night and the girls were in the back room putting on their coats, Georgette entered, slammed the door, and stood with her arms folded over her chest. "Now, listen you bitches," she said. "This kid's just fifteen years old, young enough to be a daughter of some of you gals. You know why she's working here? Because her old man tried to swap her for some money he owed, and she ran away."

Gina wished Georgette hadn't said that. It was embarrassing. She cried all the harder.

"Now, the next time one of you bitches does anything like this, I'll beat the shit out of you," Georgette said. "And if that don't work, I'll pass the word on to Papa and you can haul ass and go look for a job somewheres else. Also, the person or persons responsible for this can damn well get out their little sewing kits and put that collar back on and return it in mint condition."

After that, Gina didn't have any trouble with the girls at the Dance Casino. Her trouble was keeping awake at school. She left the dance hall as soon as it closed at four in the morning, but it took a half-hour to get home by subway, and usually it was five by the time she got to bed.

At seven in the morning, after two hours of sleep, she got up and tiptoed about getting dressed while drinking coffee. When the teachers caught her dozing in class they scolded her for running around nights and not doing her homework. Gina told no one she was a dime-a-dance girl. She stayed aloof from her classmates, who were mere children.

She read stories about rich boys home from fancy colleges for Christmas who went to dance halls for a lark. There the richest and most handsome boy fell in love with one of the dancers. She never met anyone rich or handsome from a fancy college. They hadn't heard of the Dance Casino.

Gina took typing and shorthand to get a secretarial job. She wished she could have studied languages instead. French or Spanish, which were related to Italian and would be easier to learn and more interesting than making dumb squiggles in a shorthand pad.

But she loved art class and her art teacher, Mr. Kirkpatrick. On Saturdays he sometimes took his favorite students to museums, and Gina fast became a favorite. They went to the Frick, the Metropolitan, the Museum of Modern Art, and the Cloisters, which had just opened last year. She loved the solitude and beauty of the Cloisters although she preferred the paintings in the Museum of Modern Art. Often she went alone on Sunday afternoons. Once, just once, she'd taken Georgette. Georgette had become bored. The nude statues had scandalized her. She'd giggled at them and embarrassed Gina.

Gina enjoyed having money of her own to spend on what she liked. Her biggest thrill was buying her first oil paints and canvas. In the summer, when school was out, she went to Riverside Park and painted all day, ignoring the men who tried to pick her up or the disgusted comments of people who peered over her shoulder. They informed her that what she was painting didn't look like a tree. Gina wasn't trying to paint the way the tree looked, but the way it felt.

She also bought Giuliano his Brownie camera. She wrote a brief note and tucked it in the little gift envelope, telling him she was okay and would get in touch. She didn't put on her return address.

She and Georgette visited the World's Fair to see all the wonderful things the future had in store for mankind. They went to watch Sally Rand do her fan dance, two of the few women in an audience of men. Georgette was entranced. "She's got real class," she said after the show. "I wish I'd thought of fans."

6. Diane

Summer. Early in the morning, before anyone was up, even Delia, Uncle Clayton would come into her room. "Wake up, sleepyhead," he'd say, and kiss her on the nose, then pull down the sheet so she'd lie there slightly shivering in her nightgown in the cool of the morning and be sure to stay awake. Once she was mortified when her nightgown had slipped down and a breast was exposed. He had smiled as if amused by her blushes and said he'd had no idea she was such a well-developed young lady. He'd pulled the strap of her nightgown up over her shoulder, his fingers accidentally touching her breast. For hours afterward her skin had tingled where he'd touched.

Uncle Clayton would be already dressed in a polo shirt and riding jodhpurs. While he went down and made the coffee and put it in a thermos, she donned her polo shirt and jodhpurs and met him out at the stable. Emory, the groom, wasn't even there yet. Uncle Clayton saddled his horse, Beauregard, and she saddled Lancelot. He'd given her Lancelot for getting straight A's on her report card. Lancelot was a beautiful chestnut color. At first she'd been a little afraid of him, but Uncle Clayton said there was nothing to be scared of. He said Lancelot was very gentle, and besides, if you were afraid, the animal smelled it. She hid her fear from her uncle, and apparently the horse, too, for Lancelot had started off at an amiable trot and never once acted up.

They rode fast and hard, letting the horses have their lead and work off their pent-up energy. Diane loved the feel of the air whizzing by, blowing her hair back as they galloped into the woods, where they startled birds and small animals. Both Emory and Uncle Clayton said they'd never seen anyone take so readily to the saddle, but Diane could never keep up with Uncle Clayton and now only caught glimpses of his blue polo shirt in the distance.

After a while he slowed down and they rode side by side in the semidarkness of the woods under intertwining branches. The moss hung so thick that the sun scarcely got through except for an occasional yellow patch in the dark greenness. Then suddenly there was a brightness like a sheet of aluminum, and they emerged from gloom to the bank of the Chattahoochee, where the water slipped over a wide flat stone and splashed seven feet down below creating a mist. They dismounted and drank the coffee from the thermos Uncle Clayton had brought along. He always insisted she drink first. "You'll get my germs," she said.

"As long as we keep them in the family," he said with a smile.

It was all so glorious, the air baby fresh, the sun bright as new, and the water rising in a fine white mist as if it were the dawn of creation. She smelled the tobacco of Uncle Clayton's first pipe of the day and watched the sun glint silver on his hair.

"We used to go skinny-dipping right there in that pool," he said, pointing with his pipe stem. "Your father, mother, and me."

"Mama, too?" she asked, shocked. Her mother and two boys swimming naked?

"Your mother wasn't a slave to convention. She was a Bradford, and they're pretty much like the Colquitts. We don't follow the rules, we make them. Remember that. There are two kinds of people in this world, honey, the timid souls and the adventurous spirits. The timid souls worry about what people think, and the adventurous spirits don't give a hoot what anyone thinks."

"I guess I'm a timid soul."

"No, you're not. You can't be. You're a Bradford *and* a Colquitt. That's the best combination there is. I already know you're brave, but I'll have to find out how adventurous you are. One of these days you'll have to take the adventurous-spirit test."

"What do I do?"

"You'll see." He smiled and tucked a wayward strand of hair behind her ear. "Now, come on, we'd better get back so I won't have to bolt down breakfast. I've got a busy day at the office."

Even though she hurriedly showered and dressed, she missed out on the fun of having breakfast with him. In the bathroom she heard the car start up, and by the time she got to the bedroom window, the Lincoln's tail end was just disappearing under the tunnel of oaks. She speculated on what the adventurous-spirit test would be and worried she might fail it and disappoint Uncle Clayton. She wished she'd asked him why he thought she was brave. Maybe because she didn't cry after Mama and Daddy went away. Some people didn't think that was brave, though; they thought she was stone-hearted. She'd overheard Ambrosia telling Delia that it was unnatural the way she acted. "She don't cry or nothing," Ambrosia said.

Delia said tears came easily and crying didn't prove anything. She said Diane was in a state of shock after her parents' death. That's how much Delia knew. She wasn't in any state of shock. Her parents weren't dead. But Delia couldn't be blamed; no one knew this but her, not even Uncle Clayton.

Delia called up now and told her to come right down and get breakfast. Diane said she didn't want any. She liked Delia nearly as much as Jewel, but she couldn't stand the pity in her eyes. Everywhere she went, she got that look. It was in the eyes of passersby when she went to town, in the eyes of clerks and shopkeepers, in the eyes of her teachers and classmates at Miss Mayhew's. Her classmates never called her Piggy anymore. Of course, they had no reason to, since she'd lost so much weight. She was glad school was out for the summer, though. At school, they were always overly nice to her while at the same time avoiding her as if she had some kind of contagious disease. The only one who treated her as if she were halfway normal was Cindy Wilkinson.

Now that school was out, there wasn't much to do, though. She decided to clean the fish tank, practically a whole-day project. Uncle Clayton had brought her more fish back from Atlanta and she'd had to replace the ten-gallon tank with a twenty-five-gallon one because it got so crowded. One night when she lay in bed looking at what she'd thought a peaceful aquarium scene, she'd discovered an angelfish cringing in the corner, its tail ragged from nips taken by the other fish as they darted by. When she'd waved her hand to frighten them away, she'd merely succeeded in scaring the angel. She'd gone downstairs and got a jar to put the angelfish in overnight, but the next morning found it floating belly-up. After that she'd got the bigger tank, but the fish still singled out a victim to torment.

Now she went down to the kitchen to get containers to put the fish in while cleaning the tank. "You don't eat any breakfast, and you getting skinny as a rail," Delia complained. "I baked buttermilk biscuits special this morning for you."

Diane took a biscuit to make Delia happy and went back upstairs to her fish. She put the biscuit down and forgot about it as she netted the fish and transferred them into the containers. The snails were proliferating. They were worse than rabbits. She'd started with just a few, and now they were taking over the tank, there were so many. She'd have to get rid of them, but to be flushed down the toilet seemed a cruel fate. Instead she put them in a paper bag, and while the new water was settling in the clean tank, took the snails to the river, setting them loose on the bank.

After lunch, which she ate to placate Delia, she returned to her fish, but after transferring them to the clean aquarium, there was nothing more to do. She lay in bed and thought about her parents, who'd secretly slipped off to Europe as they'd planned all along to do. They would have taken her—Daddy had wanted to—but Mama said it would interfere with her schooling.

No one had known that the caskets with the closed lids were empty and that her parents had pulled a fast one. First, they'd gone to Atlanta. From there they'd gone to New York, taking a boat to Europe just as Uncle Clayton had, docking at Southampton and going by boat train to London. After London, they'd gone to Paris and then on to Venice. Yesterday they'd driven through the Austrian Alps to Vienna. "Diane would have loved this trip," her father said. Today, which was actually night in Vienna because of the time change, her parents were at the opera.

The Viennese opera house was very beautiful, all white and gold, with velvet draperies, chandeliers, and tiered boxes. The audience was chiefly handsome officers in uniform and beautiful women with diamond tiaras. But the most beautiful people there were her mother and father. He was wearing his black dress suit and Mama her white Grecian dress with the jade clasp. They were the center of attention, stared at through lorgnettes by haughty old ladies. Instead of paying attention to the opera, the audience focused their binoculars on her parents.

The opera was *La Traviata*. No, *Madama Butterfly*. Cho Cho San was singing that beautiful aria about some fine day when Lieutenant Pinkerton would return. Tears streamed down Diane's face at the sadness and beauty of the words and music. She knew just how Cho Cho San felt.

Suddenly, right in the middle of the aria, the phone rang downstairs. Diane went rigid. Who could be calling? No one ever phoned except when Uncle Clayton was home. What if something terrible had happened to him and they were calling to give Delia the news? She became dizzy with fear.

"It's for you, honey," Delia called up.

Diane went slowly down the stairs on weak legs. "Who is it?"

"Why, honey, I dunno, it sound like one of your little friends."

She picked up the phone and spoke a hesitant hello.

"Hi," a cheerful voice said. Cindy Wilkinson.

Diane always felt a little awkward talking to her classmates, but she didn't with Cindy, who chattered away a mile a minute. "I'm having a birthday party Saturday, you have to come. It's going to be a picnic party around the pool. Bring your bathing suit, and keep your fingers crossed it doesn't rain. There'll be a lot of boys."

"Boys?" Diane shrieked, her heart speeding up.

"Boys," Cindy affirmed. "You know, the other half of the human race they never let us get near at Miss Mayhew's."

"Or anywhere else."

Cindy giggled.

"I don't know how to act around boys," Diane said, a confession she'd make only to Cindy.

"That's because you don't have any brothers. Listen, honey, *you* don't have to act. With your face and figure, all you have to do is stand there in your bathing suit and let them make silly fools of themselves."

After she hung up, Diane skipped across the floor and took the stairs two at a time. A picnic! Swimming! Boys! Oh, God, what'll I do? she asked herself, happy and alarmed at the same time. She rummaged through drawers looking for a bathing suit. She had two. The navy-blue tank suit was far too big for her since she'd lost so much weight. The pink one was elasticized and fit despite the weight loss, but it looked somewhat frayed. She remembered Cindy's remark about her face and figure. Was Cindy just being flattering? She always buttered people up. Her uncle said the Wilkinsons were *nouveaux riches* and had to buy friends because they didn't have any social standing. Diane studied herself in the mirror, uncertain of whether she looked good or bad. Once she'd gone into Emory's lodgings over the garage and had seen a picture of a girl on a calendar. She'd worn a white swimsuit and carried an adorable floppy-eared puppy. Standing on a sandy beach, she'd had one leg arched, toe pointed as if to test the water. Diane struck a similar pose.

Suddenly she heard a noise from behind and turned to see Uncle Clayton in the doorway. Her face grew hot. What would he think of her in such a silly pose?

"Well, aren't you something?" he said. His face was flushed, as if from drinking, but that couldn't be since he never drank before five, and it wasn't yet three o'clock.

She laughed a little nervously. "You're home early."

He nodded but didn't say why. He walked around her. "That's a mighty nice fit, but it looks kind of raggedy."

"It's two years old. Can I get a new one? I need something nice for Cindy's pool party. She's having one for her fifteenth birthday."

He looked startled, his face flushing more deeply. "A party? What's all this about? You didn't mention any party before."

"I was just invited a half-hour ago."

"Who all is going to be at this party? Any boys?"

"It'll be well-chaperoned," she said evasively. "Mr. and Mrs. Wilkinson will be there." She was sure Mrs. Wilkinson, at least, would.

"Now, honey, I'm your guardian and I've got to look out for you. You're just too young yet to go to a party with boys. And the Wilkinsons, they're common as dirt. They've been trying to buy their way into things for years, and now they're using their daughter."

She thought of the empty summer days with no company but her fish and Lancelot. Her parents would have let her go to the party. She could hear her mother saying it was time she met boys, and Daddy wouldn't care that the Wilkinsons bought their way in. He'd just laugh and say someone had to start somewhere sometime. "I want to go. Mother and Daddy would let me. You just don't want me to be with anyone my age and have any fun."

Uncle Clayton's eyes darkened and his lips pressed together, but only for a moment. In fact, she might have imagined it, for now he smiled and sighed. "I want you to have fun, honey, but the right kind of fun with the right kind of people."

"But there won't be anything wrong. All the girls in my class are going." She didn't, of course, know that for a fact.

Uncle Clayton came over and stood behind her. Looking at

their mirror reflections, she felt funny in her beat-up bathing suit while he looked so handsome and debonair in his pale gray business suit with his silvery blond hair. "You ought to keep covered up," he said, snapping the elastic band of her bathing suit where it had slipped up over her buttocks. "All right, if you want to go to that party so bad, you can go." He slapped her playfully on the behind. "But if you're going to be in the social swim, you'd better have a better bathing suit than that. I'm going to Atlanta on business Friday. You come along, and while I'm tending to things, you can go shopping."

She was ashamed of herself. Uncle Clayton was so sweet and generous. She put her arms around him and kissed him. "Thank you," she said. He squeezed her to him for a long time. When he let go, she felt downright dizzy. "We'll have a good time in Atlanta," he promised.

"I guess it's my place to inform you of the birds and the bees," Uncle Clayton said.

They were in the Lincoln on their way to Atlanta. It was a lovely sunny day, with few cars on the highway. Diane looked over at him a little nervously. She knew talking about something like sex must embarrass him, too. "Oh, Mother told me all about it."

"All?" he asked, smiling.

"Well, she told me not to accept candy from old men or let anyone touch me in certain places."

"I'm afraid it's not that simple. At least the advantage of my being able to tell you what to beware of is I was a young man myself once."

"You haven't told me what places to shop in Atlanta," she said, to change the subject.

"I'll not only tell you, I'll show you. I'm going to be too late for my business appointment anyway, so I'll postpone it until tomorrow."

"Tomorrow's Saturday."

"That's all right, my client's office is open Saturday mornings."

"But Cindy's party is in the afternoon."

"Don't worry, I'll see you get back in time." He reached over and patted her above the knee, letting his hand rest on her bare thigh where she'd scrooched up her skirt, not wanting to wrinkle her dress by the time they got to Atlanta. She wished she could tell him in a tactful way to remove his hand. It embarrassed her the way she found his touch exciting. He didn't realize that, because he was her uncle. She felt ashamed and wondered if she were oversexed. She moved a little, but his hand remained firmly on her leg, his fingers burning the inside of her thigh. "Now, back to where we left off," he said. "The first thing is, I'm sorry to say, that young men will often prevaricate in order to extract certain favors from attractive young ladies."

"Oh," she said. It was all she could choke out, she was so flustered.

"To put it crudely, they will swear undying love, when all they want is to get into a girl's pants."

She didn't know where to look, she was so embarrassed and excited. She kept her eyes on the white line dividing the highway, noticing the car had crossed it. Luckily nothing was coming from the other direction. He looked over at her. "My goodness, your face looks like it's on fire. I won't prolong the conversation if it embarrasses you so much, but forewarned is forearmed. I don't want to see some boy make a fool of my little girl," he said, patted her thigh, and removed his hand. Diane sighed inwardly with relief.

Uncle Clayton got them rooms at a hotel near Five Points, which he said was the hub of Atlanta. After the loneliness and isolation of Colquitt Hall, Diane was bewildered by the big-city boisterousness, the hurry and scurry of cars and people. She was glad to be with Uncle Clayton, who knew Atlanta almost as well as Columbus. He took her to small exclusive shops where only a few choice items were on display. She tried on swimsuit after swimsuit over her panties in the dressing room, then went out to show Uncle Clayton, who never quite liked anything. The salesgirls found his presence disquieting. Diane knew it wasn't just the presence of a man in a women's preserve, but of a man as good-looking and charming as he. They selected clothes, not for her approval, but for his. "It isn't many fathers who take such an active interest in their daughters' clothes," one of the salesclerks said in the dressing room.

"He's not my father. He's my uncle."

"That's even more unusual. Is he married?"

"He's engaged to be married," she said. The salesgirl was young and attractive and might pursue him.

She got two swimsuits and a good dress to wear out that night, since Uncle Clayton said he'd take her to the best restaurant in town.

"Those salesgirls get mighty confused," she told him. "They don't know if you're my father, husband, or boyfriend."

"Well, let's just keep them guessing."

It was really funny when they went to the lingerie department. The clerk didn't know what to think. Probably, she guessed that her uncle was her boyfriend the way he displayed so much interest in her underwear. She bought three pairs of panties and brassieres—what the salesclerk called a dance set. They were all lacy and each a different color—beige, black, and white—nothing her mother would ever have allowed her to buy, but Uncle Clayton said pretty underclothes were as important as pretty outer clothes, like good thoughts to good deeds.

When she became so numb from shopping she couldn't think straight, Uncle Clayton took her to an old-fashioned ice-cream parlor with white wrought-iron chairs and tables and pink, green, and white Jordan almonds in glass jars. Once again Uncle Clayton created a stir, like Prince Charming among so many sleeping beauties—not that they were all beauties.

"You can order anything your little heart desires," Uncle Clayton said, so she ordered a banana split with hot-fudge topping on a scoop of vanilla ice cream, butterscotch on chocolate, and pineapple on tutti-frutti. Topping the toppings were whipped cream, crushed nuts, and maraschino cherries. "I'll never get through this," she cried.

"Bet you do," he said. He was just having a lemon sherbet. He said he had to watch his waistline. After he finished the sherbet, he excused himself and mysteriously disappeared, saying he'd be back soon.

Diane wasn't sure if it were her imagination, but when he left, he seemed to take all the gaiety with him. Around her the women's conversation flagged, they slouched a little in their chairs and reprimanded their children, but when Uncle Clayton came back some twenty minutes later, spirits picked up again.

He was wearing a Cheshire-cat smile. "You've been up to something," she said.

She found out what, just before they went out to dinner.

She'd put on her new dress that was very grown-up and sophisticated just because of its utter simplicity. In fact, it looked rather like a slip—white, straight cut, with spaghetti straps. Wearing the dress, and with her hair coiled on top of her head, she looked at least nineteen. Uncle Clayton proclaimed her a knockout. She drank champagne from the bottle he'd ordered, the fizz going straight to her head. Down below, the streetlights had just come on. Automobile headlights came at each other from five different directions, lights shooting off everywhere like Fourth of July sparklers. "Golly, I didn't know Atlanta was so beautiful."

"Atlanta isn't the only beautiful thing," her uncle said.

He stood behind her, his hands on her bare shoulders. "Now, close your eyes, and don't open them until I tell you."

She closed her eyes and felt cool stones and warm fingers on her neck. "A necklace," she said, jumping up and down. "Can I look?"

"Not yet." Hands on her shoulders, he steered her across the room. "All right, now." She opened her eyes and gasped. Looking back at her was the person she'd always longed to be. Around that person's neck was an antique jade necklace, the stones matching her eye color perfectly.

"You're your mother incarnate," Uncle Clayton said.

It gave her an eerie feeling, looking in the mirror and seeing Mama, especially since Uncle Clayton so much looked like Daddy.

"Don't I even get a thank-you kiss?" he asked.

She stood on tiptoe and kissed his cheek. He tilted her chin with a finger and looked deeply into her eyes. "You're my favorite girl," he said.

There were more mirrors—and more champagne—at the restaurant. Their candlelit table was like a small golden island, the blue-tinted mirrors reflecting them in a sea of infinity. A five-piece orchestra played softly. While they waited for dinner, they danced among sedate couples on an ice-slick dance floor. Diane slipped and got the giggles. "Oh, oh, too much champagne," she said apologetically.

"You can never have too much of a good thing," Uncle Clayton said, and poured more champagne throughout dinner. She'd never eaten such a sumptuous meal: shrimp cocktail, *tournedos,* potato puffs, asparagus with hollandaise sauce, and a dreamy creamy dessert. Afterward Uncle Clayton ordered brandy because he said it was a special occasion. "Tonight you take your adventurous-spirit test," he announced.

"Adventurous spirit?"

"Don't you remember our discussion a while back, about timid souls and adventurous spirits?"

"What kind of test?"

"That's a secret, but don't worry, I have the utmost confidence in you."

She found this reassuring and felt elated from the drinks and the envious and admiring looks they received from other diners, who seemed as puzzled by their relationship as the salesclerks, wondering no doubt if they were father-daughter, husband-wife, or lover-mistress. To confuse them further, she smiled flirtatiously at her uncle, who obliged by gazing upon her adoringly. People will think we're lovers, she thought, and giggled again.

Uncle Clayton said it was time to get back to the hotel. She tried to guess what the adventurous-spirit test would be—something like walking a window ledge twelve stories up? It was late, she was sleepy, and not feeling particularly adventuresome.

Her uncle unlocked his door, and she stumbled into the room. He gently guided her to the bed, where she leaned back on a pillow, feeling a wave of giddiness wash over her and retreat. Wave upon wave upon wave.

Her uncle glided about the room turning off all lights but the pink-shaded lamp by the bed, so that the room looked like the interior of a velvet shell. Of course, there was no such thing as a velvet shell, she thought, smiling to herself as her uncle closed the draperies. Soon soft music came from the radio, and he was sitting beside her on the bed. He cupped her face between his hands and kissed her. "There's just you and me," he said. "We're the only ones who count."

She nodded sleepily.

"You're not going to pass out on me, are you?"

She couldn't think clearly, couldn't understand his words circling in her head as his fingers circled her breasts. Her nipples became hard as pencil erasers when he touched them. In the pink-shaded light his silvery blond hair swooped down so she couldn't see his eyes. She thought: This is all wrong, he's my uncle. Then: It's all right, since he is. Kisses followed caresses. While he kissed her breasts, he gently parted her legs. His fingers touched the secret part of her, and soon he was kissing her down there, too, his tongue flickering like butterfly wings, then going deeper and deeper. She gasped, moaned. Suddenly he rose above her, holding something long and pink and sleek, with a shiny drop of liquid at the very tip like a raindrop clinging to the end of a leaf. He was saying darling, darling, darling and nudging his way into her, and she cried out in pain, shame, and delight.

In the morning when she awoke, she heard the shower running in the bathroom. A few minutes later he came out and dressed. She pretended sleep. He bent and kissed her softly, calling her name, but she kept her eyes closed. He must have thought she was really asleep, for he wrote a note and put it on the pillow beside her before leaving. She waited until she heard the elevator door close out in the hall before reading the note:

> Precious love,
> Off to my appointment. Back soon.

But he wasn't back soon. He didn't return until nearly noon. She'd miss Cindy's party, no matter how fast he drove back. At first she felt cheated and disappointed, wondered if he'd been late deliberately. Then she felt relief. How could she face anyone after last night? She couldn't even face him.

"Oh, my," Uncle Clayton said, "I hope you're not suffering recriminations."

She looked down at her feet.

"I flatter myself you had an enjoyable evening," he said. "Better than fooling around in the backseat of a car with some inept, fumbling, pimply-faced boy."

He smiled slyly and charmingly. He didn't guess that what bothered her wasn't what she'd done, but that she'd done it with him. "It's unnatural," she whispered.

He threw his head back and laughed. "Honey, it'd be more unnatural if we didn't. They've got this Army saying, 'Rank has its privileges.' RHIP, for short. That means us. Rules are for others. Your mother never let any rules get in her way. And you just tell me, precious love, where I could find someone better than you, or you me. There's no one else our equal. We're superior in looks, brains, genes, and heritage. Hell, we're even richer," he added, smiling to make it a joke, but she wasn't so sure he was joking.

They spent another night in Atlanta, dining, dancing, drinking champagne, and lovemaking. In the midst of passion, he called her Merry. He hadn't even been aware of it. Maybe it's not me he's making love to, but Mama, she thought. And overnight the relationship between them seemed to change. Although she loved him more, he loved her less. She couldn't say how, just that he seemed not to notice her so much. She'd heard men lost their respect for women if they went all the way before their wedding night, but he wasn't like that. He was above petty rules. Besides, they could never marry.

When they got back to Colquitt Hall, Uncle Clayton made a game of fooling the servants. At night, after the servants had gone up to their sleeping quarters on the third floor, he'd come tiptoeing down the hall to her room. The creak of the floorboards signaled his arrival. In the near-darkness of her room he slipped off his robe and into her bed. The only light came from the aquarium, where the fish floated in the secret greenness.

She was sure, though, that the servants sensed something, that colored people often knew more about whites than whites knew about themselves. Diane crept up and down the spiral staircase, keeping out of the servants' way. She even dreaded passing the ancestral portraits in the hall, where accusing eyes looked down at her.

The shame and doubt she'd pushed away in Atlanta doubled in force when she returned. Atlanta hadn't seemed real, or Uncle Clayton hadn't, or the fact that he was her uncle. Now when he left her bed at night she tossed and turned on the mussed sheets that smelled of sweat and spent passion, her body aching vaguely, feeling feverish and despondent, as if she suffered from some tropical illness.

Although she despaired at their lovemaking, she despaired even more when it was no longer love. He still came to her room, he still got into her bed, they still had sex. But he left right afterward, saying it was risky to stay.

The affectionate smiles, gifts, and small attentions he'd lavished on her were also no more. Sometimes she felt she'd disappointed him in some unknown way; other times she felt as if he'd deceived her. As if after he got her, he no longer wanted her except for physical release. And maybe he hadn't wanted her to begin with, but Mama, whose name he'd called out. He might even be getting even with Mama through her. She pushed the thought away. Uncle Clayton was good and kind and generous. She was the one at fault. She'd done something terribly wrong. But when she worked up courage enough to ask him what, he laughed.

"Don't always be imagining things," he said. "There's nothing wrong. We just don't want to arouse suspicions. You've got to learn to hide your feelings and stop looking like a whipped puppy. If you want to know, that's what puts me off."

She tried to hide her hurt. In bed she found it increasingly difficult to respond to him, which irritated him all the more, however. "Now what's wrong?" he'd say. "You're as much fun as a log." But he still came to her room every night. Except when she had the curse. She began to look upon it as a blessing. She also began to fortify herself with bourbon and bought Sen-Sen to conceal her whiskey breath. She felt justified in drinking the bourbon, since he no longer plied her with brandy as he'd done that first week after they'd returned from Atlanta.

Uncle Clayton complained that one of the servants was drinking up his liquor. He suspected Ambrosia and locked the liquor cabinet. Diane found a way around that. She filched a bottle from the case he kept in the cellar and hid it among her aquarium-cleaning equipment where Delia wasn't likely to look when she cleaned.

Since Chester carted the cases of whiskey down to the cellar, Uncle Clayton switched his suspicions to Chester, who always drank on his days off. Diane was glad Chester got the blame. He informed on the other servants to her uncle. They were afraid of Chester. Delia called him a mean nigrah. But Uncle Clayton appeared reluctant to mention the missing bourbon to Chester. Although Chester seemed so devoted to her uncle for getting him out of jail after he'd carved up some people, she suspected Uncle Clayton was afraid of him, too.

Soon Diane was drinking as much bourbon after Uncle Clayton left her bed as before he came. She started taking occasional sips during the day, too. Just enough to move in a haze, keeping thoughts at a distance.

When she went back to Miss Mayhew's in September, she always had a drink before grabbing her schoolbooks and rushing off. The normality of her schooldays contrasted with the abnormality of her nights. She listened to her classmates talking about boys and kept her eyes on her shoes. They discussed the pros and cons of kissing a boy on a first date, how far to go with a steady, and what to expect on your wedding night.

Cindy Wilkinson gave another poolside picnic. It was at the end of October. Diane didn't mention the party to her uncle. Luckily he was going to Atlanta on business, and even more luckily it was during the week, when she couldn't accompany him because of school.

At the party, Diane was too shy to speak to any boy, but she soon noticed how they eyed her in her white bathing suit and showed off at the high diving board for her benefit. They weren't all as skinny and pimply as Uncle Clayton liked to think; some were slender, tanned, and muscular. One of the boys, Deke Townsend, executed a beautiful high dive and swam over to where she sat at the pool's edge splashing water with her feet. "Come on in, the water's fine," he said. She slipped over the edge and went in. "That Old Black Magic" was playing on the poolside radio. "May I have this dance?"

Deke asked, and lightly put his arms around her waist. They danced, or tried to. He smelled clean, of soap and chlorine. His skin was smooth and golden. She thought of Uncle Clayton's paunch and hairy chest.

Later, after the party, she told herself she wasn't being fair. Uncle Clayton couldn't help he was thirty-eight. And looks weren't everything. But of course there was no better-looking man than her uncle with his clothes on. He could have any woman he wanted, and she should be flattered he'd singled her out. He was generous, sensitive, and brilliant. Her misery and his disappointment stemmed from the fact that she was a timid soul and not an adventurous spirit. But she'd already begun to notice that he wasn't generous without expecting something in return, that he was shrewd rather than sensitive, and that behind the brilliance lurked a kind of madness and a possessiveness that frightened her.

This became apparent when he found out she'd gone to Cindy's party. "You deliberately deceived me," he said, his voice shaking with rage. "You sneaked off to that party the minute my back was turned. You know I don't want you to have anything to do with that white trash."

It made her mad, his calling Cindy white trash. And gave her courage. "The last time I told you about her party, I never got there."

"And you're not going to any more. Were there boys?"

"Some."

"I suppose they spent all their time pawing you."

She thought of dancing with Deke Townsend in the pool and blushed, as if it had been something indecent.

"You've got to be watched every minute," he said, noticing the blush. "From now on, when I'm not here, Chester's driving you to and from school. I'm your guardian and have to look out for you at your tender age."

"Some guardian," she said, and laughed. She wished she hadn't.

His eyes became colorless, like the blank eyes of a cartoon character. His face tightened into a fist. "Go up to your room and stay there until you learn to speak to me with respect."

She went up to her room. And locked the door. She lay on her bed wondering how he'd heard about the party. Probably from Judge and Mrs. Pierce. Marybelle Pierce, who was their granddaughter, had been at the party too. Diane had stayed overnight at Cindy's just so her uncle couldn't find out. But maybe Chester had reported she hadn't come home. Delia knew she was at Cindy's, but Delia wouldn't have told unless she was asked.

It was quiet all through suppertime. He didn't call to her to come down and eat. He came to her room, though, after the servants had gone up to the third floor. She'd expected he would. When she heard the creaking floorboards in the hall, she took a big swallow of bourbon. Her heart still crammed her chest. The doorknob turned. Turned again. "Let me in," he whispered. She tiptoed to the far side of the room, as if he might come crashing through the door with his shoulders. Now he was rattling the doorknob. "Open this or you'll regret it," he said. But he said it in a whisper so the servants in their small rooms upstairs wouldn't hear.

After more whispered threats, he left. But he came back intermittently through the long night, whispering threats and accusations. From his slurred speech she could tell he'd been drinking.

In low hisses he recited how she'd set out to seduce him, by throwing her legs around, by throwing herself at him, by going around half-naked.

She cried into her pillow so he wouldn't hear, slowly becoming aware of the name she cried out. Mama. And as he called out all those horrible things on the other side of the door, the implacable truth of her parents' death hit her. They weren't on some prolonged European tour. They hadn't been to London, Paris, Venice, or Vienna. They'd been buried under the earth all this time. They were never coming back. Never. They were dead. Dead.

She no longer heard his voice, although his vehemence increased. She no longer heard anything but that small inner voice repeating "Dead," Willy's words humming in her ear like some insidious insect: "Miz Meredith, she running with her hair on fire and blood all down the front of that white dress and chinchilly coat, and by the time we got Mistah Duncan outta that car, he black as us, crumpled up like burnt paper."

"Seductress, slut. harlot, bitch, Jezebel, cunt," Uncle Clayton called. And finally went away.

From then on she locked her bedroom door every night. He would rattle the doorknob, his voice thick and bourbon-slurred. He began with pleas, went on to demands, ended in threats. "You're oversexed," he called. "I'll just have to see you're kept away from boys until you see the light of reason."

She knew what was meant by the light of reason, but kept the door locked anyway. She also locked it during the day, for sometimes he'd return early from work and quietly come up to her room. Once he'd managed to get in, and she screamed so loud he'd had to leave before one of the servants came running.

When he wasn't there to keep an eye on her, Chester was. She was whisked to school and back in the car, and not allowed to go to a movie or to some school social function unless Uncle Clayton accompanied her. She began to eat to fill her days, since there was nothing else to fill them with. Uncle Clayton said she was becoming fat and disgusting. He lost interest in her and didn't rattle her doorknob so often. Encouraged by this, she ate more.

7. *Ilse*

"I've taken the liberty of inviting myself and my friend Major Birkner to join you and my dear sister for lunch," Freddie von Frisch said, his voice on the phone as arch as a raised eyebrow. "Wolfgang saw you onstage the other night and is crazy to meet you. He's sending a military car to pick you up."

Ilse hung up feeling despair. She couldn't alienate Freddie by telling him that he and his major weren't welcome. In fact, under ordinary circumstances she'd be glad to have Freddie along. Ursula wouldn't be so likely to make a pass. The more money Ilse borrowed, the bolder Ursula became, her hands lingering where only her eyes had lingered before. Ilse had deliberately picked a public place like the Platzgarten to ask for another loan, instead of running the risk of being alone with Ursula. But how could she ask for money with Freddie's friend the major present? She was sure Freddie knew Ursula was lending her money. Brother and sister appeared to keep little from one another. Maybe she should have borrowed from Freddie instead. No doubt she'd be safer with Freddie, whose interest was in men rather than women, although he was behaving very circumspectly now that homosexuals were in such disfavor. Certainly she should have asked for money much earlier, but she'd been reluctant to, putting it off until the very last minute. She had to meet that blackmailing Private Gertig tonight. What if Ursula wouldn't lend her more money? She didn't allow herself to think about it.

But she had to think about it. She looked around the living room for something of value to sell. For months she'd been tormented by the imprints on the rug left by the legs of the white baby-grand piano. But she no longer had the rug as a reminder. She'd had to sell it, too. Her jewelry box was empty except for the torn half of the letter Private Gertig claimed was from her father. It was hidden away under the false bottom. Ilse wondered how many more letters Private Gertig would produce, if he were now composing them himself, and if he intended to go on blackmailing her for as long as it was dangerous to be a Jew in Germany, which might be for life. But then, if someone made the discovery, her life might not last long.

Was she foolish to keep paying? Only two letters sounded authentic, the two written to Aunt Greta pleading with her to reconsider and keep their child—her. It had hurt to burn these, but she'd memorized them first. In the second letter her father had mentioned that some stage scaffolding had fallen on him and he'd had to have thirty-six stitches taken. "It left a scar on my left cheek," he'd written. "It looks very distinguished—like a dueling scar."

The torn half of the last letter had been delivered to her at the theater by one of Private Gertig's slimy friends. In the envelope was a note saying he was on military duty but he'd be back in three weeks and she'd better be at Bruno's with the money if she wanted the other half of the letter. The three weeks were up tonight.

Ilse dressed carefully for lunch, choosing clothes to create an air of prosperity she didn't have and a nonchalance she far from felt. She put on a severely tailored pinstripe suit, added a white ruffled blouse for femininity, and topped it off with a saucy hat for insouciance.

She was no sooner dressed than the military car arrived. With the major. "You are more beautiful offstage than on," he said, smiling at her across the backseat. Major Birkner was fair-haired and good-looking, his shoulders broad in the belted tunic. When he wasn't smiling, however, there was a cruel twist to his lips. Just the sort Freddie would fall for. Ilse wondered if Freddie intended using her as bait. Maybe it was just as well she hadn't borrowed any money from Freddie.

The major spoke of "poor" Freddie's hunting accident. While grouse hunting in the woods near the von Frisch castle,

Freddie had accidentally shot himself in the foot. Ilse wasn't so sure it was an accident. It left Freddie with only a slight limp, and he didn't have to worry about conscription anymore. Now he had a soft job at the Ministry of Propaganda. He jokingly referred to his boss, Dr. Goebbels, as Mahatma Propagandi. She knew better than to laugh.

The long black Mercedes rolled down Kurfurstendamm Strasse, the street of cafés. It was noon, and Berliners ate at outside tables, sunning themselves under an autumn sky. It seemed more like a holiday than a workday, and certainly there was reason to celebrate. The Germans had taken over Austria without protest, invaded Czechoslovakia, and just last month seized Poland. The sight of their smug smiles depressed her. Not even England's declaration of war had shaken them from their complacency. No one believed England stood a chance against Germany's military might. The only people Ilse felt she had anything in common with these days were the terrified and terrorized—those whom Germany had declared enemies, who tried to survive by making themselves invisible. And in order for her to survive, she must avoid them. Now when she saw old friends or met someone new, she judged them according to how they'd react if her Jewish identity were known. Would they help her or turn her in? The answer to that was obvious and depressing.

Major Birkner, who said he'd been with the first German troops to enter Austria, was speaking of Vienna. "Such a beautiful city. So sophisticated! How I'd love to show you the sights."

"How I'd love having you show them to me."

He smiled over, and she wondered how quickly that smile would disappear from his SS face if he knew, the amorous glance change to brute arrogance.

The car pulled up before the Platzgarten, old, ornate, majestic. Above the arched Gothic doors was a balcony where Hitler had stood, but then, he spent more time on balconies than Juliet. Major Birkner's driver jumped out and held the car door open, while an elderly doorman, dressed like a field marshal with epaulets and braids, sprinted down the steps to greet them and back up again to struggle with the heavy doors to let them in.

They entered to a medley of Strauss waltzes played by a concealed orchestra. The maître d' hurried forward. "We are joining Herr von Frisch," the major said, and the headwaiter bowed low as if he'd said they were joining the Führer himself. They were led past tables occupied by Luftwaffe officers with pretty girls or businessmen with pink-marzipan-pig faces. Naturally, Freddie and Ursula had the best table, where they could see and be seen.

Ilse was upset when she saw Colonel von Sachen with them. He was the same fat fool who'd paraded her around their ballroom, calling attention to her perfect Aryan features. Now he jumped up from the table while Freddie rose languorously, batting long lashes at Major Birkner. Ursula's eyes glittered as brightly as the carved-ice swan displayed nearby. She coolly examined Ilse from head to toe, dwelling on her legs and breasts in an insulting way no man would have dared. "You look very fetching," she said.

Ilse returned the compliment. She had to be nice. Ursula did look fascinating in a female-Dracula sort of way. She wore a dress of deep red silk with nail lacquer and lipstick to match. Black coarse hair fell about her thin white face, from which peered those black glittering eyes.

"I suggest we order soon," Colonel von Sachen said. "I have to return to headquarters shortly. I'm a busy man these days."

"I'm not sure I can eat," Freddie said. "I have a frightful toothache. It's that Jew dentist I went to last year. He destroyed my teeth."

"Perhaps he's cleaning latrines now," the colonel said.

"I'm sure he's more suited to the job," the major added.

"The only thing he's suited for is standing in front of a firing squad," Freddie said.

Ilse kept her eyes on the menu for fear of what they might reveal.

A long time was spent in deciding what to order. First, Ursula said she'd have duck and dumplings, but when the colonel chose goose and sauerbraten, Ursula switched to goose. The colonel, in turn, redecided on the wienerschnitzel that the major ordered, but the major changed his mind and asked for duck and dumplings. Freddie complained that everything on the menu had been deliberately chosen to aggravate his toothache, while Ursula complained of the noise. "It's like a railroad station," she said. "And look at all the riffraff who come here now. Anyone with the price of a meal can walk in."

The colonel's face reddened, making his dueling scar more pronounced. "I would not call the Luftwaffe riffraff," he said.

Freddie said he wouldn't either, the pilots were wonderfully brave and daring. His toothache did not appear to affect his appetite, after all. In fact, everyone ate in a greedy way that repulsed Ilse. It took them less time to eat than it had to order.

After they finished, conversation resumed. The colonel lit a fat cigar. Ursula took a Sobranie black-and-gold cigarette from a black-and-gold box and inserted the cigarette into a carved ivory holder. The colonel, major, and waiter all vied for the honor of lighting it, holding out matches and lighters. The major won. A smell of Turkish tobacco reminded Ilse of Private Gertig, who also smoked Sobranies. She became increasingly nervous. How would she manage to see Ursula in privacy to ask for the loan?

The waiter wheeled a dessert cart to the table. On it were cakes with various icings—caramel, chocolate, mocha, and vanilla—as well as layered cakes with fillings of apricot, raspberry, and strawberry, and in addition, cream puffs and chocolate éclairs. All beautifully displayed on individual white lace doilies.

"I'll have the hazelnut torte," Ursula said after looking everything over.

"I am sorry, Fräulein, we do not have that today," the waiter said.

"That's absurd, you always have hazelnut torte."

"Not today, Fräulein."

Ilse wondered if Ursula had asked for it because it wasn't there.

"Perhaps you'll find some in the kitchen," Freddie suggested.

The waiter excused himself and returned a few minutes later to report there was none.

"The young lady requested hazelnut torte," Colonel von Sachen said. "A reasonable enough request. You will see she gets it."

The waiter bowed and turned away.

"Immediately," the colonel added.

A few minutes later the waiter returned at a near-trot, sweat beading his forehead, hazelnut torte in hand. It was obvious he'd run to a bakery and bought it. Ursula ignored the torte when he placed it before her. She inserted another cigarette into her holder. Again the colonel, major, and waiter vied for the honor of lighting it. This time the colonel won. After blowing a perfect smoke ring, Ursula looked up at the waiter. "Take it away," she said coldly. "You were so long in getting it, it's become stale."

The waiter bowed and removed the torte. "I am sorry, Fräulein. If you wish, I will get another."

"What, and make me wait another hour? I have more important things to do with my time, thank you."

"He should be fired for insolence," Freddie said.

"I suppose so," Ursula said, "but I'm in a good mood today."

Although there were only a few diners left and the colonel had said he was in a hurry to get back to headquarters, the men remained at the table. Ilse spilled coffee and was annoyed that the hovering waiter replaced her saucer, calling attention to her nervousness.

Fortunately Freddie, who'd been prodding his tooth, announced he had to leave for his dental appointment. Unfortunately, Ursula got up to leave along with the others.

"Could I see you privately?" Ilse asked her.

"But, of course, pet, come along home with me," Ursula said, placing a thin bloodless hand on Ilse's arm.

Home alone with Ursula was the last thing Ilse wanted, but she had no choice. The major, who had insisted on paying for the meal, now bowed over Ilse's hand and told her he hoped to see her again. So did the colonel. "You always make such a hit with men," Ursula said as they preceded the men out. "If they only knew."

"Knew what?" Ilse asked.

Ursula merely smiled. Was she foisting her sexual preferences on Ilse by claiming Ilse didn't like men either? Or was she hinting that they didn't know she was half-Jewish? For a minute Ilse felt a new fear, until it came to her that if Ursula knew, she'd already be putting the knowledge to her advantage.

The black military Mercedes pulled away from the Platzgarten with the major and Freddie in the backseat, another military car carried off the colonel, while Ursula and Ilse got into the von Frisches' blue Mercedes. In the backseat Ursula smiled at her as amorously as Major Birkner. Then, when she did not get the amorous smile she hoped for in return, Ursula's voice became frosty. "And to what do I owe the honor of your presence? Not, I hope, another family catastrophe?"

Ilse was caught off guard. But, of course, Ursula would have guessed why she wanted to see her privately. "It isn't a catastrophe this time."

"What? Everything's all right? Your mother's operation went well? Your father's business is now thriving? And the house repaired after the fire damage?"

Ilse had used the excuses of sickness, near-bankruptcy, and

fire to ask for a loan. She had another one ready. "It's my little sister. She's marrying someone quite prominent in town—a banker. And the family wants to put on a big show at the wedding. I know it's ridiculous, but it would mean a lot to her and my family."

"Am I invited if I make the loan?"

"They'd be honored to have you," Ilse said. She didn't think for a minute that Ursula would seriously consider going. If so, Ilse would have to arrange a fight between the fiancé and the nonexistent sister. She had three sisters, but they were all older and married.

Ursula looked amused, as if she'd read her mind. "How innocent you look. I do love a good liar." She reached over and examined the cameo that Ilse had on a chain around her neck. She'd thought of selling it, too, but she couldn't bear to, since it was a gift from Hans.

"What a pretty cameo, and what a pretty woman. Your mother?"

It was indeed her mother, since it was a picture of Aunt Greta she'd inserted in the cameo, but Ilse thought it safer to disclaim this. "My aunt."

"You look alike," Ursula said, fondling Ilse's breasts while pretending to examine the cameo more closely. Ilse wanted to tell her she didn't care for crude schoolboy tactics, but too much was at stake. Ursula's dark eyes glittered with excitement. Ilse saw the castle turrets ahead with mixed emotions. Arriving there would get her out of the present predicament, but would she just get into a worse one? Ursula sat back and behaved as if she knew that patience was its own reward.

They drove along a winding road shaded by autumn-leafed linden trees. Ilse caught glimpses of a silvery lake through green firs between the castle towers. Although the setting was beautiful, the castle was of an unattractive yellowish-orange brick like an old factory's. At least at this time of year it blended with the foliage. The castle had a kind of ugly grandeur that was, like Ursula, intimidating. Impossible to be a baker's daughter and not be intimidated. But then, she wasn't a baker's daughter. And that was why she was here.

Horst, the driver, stopped in front, and Ilse followed Ursula inside, past old Fritz, who seemed as ancient as the castle. The room they entered was like a historical museum, the walls displaying dueling pistols, scabbards, swords, and other weapons of ancient times. Ursula's heels clicked on the stone floor between islands of Persian rugs. "Come help me pick out something to wear to the Baroness von Groot's party tonight," she said.

Ilse saw through that. The "something" was in an armoire, the armoire in a bedroom, where Ursula hoped to get her. "Oh, you know more about that sort of thing than I, and anyway, I have to get back in a few minutes. I have an interview this afternoon."

"Call and say you can't make it."

"I can't call. We're meeting at a café. It's someone from *Stern*. I've learned not to meet interviewers at my place. There's no getting rid of them."

Ursula gave her a skeptical look. "You are a clever little thing." Ilse wasn't sure whether she meant clever to get away from her interviewer or from her.

"How much this time, little liar?" Ursula asked, but she said "liar" affectionately, and, more important, had taken out her checkbook.

"If you don't believe me, come along to the Continental for the interview," Ilse said, pretending that was what Ursula didn't believe.

"I'd adore hearing the fanciful tale you dream up, but I have a fitting later. Now, how much is it going to cost me this time?"

Ilse told her the amount that Private Gertig had demanded for the other half of the torn letter.

"It gets to be more each time," Ursula complained.

Ilse wished she could tell her not to blame her but her blackmailer. Ursula wrote out a check and asked for an IOU in return, as always. Ilse didn't mind; it was only fair.

"What time is your interview?"

"At four."

"It's almost four now, you'd better hurry. Horst will drive you back to town."

Seated once again in the Mercedes, Ilse breathed a deep sigh of relief. It had been so easy. Too easy. Relief gave way to worry. Ursula wasn't the charitable type. Obviously she wanted Ilse to be in debt to her. One of these days the ultimatum would be issued: come to bed or go to prison. A thought Ilse refused to dwell on. The sun shone on Brandenburg Gate. It was a perfect autumn day. Maybe by this time next year Germany would be defeated by England, people would no longer listen to Hitler, and sanity would be restored.

She knew that her optimism was childish and groundless, but she was by nature optimistic.

She was only a few minutes late when she arrived at the Continental. Before she could tell the waiter she was joining Herr Hoffner, a tall man with polished forehead and longish hair motioned her to the back table where he stood.

"You are more beautiful offstage than on," he said, pulling out a chair for her. She'd thought a writer would be more original.

As Ursula had guessed, she made up a fanciful tale for her interviewer, describing a happy childhood on the Rhine with a kind father, adoring mother, and loving sisters. In fact, her father had been cruel, her mother critical and disparaging, her sisters far from loving. Once, jealous of the Bavarian peasant dolls Aunt Greta had brought her, her sisters had sneaked the dolls from the house and bashed in their heads out in the woods, where Ilse had found them weeks later. Little wonder that Cinderella was her favorite fairy tale. Her family, if they ever read the interview, would be amazed at her portrayal of them. Or would they? People seldom saw themselves as they were. Probably her family considered themselves good people, the way all Germans did, and the Jews deserving of what they got.

Also, illogically, she was ashamed of how her family had mistreated her, as if it were her fault. She didn't want others to know. And it was important to portray herself as living a typically happy Aryan childhood, in case doubt ever arose as to her ancestry. Of course, she didn't believe many childhoods were happy and carefree, but it was what people liked to believe.

Herr Hoffner's eyes occasionally flashed skepticism, but he listened with a smile. He was a good-natured, generous man who kept plying her with tortes and Viennese coffee. "You are like me," he said, "a nervous type. We can eat anything and never put on weight. Not so true of the others here."

Ilse looked around at the well-dressed, well-upholstered matrons gorging on pastries, whipped cream, and chocolate.

"It is not as it once was," Herr Hoffner said. "Once you came her for stimulating conversation on art and politics; now you come here merely to stuff yourself."

"What happened to the stimulating talk of art and politics?"

"What happened to Germany?" he said, then looked fearful as if he wished he could grab back his remark. Ilse wished she could tell him he could trust her, and wondered if he might be one of the few who would help her if he knew. She accepted another torte at his insistence, not because she wanted one, but it pleased him to see her eat.

When she arrived at the theater, she found that the assistant director, Helmut Bruer, was in charge. "Hans had to take his wife back to the hospital," Helmut said. "She went berserk and tried to stab some Gestapo."

Was that so berserk? Ilse wondered.

She got her usual number of curtain calls. The play was about a milkmaid seduced by a soldier who returned to war. When she discovered she was pregnant, the milkmaid planned to commit suicide, but luckily her soldier lover got another furlough, just in the nick of time, and married her. Ilse was pert and saucy in the first two acts, and suitably tragic in the last. Her dress was low-cut, though otherwise demure. The play was a hit and had been running for so long she could recite the lines in her sleep, which it sometimes nearly amounted to on stage. She longed for a dramatic part that would offer more of a challenge than just to stay awake while portraying it, but she couldn't consider leaving the theater now. Leaving would mean less pay, and she owed Ursula.

It was a toss-up whether it was worse to be at Ursula's mercy or Private Gertig's. But Ursula couldn't harm her father as long as she didn't know he existed, something Private Gertig threatened to tell if she didn't pay up.

Even though Ilse had the money, she dreaded seeing him. It wasn't just that she feared and despised him; she hated the sight of that smile and the smell of his greasy porcupine hair. She wished she could send someone in her place as she got in the taxi to meet him.

"Are you sure this is the right address, Fräulein?" the cabdriver asked pulling up in front of Bruno's. With its sleazy appearance, she could see why he asked. She thought of asking him to wait for her, but that would cost more than she could afford. She paid the driver, went down the steps and through the swinging door.

There were the usual smells of sweat, smoke, and cheap perfume, the usual women in tight showy dresses, but fewer than usual male civilians, and more soldiers. She was stared at, but not as much as before. The waiters knew her by now. So did the regulars. She made her way to the corner table where Private Gertig always sat. Tonight it was occupied by two women and another soldier. The waiter who had just turned away from their table looked at her with surprise.

"Private Gertig hasn't arrived yet?" she asked.

"You haven't heard?"

"Heard?"

The waiter took her arm solicitously, and pushing people aside, found her an empty table. "Sit down, Fräulein. I will get you a drink. What would you like?"

She was puzzled. This wasn't the sort of place where they worried about a customer's comfort. Why was he bothering about her? "A schnapps, I guess," she said.

The waiter returned with the schnapps and stood by watching as she took a few sips. He cleared his throat and looked uncomfortable. "I am very sorry to have to tell you this, Fräulein, but your dear friend was killed."

So they'd got him for his gambling debts, after all.

"He was," the waiter announced with the dignity of a war minister, "the first to be sent into Poland. And the first to die there. A fine lad. One of Germany's best."

Ilse let a few tears of sorrow squeeze from her eyes. She had never enjoyed her role as an actress as much as at this moment.

II

1942–1944

8. Susan

"It's not fair," Susan said. "Other girls my age go. And they don't have their fathers along. I suppose you think I'll sit on some soldier's lap. I'm not too young. I'm seventeen, goddammit."

"Now, honey," her father said, speaking softly, so that it sounded as if she were screaming by comparison. "Your mother wouldn't like your using profanity."

Her mother had been dead for years, but he still spoke as if she'd just stepped into another room.

He put on his hat. "I'll be home before dark," he said, and left.

A few minutes later she heard the Plymouth going down the hill. She was near tears. Whenever troop trains stopped at the train station, girls from various church groups distributed candy, cigarettes, and chewing gum. Despite the supervision by her father and Reverend Hildebrand, there were reports of misbehavior. One girl had stayed on board, riding from Leyton, Ohio, to Louisville, Kentucky, where she'd been discovered and put off. Given half the chance, Susan would do the same, which was probably why her father wouldn't let her go with him.

Susan sighed, left the supper dishes undone, and went outside. Whimpy came trotting up, his collie hair matted with burs. Together they went down to the river that looked gray-green in the twilight. Small gusts of wind rippled the water. It trembled the willows and the branches newly knobbed with buds. She trembled, too, not knowing why. Lately she was always on the verge of tears or recklessness. She said shocking things. No one understood her. But if she puzzled people, they puzzled her even more.

A fisherman sat under the covered bridge, unmoving in the hushed silence. Birds made settling-down-for-the-night noises. From a distance came the hum of highway traffic, and then the whistle of the troop train as it approached Leyton. She thought of the lucky girls who got to go on board and pass out candy and cigarettes, receiving smiles, thanks, and lustful looks in return. The soldiers were on their way to war. What if the war went on forever, and all the men were killed and she died husbandless and childless, and still a virgin? What if she were stuck here and never got to New York to see and do exciting things and meet the exciting people Miss Rice had told her about?

Miss Rice was now Mrs. Nicolas. She'd married a naval officer, a virtual stranger she'd met in the Dayton Art Museum, which had shocked everyone and thrilled Susan. Now she was in San Diego, where her husband was stationed. Before she left, she'd called Susan in for a private talk and told her she had high hopes for her. "Don't disappoint me," Miss Rice said. "Go to a good college and realize your potential." Susan wasn't even sure she'd get to college, much less a good one. Whenever she asked her father if she could go, he said, "We'll see." She'd learned his "We'll see" was a pleasant way of postponing an unpleasant "No."

"You should decide what you want to do and prepare for it," Miss Rice told her. "What *do* you want to do, anyway?"

"I want to be an international journalist and travel all over. I guess that sounds crazy."

"It sounds like hard work. Talent, you have."

"But I'm a girl."

"That didn't stop Margaret Bourke-White."

"Who's she?"

"Only one of our best photographers. You must have seen her pictures in *Life*. She covers the war on all fronts." Miss Rice patted her arm. "You'll have to be tough, Susan. I don't mean swear or chain-smoke or talk out of the side of your mouth. I mean you'll have to stick to your guns. Do what you want to do, not what people tell you to. I expect big things of you."

Susan missed Miss Rice nearly as much as she missed her brother, Eddy, who was in Marine boot camp at Camp Lejeune in North Carolina.

She sat down on the damp earth behind a curtain of green willows so that she wouldn't be seen, although the fisherman had left and there was no one to see her. Whimpy put his muzzle on her thigh. She absentmindedly stroked his head. Above her on the hill the house and outbuildings had already merged with gray.

A car rattled across the wooden boards of the bridge. The nose of a shiny blue Buick emerged. Susan knew it was a Buick because Eddy had once taught her to identify every make of car. For a minute it looked as if the the driver didn't know which way to turn—their way or the dirt road. Turn this way, she pleaded. It went the other. Maybe that was just as well. Maybe there were white slavers in that Buick. She'd heard about them. There were trapdoors in department stores where young girls fell through, never to be seen again. Or someone sat next to you in a movie and stuck a needle in your arm, and the next thing you knew, you were on a boat headed for China or Africa, where you were forced to do dirty things with yellow or black men. Sometimes the white slavers just came and kidnapped you.

Of course, she didn't believe that crap. She sighed, wishing some white slavers *would* kidnap her. She'd rather do anything with anybody than be stuck forever in the middle of nowhere, hemmed in by the horizon with nothing but fields and sky. It wasn't fair that Eddy got to join the Marines and see the world while she was left behind. He could have gotten a draft exemption for farmwork. Not that she blamed him for going. And what if he got killed in action? Only, that seemed far preferable to dying a slow death.

It was nearly dark, time for her father to be back. As if on cue, she heard the rattle of bridge boards. But it wasn't the Plymouth that emerged. It was a tan Studebaker. And turning into their drive! Someone who'd lost the way, or white slavers? She peered through the willow branches, watching as the car went up their hill. Curious and slightly afraid, she called Whimpy and started toward the house. A man was just getting out of the car as she reached the top of the hill. He was tall and slender and wore an officer's uniform with a visored cap, so handsome he snatched her breath away. When he came closer, she recognized him. Richard Lund! And here she was a mess—no lipstick, limp hair, wearing Eddy's old Levi's and a shrunken yellow sweater.

"Hi! Are you home on furlough?" she asked. Stupid. Naturally he was. He'd hardly be AWOL. He asked about Eddy, and she wondered if that's who he'd come to see, but when she said he was in the Marines, he said he'd heard.

"You've got your wings," she said, spying the silver wings on his collar tab.

"Yeah," he said, as if that were nothing. As if the Army Air Corps handed out wings right and left. He asked how she was, how her father was, how school was. She said "Okay." She couldn't think of anything more to say in his dazzling presence, and pulled up a sock that had slipped down into her saddleshoe.

"How's Clementine? She okay, too?" he asked.

"Yes, she's okay." Then she saw he was smiling, teasing

her for her bashfulness, but not minding it, understanding the way he always understood her. "Actually, she's getting a bit long in the tooth. But Millicent, that's her daughter, she won a ribbon at the county fair, too. Daddy says next August I can show her at the state fair."

Dumb. That was really dumb. What did an Army Air Corpsman care about a calf? But he'd nursed Clementine through the pinkeye, and now he asked to see Clementine, which proved he cared. She took him to the barn to see Clementine and admire Millicent.

He looked at his watch and said he had to leave. Naturally, why would he want to stay and talk about cows? It served her right. If she'd said cute, bright things, he wouldn't be in such a big hurry to leave.

"I promised my folks I'd spend my first night at home," he said, "but maybe we could go out some other night, if you're not busy."

"I'm free tomorrow night," she said, as if she weren't free every night.

"Swell. Seven okay?"

She nodded, not trusting her voice. After he left, she hugged herself, hugged Whimpy, and five minutes later, when her father drove up, hugged him.

"I'm glad you're not mad at me anymore," he said, but she'd forgotten all about that. "Guess who's home on furlough, came to see me right away, and is taking me out tomorrow night?" she demanded.

Her father, disappointingly, guessed immediately.

"But how did you know?" she asked.

"His father said last week he was coming home."

"But why didn't you tell *me*?"

"I just didn't think to. Now, honey, don't get carried away by a uniform. Richard's someone you've known all your life."

That was crazy. She hadn't fallen for him because of his uniform. She'd loved him as long as she'd known him. Of course, he did look wonderful in his uniform, better even than Miss Rice's naval officer, whom she'd seen when he came to pick up Miss Rice once after school. Susan went up to bed and for hours lay awake planning what to wear and what to say when they went out tomorrow night.

She wanted to broadcast the news the next day at school, but she was afraid if Penny Detweiler heard he was home, she'd call him, and it would be good-bye Richard. But maybe Penny knew already. Maybe she had a date with him, too. A Friday- or Saturday-night date, not an unimportant school night. But Susan had no one to blame for that but herself. She'd wanted to see him as soon as she could.

In the shower room after phys-ed period, Penny strutted around naked, swinging her behind as if boys were there to see. Susan, shy about her body, showered and dressed quickly. Just the same, she thought, I look better without clothes than she does. Her waist is too high, her thighs too thick, and her breasts might be big, but they're droopy and her nipples are pimply. My breasts are small, but they're nicely shaped and the nipples rosy. Only how was Richard to know?

As soon as she got home from school, she washed her hair and put it up with bobby pins. She told her father she couldn't do all her chores and be ready by seven when Richard arrived, so her father gave up Lowell Thomas and helped Bobby with the milking in her place. Susan hoped Bobby would leave before Richard, so he wouldn't report to Penny that Richard was home; provided she still hadn't heard.

Not long after Bobby went downhill in his pickup truck, Richard came uphill in his Studebaker. She wasn't even ready. She yelled downstairs to her father, asking him to keep Richard company, and dressed hurriedly. Her father seemed only too happy to oblige. She could hear him through the stovepipe hole from the living room to her bedroom, doing all the talking.

She swooped her hair up in a pompadour like Betty Grable's, put on her lemon-yellow Easter suit and her baby-doll shoes with ankle straps. She could tell by Richard's eyes when she went downstairs that she looked good. He sat on the piano bench, back to the piano, politely listening as her father told him how to win the war.

"Well, I guess you young folks want to be off," her father said reluctantly as Richard helped her on with her powder-blue topper. Richard put on his cap, shook hands with her father, said he enjoyed their conversation, and promised to have her home early. Finally they went out and got into his car.

"Like to go dancing?" he asked. "We can go to the Kitty Hawk in Dayton. It's supposed to be a good nightclub."

Like to? She'd love to! She'd never been to a nightclub. It seemed the ultimate in sophistication. The drawback was that it would take an hour to get to Dayton and another to get back. Her father might not let her go out with Richard again if she got home late, especially on a school night. On the other hand, Richard might not ask her out again if he thought she was such a baby she had to get home so early. Then Richard reached over and took her hand, and nothing mattered but being with him and going somewhere exciting.

The Kitty Hawk room was dark and crowded with civilians and soldiers, mostly officers, probably from Wright Field. Susan and Richard were awarded a ringside table by the dance floor. She was glad it was dark so the waiter couldn't see she was underage and refuse to serve her anything stronger than Coca-Cola. She asked for a Tom Collins. She'd never had one before but knew it was the thing to order. Richard requested a Cuba Libre, a drink she'd never heard of.

"Like to dance?" he asked, and she walked self-consciously in her baby-dolls to the dance floor. The band was playing "Poinciana." She smelled Richard's Old Spice shaving lotion and felt the long length of his body, becoming slightly giddy, although she'd had only a few sips of the Tom Collins.

As they returned to their table at the end of the set, Susan became aware that her yellow suit was all wrong, more appropriate for church than nightclub. Other women wore low-cut cocktail dresses, and some had flowers in their hair. "Ever see this?" Richard asked. He'd taken two matches, propped the heads together, and now lit them. The matches twined like legs when they burned down. She blushed at the implied sexuality, then blushed at her blushing. Richard hadn't even thought of it that way; obviously she had a dirty mind.

Richard was wonderfully entertaining. He took out a pen and drew a man's face on a cigarette, adding a bow tie. When he wasn't looking, she slipped the cigarette into her purse to keep forever as a memory of tonight. It would have been a perfect evening if she didn't keep worrying about his asking her out again.

The band started up, and the vocalist sang a song about a man wearing silver wings. She looked straight at Richard as if singing for him alone. Susan became jealous. And envious. The vocalist was very exotic. Exotic and erotic. She wore a white gardenia in her long black hair, and a long black slinky dress that shimmered over her curves in the spotlight. Her eyebrows were plucked and arched, her mouth a bright shiny red. She must be at least twenty-five.

"I think she's fallen for you," Susan said, realizing the moment she said it she'd made a mistake. In a magazine article called "Tips to Get Your Man," she'd read that you should never tell your boyfriend a girl was interested in him or he'd become interested in her.

"It's my uniform she loves," Richard said modestly.

"There are a lot of uniforms here."

Although he looked more handsome in his uniform than in civilian clothes, he was handsome to begin with. Handsome, intelligent, kind, considerate, witty, and a superb dancer. Or maybe they just danced well together because they were so perfectly attuned. What if it were something other than dancing?

"A penny for your thoughts," he said, tucking a stray strand of hair back into her pompadour.

"Oh, they're worth more than that," she told him, smiling mysteriously.

When they weren't dancing, they sat and held hands and eyes. She was sipping her second Tom Collins when he said they'd better leave. "It's nearly midnight."

"Midnight? But we just got here."

He smiled. "We've been here over three hours."

In the car he turned on the radio. Vaughn Monroe was playing his theme song, "Racing with the Moon." The station signed off. There was a small rain, just enough to feel cozy, the car like a world of their own, a small room moving down the highway.

"You're so far away," he said, and she nearly jumped into his lap. He drove with an arm around her, lips pressed to her hair, and she knew bliss. "Your hair smells so good," he said, "so fresh and clean."

She didn't know how to accept his compliment, thought of saying, "It should, I just washed it," but that was wrong, too, and ended by saying, "I thought you'd fall for that vocalist tonight," which was equally wrong.

"Oh, *her*. You could tell she's cheap."

"You could? How?"

"All that makeup and that tight dress."

Susan made a mental note to go easy on the mascara and not wear tight clothes.

"Girls like her are a dime a dozen. They pretend they're crazy about a guy and take him for all he's worth while they're playing the field behind his back. I'm no longer the starry-eyed innocent I once was."

She heard the bitterness in his voice and knew he'd been hurt. One minute she was jealous of this girl he'd cared so much about that she could hurt him; the next, she promised herself that if by some miracle he fell in love with her, she would never deceive him with another man. Not that she'd be tempted to.

"I don't want some cheap girl. I want a girl who cares. I mean, this might sound corny, but when you know you might get killed one day, you want something that means something."

She pictured his plane taking a nose dive, sparks shooting out, a plume of smoke. She shuddered and pressed against him. He couldn't die. She would love him so much she'd keep death away. He slowed down and kissed her. A long steamy kiss. Behind them a car honked. He drew away. "Sorry, I forgot you're a nice girl."

Not that nice, she wanted to say. He got another dance band on the radio and again put his arm around her. She was happy and unhappy. Happy to be with him, unhappy that he'd said she was nice. Nice was for girls who were good sports, girls boys joked with and never got serious about. All the same, he was driving slowly, as if he, too, wanted their night together to last.

Her father spoiled it all. She might have known when she saw the porch light on. A minute later he stood in the doorway as they approached the porch steps. "Do you know what time it is?" he demanded. "Nearly two. Where've you been? I was worried half to death." He went on and on. Richard apologized and fled. Susan saw the taillights disappear down the hill and knew it would be the last time she saw him.

"You scared him away. He'll never be back," she screamed.

"He'll be back. And the next time, he'll show more respect."

"There won't be a next time, you've ruined everything. I hate you," she said. She ran upstairs to bed and cried herself to sleep.

"You look awful," her best friend, Rosemary Brummit, said the next day. "What's wrong?" Susan refused to say. The obscenely sunny day made her feel even worse. It was Friday. On Friday afternoons the whole school gathered in the auditorium for assembly. It was a consolidated school, like all country schools. The first-graders sat in the front rows, the second-graders behind, and on up to the seniors, who sat in back. Susan and Rosemary sat in the very last row, along with the other girls in their class. From junior high on, the girls sat on one side, the boys on the other.

Even in her depressed mood, Susan felt a kind of fluttering around her, a stir of excitement that aroused her from her preoccupation.

"Look," Rosemary Brummit said, suddenly gripping Susan's arm. "There's Richard Lund. Oh, God, isn't he cute?"

There he stood, as handsome as a recruitment poster, tall, slender, and blond, visored cap in hand. Talking to Mr. Ashbaugh, the principal. Susan's face grew hot, her hands cold. She had an urge to crawl under her seat. How could she face him after that horrible scene her father had made last night? She felt a contradictory urge to be seen. Perhaps seeing her, he'd remember their intimate moments in the car, not her father.

But what was he doing here? Why was he talking to Mr. Ashbaugh? What were they saying? From the sixth grade to the senior class, girls smiled, whispered, and primped. One of the younger teachers had taken out her compact and was applying lipstick in front of everyone.

Susan was tempted to tell Rosemary she'd been out with him last night, but then the inevitable, embarrassing question would be: "When are you seeing him again?" Never.

Mr. Ashbaugh clapped his hands for silence. On Fridays in assembly there was always an educational movie, a lecture from Mr. Ashbaugh about their shortcomings, and a pep session for the basketball game, although now that it was April, basketball season was over. Gradually it became quieter. Susan had just time enough to see Richard and Mr. Ashbaugh sit down in the front row before the lights went off. There was the hum of the movie projector and a square light shone on the cloth drop advertising grain elevators and chicken feed before someone backstage remembered to roll up the drop cloth and let down the white screen. After unsuccessful flickerings, the movie began. It was sponsored by a cookie company and showed how cookies were made assembly-line style, with big vats of what was presumably chocolate and gigantic rollers pressing out cookie after cookie. There were a lot of steps in between but Susan was always to be ignorant of how cookies were manufactured; her mind was fastened on Richard up there in the front row.

After the movie, Mr. Ashbaugh kept his complaints short, mentioning only disturbances in study hall and wasted time at the water fountain. He cleared his throat and shot an arm out of a jacket sleeve to look at his watch, a standard mannerism that many of the boys imitated for laughs. "I have a pleasant surprise for you this afternoon," he said. "Lieutenant Richard Lund of the U.S. Army Air Corps has come here at my request to speak of his experiences. You boys in the senior class who are considering what branch of service to go into after you graduate will find Richard's remarks especially helpful. Richard, I'll let you do the talking and sit back and listen. I'm sure I'll learn something, too."

Richard stood up, and everyone applauded before he even said anything. He stood at ease, smiling, motioning for silence, but the clapping continued. He was clearly a hero, and although he wasn't more than a few hundred feet away, Susan felt he might as well be on the moon. She couldn't believe she'd been out with him last night, he seemed so distant, so unobtainable.

"Okay, let's keep it to a low roar," Richard said after a while. "Instead of talking, I'll let you ask the questions."

Arms shot up all over the auditorium.

"I'd like to ask what he's doing tonight," Rosemary whispered.

"I'd like to ask if I'll ever see him again," Susan didn't say.

Richard answered the questions easily and intelligently. The longer he spoke, the farther he was from her reach. Susan despaired. She wasn't in his league. Even the nightclub singer wasn't. Probably he'd end up marrying a debutante or someone equally rich and glamorous.

After he finished speaking, the audience clapped and cheered more loudly than before. Then the cheerleaders got up onstage. Penny Detweiler, who'd been a cheerleader for three years, was now at peak performance. She put everything she had into it for Richard's benefit, thrusting out breasts and behind as she cavorted onstage, accompanied by cute quips and faces.

"Don't you just hate her?" Rosemary asked, which was one of the reasons Susan liked Rosemary. They both disliked the same people. "And she's not as cute as she thinks she is," Rosemary added. "You're lots cuter." Loyalty was another reason she liked Rosemary.

After the cheerleading session, the students marched out of the auditorium, two by two, in time to John Philip Sousa's "Stars and Stripes Forever" played on the phonograph. The first-graders went first, the seniors last. Although Susan craned her neck, she could no longer see Richard.

As soon as the students reached the front door of the schoolhouse, they broke into a run, racing toward the yellow school buses waiting to take them home. There were four buses, one for each direction. Susan trailed behind Rosemary, wondering if Richard had already left. They went through the door and down the steps. There standing under the flagpole encircled by white gravel was Richard. "Oh, God, he's looking our way, I'm going to faint," Rosemary said. He cut across the grass, walking toward them. "Going my way?" he asked Susan. It was a moment of pure, unadulterated happiness. And triumph. In all four buses faces peered out the windows as she and Richard headed toward his car, parked among the teachers' cars. And in the car, despite the onlookers, he kissed her. It was the next best thing to announcing their engagement. Susan hoped Penny Detweiler was watching.

"I'm sorry about last night," he said. "I'll get you home earlier from now on."

He did. They went dancing, bowling, and to the movies, and he always kept an eye on his watch. If it had been anyone but Richard, her father wouldn't have let her go out every night, but no one's father could object to Richard Lund, not even hers.

What her father would have objected to were the nights they went no farther than Lovers' Lane, just beyond the bridge. At first Susan hadn't felt at all romantic, the spot reminding her of the terrible time she'd had with Champ, the basketball player from Brookville High. When Richard asked what was wrong, she told him. She didn't mention that to begin with there had been nearly the whole team in the car, and she was vague about what Champ had tried to do. Also, she didn't tell him about sending the car into the river. Richard was so nice and decent, he might have been shocked. He was, in fact, too decent, removing his hand even before she told him to—although she wasn't too sure she would have. He always stopped when their kisses were at their most passionate. He apologized, said he'd forgotten himself and what nice girls were like, which made her wonder what kind he'd been seeing.

She was invited to his house for Sunday dinner. Mrs. Lund smiled often, but carefully sized her up behind steel-rimmed glasses. Mr. Lund talked to her about cattle and crops and seemed impressed by how much she knew about farming. She offered to help Mrs. Lund with the dishes, but Mrs. Lund urged her to go into the living room and chat with the men, apparently suggesting that Susan knew more about running a farm than a house.

"My dad likes you," Richard said later. He didn't mention how his mother felt. She said her father liked him, too. That was true. And the closer it got to the end of Richard's furlough, the better her father liked him. Then suddenly it was Friday afternoon, Richard's last day home. Susan stayed home from school. Richard had to be at the train station by seven in the evening. They spent the afternoon together, walking in the woods by the river. The sun made a golden path on the rippled surface of the water. Buttercups and violets were in bloom. It was a perfect day, and Susan perfectly miserable. She knew she was spoiling their last hours with her tears.

"I'll be home again," he said. "When I get back I'll be in personnel training, teaching guys how to fly, so that should keep me there. After you graduate, you can come down and visit."

"Daddy wouldn't let me."

"Not even if you came down with Mom?"

"I don't know," she said, not relishing the idea of going to Columbus, Georgia, with his mother.

The woods was cool green, the sky a tender blue. He drew her close and kissed her, and she pressed against him, locking her arms around his neck. Their kisses lasted longer and longer. They swayed together, kneeling then lying on the grass. She pushed her knee between his legs and felt him large and hard, nudging against her. He broke away. "Oh, God, oh, no, honey, I'm trying to behave, and you're not helping. I can't stand it."

"I don't want to help," she said, and drew him on top of her, scarcely aware of the twigs and small stones pressing into her back, conscious only of the urgency to have him on her and in her, arching her body upward, opening her legs, tightening her grip. Unzipping, groping, thrusting, pain. And then a lovely throbbing, him or her? Finally they parted and lay side by side, smiling at each other.

"Shouldn't you put your clothes on?" he asked.

She was in her slip, her panties around one ankle. Her slip was all bloody. He politely turned his head away while she dressed.

"Do you think I'm so terrible?" she asked.

"You're wonderful. I'm crazy about you. Why would I think you're terrible?"

"Because I let you. Maybe I even *more* than let you."

He kissed her. "It was mutual. I should have known this would happen. If anyone is to blame, I am. And what I blame myself for is being so damn stupid and not taking precautions. I deliberately didn't bring anything, so I wouldn't do what I did. I mean, you're such a nice kid, and so young and innocent."

"I'm not all that nice. And I'm only three years younger than you. Girls are more mature than men anyway."

"If you weren't so damn nice about this, I wouldn't feel so rotten. I mean, most girls blame the guy for seducing them, but you make excuses for me. You're such a sweet kid. I think I love you."

"Think? Is that all? I know I love you."

He took her hand. "I love you, too. Very much. And I don't want you to worry. If you get pregnant, I won't let you down, we'll get married."

"I hope I get pregnant."

"You're too young to marry."

"Not when there's a war on. Not when we don't know how much time we'll have together. Not when . . ." She broke off. She couldn't say ". . . you might not come back." Putting such a thought into words might make it happen; even thinking it was dangerous.

"Oh, God, honey, I don't know. Maybe after you graduate. Maybe when I get leave again, we'll get married."

"Only 'maybe'?" she said sadly.

"Honey, I'm thinking about it from your viewpoint. What if we got married and had a few wonderful weeks together and then I was sent over and came back"—he hesitated—"war damaged? Disabled? In a wheelchair?"

"Don't say that," she pleaded. "I don't care how you come back, as long as you do. To me you'll always be perfect."

They stayed together in the woods until the last possible moment, then reluctantly walked up the hill to where his tan Studebaker was parked at the side of the house. She didn't even get a chance to kiss him good-bye. Her father came out of the house, shook hands, and wished him luck. And then he was gone.

She wrote him every day. Long, detailed letters about what happened at school, on the farm, in the community. She wrote how Bobby Detweiler had barely escaped being gored by an enraged bull, and how the fireworks factory—now making real explosives for the war—nearly blew up when someone got careless (although some people suspected sabotage). And, of course, she wrote how much she loved him. That, too, in detail. Writing filled the emptiness of her nights. And she liked writing for the sake of writing. She often rewrote an incident until it was perfect, using up nearly a whole box of stationery.

Every day after school she ran into the house and looked on top of the Philco radio where her father put her letters from

Richard. Often she was disappointed. Richard seldom wrote. He said he was a poor letter writer. Not only were his letters few and far between, but they were also brief and uninformative. He might mention going to a movie with a buddy, but not what the movie was. (Sometimes she was violently jealous, believing he'd gone with a girl.) He'd say the laundry had messed up and not returned all his socks, but he wouldn't say anything about training pilots. He said he loved her, but not how much, only putting X's at the bottom of the letters. He did ask for her picture. She sent him one she'd had taken for graduation. He wrote back that the boys in his barracks had voted her "The Girl I'd Like Most to Go on a Night Flying Mission With."

She seldom kept track of her periods and was always vague about when the next one was due. For three weeks after he'd left, she'd been hopeful, until one morning she woke up and found blood on her pajamas.

Her father was against her getting married after she graduated. He said she was too young. He said she wouldn't like living so far from home. He asked what happened when Richard was sent overseas. And who'd help Bobby Detweiler with the farmwork if she left? Bobby couldn't manage alone. "I'm not feeling well these days," her father said. He complained of dizzy spells, and with a sad, stoic smile said he was probably on the brink of a heart attack, stroke, or some debilitating disease.

"Why don't you see Dr. Boynton?" she asked, and finally after weeks of urging, he went. He came back saying that Dr. Boynton didn't know what he was talking about. "What did he say?" she asked.

"A lot of nonsense," her father said.

At first she thought her father might be covering up, protecting her from bad news of his illness, but when she thought about it, that seemed unlikely, since he so readily complained. She began to suspect it was either his imagination or that he was exaggerating so that she wouldn't marry Richard and leave him.

She couldn't wait to graduate and go down to Georgia to marry. She lived in suspended time, where nothing seemed real. Graduation activities were remote. In her mind, she'd already left school. The girls in her class seemed young and foolish to worry about what to wear to the senior prom or who would take them.

A few weeks before graduation, Susan got the news that crumbled the earth under her feet. The letter looked perfectly innocent lying there on top of the Philco. Holding it to her heart, she ran up to her bedroom to read it in privacy, although her father wasn't around to invade it. But this was part of the ritual of reading letters from Richard. She was pleased that the envelope was thicker than usual; maybe he'd written two pages instead of one. Before opening the letter, she had to make her bed, since it seemed wrong to read his letter on an unmade bed. After the bed was made, she lay propped on two pillows the way she always lay when she read his letters, and finally, when she could bear the suspense no longer, opened the envelope. And wished she hadn't.

He wrote that he was being transferred to New York and from there probably sent overseas. Maybe he'd be able to get leave before going to New York, but now wasn't the time to get married. He didn't want to tie her down. She was too young. The war might last a long time. It wouldn't be fair to her. They'd get married after the war or when he got back from overseas.

Looking up from the letter, Susan's eyes fell on the hairbrush on her vanity table. It was an ordinary hairbrush, but she was never able to look at it again, or the hundreds like it, without feeling physically ill, as if she'd eaten something heavy and indigestible that lay like a lump on her stomach.

She did, in fact, lose her appetite. She cried and grew even thinner. Her father's health improved, as did his spirits. He said Richard was "one hundred percent right. He's a sensible boy. It's all for the best, you'll see."

Maybe it was all her fault. Maybe if they hadn't had sex, Richard would want to marry her. Once in home-ec class when Miss Leach was out, they had a discussion on sex before marriage. All the girls said it was wrong, that no man would marry a girl who gave in. Only Susan and Penny were silent. "Why buy a cow when you can get free milk?" Rosemary Brummit said. Susan hated the expression. As fond as she was of Clementine and Millicent, she didn't care to be compared to a cow.

Richard didn't get leave. His next letter came from Governor's Island, New York, which he said was just a ferry ride away from Manhattan. It had taken him two weeks to write. He didn't sound terribly broken up about not getting a furlough. Susan wondered if he'd forgotten her. Why not? They'd only had two short weeks together. Now they would be separated for years. If he hadn't already forgotten her, he would. She wrote him suggesting she come visit. He wrote back, practically by return mail, that she wouldn't like New

York. It didn't even seem like America. A lot of people couldn't speak English, or spoke it with an accent. They weren't honest as in the Midwest, but out to gyp everybody, especially servicemen.

It didn't sound at all like the New York Miss Rice had described.

Susan wrote back asking if he'd gone to any plays, ballets, operas, or nightclubs where the big bands played. Richard said he'd gone to Coney Island. He said he expected to ship out any day now. Susan began to wonder if he purposely wanted her to stay away. Maybe there was another girl. She thought of Richard and some beautiful girl clinging to him on the roller-coaster at Coney Island, or necking through the tunnel of love. If there were a tunnel of love.

After she graduated, things got worse. No matter how hard she worked helping Bobby to plow the fields and care for the livestock, she still couldn't sleep at night.

She was loneliest at twilight when the dance music floated down the water from the River Inn, a few miles away. Hearing the faint strains of "Poinciana," she cried, remembering the first night she and Richard had gone out together. She went over each moment, cherishing it, fingering the cigarette with the man's face Richard had drawn. Almost all the tobacco had leaked out. It was just thin paper. "I'm seventeen, and all I have is memories," she thought.

Rosemary Brummit said she should go out more. Every Saturday night Rosemary and some girls she worked with at the fireworks factory went "stag" to the River Inn, which wasn't really an inn but a roadhouse. Susan said she didn't want to be unfaithful.

"Oh, for gosh sakes, it's okay to dance with a guy," Rosemary said. "Anyway, there's not many guys to dance with except draft dodgers and 4F's. Mostly it's just girls dancing with girls."

Susan went and was sorry. The band played the silver-wings song reminding her of Richard—as if she needed reminding. Under big striped umbrellas, groups of girls sat at tables near the river, pretending to have fun. The soft music and moonlight on the water were a complete waste. It was all so sad, especially the desperate play the women made for the pathetically few second-string men they wouldn't have noticed if there hadn't been a war on and there'd been a choice. Susan eyed the older women in their late twenties who'd never married and maybe never would. She wondered if she'd become one of them. At least, thank God, she wasn't a virgin.

She didn't know when she'd got the idea. Maybe it was that night at the River Inn or maybe those nights sitting on the porch steps, Whimpy at her side, her father in the rocking chair, the sun going down behind the willows and the mosquitoes coming up from the river. She could no longer bear the thought of not seeing Richard again, of having some woman or the war steal him away. She pictured herself sitting on the porch steps for the rest of her life while her father contentedly rocked away, of going up to a lonely, empty bed. Her father would find some excuse to keep her with him. She wouldn't get to go to college. He'd say she had to help on the farm until Eddy got back. To contribute to the war effort like everyone else. And what if Eddy didn't want to farm when he returned? He'd never liked farming.

To carry out her plan, she'd need money. She had her chicken money. And she could sell some of the pigs her father had given her in payment for farmwork. She couldn't, of course, part with Clementine or Millicent, but pigs were different. She'd sell them, take the money, and go to New York to see Richard. She couldn't risk telling him she was coming, or her father that she was going. Richard might not want her, and her father might not let her. She was sure Richard would change his mind the minute they were together. She wasn't going to let some New York girl lure him away. Even if he wouldn't marry her, she'd have something more than a few paltry memories. They'd go to plays and ballets and explore Greenwich Village. She visualized them sitting at one of the cafés Miss Rice told her about, surrounded by poets, artists, and bohemians who talked the night away.

The thought of running away frightened her less than the thought of remaining on the farm for the rest of her life.

She decided it was best to leave on Sunday. She could tell her father she was going to church with Rosemary and spending the afternoon and night at her place. That way he wouldn't worry, since by the time he expected her back, he'd get her telegram.

When her father was out, Susan phoned the bus and train stations for times of departures from Leyton and arrivals in New York. Her voice trembled when she asked for the information, and her hands shook when she wrote it down.

She considered confiding in Rosemary. But Rosemary might think she was doing the wrong thing and that it was her duty to alert Susan's father. Still, there was the problem of Rosemary's calling when she was supposed to be with her. Susan decided to wait until the very last moment and tell

Rosemary she was visiting an aunt in Dayton. Rosemary wouldn't know the aunt was nonexistent.

Friday she packed her suitcase and hid it in the closet, although she doubted if that was necessary. Her father wasn't a snoop. Saturday she went about saying silent good-byes. She threw her arms around Clementine and Millicent's necks and hugged Whimpy. She'd have liked to do the same with her father, but she couldn't, of course.

She spent a sleepless Saturday night, and had to force herself to stay in bed until the sun came up. It was a hushed summer morning. The farm had never looked so beautiful, the wheatfield so golden, the willows so green.

Usually her father helped with the milking on Sunday, since that was Bobby's day off, but she did the milking herself. She fixed him an especially good breakfast, baking biscuits, although it was too hot to use the oven. Her father was pleased. "You'd think it was my birthday," he said, "milking cows and baking biscuits." He was so trusting, so unsuspicious, that it increased her guilt. Suddenly he appeared very frail and thin. Perhaps he really was sick and would die if she deserted him. What if she were sending him to an early grave? She'd never forgive herself.

"Maybe I should go to church, too," her father said. She felt relief. If he went to church, then she couldn't go to New York. He seldom attended church, although he was active in church affairs. The next minute, however, he'd changed his mind about going, saying religion wasn't a matter of church on Sunday.

"Maybe I won't go either," she said.

"Now, it won't hurt you to, and Rosemary's expecting you. You don't want to let her down," he said with his usual conscientiousness. He and Richard were the two most honest and decent people she knew. Richard was far too wonderful to lose to some girl who wouldn't appreciate him.

Her father offered her the car, but she refused, saying he might want it later. She couldn't leave the car at the train depot. She called a cab and went upstairs to get dressed. She'd already decided on her white dress that went so well with her tan. Her hair, normally a dirty blond, was light blond from working in the sun. She looked good.

The cab came rumbling across the wooden bridge. She ran downstairs with her small blue suitcase that she'd used previously only for overnight stays at Rosemary's. She gave her father a traitorous good-bye kiss and fled. Whimpy, trotting as fast as his old legs would allow, followed her to the taxi.

Sonny Rollins was driving. His father owned the cab company, which consisted of two cabs. She sat in front, since that was customary. "Would you please hurry," she said. "I have to catch the ten-thirty train."

It was ten after ten, and the ride to Leyton took twenty minutes, not counting the extra time to reach the station.

"Hold on to your hat," Sonny said, and roared down the hill. "Where you off to?" he asked without letting up on the accelerator.

No need to lie. Sonny didn't know her well enough to guess she was running away. "New York," she said, thrilling at the words.

"Boy, some people have all the luck. Here I am stuck in this one-horse town while everyone else leaves. I'd give my right arm to get away, but the Army won't have me. Bad eyes, they say. Hell, if I can see well enough to drive, I can see well enough to shoot."

She thought maybe the Army was right, considering the close calls they had on the highway, but he got her to the station twelve minutes early. And refused to let her pay. "Give my regards to Broadway," he called sadly.

The station was mustard-colored, one room with a concrete floor and two benches facing a ticket window presided over by old Mr. Smalley. She knew it was he, since he informed her father when to expect troop trains. Luckily he didn't know who she was. Or did he? He'd never seen her before since her father hadn't allowed her to visit the troop trains. Just the same, she worried. Wasn't that a suspicious look he gave her when she asked for a one-way ticket to New York? Wasn't he taking an awfully long time making out the ticket?

The station clock said ten-thirty, which agreed with the Bulova her father had given her for graduation. The train was late. Hurry up, she told it, and went outside to pace up and down the platform past a mail cart and long-necked scales. She looked nervously down the empty sun-gleaming tracks running together in the distance, wondering if Mr. Smalley had unaccountably guessed her identity and was right now phoning her father.

A serviceman stood waiting around with his parents, sister or girlfriend. Maybe wife. They stood near the pink hollyhocks at one end of the platform. Susan remembered making hollyhock dolls when she was little, pinning the buds onto the blossoms, and floating them in a rain barrel. Finally she spied the train in the distance. Impossibly slow. Sonny Rollins should have been the engineer. Then suddenly it was pulling in beside her. Full of excitement and misgivings, she picked up her suitcase.

She felt when the conductor handed her up the steps that he was handing her into a new life. The train was crammed with servicemen, weary wives, and crying babies. Car after car was filled. A number of servicemen offered to share their seats with her. Everyone looked dingy and rumpled; many of the men were unshaven. Probably they'd been traveling all night from Chicago.

The area between the cars was crowded with standees or sitees on suitcases. She clutched her blue suitcase and pocketbook and squeezed by, excusing herself. Just as she decided she'd have to stand all the way to New York, a sailor gallantly offered, not to share his seat, but to give it to her. After he'd hoisted her suitcase up on the rack, he offered her a Milky Way, and crouched in the aisle. "Where you going?" he asked.

"New York."

"Hey, isn't that lucky? That's where I'm headed, too. I'll show you the town."

"Thank you, but I'm meeting my fiancé," she said formally, careful to give "fiancé" the right pronunciation. It thrilled her to say that word, too.

"Maybe he won't be there. Maybe he's shipped out, you never know."

Susan prayed he hadn't. The last she'd heard from Richard was a week ago Thursday. She refused to dwell on the possibility and listened to the sailor, who said he'd just come from Chicago, where it was disgusting to see so many white girls with Negroes. "Good-looking girls, too, but they can't be no better than"—he hesitated—"prostitutes."

"It's just as well you're not meeting my fiancé," Susan said loftily. "Thanks for the seat anyway." She got up and left the sailor, who wore a puzzled, indignant look on his face. Miss Rice had said they were fighting the war to rid the world of racial hatred. She'd told Susan how Hitler had walked out on the 1936 Olympics just because of Jesse Owens.

Susan wasn't sure where to go. She pushed her way through the mob in the aisles toward the women's room, where there might be a seat, but when she opened the door, she nearly gagged on the smell. She shut the door quickly and walked on. A conductor told her she might find a seat in the club car and personally led her there. She wished she could tell him about why she'd given her seat back to the sailor. As she followed the conductor, she was aware of being closely scrutinized by soldiers, sailors, marines, the Coast Guard, and the Army Air Corps. She knew it wasn't because she was such a raving beauty but because there were so few unattached women on board. It seemed so ironic, poor Rosemary and all those other girls going stag on Saturday nights so desperate to meet men, when all they had to do was jump on a train to have their wildest dreams fulfilled.

She was lucky to find a seat in the club car. It was only after she'd ordered a Coke from a white-coated waiter that she remembered she'd left her suitcase in the rack. She looked out at the fields and farmhouses rushing by and thought of her father innocently reading the Sunday paper, of how upset he'd be when he got her telegram. But as the countryside receded, so did her worries. A vision of Richard floated before her outside the train as if he were beckoning her on to New York.

The train fled past small towns, cities, and farmlands. Time passed as quickly as place. Soon it was twilight. At the first call to dinner, Susan hurried to the dining car to fulfill a lifetime ambition of eating in a diner. But there was already a long waiting line. She looked longingly at the sparkling glasses and polished silver, at the lucky people seated at tables, spreading linen napkins across their laps. A dark-haired officer seated with two elderly women and across from an unoccupied chair smiled her way. After he held a whispered consultation with the waiter, the waiter passed the other standees and came up to her. "Your friend's waiting for you to join him," he said.

The dark-haired officer had risen to his feet. He was all smiles, plus a frown—dark smiling eyes with a furrow between, and an impish grin. The contradictory smile and frown was appealing. After all, it wasn't being unfaithful to Richard just to sit across from a man in a crowded dining car.

"I was beginning to think you'd never get here," the man said, pulling out a chair for her.

Susan didn't know what to say to that, but one of the elderly ladies came to her rescue. "Oh, that mob is frightful to get through," she said.

"Frightful," the other lady added, "and the service is terrible. Why, the waiters used to be so polite. Now they slam food down in front of you and try to hurry you out."

"It's the war, ma'am, it does spoil things," the officer said.

The woman missed his irony. "Oh, doesn't it though?" she replied. She wore a navy wide-brimmed hat of straw and looked rather like the Queen Mother, as did her companion, although she wore a different kind of hat.

The man winked at Susan as he handed her the menu. "Sorry there's no lobster thermidor or oysters Rockefeller," he said.

He was wonderfully witty and sophisticated; even the old ladies chuckled at his remark. She looked at the menu. Three dishes to choose from—T-bone steak, baked Virginia ham, and roast beef au jus. He sat, pencil poised, ready to write down her choice. She hadn't even known the orders were written. She also didn't know how to pronounce "au jus," so she just said she'd have the roast beef.

She learned about the officer from his answers to the Queen Mothers' questions. He lived in New York, the war had interrupted his studies at Princeton, he was stationed in Fort Benning. Susan nearly called "But that's where my fiancé was stationed," before remembering he was supposedly her boyfriend so she wouldn't have one. She also remembered that Fort Benning was in Georgia, and wondered why, if the officer lived in New York, he was on a train going east instead of one heading south.

He was lying. He freely admitted this after the Queen Mothers left. "I'm not from New York and never went to Princeton," he said, "but they were such classy old ladies I thought they'd like that better than my being a coal miner from Donora, Pennsylvania."

She looked at him, amazed. "You're a coal miner?"

"Yeah, but the war got me out of that, thank God. My dad and brothers are still in the mines. I hated that damn town. Even when the sun was out it looked like it was raining. Always gray. I'm Michael Deal. Lieutenant Michael Deal, recent graduate of the OCS."

"What's OCS?"

"Officer candidate school, where they turn out ninety-day wonders."

She didn't understand half of what he said, but she understood someone who was glad to get away from where he lived. "I'm Susan Varner," she said. "I'm running away from home."

He didn't act surprised. Maybe he didn't believe her. "So am I. I just spent three days home with my family, and now I'm spending the rest of my leave the way I want to. Living it up in New York with a room at the Waldorf. Care to join me?"

She knew she should pretend righteous indignation, but she didn't feel it. "I'm meeting my fiancé."

"Is it love?"

She nodded. "I've loved him ever since I was little."

"I'm in love, too. All I have to do is meet the girl. I know what she's like, I just have to find her."

"What?" Susan asked, leaning forward, rather hoping he'd describe her.

"Blond, beautiful, rich, and Southern," he said, and went into a rhapsody about Southern girls, who were all lovely and charming. They spoke in soft voices. They didn't go around with their hair up in curlers. (She bet.) While he praised Southern womanhood, they got dirty looks from people still waiting for tables.

Although Susan would have loved to sit in the diner drinking after-dinner coffee, talking to him, and watching the lights of cities, towns, and cars on lonely roads pass by, it didn't seem fair to keep hungry people waiting. She mentioned this to Michael Deal.

"Oh, yeah. Yeah, you're right."

He offered to pay for her meal, but she wouldn't let him. He'd need his money at the Waldorf. He asked her again if she wouldn't change her mind about living it up with him in New York.

She said thank you, no.

"Maybe we'll meet again," he said before sauntering off. She didn't know that they actually would meet years later. In Berlin.

More people were getting off the train, fewer getting on.

Susan found the car where the sailor had given her his seat. The seat was now empty and her suitcase still on the rack. The conductor called out Philadelphia. Looking at the explosion of lights, she felt exhilaration. In two short hours she'd be in New York. She'd have to change her dress. It had been a mistake to wear white with all that soot blowing in through the windows.

She'd planned to get a hotel room and a good night's sleep before calling Richard, but there might not be any hotel rooms available. And the closer she got to New York, the less she felt like sleep.

It was all she could do to keep from bouncing up and down in her seat like a child. Then suddenly the conductor was calling out that magic name, and they were tunneling through darkness. She got her suitcase and was first in the aisle, impatiently standing behind the standees, her heart pounding along with the clanging train.

When she got off, she had numerous offers from servicemen to carry her suitcase, but she hung on to it, politely refusing, wanting not to waste words on getting acquainted with strangers, but to get acquainted with the city. Stark lights cast dark shadows along the platform. She glimpsed the Queen Mothers trotting alongside a redcap who pushed a trolley piled high with their luggage. She saw soldiers and sailors embracing girlfriends and wives.

A voice on the loudspeaker announced their arrival: New York! Pennsylvania Station! New York!

Finally, she was here.

9. *Gina*

They were seated at the Café de la Paix at the St. Moritz. One of Gina's favorite hangouts. Expensive. Fresh linen, fresh flowers, and waiters who weren't fresh. She wore a summery black chiffon dress and a hat. It wasn't much of a hat, just a flower on a ribbon attached to a tiny comb. She'd made it herself. Several of the other models where she worked at Fashion Associates had asked her to make one for them. They'd offered to pay, and she'd let them. She didn't want to, but she needed the money for Giuliano's stay at the sanatorium. And, after all, the charge was a lot less than the original hat that she'd seen at Bonwit's and copied.

Gina sipped her daiquiri and glanced at the menu.

"Pick anything you want, honey," Mr. Simms said.

That was what she intended to do. She smiled over at Mr. Simms, rather liking him despite his glasses and receding hair. He was an out-of-town buyer, one of Fashion Associates' steady customers. Mr. Freed, her boss, had warned her about him. "He's got a wife and three kids back in Cleveland," he'd said.

"Don't they all?" she'd asked.

That had shocked Mr. Freed, who considered her an innocent because she was the youngest of the models. She wondered what he'd say if he knew about her dance-hall days.

"I'll have the cherrystone clams, Maine lobster, asparagus, green salad, and chocolate mousse," she told Mr. Simms.

"How do you eat like that and keep your figure?"

"Bathing-suit models are allowed curves."

He eyed her cleavage. "You're certainly curvy, all-righty-right."

Actually, she ate only one meal a day, and that was when she was invited out. For breakfast she had coffee, for lunch a candy bar. Luckily she was invited out often. The other models did the same. That way they ate at the best restaurants, kept their weight down, and spent money on important things like clothes and cosmetics. Gina spent little money on either. She bought dresses at knock-down prices, worn once in the showroom or on the ramp. By economizing, she could pay for the sanatorium plus giving money to her mother for school clothes for her kid sisters, who'd have something decent and be spared the humiliation she'd undergone. If she had enough money saved by fall, she was going to Parsons School of Design. Mr. Freed had seen her sketches and said she had real talent. He promised to recommend her to his business friends who hired designers if she went to design school.

Mr. Simms was looking over the menu. "What's this *osso bucco*?"

"How would I know?"

"I thought with a name like Sabatini you might."

"Listen, I was born in America and speak English like everyone else."

"Oh, oh, sorry. Didn't mean to offend, sweetheart."

Why was it that just because her name was Sabatini, people thought of her in terms of spaghetti, gangsters, garlic, and small cups of black coffee? Later, when the waiter asked what beverage she'd like with dessert, she chose tea. She enjoyed the deferential way he served her, as if she were some debutante. It helped make up for childhood memories of smelling pee in the hall and sleeping five in a bed.

Mr. Simms offered her a Viceroy and lit their cigarettes.

"Where would you like to go from here?" he asked. The look in his eyes showed where he'd like to go—to his hotel room.

She smiled sweetly. "Carmen Cavallaro's at the Rainbow Room, Xavier Cugat's at the Starlight Roof at the Waldorf, and Larry Adler—he's that terrific harmonica player—is at the Savoy Plaza. But I'm sort of tired of those places. I'd rather go to Nick's in the Village—they have some really good jazz."

"Nick's it is," he said with a good-sport smile.

She realized what a good sport he was when she saw he didn't like jazz. In appreciation, she didn't flirt with the drummer. Just before they left Nick's, however, she told him about this jerk buyer she'd gone out with who'd come from the sticks and was constantly trying to paw her. "You can tell the hicks, they never know how to act with a girl," she said. It worked. In the taxi Mr. Simms kept his hands to himself to prove he wasn't a hick who didn't know how to act with girls.

At the door of her apartment building on MacDougal Street, Gina gave him a goodnight kiss. After all, it had been an expensive evening and he hadn't made passes like a lot of men despite her hick story.

Gina climbed six flights of stained marble stairs to her place on the top floor. In a walk-up, the higher the floor, the lower the rent. Lights shone under several doors, although it was past midnight. The neighborhood grew livelier every night, with more artists moving in among the Italians. She liked the artists and didn't too much mind the Italians, who weren't as poor, noisy, or nosy as on the Lower East Side.

Opening the door to darkness and quiet, she suddenly wished she were still living with Georgette. Her husband, Amazin' Harry, the magician, had magically appeared one day and talked Georgette into investing her life's savings in a bar in Pensacola, Florida, where there was a big naval base. Georgette wrote Gina she'd hired a lawyer and got everything put in her name, since Harry wouldn't be so likely to pull another disappearing act if she held the purse strings.

When Giuliano was well enough to leave the sanatorium, he could move in with her. His doctor said he was getting better every day. She figured the money she saved on the sanatorium could go for an airy, sunny place beneficial to Giuliano. She visited him upstate every other Sunday. He was the only person in her family she saw regularly. On the rare occasions she went home, she always called first to make sure her father was out. She'd had a phone installed so she could call and make sure, and for her little sisters' sakes. Angela was thirteen and Maria was eleven, the age Don Guidetti liked little girls best. Gina wished they weren't so pretty. She'd tried warning them without scaring them, saying that if her father ever mentioned visiting Don Guidetti, to call her right away. Her mother was too afraid of her father to be trusted. She was wary of Vince, who'd taken over Tuillo's dirty work after Tuillo had been gunned down. Vince was given a draft deferment for wartime work, although he worked for Don Guidetti. No doubt Don Guidetti had arranged for the deferment, which meant Vince owed him a favor.

Gina cold-creamed her face and prowled around the apartment in her slip, not the least bit sleepy. Scotch-taped to the wall were nightclub photographs of her various escorts. There were also photographs Giuliano had taken before going to the sanatorium. She was crazy about the one of the young lovers on the Staten Island ferry, but most of the other photographs were of slums, and she hated reminders, although she admired the way he'd captured the sly, fierce look of an old woman in black sitting in front of a tenement house. Suddenly she saw how cheap and superficial the girl in the nightclub picture looked by comparison to the old woman. And her escorts had a sameness about them, fat faces and thinning hair.

She thought she was so damn clever, that she'd gotten ahead in life, but had she? From a girl who danced for a dime she'd become a girl who danced for a dinner. Modeling, which had once seemed so glamorous, was just hard work, and the buyers got to feel the merchandise while you were wearing it. She never slept with them or with the rich playboy types who pursued models the way they did actresses. She didn't want any man touching her; she knew they were out for what they could get, and they weren't getting it from her. And yet there were times when she was out with an attractive man that she regretted her vow of chastity.

Now, in order to work off her restlessness, she put "Malagueña" on her secondhand phonograph, turned off the lights, undressed, and danced nude. She began with the classic Castilian dance she'd learned from Georgette, snapping fingers overhead, flinging her head back, stamping, swaying, pivoting, improvising, letting the music suggest the movement, sliding her hands over breasts and hips, offering her body to the darkness as if it were a lover, until finally she fell onto her bed. Funny, how much she enjoyed dancing, when she'd gotten so fed up with it at the dance hall. But this was dancing without a partner. Alone was better.

In the morning she had to get up early, since she was filling in for Miss Rubin, Mr. Freed's combined secretary and receptionist. Miss Rubin was on vacation. Since Gina knew shorthand and typing, she often replaced absentee secretaries, which was lucky, because although she'd been the last hired, she wasn't the first fired. A lot of models had been laid off after Fashion Associates got a government contract to make naval officers' shirts.

She got on the subway wearing a fresh cotton dress and got off wilted, as if she'd worn the dress all day.

Seventh Avenue was nearly as crowded as the subway. Pushboys shoved rolling racks of clothes down the street, yelling out for people to watch their backs. Already the streets were jammed with trucks. Later there'd be even more of a mob, with models, buyers, salesmen, and shipping clerks.

After entering a balconied art-deco building, she took the elevator to the third floor, where the offices were. The showrooms were on the fourth floor, the cutting rooms and workrooms on the fifth floor, and the sewing room on the sixth floor.

Gina sat at Miss Rubin's desk, which faced the elevator and was flanked by windowed offices. Miss Rubin had left a list of dos and don'ts for her. The first "do" was order Mr. Freed's coffee (regular, three lumps of sugar). Gina wondered how he rated three lumps with sugar rationing, and supposed if you tipped extra, the coffee shop gave extra. The last "don't" was forget to turn off the lights before leaving.

Around ten-thirty, Mr. Freed called her in for dictation, a moment she dreaded. She'd never learned shorthand properly, and wrote her own version, which she often had trouble deciphering. Also, Mr. Freed was grouchy and nervous. It was normal to be nervous in a cutthroat business where you could go broke or double your money in six months, but the grouchiness wasn't normal for Mr. Freed. That was new. Ever since his son Dan had come to work a week ago. Before he'd come in, Mr. Freed had gone about beaming and talking about his genius son who was a Yale college boy. Gina knew that the Ivy League schools had a quota system, and you had to be really exceptional to get in if you were Jewish. She didn't see anything exceptional about Dan Freed except that he was exceptionally snotty and all he did was read.

Every day he breezed in around noon carrying a pile of books as if he'd just come from the library and dressed as if he were just going to the beach. He sat at his desk reading openly. Sometimes, though, he wrote furtively on a yellow legal pad which he kept hidden in a desk drawer. When he wasn't doing either of these things, he was up on the sixth floor trying to incite mutiny among the sewing-machine operators, telling them they shouldn't put up with such sweatshop conditions. The operators, who already belonged to the ILGWU, considered him a pest. "I've got my own Dave Dubinsky," Mr. Freed said sourly. Dave Dubinsky headed the ILGWU.

Gina tried to keep up with Mr. Freed's dictation and didn't look around when she heard the elevator door open and glimpsed Mr. Freed's scowl. "Early," he said. "Only two hours late instead of the usual three. I'd fire him, if that wasn't what he wanted."

While Gina was back at her desk trying to decipher her squiggles, Dan Freed came out. He plunked himself on her desk and swung a sandaled foot. Beneath his dark glasses were full lips that would have been sensuous if they weren't sneering. Gina ignored him. She was making numerous mistakes as she typed, but she didn't correct them, so he wouldn't guess and misinterpret the fact to mean his presence flustered her. He was conceited enough to do so.

"Looks like you had a rough night," he said.

She did not dignify his remark with a reply.

"Out with another buyer?"

"None of your business," she said, not looking up.

"God, to think my own father would stoop to such things."

This time she did look up. "Stoop to what, may I ask?"

"To using his models to get orders from buyers."

"Oh, crap. If anything, he warns me about them."

"That makes it even worse. He warns you, and you don't listen."

"What's so sad is your dirty mind. Get lost, jerk."

Old Mr. Samuels came shuffling up. "Glad to see you two kiddos are getting acquainted," he said genially. Mr. Samuels was in his seventies, white-haired and shaky, but despite his shaky hands, Mr. Freed maintained he was the best cutter in the business. Mr. Samuels patted Dan's shoulder affectionately. "I've known this kid since he was in diapers. He's a good boy, just ashamed for people to know," he told Gina. Although Gina loved Mr. Samuels, she thought he had rotten judgment.

Mr. Freed peered out from the doorway. "What the hell's going on out there?" he yelled. "Some kind of Elks convention?"

"We're waiting for the fabric to arrive upstairs," Mr. Samuels said. "Sitting around twiddling our fingers."

"Thumbs," Dan Freed said.

"Thumbs," Mr. Samuels said. "See what you learn at Yale?"

"Go over to Altman's and learn what's holding them up on delivery," Mr. Freed said to his son.

"You go, I'm not your errand boy. Call him up."

"You call up, you get excuses. Now, go over there and talk to him personal. Tell him there's a war on."

After repeating he wasn't an errand boy, Dan Freed left.

Mr. Freed went back into his office. Mr. Samuels shook his head. "Kids today, they got no respect," he said; then, "But some fathers they don't deserve none, they deserve a good horse-lashing, that's what."

Gina wondered if he meant Papa, and if that was why he'd helped her. Last summer, after she'd finished high school and had gone to see her family, she'd run into Mr. Samuels on the street. When she said she wasn't having any luck job hunting, he'd said he'd speak to his boss about her, that with her face and figure she'd make a swell model. Modeling had sounded as remote as movie acting, and she hadn't really believed Mr. Samuels until he'd called and told her to see Mr. Freed. She was even more amazed when Mr. Freed hired her.

After Mr. Samuels shuffled off, Patsy Bankowsky came high-heeling up. She was skinny and snooty-looking and modeled the more sophisticated clothes. "Lend me your emery board," Patsy said. "I broke my fingernail on a zipper." Gina lent her an emery board. Patsy filed away while talking about her various insoluble problems: brittle fingernails, big feet, hair too fine to hold a set, and short men. "Like him," she said, nodding toward Dan Freed, who'd just gotten off the elevator. "Cute, but short, you know? Anyway, he's not half as cute as he thinks. He gives me a pain where a pill can't reach," she said eloquently. But all the same, she sexily draped herself over Gina's—or rather Miss Rubin's—desk for his benefit. He didn't, however, look her way.

"I suppose he thinks he's too good for a lowly model, a Yale man, boss's son, and all," Patsy said.

Although Dan Freed ignored them, his father didn't. He kept glaring out. "Listen, I have to get these letters done," Gina said.

"Tell him to shove 'em," Patsy said. "I'd never do such menial work. You ought to remind him you're a model, not a lowly secretary."

"Not when I get ten dollars more a week," Gina said.

Patsy arched an already perfectly arched eyebrow. "You do?"

It was five dollars, but the lie was worth it.

For lunch Gina ate a Hershey bar at her desk and thumbed through an art book on Goya she'd gotten from the library. She didn't feel like going out into the lunch-hour mob. The heat, however, was getting to her, the sticky air unrelieved by any breeze from the open windows. Shrill voices and honking horns carried up. She decided she'd go to the Cloisters after work. Some people might prefer the beach at

Coney Island, but she wanted to get away from humanity to where it was cool and quiet.

Mr. Freed came up.

"I'm on my lunch hour," she said.

"Did I say anything? Don't be so touchy." Then, "You call that lunch, a candy bar? You ought to have something nourishing. A sandwich, at least. Pastrami on rye. You kids, you eat anything, you'll pay for it later, you'll see. I'm going out on business. If I'm not back by closing, let me know who sneaks out."

Gina wondered if business were some woman. He didn't fool around with any of the models, but maybe he didn't want to mix business with pleasure. All married men had a girl hidden away.

The afternoon dragged on. Dan Freed, who'd been reading since lunch, was now writing on his legal pad. He tapped his teeth with a pencil eraser and stared out into space. She thought it was space; maybe he was looking at her. Hard to tell where, in those dark glasses. Then she became irritated with the way she'd been so conscious of his moves all afternoon, picked up her purse, and headed for the ladies' room, where she washed her face and put on fresh makeup.

Around four-thirty, some people took a chance on Mr. Freed's not coming back and sneaked out. Gina pretended not to notice. At five she put the cover on her typewriter and turned off all the lights except in Dan Freed's office, where he still sat, although when his father was in he was the first person out.

"Hey, turn off your lights when you leave," Gina yelled.

He didn't look up. She went to his doorway. "Listen, I have to see the lights are off, and I don't want to wait around, so turn yours off when you go, okay?"

"Where you going in such a big rush?" he asked.

"What's it to you?"

"Off for cocktails with a buyer?"

"I'm going to the Cloisters. Not that it's any of your business."

"No kidding? Are you going there for the repose of your soul or the refreshment of your spirit?"

"What's it to you?"

"Mind if I tag along?"

She shrugged. "Suit yourself, it's a free country."

He turned off his light, hooked his jacket over his shoulder by a thumb, and followed her onto the elevator, where they stood in the confined intimacy avoiding each other's eyes.

Now that they weren't arguing, they didn't know what to say. Or at least she didn't know what to say to him.

When the elevator stopped, she got out and hurried along the street ahead of him and down into the subway station. Luckily they were separated by the rush-hour crowd pushing through the train doors. People pressed against her. Mostly men. Maybe some were victims of circumstances, but not all. Just in case of mashers, she poked her elbows into ribs and stamped on feet.

By the time she got off, she was limp, perspiring, and irritated from having to stand for so long in heels and sweltering heat squashed by sweaty bodies. Dan caught up with her in the station. He was all smiles. "There's something exhilarating about riding the subway during rush hour and rubbing shoulders with the real people."

"It's not so much fun when you do it every day."

He considered this. "You know, you're right. I never thought of that. It's not fair that the Wall Street gangsters ride to work in cabs and Cadillacs while the honest working class is jammed together like sardines."

"Are you a communist?"

"Oh, Jesus, I care for humanity, does that make me a communist?"

"You have to be rich to care for humanity. When you're poor, all you want to do is get away from people."

"That's the trouble. The poor should unite and help each other."

"Oh, God," she groaned, "spare me your sermons."

He walked angrily ahead of her straight up the hill instead of along the winding drive. She hated him for his phony words, for considering the subway ride a lark, for climbing the hill so easily when she had to struggle behind in her high heels.

Then she caught sight of the tower at the top of the hill and forgot about him. Already she felt refreshed by the coolness of grass and trees. She walked through the Roman archway and into the twelfth century and thought no more of sweltering subways, Seventh Avenue, or boss's spoiled sons.

Luckily he didn't hang around. He bounded ahead and disappeared into the chapel. By the time she got there, he'd moved on. Obviously he was furious and wanted to avoid her. Good. She paused to admire a large Spanish crucifix with a sorrowing Christ, visited all her old favorites—the bronze beakers of birds and animals, the tomb where a man's feet rested on a dog.

She came across him in an arcade. Head bent, in his sandaled feet, he looked like a meditating monk, if monks wore dark glasses.

"Look," he said, pointing to the floor.

She looked and saw nothing. Then she noticed a pattern like a row of lighted candles made by the sun shining through the arcade. Not the sort of thing the average person would notice.

"Are you an artist?" she asked.

"I'm a writer. I'm going to write a novel exposing the garment industry, the back-stabbing, the treachery, the lust for the almighty buck."

"Oh, is it really like that?" she asked, impressed.

"You'd know, if you kept your eyes open, which is what I'm doing. That's why I didn't fight it when Dad wanted me to work for him this summer. You can't write living in a goddamned ivory tower. Of course, he doesn't know I'm writing. He doesn't think writing is honest work." He paused. "Listen, don't tell anyone, please, I don't want anyone at work to know."

She was flattered that he'd taken her into his confidence. "I won't," she promised. And since he trusted her with his secret, she returned the compliment by showing him what was dearest to her, although she'd vowed never to try that again after showing others, who'd politely pretended interest. "Come, look at these," she said, and led him to the crucifix, the beakers, and the tomb. He examined each thing thoroughly, silently, and with the same awe she felt.

In the unicorn room she pointed out the detailing in the tapestry. "See, that's the first time the slit technique was used, right there at the maiden's neck. The unicorn is captured because he was betrayed by a virgin. He's a symbol of Christ."

"I'm an atheist," he said.

"Oh, me, too, but I'm still on the unicorn's side. I love it where he gores the hunters. But look, there he is, poor thing, in captivity inside that picket fence. I feel like crying whenever I see it."

They had walked the length of the tapestry holding hands, not so much from affection, but like two enchanted children. Still holding hands, they went to the Cuxa Cloister and sat on a wall under an arch between graceful columns. Flowers lined the stone walks, and water splashed in a fountain.

"I feel like Roderick Hudson when he first saw Italy."

"Who?" she said.

"A character of Henry James's."

Was that Harry James, the band leader's brother? "This is Spanish, not Italian," she said. "It's called the Cuxa Cloister. Originally it was a Benedictine monastery in the Pyrenees, then it was sacked by the French." She spoke in a whisper in order not to disturb the others. There were only two. A young girl in glasses reading a book of poetry and an old man who sat with his eyes closed and face turned up to the sun. He looked like a sculpture, as if his wrinkles were carved from wood. Giuliano would have loved him.

"See that old man?" Dan said. "Isn't he fantastic? He looks like he came with the place."

He still held her hand. A new experience. Usually she had to hold a guy's hands to keep them from wandering. He turned her palm upward and studied it.

"Tell me my fortune," she said.

He gave her a dimpled, devilish smile, lightly traced the lines in her palm that sent out sparks from her central nervous system, and assumed a gypsy accent. "You veel meet a not-so-tall, not-so-charming man in dark glasses who veel turn into a regular prince of a fellow upon receiving a kiss from your rosebud lips. Together you veel sail the seven seas visiting far-off places, climbing the ancient pyramids of Egypt, gliding in gondolas through Venetian canals, dwelling in castles in Spain, and sitting in sidewalk cafés in Paris."

"Not with Nazis."

"They veel magically disappear."

"This isn't a fortune, it's a fairy tale."

"You don't like it?" he asked, back to his normal voice.

No, she didn't like it, she loved it, but she wasn't going to tell him that.

They were chased out at closing time and sat on a large flat rock on a hill overlooking the Hudson River. To their left was the George Washington Bridge. Across the river in New Jersey, the evening sun streaked the sky in candy pink and vermilion, the crinkled water reflecting the colors.

A Hudson Day Liner, stately as a steamboat, moved slowly down the river. Probably it was returning from Bear Mountain. A motorboat zipped around the liner in ever-widening circles, as if inviting it to come and play. Farther down the river, a huge grim gray battleship lay at anchor.

"What kind of ship is that?" she asked.

"A warship. An LST. Landing ship tank. People say how terrible the war is, but for some guys it's a big break. It beats dying of boredom. I mean, here's a chance to get away from the wife and kids and be considered a good guy for wanting to fight for your country. Too bad there had to be a war to provide an excuse. Me, I don't need that. I'm not getting married and tied down for life."

"Men may be tied down, but women are trapped. At least a man can get away to a job, but she's home stuck with the kids all day."

"Yeah, but what if he hates his job? Anyway, women want to get married and have kids. They only have themselves to blame."

"How do you know what women want? You're not a woman. That's not what *I* want."

"Okay, what do you want?"

She smiled. "To ride in a gondola, climb pyramids, and sit in sidewalk cafés. What do you want?"

"To be there with you," he said softly. She turned and looked at him. He'd pushed his glasses up on his head. His eyes were a lovely brown, like Giuliano's.

"I thought you didn't like me. You think I'm dumb."

"I thought you were just a good-time girl who only cared about clothes and nightclubs. You're not dumb, you're sexy and brainy."

"Brainy? Me? Ha," she said, embarrassed and pleased.

"You know a hell of a lot about the stuff here. I'm impressed."

"Oh, that's from my high-school art teacher. He used to take us to museums and explain things. I loved him."

"You sure as hell have a good memory."

"I just got out of high school last year. Anyway, I only remember what I'm interested in."

"So do most people, but they're usually only interested in crap. You have a native intelligence."

Intelligent? Her? Gina Sabatini? Most men didn't even know she had a brain, and cared less.

"Uh, you hungry?" he asked. "Let's go grab something to eat."

It was nearly dark. The sky across the river like a purple mountain range, George Washington Bridge a necklace of lights. He picked up his jacket and pushed down his glasses.

"Why do you wear dark glasses in the dark?"

"Vanity. I'm myopic. Come on. Race you down."

He ran, but she flew, her feet scarcely touching the earth.

She had climbed the other side of the hill irritated with him and the subway ride. She was running down this side of the hill in love. At the bottom of the hill he caught her by the waist and swung her around. They laughed and kissed, knowing this was love, but not breathing a word of it, as if it might break the spell.

During the day they kept their secret at work, pretending not to notice each other when people were around. At night he came down to her apartment. They walked Village streets, sometimes both talking at once in their eagerness to spill out their feelings, other times silenced by the enormity of what they felt. She'd always considered love to be like Santa Claus, something you knew better than to believe in once you were old enough. She was surprised that love lived up to its billing, that just like in a musical she felt like singing in the rain and dancing on rooftops. How wonderful to be admired for her brains instead of her breasts.

Giuliano noticed the change when she visited him. He, too, had changed. Physically. His cheeks didn't have that deathly pallor, and they now strolled the hospital grounds, even, on occasion, going down to the small village for coffee.

"You're happy," he said, smiling, pleased with this.

"I'm in love," she said. And although he still smiled, she saw jealousy flicker in his lovely brown eyes. Up to now she'd loved only him. She took his hand. "When the doctor says you can leave, I'll find us a big sunny apartment with one small dark room in back where you can develop your pictures."

"Maybe your boyfriend won't want a kid brother hanging around."

"Nuts, I wouldn't fall for a guy like that. Listen, Giuli, you'll be crazy about him. He's sensitive and intelligent and a wonderful writer." She hadn't seen his writing, but she was sure he was.

"Don't call me Giuli," her brother said. "It sounds like a girl."

She often called him Giuli, and he'd never objected before.

She told Dan about Giuliano. "God, he sounds fantastic," Dan said, "just like Hans Castorp."

"Who's he?"

"That guy who has TB in *Magic Mountain*. I'll get you the book."

They were sitting on the Gansevoort Pier, feet dangling over the edge. They frequently came here at night to escape the heat, in the company of other lovers, families, and prowling sailors whose white uniforms flashed by in the dark.

Although at first she was pleased that Dan admired her for her mind, Gina began to wish he'd notice her body. She longed for him to touch her, wanted to touch him. Sometimes she ran her hands through his dark curly hair, but she suspected it irritated him. Once she put her hand on his thigh, and he nervously moved away.

One night she deliberately created a romantic mood with candlelight and soft music. He said candles heated up the place, and turned on the lights. He said he couldn't stand trashy popular music and asked if she didn't have any Mozart.

They went to a concert at Lewisohn Stadium, where they sat on bleachers under the stars and listened to classical music interrupted by an occasional airplane. When she shivered in her sundress, he put his jacket around her shoulders. She wished it had been his arm.

He brought her Mann and Mozart and constantly corrected her grammar. She wondered if he were ashamed of her. If his real reason for keeping their feelings a secret at work was because he didn't want his father to know. But when she said she'd grown up on the Lower East Side, he was as impressed as if she'd said Park Avenue. "It must have been fantastic growing up with real people in touch with their basic emotions," he said. "Not like the bunch of phonies I grew up with."

"Yeah, they were in touch with their basic emotions, all right," she said, but he missed her irony. He considered growing up in the slums the same kind of lark as riding the subway during rush hour.

They were out on the Gansevoort Pier again when he made his shocking proposal. Marriage.

"I thought you didn't believe in it," she said.

"That was to some hypothetical girl, not you."

"But we'd soon hate each other. You'd feel tied down, and I'd feel trapped." She scarcely noticed the heat lightning flash in the sky. "Maybe we could just live together."

"We can't do that. People would find out."

"So what? I thought you didn't care what people thought."

"I don't care what they think about me, but I care what they think about you. Anyway, I have to go back to school this fall."

She heard the faint rumble of thunder in the distance. A drop of rain fell on her nose. She hadn't even thought as far in advance as fall. "What will I do when you leave?" She asked.

"You'll marry me and come along. New Haven's not so bad."

"But what would we live on?"

"What I've been living on. Dad gives me money. You know the old saying, 'Two can live as cheaply as one.' "

"Yeah, if one doesn't eat. What if your dad objects and doesn't give you any money?"

"Then to hell with him. And Yale. I'll get a job. Some night job so I can write during the day."

"And I'd have to get another job. Your dad would fire me if we got married."

She half-expected him to protest, but he didn't. "Okay, so you get a job somewhere else. I don't like the idea of buyers ogling you in bathing suits anyway."

She was both bothered and pleased. At least he was aware that she had a body. Rain peppered the water. People were leaving. "It's raining," she said, but he was oblivious of the fact, the way he became when excited about some idea. "We'll live like John and Tamara," he said. "You'll have to meet them, you'll love them. He paints and she writes. They're free spirits. He delivers Coca-Cola and she works in a coffeehouse here in the Village."

"You mean she's a waitress?"

"What's wrong with being a waitress?"

"They don't make any money. At least not the ones who work in a coffeehouse. What about my family? I have to give my mom money, she depends on me. And there's Giuliano."

"To hell with families. We didn't ask to be born, we don't owe our parents anything. Dad wants me to go to Yale so he can brag. Yale isn't going to help me run the family business, and that's what he expects me to do when he retires. The last goddamn thing I want is to run a goddamn dress factory. To hell with him."

"Why do you hate your father so much? I think you just want to marry me to spite him."

"That's crazy. I want to marry you because I love you. Come on, it's raining, we're getting wet."

"You don't act it."

"What do you mean, I don't act it? Jesus, I'm with you every night."

"And all we do is hold hands. If I make a move, you back away. What are you so scared of?"

"This," he said softly, pulled her to him, and kissed her. There was such urgency, such lust and longing in his kiss, that she was half-frightened. He crushed her against him, and together they went down onto the splintery boards of the pier, clinging to each other in the drenching rain. In his fumbling passion he went at her the wrong way. He was moaning, crying out in his frustration to get in. She was tight, scared. She felt as if she were being knifed between her legs. And then he was drumming into her as the rain drummed down. The only good thing about it was it was soon over.

He kissed her, indifferent to the rain, the splintery boards, discomfort. "So that's what the noise is all about?" he asked, smiling, but when he looked at her, his smile disappeared. "Gina, what's wrong?" he said. She extricated herself, stood up, straightened her clothes, and didn't answer.

"Oh, Jesus," he said. "I knew this would happen. I knew I'd mess up. You didn't like it, did you?"

"It hurt."

He scrambled to his feet, took her into his arms, kissed, caressed, and apologized. "I'm sorry, I'm a lousy lover. I only thought of myself."

"Let's go back, we're both soaking wet."

He walked alongside her silently and so obviously miserable that she felt sorry for him. She took his hand.

"Does it still hurt?" he asked.

"Not now."

"Oh, Christ, I'm no better than a rapist. You won't want me to even come near you now."

When they got back to her place, he ran a hot bath for her, soaped her, toweled her off, and put her to bed. "I'm okay," she said, and put her arms around him. He stayed with her all night.

"Your parents will be frantic, they'll think you've been in an accident," she said. It was six in the morning.

"I'll call in an hour when they're up," he said, and turned toward her. She kissed his freckled shoulder. He made love to her slowly and tenderly.

"You know, I think I'll learn to like this," she said.

It didn't take long.

He was more insistent than ever about getting married. "We won't be like other people. It'll be different with us," he promised.

"That's what everyone says, but it isn't."

"Yes, it is. You'll see when you meet John and Tamara. They're married and they're still free spirits."

He took her to a party to meet John and Tamara. They gave a party every Friday night. "Anyone's welcome who brings a bottle of wine," Dan said. "Not Scotch, but beer's okay. They're real people, I know you'll like them. They have a place like yours, only better."

By better he meant worse. More run-down. In fact, it resembled the tenement house where she'd grown up. Garbage and toilets in the hall.

As they made their way up the steps, a water cockroach ran across their path. "Look out," Dan cried. "Don't step on it, it might be Gregor Samsa."

She was glad he'd given her Kafka to read so she knew who he was talking about.

The party noises carried down as they climbed up. "Sounds like a real orgy," Dan said happily. When they reached the sixth floor, Dan gave a shave-and-a-haircut knock on the door. A tall, stringy blond opened the door. "Dan," she screamed, and hugged him to what would have been her bosom if she'd had one. The blond wore a seashell necklace, peasant blouse and skirt, and was barefoot. She looked at Gina. Gina wore her black summery chiffon cocktail dress. Through the door, beyond the blond, Gina saw other women in peasant skirts and blouses and men in faded shirts and dungarees. She should have known not to dress up when Dan had said beer and wine but no Scotch. Dan looked perfectly at home, since he wore his beach-resort outfit, including sandals and dark glasses, which he always wore.

When the blond left off hugging Dan, he introduced them. She was Tamara. Gina hadn't expected anyone with such an exotic name to be a tall stringy blond. He introduced her to John, who was also tall, also barefoot, and wore dungarees.

"Gina's a free spirit too," Dan said, as if it were a religion.

John and Tamara looked at her chiffon cocktail dress and appeared unconvinced. She didn't know if that were why Dan had to bring up her slum origins, but she could have kicked him when he did.

"Gina's from the Lower East Side," he said proudly.

"Really? How wonderful," Tamara said, and led Dan away, saying there were a lot of new people he just had to meet.

"Your wife doesn't look Russian," Gina told John. Or sound it, either. Her accent was more of the kind she overheard at the Waldorf or Savoy Plaza.

"She isn't," John said. "Her real name is Lois. Don't tell her I told you. She thinks 'Tamara' sounds more artistic. Maybe I should change my name, too. 'John' doesn't sound like much of a painter, but then, maybe I'm not much of one."

Gina looked around at the paintings of desert scenes: some

sand and rocks; some sand and sunsets; some sand, rocks, and sunsets.

"I think I'm in a rut," he said.

"They remind me of Georgia O'Keeffe," she said politely.

"Yeah, well, she's a favorite of mine. I don't know, I was thinking maybe of taking some class at the Art Students League this fall and going to some lectures at the New School. They've got some great painters there now. European refugees. Excuse me," he said, and went to greet some new arrivals.

Gina stood alone in the crowd drinking wine from a leaky paper cup. A social outcast in her cocktail dress. Men took one look and shied away. She wasn't used to that. The apartment was small, dimly lit, and horribly hot. Nearly everyone sat on the floor or crammed together on a couch. A table held contribution bottles and a leaning stack of paper cups. A candle in a Chianti bottle dripped wax like red spaghetti. Tamara was still hanging on to Dan, gazing adoringly down at him.

Gina became aware of a crying baby. Heartbreaking yowls. Dan hadn't said that the free spirits had a baby. Weren't they being a bit too free in spirit, ignoring those cries? Maybe it was so miserable because it couldn't breathe in this heat. Despite the hot night and crowded room, the window by the fire escape was down. She stepped over stretched-out legs and went to open it.

"Don't!" a man screamed. "You'll let Sweetpea out."

A baby couldn't climb out a fire-escape window, could it?

"She's in heat," the man said. "She's always in heat. If she gets out, she'll have another litter."

"If I don't get any air, I'll pass out," Gina said.

"Aw, come on, it's not that bad. It's all mind over matter. Forget about it, enjoy the party. John and Tamara give great parties, don't they? Everyone's a free spirit here," the man said, bouncing up and down on his feet. He had dirty yellow hair and a dirty yellowish shirt to match. "Hey, do you ever go to the Waldorf? There's a great gang hangs out there, too."

"I've been there a few times," she said, not wanting to brag. She hoped he changed his shirt before he went.

"That's where Max hangs out."

"Who?"

"Maxwell Bodenheim. You don't know who he is? He's America's greatest living poet. He has this coterie at the Waldorf. Old guy, sits around with a glass of water until someone gets him something at the counter."

She realized that they were talking of two different Waldorfs. His was the cafeteria near Eighth Street.

"That's how America treats her poets, lets them starve. Of course, give him money, he buys booze. But why the hell not? I got a poem he wrote me in swap for a drink at The San Remo. Just a sec, I'll show you. Terrific poem. Hell, it's here somewhere."

While the man turned his pockets inside out in search of the poem, Gina looked for Dan and saw him deep in conversation with a pretty redhead. They stood in a corner away from the crowd. She left the man searching, and stepping over bodies, made her way over.

"Hey, I wondered where you'd got to," Dan said, as if she hadn't been in plain sight all evening. "This is Emily. As in Dickinson. She's a poet. Gina's a painter," he told Emily. She could scarcely qualify as a painter, since she painted only on Saturdays, but she supposed he called her one since they were among creative people. Emily smiled. "We were discussing Prufrock," she said, and repeated a line about growing old and wearing trousers rolled.

"Prufrock's one of my favorite poets," Gina said.

A sudden deadly silence.

"Honey," Dan said, "Prufrock is the guy in the poem, not the poet. That's T. S. Eliot." He turned to Emily. "Gina's from the Lower East Side. Isn't that fantastic?"

"Oh, God, fantastic," Emily said. "What material! I envy you."

"Yeah. It was really fun—rats, rickets, and no heat in the winter."

She turned and made a beeline for the wine. A man in paint-smeared pants was slopping wine from a gallon jug into a paper cup. "Hey, have some dago red," he said handing the cup to her. She splashed it on his pants, adding a new color.

The night grew hotter, the crowd noisier. Dan had disappeared. The cat yowled in despair. She knew how it felt. Emily, the redheaded poet, was now sitting on someone's lap on the couch, but where was Tamara? With Dan? John sat on the windowsill by the fire escape, strumming a guitar and humming to himself.

"Do you know 'Malagueña'?" she asked.

He struck the opening chords. Gina kicked off her high-heeled sandals and began to dance. Some floor sitters drew up their feet to provide more room. Others gathered to watch. She ignored them all, intent only on the music. John increased the tempo. She stamped her feet, snapped her fingers, flung her head back.

Her narrow skirt was inhibiting. Scarcely missing a beat, she pulled off her dress and tossed it into the air, dancing in her black lace brassiere with panties to match, appropriately called a dance set.

The room throbbed with music and heat; even the candle flame pulsed to the rhythm. "*Olé, olé,*" a drunk called, apparently thinking he was watching a bullfight instead of a dance. Someone shushed him. Around her, rapt faces became pink shiny blurs as she whirled, swayed, and pivoted, dancing faster and faster, until John hit a final chord and she came to an abrupt stop with a stamp.

First silence, then an outbreak of applause and cries for more.

She walked to the vicinity of the spot where she'd tossed her dress. A hand held out the dress along with her shoes. Dan's hand. "Put these on," he said. She started to put them on. "No, not here. Jesus, you've made enough of a spectacle of yourself," he said, pulling her toward the door, then out to the landing.

"I was just being a free spirit," she said, slipping into her dress.

"You were showing off. How do you think I felt with all those guys ogling my girl in her black lace underwear?"

"How about you running after Tamara and Emily?"

"Oh, Christ, they're old friends. Can't I even talk to a woman anymore? After your exhibition, you're hardly the one to criticize."

"You ignored me on purpose. You're ashamed of me."

"I wasn't, but I am now."

"You don't have to be any longer," she said.

She ran down the stairs and out on the street, clutching her shoes and sobbing, ignoring the stares of passersby.

Not until she'd run for two blocks did she realize she had no reason to. He hadn't followed her. He'd returned to the party. Obviously to teach her a lesson, show his independence.

She went to her apartment, knowing he'd be back soon. She knelt at the window watching. Whenever she saw a lone figure in the darkness, her heart picked up speed.

She was still at the window when the buildings stepped out of the night and the sky changed to gray to blue to pink. She knew then he'd long ago left the party, maybe to see the redheaded poet home.

Of course, she should have realized he couldn't be trusted more than any other man. Back with his friends, he'd seen his mistake, considered her beneath them, and used her dancing in her underwear as a convenient excuse.

Okay, she'd show him she didn't need him, either.

Monday she got off on the third floor. Miss Rubin looked at her curiously as she passed her desk, as if she might stop her. It was ten-thirty, and Dan wasn't in. Disappointing but not surprising. She went into his father's office. "Consider this official notice of my departure," she said.

"Huh?" Mr. Freed said.

"I'm leaving."

"Gina, I thought you liked it here."

"I'm not realizing my potential. I'm an artist. Working here is a waste of time."

"You sound just like my son."

Since Gina was back working on the showroom floor, she seldom saw Dan. When they met, they both looked in opposite directions.

Of course, she couldn't just quit and paint. She had to get another job to pay for Giuliano and her kid sisters' expenses. She hunted around and got a modeling job at the Simon Brothers'. But this fall she was signing up at the Art Students League. She'd show Dan and his friends what a real artist was.

10. *Ilse*

They sat on the terrace of a small café near Rudesheim, surrounded by schnapps-drinking SS men celebrating the new German offensive in Russia.

"To Stalingrad," an SS man said, raising his glass.

"To Stalingrad," the others echoed, raising theirs.

Hans, who usually drank little and talked a lot, was now drinking too much, and was gloomily silent. In less than an hour he'd almost single-handedly downed a bottle of Rudesheimer wine. Ilse wondered why he'd bothered to waste her precious time and his precious petrol for a Sunday drive to the country, only to ignore her, especially when he'd been so successfully ignoring her at the theater. Ever since his wife's death he'd avoided her as if she were responsible. Guilt. She was a constant reminder of his unfaithfulness. This morning he'd phoned to suggest the drive, saying he had something to tell her. But so far he'd told her nothing.

The SS men flirted with her covertly, perhaps thinking Hans was her father. It hurt to see how he'd aged, his horn-rims dominating his now thin, haggard face.

Down below, the Rhine lay sparkling between sloping green hills. In the distance, across the river, grazing sheep dotted the hillside like gray stones. If it weren't for the river traffic of coal-carrying barges and tankers flying the scarlet flag of the Third Reich, she wouldn't have guessed there was a war on.

But war was a way of life now, peace difficult to recall. She'd forgotten the pleasure boats she'd watched as a child, cruising up and down the Rhine from Amsterdam to Basel. Not far from here was Einberg, where she'd grown up. For six years she'd neither seen nor heard from her family. Soon nothing in her childhood would remain. Every time she viewed fresh destruction by aerial bombs, she was torn between despair at seeing beautiful Berlin destroyed and hope that the Nazi mentality would also be reduced to rubble.

The SS men who were drunkenly singing patriotic songs were now singing the one she hated most, "The Horst Wessel Song." "When Jewish blood flows, everything will be good," they sang boisterously, and motioned the civilian patrons to join in. They didn't need any encouragement.

"Sing," Hans commanded. He'd raised his glass and was singing with gusto.

Wineglass trembling so that she had to hold it with both hands, she obeyed, skipping the word "Jewish" and substituting "Nazi" in her mind. Everyone smiled affectionately at each other, united by hate—the SS, waiters, patrons, the proprietor, his wife. Ilse was surprised a passing dog didn't smile and join in.

Hans was grinning broadly, stupidly. She wondered how she ever could have loved him. After "The Horst Wessel Song," an SS officer came over to their table. He put a friendly arm around Hans's shoulder, and together they sang a dirty duet about a lonely shepherd and what he did with his flock at night.

"I'm leaving," Ilse said, glad to use the song as pretext. She gathered her sweater and purse and got up. Hans's new friend, the SS man, tried to detain Hans by telling him she'd get over it. Hans, however, followed her to the car amid calls of friendly good-byes.

Seated beside him in the Minerva, driving through the green-and-gold Rhine Valley, she was glad she hadn't told Hans about her father. Three years ago, she'd been so amazed at the news that she'd felt if she couldn't tell someone she'd burst. At least she no longer had to worry about anyone learning her secret, now that Private Gertig was dead and Ursula paid off. But although she could avoid Ursula, turning down her dinner invitations, she couldn't avoid Hans unless she left the theater.

"Sorry I got so drunk and acted like an ass," he said.

"So am I."

"There's a *Lebensbun* near here. That's where the SS donate stud service to unmarried Rhine maidens, producing more pure-blooded monsters," he said.

Clever Hans. First he played up to the SS; then, suspecting her anti-SS sentiments, he played up to her. And if he suspected, she'd have to be more cautious. "You shouldn't talk like that," she said.

"I shouldn't talk. I should shut up. But I get sick of shutting up. I can't speak out in the theater, I can't speak out in my own home. My son, my darling little Nicolas, has joined the Hitler Jugend. He spies on me—listens in on the phone, goes through my papers. What a joy it would be for him to turn in his father and prove what a good little German he is."

Ilse was completely confused. Which was the real Hans—the one who sang along so lustily with the SS, or the one who spoke now?

"I thought you invited me for this delightful ride because you had something to tell me," she said.

Silence. A long silence. He touched his glasses with a familiar nervous gesture. They'd slipped down his nose, which looked long and lonely on his thin face. "I think you should find a theater more suitable to your talents," he said with a stilted formality.

"Oh, you mean you want to get rid of me?"

"It's obvious we're not doing anything worthwhile."

"What theater is? As you so frequently lament, it's either farce or Fatherland."

He said nothing.

"If you don't want me around because it makes you feel

guilty now that your wife is dead, why not be honest and say so?"

"All right, I'll be honest and say so."

She wished he hadn't been. She hadn't expected it to hurt so much. That's just your pride, she told herself. You were ready to leave a minute ago, but now that he's urging you to, you're upset. "What about the new play?" she asked. "If I go now, you'll have to find someone else and postpone opening night."

"Yes, okay." He reached out for her hand. "You know this has nothing to do with how I feel for you, Ilse. I love you."

"Of course," she said in a bright, hard voice.

"I was lying just now. I don't feel guilty about seeing you while Eva was alive, what I feel guilty about is her death. If I'd taken better care of her, she'd be alive today."

"That's silly, Hans. She died of pneumonia in a hospital. How could you help that?"

"She was murdered."

Ilse looked at him in amazement. His knuckles were white on the steering wheel. Had Eva's death affected his mind?

"Do you know what TP stands for?" he asked. "Test person. A human guinea pig. That's what Eva was. I admit I was shocked when the doctor told me she'd died of pneumonia when she hadn't even had a cold, but I accepted it. Until I was talking to this writer. I say 'talking.' He was the one talking. Drunk. Smashed.

"At first I thought he was raving. I wanted to. He said he'd just finished an assignment on Germany's glorious advances in modern-day medicine. He mentioned the mental institution where Eva was, not knowing, of course, that she was my wife. The doctors there boasted to him about what great feats they were accomplishing, while repeating that certain things were off the record. They were performing brain operations, running tests on pregnant women, horrible things. Experiments. They even showed him the patients. Patients, hell—victims. The mentally ill, the politically unpopular, and, of course, the Jews. The guy was weeping when he was telling me this."

Ilse felt a chill despite the bright sunlight. "Maybe he was making it up."

"No, he's a respected writer for a respected magazine. He was drunk, but he wasn't making it up."

"Was his name Hoffner?"

Hans shot her a look. "Why do you ask?"

"He interviewed me once."

"No, someone else," Hans said, too quickly. Then, "Don't breathe a word of this, you'd put all of us in danger."

He drove silently the rest of the way back, double-parking in front of her apartment building. A bomb had struck next door, exposing various levels, like a stage setting with open kitchens, bedrooms, and living rooms. Stairs led to nowhere, a door was ajar to a twilight sky.

Just before she got out, he repeated his warning to tell no one. As she walked toward the door, she wondered why he'd confided in her. Maybe because he'd found the burden too much to bear alone. At least that meant he trusted her. They were still friends if not lovers. Why, then, was he in such a hurry to get her out of the theater, when they both knew she was a drawing card?

She had nightmares that night about the hospital where Eva had died. It was an animal hospital, or rather the staff were animals, baboon doctors in surgical masks, donkey nurses in white caps screeching and braying over hacked bodies with spilled entrails and red wormlike brains. When she awoke, she was afraid to go back to sleep for fear of the nightmare returning.

She stayed awake. She had to get to the theater early anyway in order to find the right costume for the servant girl, Gisella, she was portraying. Gisella was a little country girl who left to work for a rich uncle in the city, leaving a boyfriend behind. A friend of her uncle's son professes love and seduces her, only to callously drop her and marry a rich girl. Gisella, heartbroken, returns home and marries the peasant boy, realizing it was him she'd loved all along. A stupid play called *Country Cousin*, bound to be a hit. Why didn't Hans want her playing a role she was, unfortunately, so eminently suited for?

She had to have Gisella's costume for dress rehearsal this afternoon. Her problem was getting past Frieda, the wardrobe mistress. New costumes were impossible to come by now, old ones worn out. Frieda kept the moth-eaten clothes in tip-top condition and guarded the wardrobe room as if from enemy invasion. Worse yet, Hans humored her. Perhaps because of Frieda's advanced age. She'd been at the theater for years and was a surrogate mother to Hans.

Frieda kept the wardrobe room locked, but Hans also had a key.

Ilse, arriving at the theater before anyone else, went to Hans's office to get the key from his desk. She felt guilty rifling among his things in the desk drawer, and the key wasn't there anyway. Spying his old tweed jacket hanging from a hook, she looked for the key in his pockets. For her trouble she found a few grains of tobacco in the lining. Just as she was about to give up, her fingernail caught on some loose threads. Probably there was a hole that the key had slipped through. There was. She felt the key in the lining but had trouble working it up through the hole. Funny, that. How could it have slipped down, when it was so hard to work up?

Key in hand, she hurried to the wardrobe room. It was one flight up from the dressing rooms, in back of the theater. Another short flight of five iron steps led to the door. She unlocked it and went in. The room was without windows, dark and shadowy. Turning on the light made little difference since the light bulb was of low wattage and high up in the ceiling. Row after row of costumes hung from metal poles: red hunting coats, Prussian uniforms, smoking jackets, negligees, feather boas, peasant costumes, some ratty fur coats, a worn black velvet cape. Practically everything was threadbare and shiny.

There was an eerie silence. As she walked along the rows, stopping here and there to inspect something promising, she had the peculiar feeling she wasn't alone. As if to back her up, she heard a scrabbling sound in a distant corner. Rats? She smiled at the idea. Frieda wouldn't allow a rat in her domain. But there was a definite scampering. It stopped the minute she began sliding the costumes along the rack.

Soon she forgot about the noise. After an intense search, she found a low-cut dress with a frilly little apron and a maid's cap pinned to a sleeve. Just the thing. As she unpinned the cap, she heard the noise again. Closer this time. More scampering. A voice. A child's frantic whisper: "Anna, Anna, come back here."

And then a woman's voice, hissing, desperate: "*Kinder.*"

Quickly Ilse pushed the clothes apart. She could only stare.

There, frozen in a tableau, were a woman and two children. The woman's hair was dark, dull. She wore an old brown dress. One bony hand clutched each child's shoulder. All three were thin and ragged. The smaller child, a girl, looked to be about four. The boy appeared to be eight. The woman seemed too old to be the mother of such young children, but the fierce protective look on her face told Ilse otherwise.

The little girl began to whimper. The woman drew her closer. The boy's eyes were enormous in his small pale face.

"What are you doing here?" Ilse asked, but the little girl

only whimpered louder, the boy's eyes grew larger, while the woman clutched her children more tightly. Suddenly Ilse knew why they were here. Hiding out. Refugees. Jewish refugees. But how did they ever manage to get into this room Frieda so jealously guarded?

"Don't be afraid," she said gently. "It's all right. I won't tell anyone. Are you hungry? Here, have some chocolate." She dug into her pocket and got the candy bar she always kept for emergencies when she was too rushed to eat. She held out the candy. The little girl stopped whimpering and reached for it. The mother's hand clamped down on the child's wrist.

"You can't stay here," Ilse said. "The wardrobe mistress is bound to come in any minute." Aside from the fact that Frieda was a staunch patriot, she'd hand someone over to the Gestapo for nothing more than invading her territory.

The woman stared silently at Ilse.

"Please, come to my dressing room. Quickly, while there's a chance. Before anyone else comes in. You can hide there until I think of something." Someone in the theater must have led them up here. Who? Certainly not that fascist Frieda. Nor Hans. He'd have more sense than to hide anyone where Frieda could find them. Willy, the stage doorman? He was always hanging around. Perhaps for good reason. But she couldn't just stand here wondering and wasting time.

The woman remained silent. If Ilse hadn't heard her call out to the children, she'd have thought her a deaf mute. Ilse became impatient. What was wrong with that fool? Why wasn't she thinking of her children's safety? "Come with me. You *must*! You can't stay here. You'll be caught and turned in."

She'd no sooner spoken than she heard footsteps rattling on the iron stairs. Frieda! Now what? She turned to the woman. "Hide," she said. "Over there by the door, so you can slip out. I'll divert her attention. Get her away from the door. Wait just below the iron steps, it'll be only a few minutes, then I'll take you to my dressing room. Quick, now."

The woman and children disappeared behind the black cape just as Frieda's key clinked in the door. Frieda entered, walking briskly. When she saw Ilse, her white frizzy hair fairly stood on end. She raised a string bag crammed with packages as if she might strike Ilse with it. "What are you doing here? How did you get in?"

"Oh, I borrowed Hans's key," Ilse said lightly. "Now, Frieda, don't be mad. It's just that I suddenly realized that dress rehearsal was today and I didn't have Gisella's costume. Come look," she said, trying to lure the old woman away from the door. "What do you think? Isn't this perfect for a little servant girl?" she wheedled. "For Gisella?"

Frieda ignored the dress. She glared at Ilse through rimless glasses. Suddenly she cocked her head as if she'd heard a noise, but the only noise was Ilse's wildly beating heart.

"No one is allowed here when I am not around," Frieda said in her baritone. "Take that dress and go."

But she couldn't leave. She didn't know if the mother had slipped out with her children or was still hiding behind the black cape, too petrified with fear to move. "Shoes," she said to Frieda. "I'll need shoes, too."

Frieda also kept the shoes under lock and key in the shoe closet. She was even more possessive about the shoes than the costumes. "You'll have to unlock the closet and find something for me," Ilse said. For a split second she thought she saw fear in Frieda's eyes glinting behind those glasses, but apparently it was only indignation. "I do not have time to fool around with shoes," Frieda said crossly. "Tell me what you want and I will bring them to you later."

Ilse described the kind of shoes she wanted in detail, to stall for yet more time. "They must be old-fashioned, high-button shoes, but also high-heeled. Not brown. Maybe black or cream-colored. Yes, cream-colored. No, perhaps they should be brown after all."

Frieda wasn't standing for any more of this nonsense. She took Ilse by the arm, steered her through the door, and before Ilse knew it, the lock clicked behind her. Wasn't that going too far, locking the door? And what if the mother and children hadn't got out? They'd be locked in. Ilse's heart plunged. How would they escape now? But maybe they'd already escaped and were hiding somewhere on this very floor. She ran down the iron steps, her heart running ahead of her. She made a panicky search of each room, found no one, and flew down the other flight of steps to continue her search of the dressing rooms, the prop room, even the water closet. "Anyone here?" she called softly. "Please answer," she begged.

She was still searching when she heard Willy. He came around the corner, down the hall with Hans, complaining about something. Was that to divert Hans's attention? Willy was in his sixties. Like Frieda, he'd been at the theater for ages and exaggerated the importance of his job. Hans wasn't as lenient with Willy as with Frieda.

"Yes," Hans said curtly to Willy's complaints. "Yes, I'll look into it later." He walked on, leaving Willy to stand grumbling to himself before turning on his heels and going back to his post.

All right, she was almost positive it wasn't Willy. But it might be the assistant director, Helmut Bruer, so quiet and self-effacing and ingratiating. Maybe he didn't want to make enemies and call attention to himself for the sake of what he was doing. But why wasn't he here seeing to his charges? Did he assume they were safe? Fool. She wondered if she could trust Hans enough to enlist his help in getting the refugees to safety, but she remembered the lusty way he'd sung "The Horst Wessel Song." Still, that hadn't been an act when he'd talked about Eva. Oh, God, what to do? Then she heard brisk footsteps along the hall and glimpsed Frieda's upright back as she marched into Hans's office.

Immediately Ilse ran back upstairs to the wardrobe room to rescue the fugitives. The key was damp in her palm as she turned it in the lock. She entered, calling softly. "Are you here? Answer. Please answer. Quickly, while I can get you out."

The silence was deep. Were they hiding somewhere behind the costumes, as afraid of her as of Frieda? She made a hasty search of the room and managed to get out before Frieda got back.

There were voices. Others had arrived for rehearsal. How could she possibly spirit the mother and children from the theater while people roamed the halls? And even if she accomplished this miracle, what would they do once out on the street in broad daylight? Stand there and wait to be picked up by the Gestapo?

Ilse went into her dressing room. She was surprised to see she still carried Gisella's dress over her arm. She flung it onto the cot and sat down at her dressing table, head in hands, trying to think what to do, pressing fingers to forehead as if she could make an idea pop out.

An abrupt knock, and Hans came striding in. It wasn't like him just to burst into her room. "Frieda said you snitched my key and went to the wardrobe room without her permission."

"So what? Since when is that a crime? I needed a costume for rehearsal."

"I'd like that key back, please," he said, thrusting out an open palm.

"Oh, my God, all this fuss about a stupid key," she said. Although she could control her voice, she couldn't control her trembling. She dropped the key into his palm and noticed his hand trembled, too. Their eyes met. He *knew*. Frieda must have discovered the fugitives and reported it to him. And then she saw that look in his eyes. Dark with worry and fear. Of course he'd sung along with the SS. He'd had to.

"You saw them?" he asked, his voice low, as if someone might be listening outside the door.

She nodded.

"Please forget what you saw."

"You knew they were up there all along?"

He sighed, sat down on her costume where she'd flung it on the cot, unnoticing. "I want you out of here, it's dangerous."

"You mean you and Frieda are helping people escape?" In her relief she spoke so loudly that he winced. She had to do a complete turnabout in her opinion of Frieda. She wasn't just a cranky old woman possessive of her domain; she'd had reason to guard the wardrobe room. And that's why Hans had backed her up. "For a director, you make a good actor," she said.

He smiled rather slyly.

"Only, how do you know I can be trusted?"

"How do you know anyone can be trusted these days?" he said. "I noticed you skipped a certain word yesterday during our songfest." He made a wry mouth at the word "songfest." "And Frieda told me the mother told her you'd wanted to hide them."

"So why did you come in here so angry with me?"

"Because you give me a new headache. I worry about you, now that you know."

"Who else knows? Who else is in on this?"

"*Liebchen*, don't ask. We're just a few links in a long chain. Leave it, sweet. I've lost one person dear to me, I don't want to lose you, too."

"Maybe she died a natural death," Ilse said to comfort him. "After all, you saw her afterward, you didn't notice anything."

"I wasn't looking for anything. No, I guess I should be grateful. She might not have been tortured like the others, maybe just infected with bacteria." He covered his glasses with his forearm, as if he couldn't bear the sight of what was in his mind. "To think there was a time I considered myself above politics. Let the bullyboys take over, what the hell could I do to stop them anyway? None of that was my business. The theater was my business. When atrocities were hinted at, I told myself they were exaggerations. When friends disappeared, I told himself they never existed. The lies I told myself. Unbelievable. Then it hit home. Something snapped. I can't live with myself now without doing anything. It's a kind of dedication to Eva's memory."

"But what happens if you do manage to get people out of Germany? They just go to another country occupied by Germans."

"I don't know. I only know what hell it would be if they don't get out. This way, there's always hope. The safe places are Sweden and Switzerland, but if they reach one of the more civilized countries—Holland, Denmark, Norway—there's a glimmer of hope they'll be hidden or able to get a boat to safety until this madness is over. If it's ever over."

"Hans, I want to help."

"I was afraid you'd say that."

"Not afraid I wouldn't?" she asked, standing before him.

He smiled and drew her to him. "I don't know which is worse."

"You're sitting on Gisella's dress," she said. He moved over, she rescued the dress, then threw her arms around him. "Just when I think it's all over between us, it's back together again."

"Is that so bad?"

"It's confusing," she said, kissing him. He traced her ear with his finger. He always found her ears erotic. "It's been so long between drinks," he said. Then, "Oh Christ, the world's shot to hell, rehearsal's in ten minutes, and all I want is to take you to bed."

She smiled. "Sometime soon. Now, tell me how we get those three out of here. You can't just let the children run around the wardrobe room."

"They weren't supposed to. I guess their mother thought they needed the exercise and it was safe to let them out in the morning."

"Out of where?"

He hesitated. "A small room behind the shoe closet. A cubbyhole, really. The shoes along the wall hide the door, but you wouldn't know it was a door. It looks like part of the paneling. They've been there five days. Tomorrow they're to be taken to someone who will try to get them across the border."

"Let me take them. And don't tell me about risks, I know."

"You'd be too easily recognized. If you're caught, it would

lead the SS back here, and this is an important part of the escape route. More people are scheduled to come through."

"Don't worry, I'll be in disguise, I've had plenty of practice."

"Ilse, I don't want to get you into this." He sighed. "But we could use your help. I'm bat blind without these damned glasses, so I can never vary my disguise. And poor Frieda, she's a staunch old lady, but it's a strain on her."

"So what do I do?"

"It should be fairly simple, but something can always go wrong. They're having a parade tomorrow to show Germany's military might since her recent losses in Russia. You and the woman and children join the onlookers. An elderly man wearing a blue bow tie with three fountain pens clipped to his pocket will join you and lead them away. He's an old German aristocrat and isn't likely to be suspected."

"And he's helping fugitives? It almost restores my faith in humanity."

"He's helping because he's a patron of the arts and the little boy is a prodigy. At age eleven he plays Mozart marvelously."

"Eleven? He looks eight."

"He hasn't eaten much lately. Jews can't buy anything, even if they have the money. And that poor woman's had a hell of a time just surviving."

"What happened to her husband?"

"I don't know. Whenever she starts to talk about it, she breaks down and cries and becomes incoherent."

There was a knock at the door. Ilse jumped nervously.

"Do you know where Hans is?" Erica Blount called. She was the mother in *Country Cousin*. "We're all onstage waiting."

"Be right with you," Hans called.

Ilse wasn't in the first scene and didn't have to go out immediately. She put a detaining hand on Hans's arm. "Bring Nicolas's Hitler Jugend uniform tomorrow," she said.

"What for? My God, the kid lives in it."

"Say it has to be cleaned, then say the cleaner lost it."

"He'd turn the cleaner over to the Gestapo, and me, too."

"Just bring it. You're bigger than he is. We need it for that little boy upstairs. He'll be safer in that uniform. Frieda can fit him. She's a wizard with the needle."

Hans said he'd try, and left. Ilse put on Gisella's dress and joined the rehearsal group.

Another nightmare night. This time she dreamed the elderly man in the blue bow tie suddenly changed into a Gestapo officer in black boots. She sat up abruptly. What if the dream carried a warning?

Again she arose early. She was too nervous to eat breakfast and had only coffee, which increased her nervousness.

At the theater she got her disguise ready so that she could make a quick change. Hans came in and gave her the details. She and the mother and children would leave right after her matinee performance. They were to station themselves in front of a cinema showing a Zara Leander movie. He'd also brought along Nicolas's Hitler Jugend uniform and had already given it to Frieda for alterations. "Give these to the kids to wave during the parade," he said, handing her two small swastika flags.

And then it was time to go onstage. The plot was improbable, but less so than in life. It was the same old play that had been running for nearly a year now, although the new play wasn't that much different. She played her part automatically, her mind on the more difficult role she was to play when the curtain descended.

After the last curtain call she hurriedly changed into her disguise: dark curly wig, dark summer suit, dark glasses, and low-heeled oxfords. With dark hair she wouldn't be so noticeably different from the mother whose sister she was supposed to be. The young, unmarried sister, Fräulein Steimetz. Hans had given her an identification card made up in that name. The mother's name was Frau Gantz, Hans said. He didn't know, or at any rate pretended not to know, who had procured the ID's. They both worried that the ID card for the boy, made up for his correct age, seemed falsified, since he looked so much younger.

Once dressed, Ilse hurried out of the theater, where the mother and children waited in the postmatinee crowd. She'd changed so quickly that she was able to join some stragglers leaving the theater.

As she walked toward the woman she knew only as Frau Gantz, she became conscious of being watched. Without turning her head, she scanned those within eye range. Her heart came to a standstill. There were Ursula and Freddie von Frisch with another couple, a young SS officer and a smartly dressed elderly woman, the Baroness von Groot. Ursula was staring at Ilse as if she'd seen straight through her disguise. But maybe she just stared at all young women, and maybe she didn't find her disguise that attractive, for a minute later she and the others were climbing into the blue Mercedes. I don't have to worry then, Ilse thought. Or did she? Ursula and Freddie had already seen the play. Why would they want to see such a lousy play twice?

Ilse went up to Frau Gantz and greeted her in a sisterly way. The little girl played her part perfectly, accepting Ilse's kiss as if she were a favorite aunt. Ilse took her hand while Frau Gantz walked alongside her holding the boy's. Although his sister was too young to recognize danger, it was clear he was terrified. He walked as stiffly as a mechanical toy. At least Frieda, bless her, had done a beautiful alteration job. The Hitler Jugend uniform fit as if made for him.

As they left the anonymity of the crowd, Ilse began to feel uneasy, as if a spotlight were trained on them as they walked along the street. But the few passersby paid scant attention. After all, what was so unusual about them? The little girl, still holding Ilse's hand, skip-walked alongside. Ilse tried not to hurry in order to hide the appearance of urgency or to tire the child. It was a fairly long walk.

It looked like rain, and Ilse worried that the crowd might not stretch as far as the movie house, then assured herself that a little rain wouldn't deter the patriotic from watching a parade. They passed bombed-out buildings where a slight breeze stirred dust in the rubble. An incendiary bomb had scored a direct hit and split a building in two. Another had twisted the framework of a building as if it were modeling clay. A block of important government buildings was completely undamaged, however. Over the buildings stretched a vast net canopy with patterns of leaves and branches interwoven, so that from the air it would look like a park.

Soon they were caught up in the parade crowd. Ilse slowed down and delved into her handbag. She brought out the swastikas and handed one to each child. At first Frau Gantz gave her a furious look; then, noticing the other children waving swastikas, she smiled conspiratorially. Ilse wondered how Frau Gantz could retain her sense of irony after the horror she'd lived through, but then, how could she have lived through it if she hadn't?

The crowd was growing. Ilse picked up the little girl, for fear she might get trampled. The child leaned trustingly into her arms, waving the flag and smiling. Feeling the precious warmth, Ilse hugged the child to her, wishing she could carry her across the border to safety, charged with strength to walk no matter how many miles for no matter how long.

They reached the cinema. Ilse glanced around but saw no elderly man in a blue bow tie. She really didn't expect to; the parade had barely begun. There was a sound of rolling drums. Beyond the onlookers' heads she saw rows of helmeted soldiers, faces remote and brutal. While the crowd cheered, she noticed a disagreeable odor more and more prevalent these days where people gathered, the gassy stink from the bran bread everyone now ate.

After the marching troops came soldiers in jeeps, and then huge panzer tanks, monsters on tread wheels, ready to kill or crush anything or anyone in their path. A man with flowing white hair, looking like a distinguished poet, suddenly stepped up beside her. He wore a blue bow tie. In his breast pocket were three pens. Remembering her nightmare, Ilse half-expected his craggy features to become an impassive Gestapo face. She shuddered as he took the little boy's hand, as if he might crush those delicate fingers so that they could never play Mozart again. Frau Gantz took the little girl from her arms. As their hands touched, Ilse tried to convey her love and give her strength to this woman she'd so stupidly considered a fool. Courage, the woman didn't need. She watched the small group of four walk off, so frail and defenseless, an old man, a woman, two children. While others cheered and stomped and waved the soldiers on, she prayed that the boy would grow up to realize his genius and the little girl grow up to realize herself, or merely, dear God, that they grew up.

She left shortly afterward.

From then on she joined Hans and Frieda in helping the fugitives. They arrived nearly every other week. Hans told her little about where they came from or where they were going after they were delivered to another stopover place. He said some of them had been living in concealed quarters of gentile homes until suspicions were aroused. He said it was best not to know. No matter how brave, people talked under torture. Each night before an assignment, Ilse lay awake trembling with fear, but when the time came to act, she was calm and amazingly clearheaded after the sleepless night.

To allay suspicions, she did what she hated most—went out with the SS. Only the fact that she was outwitting them by helping the refugees made it possible to tolerate their presence. She didn't, however, tolerate their amorous advances. Luckily, just strutting about with a theatrical star on their arm seemed to satisfy their vanity. Whenever she went out, she always made sure it was for dinner, and ate enormous meals. In this way, she saved her food coupons. While she hungrily wolfed down food, she would sigh and charmingly complain how inadequate the coupons were for someone who used so much energy onstage. Frequently her escorts took the hint and obliged by getting her additional coupons. With these, and the coupons saved from eating out, she would go to the Konsum, a cooperative store, where she was able to procure enough food to stock the secret room for future refugees. In order to avoid becoming a too familiar customer at the Konsum, and thereby arousing suspicions, she shared the coupons with Hans and Frieda, who also bought supplies.

Often the refugees didn't look at all like their ID's. Ilse would take her makeup kit into the small room and carefully alter their appearance to match that on the card, then choose appropriate clothes from the wardrobe room. Sometimes Hans and Frieda didn't recognize the fugitives after she'd finished her handiwork.

She became intoxicated with her work, which was far more demanding—and rewarding—than anything she'd done onstage.

"Don't take chances," Hans warned. "This isn't a game."

Frieda was openly admiring. "You're a regular little daredevil," she said.

As Ilse helped the refugees, she hoped that somewhere someone might be doing the same thing for her father. She couldn't believe he was dead, even though she knew there was little chance of his being alive, but she kept wishing for the miracle of his survival and that one day they would meet.

By agreement the three of them—she, Hans, and Frieda—spoke only of their work when necessary to impart information. They spoke in code. Whenever a new refugee arrived, Frieda would say that she had a certain item of dress—stockings or gloves, for example—that Ilse had wanted for her role, while Hans said he'd just received a new script.

But Willy, the doorman, had become increasingly suspicious. Unfortunately he was so keen on his job, he was at the door when there was no reason to be. Fortunately he reported his suspicions to Frieda. "Suddenly, there's Herr Lessing leaving with this guy, someone I never saw come in," he said, "and I was at the door all day."

"When you weren't at the corner café drinking," Frieda said.

Willy was indignant. "I only went there once and wasn't long. I don't get drunk on duty. If you ask me, something queer's going on."

Frieda advised him to keep an eye out, knowing he'd do that anyway. Willy went one step further than keeping an eye out. Not long afterward, they noticed the Gestapo patrolling the street near the theater at odd hours. Frequently people were stopped on leaving the theater and asked to show their identifcation.

It was Ilse's idea for Hans to sneak a respected person in, someone with influence in the party. Hans made an appointment with a lawyer high up in the Nazi hierarchy. Just before the lawyer was due to arrive, Frieda lured Willy to the café for a beer. After consulting with the lawyer on various theatrical procedures, Hans accompanied him to the stage door, where Willy was back on duty.

Willy must have immediately given the nod to someone, for the lawyer hadn't gone twenty feet before the Gestapo appeared demanding to see his ID card. The lawyer indignantly protested, thus making himself more suspect in the eyes of the Gestapo, who hauled him off to headquarters. A telephone call from the lawyer to a high-placed official established his racial and political purity. The lawyer was furious, the Gestapo embarrassed, and no longer was anyone asked for identification when leaving the theater.

Just the same, Hans passed word to his underground contact to reroute all refugees until things had cooled off. Ilse even accepted an invitation to the von Frisches' party. The invitation, embossed in gold, arrived one day in her mail. The party was to follow a concert benefit to raise war funds. Ursula called to make sure she'd be there. "You can't bow out of this one, since it's after the theaters are closed. And we're having a very important guest." Ursula paused for dramatic effect. "Herr Göring."

Ilse picked up her cue and pretended to be in girlish ecstasy at the opportunity of meeting such an honored person. Privately she hoped it would be a big party with so many people clamoring to meet him that she'd be overlooked in the excitement.

The only good thing was that Hans was invited, too. At least they'd have each other for moral support.

For the party Ilse chose a white tulle dress that stressed Aryan purity. Hans said she'd never looked more beautiful. "Like a bride," he added wistfully. "In a saner world, I'd ask you to marry me."

"And I might just be crazy enough to accept," she said, putting her hand over his. He drove with one arm around her shoulder as in their courtship days. She held on to his hand for reassurance. "We'll be alone in enemy territory."

"We are every day," he reminded her.

She was suddenly tempted to tell him of her father, but she held back, remembering his remark that even the bravest cracked under torture. Although she loved Hans, she wasn't blind to the fact that he couldn't bear physical pain.

Because of the constant bombardment, Berlin had been in total blackout, so that it was hard to tell when they'd left the outskirts and were in the country. Ilse wasn't aware that they'd reached the von Frisches' until the headlights shone on the summer-green leaves of the tunnel of linden trees. The castle, too, was in complete darkness, but when the car lighs swept the courtyard, there was the gleam of long black official cars as if they'd arrived at military headquarters.

"We'll be very nice, very polite, very charming, and leave very early," Hans said.

"I wish I'd thought to bring a bomb. Just think how many top officials we could polish off."

"Twenty more would spring up in each one's place," Hans said.

Standing before the double Gothic doors, Ilse felt apprehensive. Again her hand sought his.

The elderly butler, Fritz, let them in and directed them to the ballroom, where an orchestra played Strauss waltzes. Chandeliers, like illuminated waterfalls, showered light on Germany's elect. With their expensively gowned and beautifully coiffed women, they stood in small affable groups, smoking, smiling, and drinking. Waiters passed among them with trays holding slender-stemmed glasses and canapés. Although Ilse had been to the von Frisches' parties before, this one was by far the most dazzling, even the more so considering all Germany subsisted on a stringent wartime diet.

"Let's at least get something out of this," Hans said. He guided her toward a buffet table laden with numerous delicacies, paté de foie gras with truffles, blinis and caviar, tiny shrimp, quail eggs, oysters, fat black Spanish olives, and thin slices of Italian ham. "Don't they know there's a war on?" he whispered.

Excitement rippled out from the center of the room. Ilse soon saw the cause. Herr Göring. He, too, was in white—a white suede suit with red sashes crisscrossing a matronly chest adorned with an array of medals. It looked as if he'd raided their theater's wardrobe room. She was tempted to whisper this to Hans, but luckily didn't. Freddie von Frisch came limping up. The longer the war, the more pronounced his limp. "Did you see?" he asked, nodding in Herr Göring's direction. "I wish he'd worn his green velvet suit. It would have been so much more suitable for the occasion. Suede seems so sporty. But look at darling Ursula. She's in her element. And doesn't she look stunning?"

"Stunning," Ilse repeated. Darling Ursula's black hair was arranged as carefully as a geisha's, piled high above her stark white bony face. She wore a black satin dress with a skirt so narrow that it impeded her walk, so that while Freddie limped, she hobbled.

"Come let me introduce you," Freddie said, taking Ilse's arm. He meant to Göring. Ursula stood proudly at his side. Together they looked like a comedy team: he short and plump in white, she tall and thin in black. Ilse looked frantically about for Hans, needing him beside her when she encountered this monstrous little man, but Hans had slipped away. Worse yet, Hermann Göring, upon catching sight of her, was coming in her direction. They met halfway. He grabbed Ilse's hand even before Freddie introduced them, enclosing it between two damp, plump paws, and gazed rapturously up at her. "And who is this beautiful young lady?"

"Our little Ilse," Ursula said, stepping forward. "The star of *Country Cousin.*"

"An actress? Oh, now that I've seen you, I must see *it,*" he said, his look more adoring. But of course, he had a weakness for actresses. He was married to one.

"I'll see that you and Frau Göring are sent tickets," Ilse said, hoping to scotch any romantic intentions by mentioning his wife.

"For such a thoughtful gesture you will have to come visit us at Carinhall."

Ilse smiled and said she'd be honored to, at the same time sickened, not just by the man himself, but by the overpowering smell of perfume and pomade such as she hadn't smelled since that blackmailing Private Gertig. She was relieved when an overdressed, bejeweled woman thrust her way forward and reminded Herr Göring that they'd met in Munich.

Ursula eyed Ilse admiringly and jealously. "Carinhall, indeed. How did you wrangle that invitation in a few short minutes?"

"Oh, I doubt he's serious," Ilse said, fervently hoping he wasn't. "And it's you who've pulled the rug out from under everyone by managing to get him to your party." Ursula was only partially mollified. "Not just him, but the cream of the SS. What a treat for a baker's daughter," Ilse raved. Finally Ursula smiled.

She had, she hoped, made enough of an impression on Ursula that she wouldn't be suspicious when she discovered she'd left early.

As soon as she could manage to get away from Ursula, she went in search of Hans. He was waiting near the door. Luckily it was summer and they didn't have to worry about making a show of leaving by putting on coats. Without a word, they left.

"I was very nice, very polite, and very charming," she said in the car, "and I feel very much like throwing up."

Perhaps it was Ilse's overconfidence that got her into trouble with the Gestapo. She had such success in escorting the fugitives to their destinations that Hans and Frieda came to depend on her judgment more and more. At least Frieda did. Hans warned her, but she told him he was being an alarmist. She let Frieda see to the fugitives' comfort while they hid out in the secret room, she let Hans arrange for their arrival, but she considered herself responsible for their departure. She found it best to look ordinary enough not to be noticed but attractive enough to smile her way out of trouble.

It was midsummer, the theater closed for a few weeks, and she was to take the most recent refugee, a young student of sixteen, to his next stopover point. Because he was of draft age, the person in charge of procuring proper papers had put him on furlough, although he arrived as a civilian.

Ilse got the uniform an actor had worn as her soldier lover, and Frieda altered it to fit the student. She decided the best time to deliver the student-soldier to his assigned place was after the air-raid sirens sounded. Then everyone was so intent on getting to a bunker they didn't notice others.

She and the student-soldier stood inside the darkened threater waiting. Since the theater was officially closed, she didn't have to worry about Willy stationed at the door, but she had the worries of whether someone might see them leave the theater and of whether or not there'd be an air raid. Still, the bombing of Berlin was relentless, and there was no reason it wouldn't happen again tonight.

Ilse took the student's hand, knowing that waiting was always more torment than doing. She'd dressed to look like his girlfriend, wearing a demure blue dress with white lace collar and hoping she looked more his sixteen than her twenty-two. He clung to her hand as if she were his mother, however.

Finally the air-raid sirens sounded. Quickly she and the student squeezed out of the theater door into the darkness of blacked-out Berlin. There wasn't a crack of light anywhere.

Around them, shadows hurried toward bunkers, some carrying suitcases, prepared, if necessary, to spend the night.

She heard the overhead drone of planes and explosions just a mile or so away. If they risked bombs, at least they didn't risk the Gestapo. Wrong. Through the darkness, shoulder to shoulder, bootsteps echoing in the narrow street, came two Gestapo soldiers.

"Where's the nearest bunker, please?" Ilse asked before they could ask any questions. Perhaps that had been the mistake. Perhaps she and the student should have walked on, and the Gestapo would have paid no attention.

"You just passed it back there at the corner," she was told.

A flashlight beam suddenly shone in her eyes. It skipped to the student. "Let's see your papers, soldier."

The student, eyes shining with terror, fumbled through his pocket, while the other Gestapo, the untalkative one, kept a hand on his holster. Finally the student produced his furlough paper.

"This is not valid. It was up two days ago."

Ilse squeezed the student's arm to give him courage. What an idiot she'd been not to notice the date on the paper. Probably the issuer hadn't thought of delays en route.

A bomb struck so near it shook the earth under their feet. Ilse felt a tremor run through her body, but she didn't know if it was from the bomb or fear. She hoped the Gestapo would worry about their own skins and flee, but instead they rudely shoved the student forward, hurrying them both to the corner bunker, where the silent Gestapo suddenly made himself heard by pounding on the iron door and demanding admittance. A man in a steel helmet with an air warden's armband opened the door. He started to complain about the inconvenience of having to let in late arrivals, when he saw the Gestapo behind Ilse and the student, ceased his complaint, called out "Heil Hitler!" saluted, and jumped back so they could enter.

Women, children, and old men stared as they came in with their Gestapo escorts. The student appeared dazed. He stumbled over a suitcase. Ilse took his hand and clung to him as a scared sixteen-year-old girl might cling to her boyfriend. She was scared, all right. An old woman gave her and the student-soldier a sympathetic look as they passed by, the student in the Gestapo's grip. "*Kinder,*" she whispered to another woman. "Why, they're just *kinder.*"

It was as if a script had been written to which Ilse had forgotten the lines, for on hearing these words, she picked up her cue. She looked up at the Gestapo with tears in her eyes, not to melt their hearts, since they were heartless, but to affect those around her. Speaking in a shy, frightened voice, she begged them to release her fiancé, who'd been in battle and suffered from shell shock. "He's overstayed his leave because of me. You see, I discovered I'm pregnant, and we were to be married tomorrow."

The student-soldier certainly looked shell-shocked in his terror.

She had spoken in a stage whisper, as if her pleas were meant only for the Gestapo's ears, but, of course, loud enough for others to overhear.

The Gestapo merely leered over the fact that she and the soldier had indulged in illicit sex, but the bunker audience appeared increasingly sympathetic.

"If he's taken in, our child won't have a name," Ilse sobbed. "He may not return from battle if he goes back, what then?" she asked, wringing her hands.

"*Kinder*," an indignant woman said. "It is becoming a war in which our children fight. See what it does to them, they grow up too soon."

But the Gestapo were also young, scarcely twenty. They began to look uncertain among their critical elders.

Ilse threw her arms around the student-soldier and cried harder.

"Won't let him make a decent woman out of her, and she's a mere child."

"And what happens to their baby when it grows up without a name?"

The whistle of falling bombs, the onrush of an occasional incendiary, the steady gunfire were ignored by the bunker inhabitants, who were used to these every-night sounds and more caught up in the drama of the young lovers.

Voices increasingly took their side. The student had sufficiently recovered from his fear to put an arm around Ilse. The Gestapo were becoming nervous. They stepped away from the others and held a whispered consultation while the bunker inhabitants spoke consolingly to the young battle-shocked soldier and his pregnant fiancée.

Suddenly blasts sounded announcing the all-clear. The air warden opened the iron door. People began filing out, but a small mob accompanied the Gestapo, Ilse, and her soldier. Outside, however, the two Gestapo just kept on going, walking with a studied indifference and disappearing into the night.

Ilse turned to thank her befrienders. With tears and smiles, she said she wished she could invite them all to her wedding tomorrow.

11. Diane

It was a Saturday night in June. They were gathered in the inner courtyard of pink Savannah brick at Miss Mayhew's School for Young Ladies. The air was soft and smelled of magnolias, the creamy blossoms so large and profuse they dragged at their branches.

"Why, don't you look devastating! That green dress is the exact same color as your eyes," Miss Emerson said. "And I'm just so glad your uncle saw the light and let you come after all."

Actually, Uncle Clayton was in the dark. She'd sneaked off. Diane looked apprehensively through the arched entrance to the courtyard, hoping to catch sight of the Army buses that were to take them to the dance at Fort Benning, afraid she'd see her uncle's Lincoln first.

Around her was the honeybee hum of Southern voices of pretty girls dressed their prettiest. The smell of perfume mingled with that of magnolias. Although Diane had lost twenty-five pounds, she still felt fat. And scared. Scared of the dance and scared she wouldn't get there.

When she'd told Miss Emerson this spring that Uncle Clayton wouldn't let her go to the Fort Benning dances, Miss Emerson had been indignant. "Why, I could see his objecting to a dance for enlisted men, but this is for officers and gentlemen."

Uncle Clayton had found plenty to object to. He claimed they were all Yankee trash at Fort Benning, officers included, who'd been nothing but butchers or delivery boys before induction and going to Officer Candidate School. He said she was too young to go to those dances, especially if they were chaperoned by two silly spinsters like Miss Bibb and Miss Emerson. Miss Bibb, who was twenty-seven, could hardly qualify as a spinster, but Diane didn't argue that. When she said girls from good families went, he said no family was as good as theirs, and if those girls' parents let them go, he couldn't stop them, but, by God, he was her guardian and he was going to protect her.

That was a laugh. What he wanted was to keep her prisoner. Ever since she'd locked him out of her room three years ago, he'd seen to it that she went nowhere, under the guise of protecting her. He drove her to and from Miss Mayhew's, and if he was away on a business trip, Chester drove. Chester also reported on her to Uncle Clayton. She just hoped he hadn't phoned and reported she'd gone to stay with Cindy overnight. Again she looked for the buses.

"It's all right, he's way out there on Jekyll Island, he can't know," Cindy Wilkinson said, placing a comforting hand on hers.

"I know, but I can't help being nervous," Diane said. This morning Uncle Clayton had taken the train to Brunswick, where he was meeting his friend General DeWitt. Together they were taking a boat to the island to spend the weekend at Uncle Clayton's club. Her uncle was proud of belonging to the Jekyll Island Club, whose members were Whitneys. Macys, Pulitzers, and Vanderbilts. But if he suspected anything, he'd sacrifice golf and sailing just to catch her. And how did she know he'd taken that train? Maybe he'd just pretended to and was biding his time.

There was an increasing hum of excitement, and with enormous relief Diane saw two olive-green Army buses pull up to the curb.

"Come on," Cindy said.

In a swirl of others, they approached the bus, boarded it, and sat toward the back. "These seats are hard," Diane said.

"Well, honey, you can't always expect chauffeur-driven Lincolns," Marybelle Pierce said from the seat in front of them. "You'll just have to learn to live in discomfort like the rest of us mortals."

"I wasn't criticizing, I was commenting," Diane said.

"That's telling her off," Cindy whispered, squeezing her hand.

Diane was grateful to Cindy, who always made her feel as if she were witty and beautiful. She didn't know how she'd live without her. But she worried that Marybelle might, just from spite, mention that she'd gone to the dance. All she had to do was tell her grandparents, who were friends of Uncle Clayton's, and then the cat would be out of the bag. Although Miss Bibb and Miss Emerson didn't know she was going to the dance against her uncle's wishes, her classmates did.

Finally the bus was full. Diane was just beginning to

breathe easier when Miss Emerson clapped her hands and called for attention. "I have a few words before we leave," she began. "Now, I want you all to comport yourselves as becoming to young ladies of privileged background representing the flower of Southern womanhood."

Scattered giggles. "I suppose," Miss Emerson said sternly, "this may seem humorous to you, but it's no laughing matter. The young men whose company you will enjoy tonight may soon be on a distant battlefield defending our way of life, where the memory of a lovely young lady will sustain his darkest moments. This is not to suggest," Miss Emerson said acidly, "that you exceed the boundaries of propriety in the name of patriotism." Miss Emerson's few words took fifteen minutes and ended with a roll call.

Diane groaned. "Oh, God, couldn't she have made that roll call before?" she whispered to Cindy.

At long last the bus started up. The other bus was a mile or so ahead. Miss Bibb wasn't as long-winded as Miss Emerson. Now that Diane didn't have to worry about being prevented from going to the dance, she worried about what happened when she got there. "I just know I'll be a wallflower," she wailed.

"Honey, there's no wallflowers at these dances, not with all those men," Marybelle Pierce said, obviously listening in.

Cindy said that since she'd lost all that weight, she didn't have a thing to worry about.

"I've still got ten pounds to go," Diane protested.

"You don't want to get skinny, you're just right," Cindy said.

Two months ago, before she'd gone on a diet, Diane had weighed close to a hundred-fifty. Now she was down to a hundred-twenty-five, but that was still too much for someone five-feet-five with small bones. Other girls' weight might vary by ten pounds or so, but no one had such wild weight fluctuations. The trouble was, now that she'd lost so much weight, Uncle Clayton was back rattling her doorknob at nights.

"You don't have to worry about not dancing," Cindy said. "What you have to watch is where they put their hands when you dance."

"Dancing's the last thing some of them are interested in," Marybelle said.

"What's really awful," another girl said, "is when I was dancing with this boy and all of a sudden I felt his . . . thing, I just thought I'd die from embarrassment." She giggled. The others giggled, too, and Miss Emerson, seated in front, cast a cold look in their direction, as if she knew what the giggling was all about.

A jeep with two MP's in white helmets passed by. The bus slowed up at a sentry box, where a soldier waved them through. Then they were bouncing down a rutted road past ugly green buildings and barracks, coming to a standstill alongside a low building with a veranda, not quite as ugly as the others.

Miss Emerson made another speech before they disembarked. No one was to take one step off that veranda, and everyone was to promptly return to the bus once the dance was over. Any departure from these rules would result in exclusion from future dances.

Outside, some soldiers had gathered. Enlisted men. They watched as the girls descended from the bus. "Yeah," one said, "we get the dogs, and the officers get the pretty ones." He was looking straight at Diane. She wasn't a dog after all, she was pretty. She held her head high and her stomach in.

"Stick close," Cindy said. "You're such an innocent, I have to keep an eye on you."

Innocent? If Cindy only knew. She pushed away the dark memory of those nights with her uncle and tried to think of herself as just another girl from Miss Mayhew's, pampered and protected and virginal, knowing she was a walking lie.

They passed public-school buses parked nearby, which meant the town girls were already here. A dance tune floated out. There were a few tense giggles as they entered the big barnlike building, where balloons hung from rafters. Officers in summer pinks stood in groups, sat at tables, and swiveled around on bar stools to eye them appraisingly.

"The more discriminating don't have anything to do with the town girls, they're waiting for us," Marybelle Pierce said.

And she accuses me of being a snob, Diane thought. Her palms were wet, face warm. So many men. What would she do? Say? She scarcely ever talked to boys, much less men. And what if, dancing out there, something embarrassing happened like they'd been giggling about on the bus? She began to wish she hadn't come. But maybe she wouldn't have to worry. Maybe no one would dance with her.

The band was playing "Sunrise Serenade." Around her girls were asked to dance, led out to the dance floor. Oh, God, I'll just stand here by myself, the only one ignored, the first wallflower in the history of Fort Benning dances. And then three men descended at once. She would have chosen the good-looking blond captain, but she had no choice; a dark-haired lieutenant who both smiled and frowned outmaneuvered the others.

"You're new here," he said on the dance floor. "I've never seen you before."

"There must be a lot of girls you've never seen before tonight."

"Yes, but I'd have noticed you." He spoke with a Yankee twang.

The captain tapped his shoulder, "Sorry, Lieutenant," he said.

But a second later the lieutenant was back tapping the captain's shoulder. "Sorry, Captain."

She didn't have to worry about what to do or say, all she had to do was smile. "Sunrise Serenade" ended and "Moonlight Serenade" began. Or was it vice versa? She was confused but happy. Men were always cutting in. Marybelle was right, there were no wallflowers. And although all the girls were popular, she was the most popular of all. She felt as light and airy as the balloons.

When the band ripped into "Tuxedo Junction," she headed for the sidelines, declining those who stepped forward and asked her to dance. The dark-haired Yankee with the impish grin was back. He didn't take no for an answer, however. "I can't dance to that," she said.

"Sure you can, just let yourself go," he said, swinging her out and pulling her back. Although their fingertips scarcely touched, he magically directed her steps, spinning her about until she got dizzy, her skirt flying high around her thighs so she was afraid her panties might show. She was sure Miss Bibb and Miss Emerson would both run out and drag her off the dance floor.

When the set ended, he did not release her hand. "I'm Michael Deal, what's your name?"

She didn't want to say. He might have noticed it somewhere flashing from a factory sign. She wanted to be liked for herself. "Diane," she said.

"It should be Diana, like the goddess."

"Oh, you Yankees and your lines."

"It's not a line. The minute you walked through that door, I knew you were for me. The girl I'm going to marry."

She laughed. "Are all Yankees crazy?"

Cindy was signaling from where she sat at a table with Marybelle and two officers. "Excuse me, there are my friends," she said.

He looked over. "Isn't that a coincidence, they're my friends, too."

But they weren't. Not only didn't he know Cindy and Marybelle, but he didn't know either Lieutenant Pickering or Captain DeWitt. Captain DeWitt turned out to be the nehpew of her uncle's friend General DeWitt. Now she was sure her uncle would find out she was here, either through Judge Pierce or General DeWitt, but she was having too much fun to care. "I'll worry about that tomorrow," she told herself, remembering Scarlett O'Hara's philosophy.

Later, dancing with Michael Deal again, she confronted him with his lie, but he only grinned and said they were his friends now.

It would have been a perfect evening if she hadn't done the dumbest, most stupid thing imaginable. She had somehow let Michael Deal talk her into inviting him to Colquitt Hall. Not only him—that wasn't so bad, she could have weaseled out of that—but she'd also invited Cindy, Marybelle, Lieutenant Lee Pickering and Captain Gordon DeWitt all for a picnic celebration of her eighteenth birthday next Sunday. She didn't even have drinking as an excuse, since she'd had only one daiquiri.

Heading toward town on the bus, she sat with clammy hands in her lap, wondering how she could get out of this. Easy enough to tell herself when she was having fun that it didn't matter what Uncle Clayton said, but what he'd say to the dance was nothing compared to what he'd do about her inviting a bunch of people to Colquitt Hall.

She could hardly bear the happy chatter around her. "I just danced my feet off," Marybelle said; and, "Cute! Lordy, is he cute," someone else said, "but you have to watch those piano fingers every minute."

"What do you mean, piano fingers?"

"I mean they wander all over."

Cindy, too, was chattering away, asking Diane if she didn't think Gordon DeWitt was just darling. Diane nodded. Marybelle, who was sitting in the same seat going back as she had coming out, turned around to face her. "I'm just tickled pink you're having that picnic, Diane. I swear I've been waiting weeks for that little lieutenant to ask me out, and tonight he said he'd take me to your picnic."

"No, he isn't, Cindy said. "Michael's taking us in an official miltiary staff car with a chauffeur. He can do that, since he's head of the motor pool."

"I'm not going in any dumb old staff car," Marybelle said. "I'm going alone with Lieutenant Lee Pickering."

The more they argued, the more the picnic became a fact, and the more frightened Diane became. Word was spreading throughout the bus about the picnic at Colquitt Hall, and all the girls started playing up to her, hoping for an invitation. Suddenly she was popular, something she'd always longed to be, and she couldn't even enjoy it.

Although the Army bus had picked them up at Miss Mayhew's, they were dropped off at their homes. Diane got off with Cindy. Cindy's house was practically brand-new and resembled a Spanish villa, with its white stucco exterior and red tile roof. Uncle Clayton said it looked like it belonged to a Miami gangster.

Cindy's parents were in bed, the house quiet. They tiptoed to Cindy's bedroom in back. It opened onto the terrace by the swimming pool. Sometimes when Cindy had slumber parties, they'd slip out late at night and go swimming. Cindy was always having friends sleep over, but Diane seldom got to come unless Uncle Clayton was out of town. Delia never told that she was away, but she could still go only when Chester was off on some drunken toot. Diane thought how lucky Cindy was to be able to have friends over. She felt guilty not inviting Cindy out to her place, but Uncle Clayton said he didn't want people invading his privacy.

Once again, fear struck. How was she going to get out of that picnic? Cindy and Marybelle would never speak to her again if she backed out. And what would Lieutenant Pickering and Captain DeWitt think? She didn't particularly care what Michael Deal thought, since it was all his fault to begin with.

In the bedroom, Diane took off her dress and brassiere and hurriedly slipped her nightgown on before taking off her underpants. She didn't want Cindy or anyone else seeing her naked, as if they could guess from one look at her what had happened with her uncle.

"You have such a beautiful body, why do you hide it?" Cindy asked. Cindy certainly didn't hide hers. She paraded around in white panties and brassiere, showing off her fantastic tan.

"I guess it's habit from hiding my ugly fat," Diane said. That was also true. She slipped in between the sheets.

Cindy sat up in the other twin bed, a sheet banding her breasts so that Diane could tell she was naked. "I should do something about this room, it's so babyish," she said. "Only it seems silly to bother since I won't be home this fall anyway."

"Lucky you, going all the way to New York, while I only get as far as Atlanta," Diane said. Cindy was going to Vassar, Diane to Agnes Scott.

"You could go to Vassar, too."

"No, I couldn't. Uncle Clayton wouldn't let me go that far away."

"Why do you let him boss you around like that?"

"What else can I do? He's my legal guardian."

Cindy gave her a funny look. "Some guardian."

Diane's heart gave a leap. Had she guessed? "What do you mean?"

Cindy didn't answer right away. She got a pack of Lucky Strikes from the night table and offered Diane one. Diane didn't smoke, but took a cigarette to be companionable. There was a distressingly long time while Cindy lit Diane's cigarette, her own, and then inhaled deeply, blowing out a smoke ring. "He's stealing you blind," she said.

"Stealing?"

Cindy nodded. "Siphoning off the money coming to you from your inheritance and investing it as his. That's what Mr. Wendall says, and he should know. He's one of your uncle's legal-eagle assistants. A friend of Daddy's. Daddy was telling Mama about it the other night at supper. He says Mr. Wendall says the reason your uncle's such a good friend of Judge Pierce is he'll need a friend in court if the law ever catches up with him."

Diane was stunned; her thoughts flagged behind Cindy's words. She was ready to believe anything of her uncle, but this? Why did he have to steal from her, when he had money of his own? "He's got his own money," she said.

"Some people are just plain greedy," Cindy told her. "If I were you, I'd let him know you knew what he was up to. That would stop him. Don't mention names. You'd get Mr. Wendall into trouble, and God knows what would happen to Daddy. I mean, we're considered upstarts, and he's from an old established family. People would take his word against Daddy's or Mr. Wendall's any day. What you do is just strongly hint. Tell him he'd better straighten up and fly right, because when you're of legal age or married, whichever comes first, you goddamn well can throw him out of Colquitt Hall right on his ass, because that place belongs to you, not him."

Diane laughed. "That's not a hint, that's a threat. Anyway, he wouldn't pay any attention to me. And he considers himself above the law. If people knew what he did, he'd be tarred and feathered and run out of town." Or would they say there wasn't any smoke without fire? That she'd seduced him, the way he said she had.

Cindy was eyeing her. "What did he do?"

The breeze ballooning out the ruffled curtains, bringing in the faint smell of honeysuckle and chlorine from the swimming pool, was suddenly overpowered by the stronger smell of dampness and decay that pervaded Colquitt Hall. She could never tell anyone, even Cindy, what had happened. "I can't . . ." she said. The words hung in the air. ". . . talk about it." She turned her head away so that Cindy couldn't see her tears, but maybe not soon enough, for Cindy bounded from her bed to Diane's and put an arm around her. "You can tell me."

Diane shook her head violently. "You're my only friend, and you'd never speak to me again, even if you did believe me."

"Tell me, or I'll think the worse," Cindy said, smiling, trying to joke her into telling.

"You couldn't come close," Diane said, and began sobbing. "Maybe it's me. Maybe I *am* a bad person."

"Oh, nuts," Cindy said, and kissed her. "You're the sweetest person I know, and not a bit snooty. There's nothing bad about you."

But Diane felt something bad now. Lying there, pressed so close to Cindy, she became aware of Cindy's breasts against hers, of the small, silky body separated only by a thin nightgown, of Cindy's perfume. Diane sweated desire from every pore, and hated herself. She turned away, but Cindy, in the unrelentingness of innocence, turned with her, pushing against her buttocks, clasping her breasts, until Diane, overcome, turned toward her. They kissed and twined together, embracing and exploring. Cindy, making funny little cooing sounds in her throat, instructed Diane what to do by gesture. Finally, passion spent, they slept.

Or Cindy did.

Diane lay awake staring at ghostly objects in the moonlit room. I'm bad, I'm evil, I seduced him, and now her, too. Perhaps her parents had deliberately plowed into that truck, knowing they'd given birth to a monster.

But in the morning everything looked different. The sun shone cheerfully on ruffled pink organdy curtains and bed canopies, casting a pink light on Cindy's face. She yawned and stretched. "Some night," she said, smiling over at Diane. Maybe it was all a dream.

When they sat down to breakfast, though, it was as if Cindy's mother had guessed. She gave Diane a disapproving look. Usually she fawned over her to the point that Diane was embarrassed and wondered if her uncle was right after all in claiming the Wilkinsons used her friendship with Cindy to promote themselves in society. Mrs. Wilkinson overdressed, even for breakfast. She wore a pair of smart yellow satin lounging pajamas with mules to match, and dangling earrings. "You'd better hurry and finish your breakfast," she told Diane. "Your uncle's sending in Chester to take you home."

Diane didn't dare look at Cindy. How could Mrs. Wilkinson have known? Had she peeked through the keyhole? But her next words clarified the matter. "I was just about to come in and wake you. My, I had a time of it explaining things to your uncle. Before I'd even had my coffee, he called and asked for you.

"I told him you were sleeping late because you two girls had been to the dance last night. He was enraged. He said he'd forbidden you to go to those dances at Fort Benning." She gave Diane a reproachful look. "I'm afraid you're going to be in serious trouble for practicing deceit. And you, too, young lady," she said to Cindy, "for aiding and abetting. I told him I didn't know you two had gone against his wishes, but I'm afraid he didn't believe me. I don't know what he must think."

"Oh, my God, Mama, what do you care what he thinks? The way he's cheating Diane out of her money, and then pretends to be so concerned for her welfare."

"Now, you hush, what's said in this house is to be kept under this roof."

"Not when it means Diane's getting swindled."

"You don't know that for a fact," Mrs. Wilkinson said. "You just watch what you say, that big mouth of yours could land us all in trouble."

"Well, I know what Mr. Wendall told Daddy," Cindy said defiantly.

Her courage gave Diane courage. "That's okay, Mrs. Wilkinson, I'll explain to him you didn't know," she said. She was no longer afraid of him. His cheating her was something that could be made public. She even let Chester sit and wait outside in the car while she slowly finished breakfast, and then took her own good time putting things into her overnight bag.

Cindy said good-bye to her under her mother's eyes. Her

fingers lingered on Diane's arm, and they exchanged glances. Last night hadn't been a dream. Diane was excited and frightened.

Chester had a big smile on his face when she got into the backseat. He greeted her with a cheerful good-morning. "Mistah Clayton, he back early this morning and he mighty upset when he find you away."

And I just bet I know who I can thank for that," she said.

"Now, I don't know what you mean. He done come back because someone sighted a enemy submarine right out there near Jekyll Island, and everyone was ordered off."

Oh, sure.

Chester drove the Lincoln as if it were a race car. It always scared Diane to go fast, and she sat tensely in the backseat, almost glad when they turned up the oak-lined drive toward the house.

"There he be waiting," Chester said, pulling up.

Uncle Clayton stood on the veranda steps, tan, his graying hair sun-silvered. He wore a blue polo shirt and white slacks and a furious look.

She got out of the car with her overnight bag and walked up the steps toward him.

"You march right up to your room, young lady. We're going to have a good talk about this."

A good talk in her bedroom? Was he going to say he'd let her off lightly if she let him get into her bed? She wasn't going to take a chance on that. And if he was swindling her, he was the one in trouble, not her. She stood her ground. "I'm not going to be treated like a child anymore. I went to that dance, and I had a real good time, and furthermore, I invited some friends to a picnic next Sunday."

His eyes darkened. "I'm not standing out here and discussing our private affairs for others to hear."

He must mean Chester, since the other servants would be in church.

"That's fine with me, there's nothing more to discuss."

She started past him on the steps. He grabbed her arm right where Cindy's fingers had lingered, his fingers pinching her flesh. "You come along with me," he said in a whispered hiss. "I'm not taking any sass from you."

For a minute she was afraid he'd drag her up to her bedroom, but he steered her into the library, nearly flinging her into a leather chair. He stood over her, face flushed under his tan. "Just who all did you invite on this picnic you're going to have to uninvite?"

"I invited Captain Gordon DeWitt, your friend's nephew, and Marybelle Pierce, your friends' granddaughter. Among others. I don't know about Captain DeWitt, but I know Marybelle's going to put up a hue and cry to her grandparents if I have to uninvite her. And I asked my best friend, Cindy."

"Who's that because of your money and social standing."

"My money? Why, thank you. I thought it was yours, the way I hear you've been spending it."

A small vein jumped in his throat. She watched it pulsing. It looked as if he'd lost his power of speech; then he said in a choked voice, "Where'd you get that nonsense?"

She didn't answer, remembering Cindy's warning about getting her father and Mr. Wendall in trouble. Offensive was better than defensive; she'd learned that from him. "I invited my friends to celebrate my birthday. And I made it a picnic to make up for the one I missed out on on Cindy's birthday when we were in Atlanta. I expect you remember that."

His face was no longer flushed, but pale.

"I'll be eighteen a week from today. In three years I'll be of legal age and come into my inheritance. It's going to look mighty peculiar if there's nothing there."

He laughed uneasily. "You're talking crazy. In three years you'll be in a loony bin, the rate you're going. Now, get out of here."

By the time she reached her room, she was shaking, no longer feeling brave. All she felt was his hate vibrating through the house. She saw his plan. He'd say she was crazy and put her in a mental institution and never have to account for a penny of her inheritance. He'd say her parents' death had affected her mind. Even what he'd done to her he'd turn to advantage. If she dared breathe a word, he'd say that was part of her craziness, imagining him seducing her. And she knew whom people would believe.

She heard his footsteps on the stairs and quickly turned the key in the lock, her heart pounding as the steps paused before her door. She was alone in the house without anyone to hear. There was only Chester, who wouldn't hear from his room over the garage and wouldn't help if he heard. The doorknob rattled. She backed off into the bathroom, ready to lock the door there, too. But he went on to his room. Or maybe he only pretended to and would tiptoe back. She waited for what seemed forever, and hearing nothing, cautiously opened the door. He was nowhere around. Quickly she ran down the steps and out the back door to the stable. If he followed, she'd ride for help to a neighbor's, although the nearest lived miles away.

She bypassed his horse, Beauregard, and kept out of kicking distance of Lucifer, who was so wild and ill-tempered that even Emory, the groom, steered clear of him. Uncle Clayton laughed at them, but she noticed he kept a careful distance, too. Emory said she was the best horsewoman he'd ever seen and could sit anything, but she had enough sense not to try Lucifer. She didn't know why her uncle kept Lucifer. He said the horse would make a good sire.

She mounted Lancelot and headed toward the river. Although it hadn't rained for weeks and the earth simmered with heat, under the oaks there was a dampness where the sun never penetrated the thick moss and leaves.

She emerged from semidarkness to the bank of the Chattahoochee. The falls splashed rainbow-hued in the sunlight. Below the falls was a deceitfully placid pool with a treacherous undertow, reminding her of Uncle Clayton.

At least she'd given him the slip. She wouldn't go back until it was time for Delia and the others to return. She dismounted and let Lancelot graze while she leaned against the trunk of a giant oak listening to songbirds and wondering why nature was so beautiful and human nature so ugly. Last night she had gone against nature. But maybe it wasn't all her fault. Maybe it wasn't any of it her fault. She remembered Marybelle and some other girls at Miss Mayhew's always complaining about Cindy's touching them. Marybelle said it was icky. Of course, Marybelle was jealous of Cindy because she was cute and popular and president of the senior class. Cindy wasn't at all like Miss Gregory, who wore tailored suits, flat heels, and her hair cut short. She was the phys-ed teacher, and there was a lot of speculation about her. But she looked mannish. Cindy was the epitome of femininity. Well, so was Diane herself, for that matter. According to Michael Deal, she was every man's dream girl. Ha. But maybe he'd meant it. He'd been so worshipful it had embarrassed her. But brash, too. Yankee brash. He said he was going to marry her. Was he crazy, or was that some Yankee line based on the premise that if you mentioned marriage you could get in a girl's pants, as Uncle Clayton put it.

What if he'd meant it, though? Then Uncle Clayton couldn't put her in any insane asylum. Cindy said she'd get her inheritance when she was of legal age or married. Uncle Clayton would never allow that. She'd have to elope. She tried to picture Michael Deal on a ladder and her handing him a suitcase out the window, but it just looked like something in the funny papers, a cartoon elopement.

She flopped down on the grass, smelling the lovely mushroomy smell of the earth, and gazed up at sunlight splintered by leaves. She shut her eyes and her mind, refusing to think anymore of Uncle Clayton or Cindy or Michael Deal, and lay on the warm earth, feeling the sun on her eyelids, the sound of the splashing falls becoming fainter and fainter.

At first she thought it was her heart thudding, galloping crazily in her chest, and then she felt a shadow fall across her. A high, piercing whinny.

She opened her eyes, and a scream tore from her throat. Above her the broad brown underbelly of a horse rearing up. In a flash she noticed the white tuft of hair around the horse's penis, the split in the front hooves as they paused suspended in the air. She lay frozen, the sour smell of the horse's sweat mixed with the smell of her fear, and she saw with certain knowledge that the hooves were going to descend on her. She lay waiting, too weak with fright to move, glimpsing a blurred sun, double-edged leaves, and triumph on his face. The hooves came toward her, and she rolled away just as they slammed into the earth a fraction of an inch from her head.

He slid down from the horse and flung the reins over a low branch. Shiny riding boots strode over to where she lay shivering. "You all right, honey? That sure gave me a scare." With solicitous fingers he brushed her off. She looked up. The concern in his voice did not match the look in his eyes, fractured with a strange light. One hand groped for her breasts, the other lifted her skirt. She jumped up. Ran. His footsteps thudded behind her; he tackled her around the legs. She kicked, clawed, and hit. They struggled in sunlight and silence, the only sound that of heavy breathing. She got away, ran over to the horse, grabbed the reins, and scrambled up.

In a minute she was flying over the earth, trees streaking by in a blur, as from the window of a speeding car. She was riding Lucifer. "Just hang on," she told herself, and glued her body to the horse's, gripping the reins in a fist and his flanks with her knees. She prayed she could hold out as long as the horse. Beneath her, his lightning hooves flashed over the earth, and then all of a sudden the horse halted, reared up. She was standing in the stirrups. She was sailing off into space.

* * *

The pain came in spasms. It was chiefly in her shoulder, as if a spike had been driven in. And then blackness.

Someone was sobbing. Delia. Crooning over her, another voice. And then *his*. "I told her she was taking her life in her hands, riding that horse. She wouldn't listen."

A big sun-flooded room. Flowered drapes and two easy chairs to match. She was trussed up. In some cheerful place for the crazy. He had her where he wanted her now.

She lay aching as if she'd been whipped into submission. A plump gray-haired nurse looked in on her. "Well, hello there, we're awake finally. How are we feeling?" A false smile and appeasing tone for the insane.

"Get me out of this straitjacket, please," she begged.

"Why, honey, that's no straitjacket. You're in traction. You're a very lucky little girl."

Dr. Jasper said the same thing later. Light glinted on his domed head and glasses. "A quarter of an inch lower, and your eye would have been put out. Must have been a sharp stone. Required thirty-six stitches."

"Will it leave a scar?"

"Maybe a small one. Now, don't you worry. Your eyebrow will hide it when it grows out. We had to shave it off. You've got a dislocated shoulder, some broken ribs, and a mild concussion. I think it's mild. Never know about those. I want to keep you under observation for a while."

"How long?"

"A week, two weeks, no longer."

And then weak, bandaged, taped up, she'd be at her uncle's mercy.

"I'm in no hurry."

Dr. Jasper looked at her oddly. A patient who wasn't in a hurry to leave a hospital? "Well, I hope you're not in a hurry to climb back up on that horse again. Your uncle says he warned you not to. You ought to listen to him, honey." He patted the bed in the vicinity of her feet and left.

The cheerful room was comforting. If only she could stay here. On the wall were pictures of horses. Ironically, the chestnut resembled Lucifer. Well, if she couldn't stay here, she knew one thing. She wasn't going back. He'd intended murder, not rape. He'd let her get away too easily. Put Lucifer within reach, knowing she'd jump on the horse to escape him, hoping the horse would bash her brains out.

And he wasn't out to kill her for some trifling reason like sneaking off to a dance or inviting her friends on a picnic without his permission. That might spur him on, but his real reason was to keep her quiet about his swindling her out of her inheritance.

A hospital would be a perfect place for attack. She was like a sacrificial victim lying here strapped down and helpless. Holding herself perfectly still, she tested her ability to fight back, moving first her fingers, then hands, arms, legs, feet. Besides the shattering pain she felt when she tried to, she could scarcely move the upper half of her body. She could kick; that was about all.

If she could only tell someone, get help. Dr. Jasper? He wouldn't believe her. Suggest she was making things up. Maybe even mention to her uncle that she was in a bad way mentally. That's all Uncle Clayton would need. Then she'd be where she thought she was this morning. He wouldn't have to go to the bother of killing her, just lock her up for life and have free rein with her money.

The nurse came in with a lunch tray. Her name was Nurse Garnet. "We'll feel better after we eat," she told Diane, adjusting the tray over her chest. She stood by making encouraging comments while Diane poked a listless fork at the food. Maybe she could get Nurse Garnet's help. "Isn't this a lovely room?" Nurse Garnet asked. "The best in the hospital. Your uncle thinks mighty highly of you. He was just worried sick when he brought you in."

So much for Nurse Garnet. But there was Cindy. Only, would her mother agree to her staying with them?

Visiting hours began at one. Uncle Clayton arrived on the dot, bringing roses and brimming solicitude. Nurse Garnet showed him in and hung around, as adoring as a schoolgirl. Diane was glad at least that she hung around, and she was even gladder to see Cindy and Marybelle come in. Safety in numbers.

Uncle Clayton smiled charmingly at Marybelle, ignoring Cindy.

"Oh, Diane," Cindy said, "you look like a mummy all taped up."

"My heavens, I thought I'd just die when I heard," Marybelle said. "How did it happen?"

Diane didn't get a chance to tell. Uncle Clayton jumped in immediately with his version. He sat in the chair nearest her bed, movie-star handsome in his beige summer suit, showing just the perfect touch of concern and admiration. "I warned this little daredevil not to go near that horse, but she considers any risk a challenge," he said, thereby laying the groundwork for when she went back to Colquitt Hall and broke her neck in some unlikely way.

"If it hadn't been for Delia and the others finding her lying there unconscious, I'd hate to think what would have happened," he continued. So would I, Diane thought. He'd have finished me off.

"Where'd they find her?" Cindy asked. Diane wanted to know, too.

"In the woods. They were taking a shortcut back after some church doings."

"Oh, golly, wasn't that lucky?" Marybelle said.

Cindy shot Diane a look. She'd guessed something. If only her uncle would leave so she could tell her. Not much—she couldn't say much in front of Marybelle—but Cindy would catch on.

Uncle Clayton said he was having the horse shot. "It's a menace to humanity." Diane felt almost sorry for Lucifer, who was to be shot merely for failing to carry out his mission successfully.

Her uncle stayed until the others got up to go. They all trooped to the door together. Nurse Garnet came bustling in carrying a huge bouquet of deep red roses. "Would you look at these? We had one heck of a time finding a vase big enough to put them in."

"Oh, aren't they be-yoo-ti-ful," Marybelle cried.

"I'll just see who they're from. Don't want this little girl dislocating her shoulder again just to reach a card," said Uncle Clayton, plucking the card from the roses.

"Give it to me," Diane said fiercely. They all—even Cindy—eyed her reproachfully for talking to sweet Uncle Clayton like that. He reluctantly handed over a small envelope. Diane opened it, read, and giggled. "My, my," she said.

"I'm consumed with curiosity," Marybelle said.

So was Uncle Clayton. His eyes bored holes through her and the card. Diane felt a childish glee withholding her information. If her uncle could have snatched the card away, he would have. But he wouldn't have learned much. The card was signed, "A Secret Admirer." Scrawled at the bottom, "Tonight at eight!"

Diane scarcely noticed her visitors leave, hardly felt sharp aches or dull pains. Forgot fear. Who was he, her secret admirer?

Right after supper she had Nurse Quimby get her makeup from the drawer of the bedside table. Nurse Quimby held up a mirror. "Oh, I'm hopeless," Diane cried. There were scratches on her cheeks like claw marks, tiny abrasions yellowed from iodine going all the way up to her hairline, white tape X'd above an eye. But she didn't look like a mummy. Cindy and her exaggerations.

"Why do you want to put makeup on so close to bedtime?" Nurse Quimby asked.

"I feel naked without lipstick," Diane said.

"There's nothing like a little powder and lipstick," Nurse Quimby agreed. She was the night-duty nurse. Young, red-haired, freckle-nosed, and friendly. Diane liked her a lot. Would Nurse Quimby take her home with her? She wished she'd stick around now so they could get better acquainted, but Nurse Quimby had other duties. She put down the makeup mirror, closed the draperies, and left.

A breeze pushed out the draperies. Or was it a breeze? Suddenly Diane was scared. What if this was a ruse of her uncle's? He'd sent the roses and that card. Posing as someone else, he'd sneak in and strangle her while she couldn't fight back. She found the card and studied the handwriting. Scrawly. Uncle Clayton wrote such a small neat script it was hard to read. But he might have scrawled in order to disguise.

The noises in the hospital were fewer but sharper. She strained her ears. And kept a hand by the nurse's bell. The draperies moved as if someone moved behind them. The table lamp was out of reach. There was only a thin night light. She looked at her watch. After eight. He wan't coming, then.

All of a sudden the doorknob turned. Diane's heart pounded.

Nurse Quimby poked her red head in. "Are you decent?" she whispered. "You have a visitor."

"Who?" Diane asked, but Nurse Quimby had disappeared.

Diane's flailing heart threatened to push through the thin shell of her chest.

More whispers out there, some giggles identifiable as Nurse Quimby's. Diane half-expected to see Uncle Clayton enter disguised by a black mask and long flowing cape. Instead a dark-haired Army lieutenant came in. He wore his cap at a jaunty angle, a frown between his heavy eyebrows, a smile on his lips. Michael Deal!

"Hi! How you feeling?"

She was vastly relieved it wasn't Uncle Clayton, but disappointed to see this brash, smiling Yankee. "How did you get in?"

"With my looks and charm, it was a snap."

"How did you know I was here?"

"Called your house. I'd have come at visiting hours, but I couldn't get away from the field. You look beautiful, even bandaged up."

Delia must have told him. "Lucky Uncle Clayton didn't answer. He wouldn't have told you a thing."

"Why?"

"Because he wouldn't. Because he won't let me see boys."

"You're kidding? Why not?"

"He doesn't think there's anyone good enough for me."

"There isn't," he said with that smiling frown. "Except me."

"He thinks they're all fortune hunters."

"I like money. I'm crazy about it. But I wouldn't marry for money. I'll get rich on my own." A smile again, a certain shyness in his eyes. She liked him. "I thought," he said, "since you couldn't have a picnic, we'd have one here." He nodded toward the wicker hamper.

"But that wasn't until my birthday this Sunday."

"We can have one then, too." He opened the hamper. It was as attractively packed as something in the food section of a women's magazine. He'd thought of everything—checked napkins, chilled champagne. Even glasses. Although she'd hated champagne ever since that night in Atlanta, she took a few sips to please him. She also sampled the shrimp salad and chicken. The rest—the ham, and the various salads (bean, potato, cucumber), the angel- and devil's-food cakes—she couldn't eat.

"Aw, come on, you can do better than that," he coaxed. But he wasn't eating either. The smile had gone, the frown remained. "Tell me how it happened," he said.

She gave him Uncle Clayton's cleaned-up version. He listened aggressively, his long thin body alert. He seemed to be in perpetual motion, even when perfectly still.

"Uncle Clayton's having the horse shot. He says it's a menace to humanity," she said, finishing her story.

"Sounds like someone should be shot," he said. He was smoking, using as an ashtray a saucer he'd taken from under a gift plant. She stared at him in wonder. "What do you mean?"

"Why'd he have that horse around if it was so mean-tempered? Especially if he knew you might be tempted to ride it?"

He was wrong in his deduction, but right in his suspicion. He didn't trust her uncle, sight unseen, but maybe that was why he didn't.

Nurse Quimby came tiptoeing in. "You have to leave before lights-out," she whispered conspiratorially. "They'd notice if there was a light under the door." She waited to see that he did. Michael touched Diane's hand, a surprisingly light, gentle touch. "See you tomorrow," he said. "Same time, same place."

It was Nurse Quimby who spied the gift-wrapped box on her pillow. "Oh, open it," she cried. Diane fumbled the ribbon, tore off the wrapping. Inside was a gold chain bracelet with a dangling heart inscribed June 27, 1942.

"Oh, isn't that darling?" Nurse Quimby said. "And isn't he sweet? He gave me a box of chocolate-pecan caramels." She looked slyly at Diane. What happened June 27?"

"That was the night we met."

"But that's just a few days ago! He said you two were getting married, or I'd never have let him in tonight. As soon as you got out of the hospital."

"Don't you believe in love at first sight?"

Nurse Quimby certainly did. She was more excited than Diane. Diane gave her the picnic basket with the mostly untouched contents, and made her promise not to tell a soul about Michael's visit.

"How could I? If anyone found out, I'd be fired." She giggled. "Oh, this is so romantic. Oh, I wish I could tell." She danced out of the room with the picnic hamper.

He arrived every night at eight. When he found out she preferred Dr Pepper to champagne, he brought in a case and bribed Nurse Quimby to keep it on ice. Or maybe he didn't have to bribe her. Nurse Quimby was ready to risk her job or even her neck for their romance.

Since his visits were brief and they had to speak in whispers. Diane didn't get to know much about him except that he was from some mining town in Pennsylvania, where his family and relations were coal miners. Perfect. Think how upset Uncle Clayton would be when he found out her husband was what he'd call a common, lower-class laborer. She only wished Michael's manners and grammar were worse, and cherished each double negative. He made no demands except to marry her and bestow worshipful glances. She could live with that. Lucky for her he was so nice. She'd have married anybody to get away from home.

Diane celebrated her eighteenth birthday in the hospital, with Uncle Clayton, Cindy, and Marybelle in attendance. Uncle Clayton brought a birthday cake decorated with rosebuds and pink candles. He said her real gift would arrive in a few days, and it would be a big surprise.

Not nearly as big a surprise as the one he'd get.

Michael and she planned their elopement. The only thing left up in the air was the date. That would be decided by Dr. Jasper.

It was decided Tuesday morning, when Dr. Jasper patted the bed in the vicinity of her feet, as was his habit, and announced she could leave Friday. "That way you don't have to spend the weekend here. You'll be pretty much okay as long as you don't take up tap dancing. Your uncle thinks you'd be happier at home in your own bed."

With him? In bed or dead. Take her choice.

Uncle Clayton was in a frighteningly happy mood that afternoon.

"Diane's going home Friday," he told the other visitors with a smile. Besides Cindy and Marybelle, Miss Emerson had dropped by.

"I certainly hope you don't get back up on that horse," Miss Emerson said coyly.

"She won't. He's been shot," Uncle Clayton said.

There was a short silence. "Well, I . . . Couldn't he have been put out to pasture?" Miss Emerson said. Uncle Clayton repeated his remark about the horse being a menace to society.

"We'll come visit you and see you behave," Cindy said brightly.

Diane was beginning to think Cindy had switched sides. No longer were there shared glances between them. These days Cindy seemed to sparkle for Uncle Clayton, who appeared to forgive her the sin of being nouveau riche. For a moment Diane thought how much fun it would be if her uncle and Cindy got together, comparing notes on her in bed, both claiming she'd seduced them.

"I'm leaving Friday morning," she told Michael that night.

"No, we're leaving Thursday night," he said. "I'll get a four-day pass. We'll go to South Carolina. Someone at the field said Alabama's where you get a quick divorce and South Carolina a quick marriage. I'll ask around about a justice of the peace near the state line. I wish it could be a church wedding. I wanted to see you coming down the aisle in white lace carrying white roses while the organ played Mendelssohn."

"Lohengrin. Mendelssohn's for afterward. I thought men considered church weddings romantic nonsense."

"I like romantic nonsense," he said, kissing her on the eyebrow that hadn't been shaved.

Wednesday night he arrived to report triumphantly that he'd gotten two weeks off. "We'll have a real honeymoon," he said. Suddenly she thought of marriage as something other than just getting away from home. Men expected virgins. What would he say when he found out she wasn't? She could say it was from horseback riding. That happened, didn't it? Losing your hymen that way. And he always accepted everything she said. He was so sweet, so nice and normal. To think she'd have a husband, a home, and children, just like everyone else.

Thursday she spent the morning walking up and down the hospital corridor in her robe. She didn't want to get dizzy when she walked out tonight. She was the nurses' pet, and they all greeted her with smiles and laments about how much they'd miss her. Often other patients came to their doors to watch her pass by, as if she were some sort of celebrity.

Cindy, Marybelle, and Uncle Clayton arrived together at visiting hour. Uncle Clayton had brought her overnight bag as she'd asked, telling him what to tell Delia to pack—her white sundress and jacket. At least she'd be wearing white for Michael.

"Come over here, honey, I want to show you something," Uncle Clayton said. He was standing by the window. She went over. He couldn't very well shove her out with witnesses. But both witnesses wore big smiles. For an irrational moment she suspected conspiracy. She looked down to where he was pointing. "There! Do you like that? That's your birthday present. I thought it'd keep you off a horse."

Down below, smack in front of the hospital, making every other car on the block look shabby, was a brand-new white convertible.

She knew instantly what he planned. She'd die in a car crash like her parents. But he wouldn't be fool enough to do anything so that it would happen immediately. Two accidents in a row would be suspicious.

"Oh, Uncle Clayton, it's be-yoo-ti-ful. I'm so excited. A car of my very own! Could I just keep the keys with me?" she asked, pouring it on thick, kissing him. She hated touching him, but she managed it with revenge in mind.

And for once she'd fooled him. His tan, handsome face registered confusion. He might expect her to show gratitude before others, but a kiss? A minute later he was looking pleased and smug. Maybe he thought he'd be able to coax her back in bed with a white convertible. Or do it in the backseat.

Cindy and Marybelle were smiling in anticipation. Uncle Clayton magnanimously handed over the keys, accompanied by a mock courtly bow. "The biggest headache was getting a tankful of gas," he added expansively. "Took all my gas-ration coupons."

She felt happier and happier. Not only was she going to use his gift to elope in, but also he was supplying the gas. She wished she could see his face tomorrow morning when he arrived and found her and the car missing.

Finally they left. Finally it was suppertime. And finally it was dark and time to get ready. Michael wasn't coming until eight-thirty, because they had to wait until dark. But tonight it was dark earlier than usual. And raining. Not hard; not yet, at least.

Nurse Quimby came in to help her dress. Naturally, they'd had to let her in on the elopement. They couldn't have gotten away without her noticing, and anyway, she was eager to help. "I brought you something," she said, and twirled a blue garter on a finger. "Something old, something new, something borrowed, something blue," she sang. Then, "Oh, you look beautiful," she said, gazing at Diane in her white dress. "Like a real bride. Put on this garter, don't forget. Now, you're ready. Wait here, I'll go see if the coast is clear."

She came back a few minutes later smiling and breathless. "Okay," she whispered, "but the door's open to the nurses' station. We'll just walk by naturally. If anyone asks questions, I'll say I'm showing you around. Put your robe on, just in case. I hope nobody notices your high heels."

Diane tiptoed alongside her down the corridor. She still felt a little shaky, but that was mostly due to nervousness. None of the nurses looked up when they passed the open door. They were all listening to President Roosevelt's speech on the radio.

Nurse Quimby led the way down three flights of back stairs to the rear exit, where Michael stood, hands in pockets, shoulders hunched, shivering in the rain, but when he saw her, his face brightened as if the sun had come out. He kissed her, then remembered it was raining and said they'd better make a run for it. "I forgot an umbrella. Better keep your robe on until we get to the car. It's a half-block away."

"We don't have to go that far. We're taking mine, it's parked right in front." She had to waste precious minutes explaining it all.

Michael was doubtful. "But I've borrowed my buddy's car. I can't leave it on the street."

"I can't leave mine, or he'll take it back."

"If you all don't hurry, it's not going to matter whose car you take," Nurse Quimby said. "I'll drive your buddy's car back when I'm off duty. Just give me the keys and tell me where to take it."

He gave her the keys and directions; then they hurried through the rain, Nurse Quimby with them. Diane wondered if she planned to come along, but she stopped short of the car and looked at them wistfully as they started to get in. "I wish I were going with you," she said. Diane squeezed her hand and said how grateful she was for her help and the blue garter, and promised to tell her all about it when they returned.

Michael stood holding her door open. The convertible gleamed brightly in the rainy darkness. They got in and waved good-bye to Nurse Quimby.

They were off. While Michael drove, she took off her wet robe and fluffed out her damp hair.

"Happy?" he called over to her.

"I'll be happier after we cross the state line."

"I'll be happier after we're married," he said, taking her hand.

The rain stuttered on the convertible roof. Driving required all his attention and both hands. When he took his hand from hers, hers felt deserted. Despite the rain, he drove fast, and although ordinarily speeding made her nervous, tonight she was more nervous about getting away. Even though Uncle Clayton couldn't know, she still sometimes believed he had supernatural powers. She thought of his wrath when he found out she'd eloped, and hoped he didn't learn about the part Nurse Quimby had played. At least he couldn't have her shot.

The car hit a bump, and Michael reached out to her. "Sorry, darling, I didn't see that one." His protectiveness made her feel more secure. To think she'd never have to worry about Uncle Clayton again. She pictured him sitting in the library drinking bourbon and making plans. How he'd fix the brake so it wouldn't work and she'd die in flames like her parents. "I told her she should get those brakes looked after, but she just kept putting it off."

She laughed.

Michael smiled over and lifted her hand to his lips. "I love you," he said, and when she didn't answer, asked didn't she love him, too.

"Why else would I marry you?" she said.

Finally they crossed the state line. On either side of the highway were clumps of brambly bushes and scraggly trees.

"My buddy said it was backwoods country, but he didn't say it was this far back," Michael said.

Occasionally they passed a dirt lane with scattered shanties, a few dim lights in the windows. Gasoline lamps. Electricity didn't extend down dirt roads.

They came to a sign saying "WELCOME TO COOLEYVILLE, POP. 843."

A few blocks later another sign said, "We hope you enjoyed your visit. Come see us again."

"The sign's bigger than the town," Michael said.

And then there was silence again except for the rain stuttering on the roof. Michael drove slowly now. "I don't think it's much farther. Sorry I couldn't give you sunshine instead of showers."

"You couldn't have supplied sunshine at night. Not even you."

"For you, anything."

Headlights shone on a rickety house. In front a sign said "LAIRD AVERY TAXIDERMIST," and under that, "JUSTICE OF THE PEACE."

"Looks like he's not missing out on anything," Michael said, stopping the car. "Okay, darling, this is it. Run for it."

Luckily they didn't have far to run to the porch. The house was dark. Diane stood under a part of the porch roof that wasn't leaking while Michael pounded on the door. After a while a light came on inside and a man's voice called, "Coming. Just hold your horses."

The door opened and a man peered out at them. He wore baggy trousers held up by suspenders over a yellowish underwear top. "I suppose you're after getting married," he said.

"That's right, that's what we're after," Michael said.

"Well, come on in outta the rain."

They entered, and he closed the door behind them. "Hey, Corny, come on down. Folks getting hitched," he yelled.

A gaunt woman shuffled into the room a few minutes later. She wore men's shoes and a faded housedress. Her blue eyes were also faded and her gray hair stringy. "This is my wife, Cornelia," the man said. Then, " 'Scuse me while I just go put a shirt on."

He disappeared. The woman stood with her arms crossed forbiddingly across her chest. "You sure picked a poor night to get married."

Michael said, yes, he might have picked the wrong night, but he'd certainly picked the right girl. The woman looked Diane over critically. "Looks like you've been in some kind of scrap," she said.

"I was thrown from a horse," Diane said. The woman continued to look at her skeptically, as if she didn't believe this. Diane looked away. All around the room were stuffed birds and animals. There was even a cage holding a stuffed canary. A bushy-tailed squirrel with button eyes shared the mantel with a fierce-beaked eagle. In between, Diane envisioned a stuffed, beady-eyed Uncle Clayton.

Laird Avery returned with a shirt on. It was buttoned up wrong.

"Well, let's get going," he said.

12. *Susan*

The Sunday sports section hid all but his long legs in suntans and polished brown oxfords that gleamed reproachfully at her.

"Richard," Susan said, "I'm sorry."

No answer. The newspaper barrier remained.

"At least tell me why you're mad at me."

"Who said I was mad?"

"Okay," she said, and walked slowly up the spiral staircase. When she turned to look down, he was squinting up at her. It was a look she loved, as if he were flying into the wild blue yonder, as in the Army Air Corps song. "Mom always had chicken, mashed potatoes, and gravy for Sunday dinner," he said before returning to the newspaper.

She'd messed up again. Because it was so hot, she'd made shrimp salad and lemon mousse. She'd cut the recipes out of the New York *Times*, taking their word for it that it was the perfect summer Sunday lunch.

Upstairs she ran hot water in the bathtub. She'd heard hot water was cooling. She took off her harem hostess pajamas, letting them fall onto the tile floor. They, too, were a mistake. An expensive mistake, taking the last of her pig money. But the saleswoman at Saks Fifth Avenue had said they were just the thing for leisure wear and informal entertaining. Richard said he didn't care if they were called hostess pajamas, they looked just like plain pajamas to him, and what would people think of her wearing pajamas in the middle of the day. So much for gracious living.

She poured half a jar of bubble crystals into the bathwater before getting into the tub. She especially loved bathrooms, since she'd grown up on a farm without one, and she especially loved this bathroom with its pink enamel tub, sink, and toilet. There was a long window she could look out while luxuriating in the bath. Richard said she was exhibitionistic, but who could see in through the thick green leaves outside? The branches practically poked into the window. It was like taking a bath in a tree house.

She spent hours in the bathroom, either taking showers or lying amid scented bubbles in mindless ecstasy. Except today ecstasy didn't come. What had gone wrong? Why weren't they happy? Or rather, why wasn't Richard? She'd be happy if he were. She was in a city she loved, living in an apartment she loved, married to a man she loved. But everything she did to please him only irritated him.

Maybe he'd never forgiven her for coming to New York. He'd been so sweet when he'd met her at Penn Station, she hadn't guessed. And it must have been a shock to him, hearing her voice on the phone at seven in the morning saying she was in New York, when he'd thought she was in Ohio. She'd at least waited until morning to call, though. After she'd arrived at the train station, she'd sent her father a telegram, then gone out and walked for blocks, taking note of landmarks so she wouldn't get lost. The city had looked just like it had in the movies, with its tall buildings profiled against the night sky. It had been the most thrilling time in her life, seeing a city sunrise. Far more beautiful than sunrises on the farm. First, a delicate pink edging white clouds that bloomed pinker and pinker, like giant peonies, and then the sun flaming in top windows of buildings, blazing a golden path down the street, where early-morning risers made their way to work. She thought of Caesar's words in her Latin textbook: *Veni, vidi, vici*—I came, I saw, I conquered. She wasn't sure what she wanted to conquer, only that the city threw out a challenge she had to meet. She went back and phoned Richard.

Forty-five minutes later he'd arrived at the information booth, where they'd agreed to meet. He was fresh-shaven and pink-faced and puzzled. "Honey, what are you doing here?" he asked.

"I couldn't live without you," she said, and threw her arms around him. He kissed her, and she worried that the soot from her white dress would spoil his uniform.

Later, over coffee, he'd said that, of course, now that she was here, they'd have to get married, saying what she supposed was the honorable thing. And being responsible, too, he'd insisted she call her father. A telegram, he said, would be too much of a shock. It had been a terrible fifteen minutes on the phone. The telegram hadn't arrived, and her father hadn't known what she was talking about. He'd thought she was calling from Rosemary's.

They had gotten married at City Hall, along with dozens of other servicemen and their girls. The ceremony was swift, assembly-line style, so that afterward she hadn't felt married. Richard had supplied the witnesses, two of his bowling-baseball-basketball buddies from Governor's Island. She'd wanted to eat in Chinatown, so they'd gone to a Chinese restaurant there for a celebratory dinner. Richard and his buddies had agreed afterward that they didn't feel "full."

For nearly a month they lived in a barrackslike house for married officers on Governor's Island. Although Susan loved the idea of living on an island, she preferred the island to be Manhattan. Richard spent his time off bowling or playing ball and didn't care to explore New York. She took the ferry to Manhattan and went apartment hunting. It was very discouraging. Everything was too expensive and there were few vacancies, none in Greenwich Village, where she had her heart set on living. The closest she could get was London Terrace in the West Twenties, and the rental there was high—from sixty-five dollars to one-hundred-thirty. Every morning she dashed over to the officers' club to read notices posted on the bulletin board about apartment rentals. The morning she saw an apartment for rent in Greenwich Village, she jumped on a ferry, not even wasting time on a phone call.

Lucky she hadn't. Captain Mercer, who lived in the apartment, said he'd taken the phone off the hook after the first fifty calls.

"You're the first to arrive in person," he said. He stood in the doorway blocking her entrance. "You'll have to wait your turn."

Wait her turn after fifty others? It would be gone by then. "Oh, can't I just look now that I'm here? I've always wanted to see an apartment in Greenwich Village."

"Why? What do you expect to see?"

"I don't know, that's why I want to see one."

"I suppose it won't hurt to look, but it won't help," he warned. "I always keep my promises, and there're fifty people ahead of you."

Did he have to keep saying that? He was a thin man with a blond mustache who said he was subleasing the apartment for the six months he was on temporary duty in Washington, D.C.

Susan would have wanted an apartment in Greenwich Village even if it had been a hovel, but she liked this one the minute she saw the sunny kitchen with the checked café curtains and white ice-cream-parlor chairs and table, loved the living room with its fireplace flanked by bookcases, and desperately loved the wrought-iron staircase spiraling up to a bedroom and bath. Never had she seen a place she wanted more, and none had been in that glorified stratosphere of creativity that Miss Rice had raved about—Greenwich Village.

She had to win over Captain Mercer and get this apartment, but she wasn't sure how. She looked for clues among the books in the bookcase, but they were all classics, nothing she'd read: *War and Peace, Crime and Punishment, Remembrance of Things Past*. Finally she saw something she had read, thanks to Miss Rice. "Oh, you've got *Winesburg, Ohio*, one of my favorite books."

"Yes, I'm fond of it too," he said. (Thank God, she thought.) "I'm curious, what story did you like best?"

Testing her? Did he think she hadn't read it? " 'Hands,' " she said promptly, although she'd liked better the one about the schoolteacher in love with the minister and didn't know why she'd chosen "Hands." Later she was to discover that there was some lucky star guiding her whenever what she wanted was crucial, but she didn't know that now. She only knew by the responsive light in Captain Mercer's eyes that she'd found the key to his heart. "It's a beautiful, sensitive story," he said, touching the book's spine gently. He had thin, tapering fingers, tactile, like the man's in the story.

From then on it was easy. "I know this is unethical," he said. "I should let the others see the apartment. On the other hand, you respect my possessions. I can trust you."

"I'll take good care of everything. Dust your books every day, and if you don't mind, read them."

He smiled. "You're young, aren't you?"

"I'm twenty," she said, adding three years, but he thought twenty was young. She told him that her husband was older and a very responsible person.

"No children, I hope," he said, looking alarmed. When she assured him on that score, he said the rent was sixty a month.

She blinked. "Oh."

Surprisingly, he came down five dollars. She gave him the grocery money in partial payment, "so no one will take it from me."

"Oh, it's yours. But what if you husband doesn't like it?"

"He'll love it," she promised.

Richard had loved it when he saw it, but he'd been angry at the idea of her renting an apartment without consulting him, and it had taken all her powers of persuasion to get him to look at it.

The bathwater was cooling. She must go down to Richard and make things up. They'd had two months together; they wouldn't have much longer. He was doing special work that he described as being highly technical and temporary. When that ended, he'd be sent overseas. But she didn't have to go to him. He was coming to her. She heard his footsteps on the iron stairs and arranged the few remaining soap bubbles as becomingly as possible.

There was a knock on the bathroom door, and a second later he stepped in. "Not in the bathtub again! You'll shrivel up," he said, but his voice was tender.

She smiled up at him. "Come join me."

He looked shocked. "There's not room for two."

"Come see."

First he picked up her hostess pajamas and hung them on a hook. "My little messy, sexy Susan," he said, undressed, and got into the tub with her. She soaped him, kissed him, blew in his ears, and touched the tip of his penis.

"Oh, my, where did you learn these things?" he asked.

"I read them in *Sally Stewart, Student Nurse,*" she said. He gave her a puzzled look, not always sure when she was joking.

His penis emerged from the water like a pink submarine periscope, and then he submerged into her.

Afterward they went for a walk in Washington Square Park, where Italian women sat on tree-shaded benches, children and dogs romped, and men played chess, fingers to forehead, scarcely moving. Susan, ever on the lookout for bohemians, was delighted to see a woman in a gypsy skirt and peasant blouse. "Maybe she's a poet," she whispered to Richard.

Holding hands, they went to watch the children splash in the fountain pool. A small blond boy in red trunks dumped a pail of water over his head. He looked like Richard. "I want a baby, a little Richard," she said. Richard squeezed her hand. "We'll have dozens when I get back."

"No, now," she said. She didn't say "in case you don't," not allowing herself to put the thought into words. She clung to his hand as if to prevent his going.

They passed Washington Square Arch. "You know, I think someone's hiding out up there," she told Richard. He laughed. "No, honestly. Once I was here when it was just getting dark, and I saw a màn hanging around the arch, and suddenly he disappeared."

"Why were you hanging around here in the dark?"

"It was your bowling night. I went for a walk."

"Honey, please. Promise me you won't run all over town when I'm not here."

"I promise," she said, and didn't mention the lovely afternoon she'd spent sipping a martini at the sidewalk café at the Brevoort, feeling as sophisticated as a real New Yorker.

When they returned to the apartment, they made love again. This time in bed. It was a perfect ending for a day with an unpromising beginning.

In the morning Richard ate a hurried breakfast and left for Governor's Island. She went out and bought a New York *Times* and returned to the apartment. Next to exploring the city, she enjoyed most sipping coffee and reading the *Times* while listening to street noises from below. She read that Barbara Hutton had married Cary Grant and that Churchill had attended a party in his basement quarters at 10 Downing Street wearing his siren suit. Jugged hare and cherry tart were served. Susan admired Mr. Churchill and the British enormously. Every night the Germans dropped bombs on London, but the British carried on.

She turned to the help-wanted section. Richard often complained about the high rent. A job would help pay for the rent, and she'd be too busy to do what he so strenuously objected to—explore the city.

Under "Secretarial" she saw that the New School for Social Research was looking for a girl Friday. The salary was low, but you could attend classes for a reduced rate. Also, the New School was only a block away. She put on her brown-and-white-striped seersucker suit and brown-and-white spectator pumps, then combed her hair in a pompadour to look older. But by the time she arrived at the New School, her pompadour had collapsed.

She was interviewed by a Mrs. Beck in Administration. "Where did you work before?" Mrs. Beck asked.

"I just graduated this June."

"You've never held a summer job?"

Susan didn't mention haying or plowing, since they weren't required of a girl Friday. "I can type eighty words a minute and was class valedictorian," she said, also not mentioning that there were only twenty-three in her class.

Mrs. Beck had peroxide-blond hair and a button nose. Despite the fact that she wore an unbusinesslike white eyelet blouse showing an unbusinesslike lacy slip, she was all business. "Do you know anything about the New School?"

What was there to know? "It has night classes," she said.

"It's known as the University in Exile," Mrs. Beck said. "Alvin Johnson, who heads the school, is devoting all his time and energy in an effort to bring to the United States French liberal and Jewish professors to save them from Hitler's hounds. You see, a school can issue invitations, giving non-quota visas. But if these people don't have jobs promised, they won't get away. Their loss will be the world's."

"They just can't come over here first and then get a job?"

"No, they have to have the job first."

"But how can they get a job in America if they're in Europe? Why can't they come here?"

"Ask President Roosevelt. Ask the American people, who are deaf and blind to what's going on. Here, I'll give you some information on the subject."

Mrs. Beck crossed the room to the filing cabinet. Susan had the distinct feeling she'd get the information but not the job. The phone rang at her elbow. Mrs. Beck kept digging away in the filing cabinet. Susan picked up the phone. "New School for Social Research, may I help you?" She put her hand over the receiver. "It's a Miss Dorothy Willis about the job."

"Well," Mrs. Beck said, "you're certainly an enterprising young lady. Tell her the job has been filled."

Susan was delighted but puzzled. She was more at home among strangers in New York than people she'd grown up with in Ohio. Except for Miss Rice, she'd been treated with suspicion, her ideas thought silly, and she'd often felt inadequate. Here she felt she could do anything.

When Richard arrived home, she ran to the door and hugged him. "Guess what? I've got a job. Isn't that wonderful?" She told him about being able to attend classes at reduced rates and how she'd be helping to save Europe's best minds and talent from Hitler's hounds. As she spoke, she saw him grow tenser, straighter. Her words trailed off.

"I don't want my wife working. I want you home where you belong."

"But it's just a block away. I'll be home before you get back. You said the rent was too high. This way I can help pay."

"You didn't even consult me. You just went out and got it, the same way you got this apartment behind my back."

"I wanted to surprise you. I thought you'd be glad."

"You surprised me, all right. Tell them you're not taking it."

"But they've turned down others. That wouldn't be fair."

Probably they could find someone else easily enough, but she thought it best to appeal to Richard's sense of fairness. He was unmoved, however. He gave her the silent treatment. Since he wasn't ordinarily talkative, she shouldn't have minded, but she did. Instead of serene silence, this was tight-lipped tension.

In bed that night he lay with his back to her. When she moved toward him, he moved away. She stroked and caressed him. "It'll keep me from walking the streets," she said, and heard suppressed laughter. He took her in his arms. In the morning he made love to her again. She'd have enjoyed it more if she didn't have to worry about being late on her first day on the job.

The work wasn't very exciting, just typing, filing, and phone answering, but she told herself she was doing it for a cause. She had read the information Mrs. Beck gave her and admired Alvin Johnson enormously. She'd like to meet him, but he was always in Washington, D.C., trying to convince various committees of the importance of bringing refugees over, or out raising funds to cover the cost of their travel if he succeeded.

Since Richard wanted her home whenever he was, she could take a class only on his bowling night. She signed up for a series of lectures on twentieth-century literature given by Professor Jean DuPres. His lectures turned out to be more on life than literature, and he went so far as to assign homework in the form of writing essays. The class grumbled but complied. Perhaps because they were afraid of Professor DuPres. Despite his limited English, he could make devastating comments that reduced the class to quivering jellyfish. Professor DuPres justified his essay assignments on the premise that literature could be appreciated only with an open mind and open eyes, and they were to write on what they observed.

Professor DuPres worked for the Bureau of International Affairs for the New York *Courier*. In Paris he'd been a journalist on a French newspaper called *Le Monde*. He'd also taught at the Sorbonne. He was thirty-three, married, with two children. Susan knew all this because she had looked up his record in the office file.

On class night Susan ate at the school cafeteria, since Richard was out at Governor's Island. While munching a tuna-fish sandwich, she rewrote her assignment, trying to ignore the chatter from nearby tables. She'd written about the family living in Washington Square Arch. She'd been right about seeing a man disappear into the arch. And after keeping close watch, she'd been rewarded by seeing some clothes hung out to dry. One day she'd tailed the man to and from a grocery store, approached him on the way back, and said she knew he was living up in the arch. After swearing her to secrecy, the man confessed he'd moved his family into the arch when they hadn't been able to find anywhere else to live, and had stayed on because there was no rent to pay and they had no money to pay rent with.

Susan was rewriting her piece for the third time. Professor DuPres's spoken English might leave much to be desired, but his knowledge of written English was better than native English speakers'.

"Okay if I sit here?" a voice asked. From the awful New York accent Susan expected to see a gum-chewing girl dressed all wrong. She was surprised when she looked up to see a girl in coed cardigan and plaid skirt—cute, curvy, and curly-haired. No, not cute. Cute was turned-up nose and hi-there smile. This girl had a classic Roman nose and cynical mouth. She put her tray down, not waiting for Susan's answer. "I don't want to sit at an empty table and be bothered by some jerk," she said. After that she paid no attention to Susan, but ate an egg-salad sandwich while leafing through an art book that took up half the table, leaving Susan little room to write.

Susan was on the last paragraph when she heard a startled gasp beside her. "Look, isn't that beautiful?" her tablemate asked, pointing to a photograph of a tall slender building in pink and white. "That's Giotto's Tower. It's in Florence," the girl with the awful accent said. "That's also where Michelangelo's David is, the Uffizi Gallery, and where Dante met Beatrice."

Susan was impressed by such knowledgeability and could

only add that all Italy was famous for its painters and sculptors.

"Oh, I thought Italians were gangsters and garlic eaters."

"You omitted spaghetti," Susan said sarcastically, imitating Professor DuPres. The girl reminded her of Richard, whose one bad trait was to think any nationality or religion different from his automatically inferior.

"I was just being funny."

"It isn't so funny," Susan said, but didn't want to dwell on the subject. "Are you interested in art?"

"I'm studying painting at the Art Students League and going to lectures here. Our lecturer is wonderful. He's a European refugee and has been everywhere and seen everything."

"So has our professor, but he's supposed to be lecturing on twentieth-century literature and talks about journalism instead. He's a journalist."

"Why don't you say something to him about it?"

"Oh, I don't mind. I'd love to be a journalist."

"I bet you'd be good. You don't jump to conclusions. My name's Gina Sabatini."

"I'm Susan Varner—I mean Lund. I just married recently."

"Marriage—that's not for me."

Susan was amazed. Every single girl she knew wanted to get married. "Why not?"

"If I had a week's time, I'd tell you." Then, "Don't mind me, I'm just bitter. My boyfriend and I broke up a few months ago, and the longer it gets, the worse I feel."

"You still love him?"

"I hate him," Gina Sabatini said. She smiled a sad, wan smile. "Yeah, I guess I do. Maybe we could meet after class for coffee. It gets kind of lonely."

"I'd love to, except I have to get home to my husband. We could meet next week, though, same time, same place."

They met every week after that.

Susan saved up things to tell Gina she no longer told Richard, since they upset him so much. Whenever she repeated Professor DuPres's words of praise, Richard either said "Bragging again" or claimed it wasn't her mind her professor was interested in.

"Professor DuPres asked me to read aloud in class what I'd written on that family living in Washington Square Arch. He said it was an example of keeping an open eye," Susan told Gina.

Gina was as happy to hear this as if it had happened to

her. "That's funny, you know. Your teacher says you have an open eye, and mine says I have a fresh eye. I think what they mean is originality," Gina said somewhat immodestly.

"An artist needs originality, talent, and discipline. Plus perseverance," Susan said, rather proud of this pronouncement, although saying it made her a bit self-conscious. Girls talked about clothes, cosmetics, and men, not art. Because she was so unused to talking about such things, it sounded silly and pompous.

"Plus courage to believe in what you do," Gina added.

"Otherwise stated, guts," Susan said.

"Otherwise stated, balls," Gina said.

Susan was used to shocking people, but not to being shocked.

Gina talked frequently about her ex-boyfriend, Dan. "We broke up two months ago, and every day I miss him more. He got mad at me because we went to this party and I danced with my clothes off."

"You took your clothes off?" Susan asked in shock and admiration.

"Well, not everything, just my dress. It was hot, and my skirt was too narrow. I didn't see anything wrong with it. He was always talking about being a free spirit. Of course, men say one thing and think another."

"Not my husband, he's very consistent," Susan said. She'd like to tell Gina what an honest, intelligent person Richard was, to restore Gina's faith in men, but she was late for class.

When she entered the classroom, Professor DuPres paused dramatically in mid-sentence, the better to point out her tardiness. She self-consciously squeezed past knees to the nearest seat. She always chose a seat near the door, since she always left class early to be home before Richard. She felt herself blushing while she waited for Professor DuPres's inevitable sarcastic comment. She didn't have long to wait. "I am afraid I bore Mrs. Lund," he said to the class. "She is not only leaving early but now arriving late."

Titters from the class. Actually, the criticism was mild for him. He went back to his discussion of book burning in prewar Germany. "It should have set off world alarm, but few took notice. Now there will be books lost forever to history. It will not be known what they are. But what is worse is that destroying a product of the mind is the first step in destroying the mind of the human being or that human being himself. You will note I speak this more clearly than most thoughts. That is because I wrote it down because it is of the very most importance." His prim, unusually red lips formed one of his rare smiles. He was small and neat and had a small neat mustache. In his neat pin-striped suit and vest he looked like a foreign diplomat.

Just before class ended, Susan got her things together. Most of her classmates stayed on, hoping to persuade Professor DuPres to go with them to some bar or cafeteria after class. Occasionally he went. Susan wished she could have gone along at such times. She got up from her chair and headed for the door.

"Mrs. Lund, might I speak to you?" Professor DuPres called.

Was he going to scold her again? Her classmates appeared to be eagerly awaiting a display of his cutting wit, which they enjoyed when not directed at them, and especially enjoyed since she was more often praised in a class where praise was stinting. It didn't help that she was the youngest and hadn't been to college, as most of the others had been.

"Class dismissed," Professor DuPres said.

Her classmates took the hint and left with disappointed expressions.

Professor DuPres eyed her from under shaggy eyebrows that were in sharp contrast to his small neat mustache. "Always you are in a hurry. What is this hurry?"

"Oh, I try to be home before my husband. Tonight's his bowling night."

"And did you choose this class because he bowls tonight?"

She nodded. "But I was lucky. I didn't know it would be so good."

Professor DuPres appeared not to notice the compliment, but she saw a small light go on in his eyes. Even the most brilliant like to be complimented.

"You are working here during the day?" he asked. And she wondered if he'd checked her records, too.

She nodded again. "It's not terribly exciting, typing and filing, but I get this class at a reduced rate, and it's for a cause. I feel I'm helping to save people from Hitler's hounds," she said, using Mrs. Beck's phrase.

"Typing and filing, others can do, no? Reporting, this is something else. In my department there is an opening. The salary is a pittance, and there, too, is typing and filing, but also some writing. It is a job requiring training, but you will learn, I think, quickly."

Because of the phrasing and heavy accent, it took her a moment to figure out that what he was offering her was an in-training job for a reporter on the New York *Courier*. Professor DuPres wasn't aware of the cause for the delay. "I regret the typing and filing, but it will not be forever," he added.

"When can I start?"

"I shall speak tomorrow to the person in Personnel, and they will contact you. Even so, I have the final word, and I think however that my recommendation it is sufficient."

A newspaper reporter. A job she'd dreamed of. She suppressed an impulse to hug Professor DuPres, but she couldn't suppress her idiot smile. Professor DuPres extended his hand. She realized he meant to shake hands on the deal. So European. After thanking him too often, she said good night and floated out the room and down Twelfth Street toward home.

It was a beautiful October night, and a full harvest moon floated along with her. She remembered how isolated and lonely she'd felt on the farm looking at that same moon. Now, here she was in New York, with everything she wanted—Richard and a newspaper job. And Professor DuPres had chosen her over all her older, better-educated classmates. Her triumph abruptly turned to worry. What if Richard were right, and it wasn't her mind Professor DuPres was interested in? No, that was ridiculous. He might invite her out for a drink and make a pass, but he wouldn't offer her a job. She was late. She hurried. Richard would wonder what had happened to her. She wanted him to be in the right frame of mind when she told him about the job.

The moment she opened the door, she saw he was upset, but before she could explain, he drew her to him and kissed her. Had he missed her all that much? Maybe she should be late more often. He held her against him. "They came," he said. "My overseas orders. I leave tomorrow."

She felt as if she'd been punched in the stomach. That wasn't fair. Just when something good happened, something bad had to happen to ruin it. "Tomorrow? They can't send you away so soon without telling you beforehand."

"It's not their way to give advance notice. Come on, squirt, I'll fix you a drink, you'll feel better," he said, tilting her chin and kissing her. "Squirt" was what Eddy used to call her. Richard called her that in affectionate moods. "Guess Captain Mercer won't mind our drinking some of his Scotch, under the circumstances," Richard said.

He poured the liquor into two glasses, added water and ice, and handed her a glass. They sat side by side on the sofa. She leaned her cheek against his shoulder, holding the drink in one hand while clinging to his arm with the other.

"Where are they sending you?" she whispered.

"I think England. I won't know until I get there."

"You'll fall for some English girl. One of those Wrens or whatever they call them. During an air raid. You'll meet in a shelter and she'll throw her arms around you when a bomb explodes outside, and since you're over there and lonely, you'll think it's love."

"Honey, where do you get such crazy ideas?"

"It might not happen exactly like that, but it'll happen. I read somewhere that war intensifies love."

"I love you, I married you. Don't you trust me?"

"I trust you, but you always hear about men having to gratify their carnal desires."

He squeezed her to him. "I'll never gratify my carnal desires with anyone but you. Come on, let's go to bed and gratify them now."

But it wasn't carnal gratification. At least on her part. She was too conscious of the body she'd soon be separated from, and tried to memorize it with kisses and caresses. How long until they made love again?

While he slept, she purposefully remained awake, not wanting to miss out on a moment of her last time with him. But she fell asleep in the early-morning hours. Worse yet, she overslept. He woke her with a kiss. "Honey, I'll have to leave soon," he said. They made hurried love, and she fixed a hurried breakfast. She couldn't eat, but sat sipping coffee and trying not to cry.

"You'll have to get someone to rent the place," he said. "It won't be hard. All you do is put a notice on the bulletin board, it'll be snapped up."

"But I can't leave. I forgot to tell you in all the excitement last night. The reason I was late getting home was Professor DuPres offered me a job on the New York *Courier*."

"You're not taking it," Richard said softly. "You're going home."

Susan heard echoes. He'd objected to the apartment, the New School job, and now this, but he'd change his mind as he had before. "I already told him I'm taking it."

"Tell him you can't. I'm not having you here in New York alone. I don't want to be worrying about you on top of everything else, especially about some dirty Frenchman trying to seduce my wife while I'm away."

"He's not seducing me, he's offering me a job."

"He's seducing you with the job."

"He wouldn't stoop to that and risk hiring someone incompetent. It's a dream job. A chance in a lifetime. And it's so lonely on the farm. I'd go crazy there worrying about you. At least this way I'll have a job to concentrate on."

Richard looked at his watch. "We have just five minutes left. Our last five minutes. Don't spoil them for me. Promise you'll go home."

"I promise."

He took her in his arms, and they held each other. Then he was gone.

Dear Susan,

Nothing you do should surprise me after you ran away to New York, but this does. I talked to Richard's folks, who say he is very distressed. They can't understand you, and I can't either. You are worrying that poor boy to death. What if he dies on foreign soil? I'd hate to have that on my conscience.

I know I was too lenient with you after your mother died, but I tried to make up for her loss. I see now I should have been more strict. I won't mention my poor health. I guess it means nothing to you that I have to do the farmwork when I'm feeling so bad.

I can only hope you come to your senses and realize what this is doing to such a fine young man as Richard. Think of how he feels, fighting over there while you're carrying on in New York.

Your loving father,
Dad

Dear Susan,

Richard wrote you wouldn't go home after you promised him to. He said you might listen to me because you'd always looked up to me. So here's a try.

You're acting like a spoiled brat. You're not just upsetting Richard. Think of what you're doing to Dad. It's bad enough you ran away, now you won't go back and help out on the farm when he's so sick.

What are you up to in New York anyway? I

know a lot of guys from camp here go up there on leave and pick up cheap girls. You should hear how they talk about them. I'd hate to think my sister is one of them, but sometimes I wonder. Don't tell me you're staying there because of some job. I know better.

That poor guy is over there risking his life for you while you're running around having a good time. I'm ashamed of you. Now, get your tail back home.

Your disgusted brother,
Eddy

Dear Susan,

I never expected you to lie to me, to practice deceit. You gave me your word of honor you wouldn't take that job and said you'd go home, all along knowing you had no intention of doing so. And this after you trapped me into marrying you. If you hadn't run away to New York, it would never have happened. It makes me wonder if you came to New York because of me or because you wanted a good excuse to go there.

My folks keep writing asking when you're coming back. It's embarrassing to say I don't know. What I'd like to know is what's going on between you and that Frenchman. No, on second thought, maybe I wouldn't.

You'll never know how much you've hurt me. I keep wondering what happened to that sweet little girl I knew back in Ohio. Please, if you love me, go home.

Your hopeful husband,
Richard

The only cheering letter was from Captain Mercer. Cheering to her, not him. He said his temporary stay in Washington was extended for another six months. Could he put up in his place if he came to New York for a visit? He'd sleep on a couch or pay for her hotel room. He was just homesick for his apartment.

Susan wrote him and said that of course he could stay in his own bed in his own apartment. She'd sleep on the couch or stay with a friend. Gina, she supposed, would put her up for a week or two.

The other letters she shoved in a drawer, intending to answer them when she was able to rationally. Miss Rice had said she'd have to be tough and stick to her guns if she wanted to be a journalist. She tried to be tough, telling herself Richard could get shot down no matter where she was—in Ohio or New York. The Germans wouldn't shoot him because she was here. On the other hand, he might take some silly risk, or not have his mind on flying, imagining her and Professor DuPres in bed together.

But was it her fault he didn't trust her? Professor DuPres—whom everyone at work called either Mr. DuPres or Jean-Paul—took no notice of her whatsoever as a woman; his concern was that she do things precisely the way he wanted. She had a cubbyhole next to his office, where she could hear him talking to his wife every day. Her name was Natalie. Susan wasn't sure what he said, since he spoke to her in French. She was, however, taking a course in French, not to understand the phone conversations but because she yearned to speak a language that sounded like poetry.

She was also taking a course in art history with Gina, for her own edification and for Gina's sake. Her brother Giuliano had died in a sanatorium upstate, and Gina, who was so vitally interested in everything, had become completely withdrawn. Susan had had to push her into taking the course. Giuliano, Gina said, was the only person she'd ever really loved. He was sweet and gentle and on his way to recovery. She couldn't understand his sudden death. Gina didn't cry, she just looked stricken, which was worse.

With her work and her classes, Susan had little time to feel guilty about Richard. Or so she'd thought. In the mornings before going to work, she became physically ill and threw up, the guilt a kind of morning sickness. Morning sickness? She paused and looked at her pale mirror image. When was the last time she'd had the curse? And why did they call it a curse when it was sometimes a blessing? She couldn't remember when she'd had her last period. She was never good at keeping track of such things, so that when she got her period it surprised her more often than not.

She became worried. Richard had been gone for almost two months, and she couldn't remember having a period since he'd left. But maybe her nervous system had gone haywire.

She got the name of a doctor from a co-worker and made

an appointment for that afternoon. She sat tensely in a waiting room along with a mob of others looking at pictures of pastoral scenes and patriotic posters. One showed Uncle Sam's hand clamped over a man's mouth, saying, "Loose Talk Costs Lives." Another said, "Even the Walls Have Ears." Finally the nurse-receptionist called her name. "What is the nature of your visit?" she inquired.

"I want to see if I'm pregnant."

The nurse-receptionist wanted to know why she hadn't said so earlier, and told Susan to bring in a urine specimen. Susan wondered why the nurse-receptionist hadn't inquired earlier. She took in a urine specimen in a Skippy peanut-butter jar carried in a brown paper bag. She worried all the way to the doctor's office that it might spill. The nurse-receptionist said to call Monday for the results. It was Friday. Susan spent a suspenseful weekend. She told herself it would be wonderful to have a beautiful blond little Richard to look after. It would make Richard so happy. But it would also give him more reason to insist that she quit work and go home to Ohio. How could she leave a job she loved so much? Also, it wouldn't be fair to Professor DuPres, who spent so much time training her to be a good reporter.

All weekend she looked hopefully for blood on her underpants.

Monday morning she called the doctor's office at nine, only to be told the report wasn't in yet. After she called a half-dozen times, the nurse said she'd call her. The call came late that afternoon. "Good news," the nurse said. It took a minute for Susan to realize that the nurse meant she was pregnant.

Susan hung up the phone and sat at her desk stunned by the news, barely acknowledging the good-nights of her co-workers as they passed her door on the way out. When the last footsteps faded, she bowed her head on the typewriter's gray metal surface and enclosed it in her arms as she might a lover. She smelled the lovely smell of printer's ink that permeated all the offices and asked herself what she'd do now. She loved her job, she couldn't leave it. Should she write Richard and make him happy about being a father, only to make him unhappy when she refused to go home? Maybe she should go. After all, Ohio wasn't Siberia. She could always come back. But not to this job or that apartment. And she knew that once on the farm, she'd never get away. Especially with a baby.

A hand lightly touched her shoulder. "It is bad news?"

Professor DuPres. She'd thought he'd gone home, too.

"Your husband is all right?" he asked, looking concerned.

Of course, here she was acting as if she'd heard of a death instead of a life. She looked up and tried to smile. "No, just feeling sorry for myself."

"Come along, we will have a drink and you will feel cheered."

She got her coat—a new coat. Her father had refused to send her winter clothes to New York, as if she'd come back to Ohio to get them. The new coat had a fitted waist with a flared skirt. Black. Sophisticated. Since she didn't want to keep Professor DuPres waiting while she went to the ladies' room, she settled for a quick surreptitious hair-comb. She'd switched from a pompadour to wearing her hair over one eye after seeing Veronica Lake in *This Gun for Hire.*

"*Très comme il faut,*" Professor DuPres said.

"*Vous l'aime? Merci.*"

He smiled and asked where she'd learned her French. She worried then if she'd asked him did he like her coat or love her. "I'm just learning, as you can no doubt tell," she said.

They passed the city room with its rows of desks where reporters and deskmen sat about idly talking or reading. Some looked out at her curiously and nodded at Professor DuPres respectfully. They went down the back stairs, where the smell of printer's ink became stronger, and she heard the throb of running presses. The New York *Courier* was in the shadow of the New York *Times*, literally and figuratively. It was also on Forty-second Street, but it wasn't half as big and not nearly half as prestigious. Just the same, it wasn't as bad as the *Daily News.*

They went through the door and out into a street silenced by snow. Big thick flakes of the kind she'd cut out in grade school to paste on windows for Christmas decorations.

She hoped he'd take her to the bar where *Times* newsmen hung out. She'd never dared go in alone. Although some of the *Courier* staff went there too, it was like a club. You didn't go in unless you were a bona fide reporter. She was still in the lower ranks. He walked on by. Perhaps he wasn't taking her there because she was an underling. Or because it might get back to his wife.

"We will go to the Algonquin, okay?" he asked. He often used "okay" as if that made him sound more American.

"Okay," she said. Going to the Algonquin almost made up for not going to the bar. She'd wanted to go there ever since she'd read about the Round Table, where Tallulah Bankhead,

Dorothy Parker, and famous Broadway wits and newspaper columnists had gathered.

At the Algonquin, Professor DuPres led her into a roomy lounge where smartly dressed people with witty faces sat on sofas and in easy chairs. Cigarette smoke, combative smiles, clinking ice, competitive voices. Suspicious laughter. No spontaneous combustion here. It made her nervous. Since it was so crowded, they were forced to share a sofa with two others, who looked pained when they sat down.

"Would you not like to take off your clothes?" Professor DuPres asked, then corrected himself, ". . . coat?" She jumped up and foolishly giggled, wondering if that was his faulty English or a slip of the tongue. It had been a mistake to get up, for he politely stood too, reaching upward to help her off with her coat, since she was so much taller. Then she caught her wristwatch in her coat sleeve and there was a struggle before the coat came off. After that there was the problem of where to put the coat. He carefully laid it between himself and the other two sofa occupants, as if it were some kind of dividing line.

A waiter appeared, asking what they'd like to drink. "I suppose you want one of those awful gin concoctions you Americans are so fond of," Professor DuPres said. She nodded. He asked for martinis. "When in Rome . . ." he said resignedly.

Susan spilled the martini down her front. He deftly wiped at the spot with a cocktail napkin, his fingers lightly brushing her breast. She wondered what someone so French and suave and debonair must think of someone who clumsily spilled drinks and got tangled in coat sleeves.

"It is nice here, no?" Professor DuPres asked. "Not so much hurly-burly or noisy as in bars. More relaxed, as in our cafés, although during my last days there it was far from relaxed. We were very tense, very nervous, all. We have lost our teaching jobs, there is nothing to do but sit in the café and wait, wait, wait."

"For what?"

"For news that we are to teach in America. Sometimes someone comes in flashing a cablegram, we are all jealous but also happy that at least one of us escapes. Every day the situation becomes more dangerous, especially for those who are Jewish, but also for those in trouble politically. We wait through the spring, the summer, then it is October. If we are to escape, we will have to leave soon. The only escape route is by the Pyrenees, impassable when the snows come. And there is the question of our children. The youngest is then five, the oldest eight. One day I say we take them with us, my wife says no. The next day I say yes, you are right, we leave them in a Catholic orphanage where they will be safe. But my wife she says no, she cannot bear to leave them. Children survive the rigors better than adults, she says. Back and forth, to and fro. We cannot decide, but we must. It is bad for me because I am considered a political enemy, it is worse for her, she is Jewish, and then the children, what chance do they have, you see?"

The waiter interrupted, asking if they'd like something to drink. Susan was irritated. She couldn't bear the suspense of the story even though she knew its outcome, since Professor DuPres was here seated beside her replying that they would have two more martinis.

Professor DuPres didn't speak until the waiter brought their drinks, and then only at her instigation. "So what did you decide?" she asked, conscious and unconscious of the drink pinching her nose, the smell of lemon.

"We take the children. There are two others who accompany us, a printer of a radical newspaper and a resistance fighter whom the Nazis are now looking for. He is young, strong, a carpenter. We will have two guides, one French to take us to the border, one Spanish after we cross it. By the time we reach the border, things go bad. An early snow. It is cold, slippery, we cannot travel fast. My younger son he tires and has often to be carried. The older one sprains an ankle, and he too, has to be carried. The young, healthy carpenter catches pneumonia. We leave him behind at a farm.

"Our Spanish guide robs us one night and disappears. Fortunately my wife has foreseen such an occurrence and has hidden half our money in a teddy bear our youngest son has insisted on bringing along. She has taken out the . . ." Professor DuPres searched the lounge for the word.

"Stuffings?" said one of the other occupants of the sofa, who were both listening.

"Yes, thank you, stuffings," Professor DuPres said, unperturbed that his audience had increased. "These stuffings she has taken out and replaced with money. We have luck in finding an old farmer who lends us his grandson to take us the rest of the way. Even so, we do not reach Lisbon until nearly a month later. But again luck. The cablegram is there waiting. The irony is that had we stayed in Paris one day longer, I would have received it. It was sent on after we left, and went wandering around in search of us. Thank God, it found us."

Susan sank back on the sofa as exhausted as if she'd crossed the Pyrenees with them. But there were questions. She took a long sip of the martini to help overcome her shyness and asked: What happened to the carpenter who caught pneumonia? How had they managed to carry two little boys? What would have happened if the cable hadn't arrived? What about all the others in the café waiting for cables? Why was he considered a political enemy to begin with?

"You see," he said, smiling, "I have trained you to be a good reporter." Under the small neat mustache his lips touched the rim of the glass. She saw before her a hero. This small neat man in his three-piece pin-striped suit had managed to cross the mountains to take his family to safety, something that the young, healthy carpenter hadn't been able to do for himself.

The lounge was nearly empty now; even the couple sharing the sofa had left, giving them more space. But they remained seated close together. "To answer your last question first, I had done very little except to denounce Nazi doctrine in the classroom. Under a pen name, I write for a radical newspaper. That is discovered. I do not like to think what has happened to the others at the café. I do not know either what happened to the carpenter. Before my older son hurts himself, I carry my younger son. After that, I carry the older boy and my wife and the printer carry the younger one."

"Is the printer the one who printed the radical paper you wrote under a pen name for?" she asked, and wondered if Professor DuPres's sometimes fractured English was influencing hers.

"Yes, and now I must get home, and so must you."

Although the sofa pillow tilted them together at the slightest move, he had been careful not to so much as touch her. Richard would never have believed it. He was so sure that Professor DuPres was a dirty old Frenchman out to seduce her. She almost wished he were. Still, when he offered to see her home in a cab, saying they lived in the same neighborhood, she thanked him and said she would walk.

"Walk? All that distance?"

She nodded, smiled, thanked him for the drinks, and called good night. She needed to walk; she had so many things to assimilate. It was thirty-some blocks to her place. If she got tired, she could always take a subway. On the corner a Salvation Army Band played "Joy to the World." It seemed a poor choice in view of the war. She thought of Eddy playing his trumpet with the Salvation Army Band back in high school. Now he was at Guadalcanal.

She passed store windows with twinkling Christmas lights, Santa Clauses, and reindeer. The tops of tall buildings were obscured in a white mist. Her thoughts were as formless as the snow, swirling in her head, mixed with memories of past Christmases, of ice-cream hills and fir trees, of the covered bridge wearing a slanted hood of snow, and underneath, the river iced over, a white lake. She thought of her father home alone, hanging a wreath at the window. No reason for a Christmas tree with her and Eddy absent.

She was just about to step off the curb, when a car came at her, missing her by inches. She could have been killed. She and her baby. Her baby. How could she have forgotten? Sitting there tonight smoking and drinking. Alcohol was bad for a fetus. From now on it would be orange juice, fruits, and vegetables. A baby needed every advantage in life, including good health. At the Algonquin with Professor DuPres, she'd forgotten about being pregnant, forgotten Richard. How could she? Suddenly she visualized Professor DuPres crossing the Pyrenees in his pin-striped suit. She had to smile at the image. Undressed, he'd no doubt be a big disappointment. Spindly legs. Hairy. Richard had lovely long legs with blond curly hair.

She came to the Flatiron, her favorite building in New York next to the Woolworth Building. It divided the street in two. She went down Fifth Avenue toward home, and although there was little traffic, she crossed the streets carefully, conscious of the other life she carried.

When she reached her apartment, the phone was ringing. She hurriedly unlocked the door and searched for the phone under a pile of newspapers, hoping it wasn't Captain Mercer announcing he was in town. The place was a complete mess. She picked up the phone and said a hesitant hello.

"Finally. You are all right? I was becoming worried."

"Yes, except for sopping-wet clothes and frozen toes."

"You must this minute take them off and get into bed."

"My toes?" she said teasingly.

"Gently immerse the feet in warm water. There is a possibility of frostbite. You do not perhaps feel anything after those corrosive martinis. I suppose you have not eaten? No food in your house? Am I or am I not right? No hot soup? I could bring to you some soup."

"Don't worry, Professor DuPres, I have food. I'll be okay."

"Jean-Paul, please. I cannot help but worry. I am a mother hen. It is my nature to worry."

That turned out to be true.

Susan and Gina had a lonely Christmas dinner together at Gina's studio on MacDougal Street. Gina served spaghetti in marinara sauce, which Susan knew was a tribute to their friendship, since Gina wouldn't admit to a preference for anything Italian to others.

New Year's Eve they went to the movies. Susan had wanted to see *My Sister Eileen*, which was about two girls from Ohio living in Greenwich Village. Gina wanted to see *The Black Swan*, because it was based on a book written by someone named Sabatini. They compromised and went to see *Casablanca*. They both loved Humphrey Bogart.

"He reminds me of Dan," Gina said. "So goddamned cocky."

"Ingrid Bergman's husband reminded me of Jean-Paul."

"Jean-Paul?"

"You know, Professor DuPres. He said to call him Jean-Paul."

"Do you love him?"

"What a question, just because I call him by his first name?"

Gina gave her a look.

"He came over and nursed me when I was sick in bed," Susan said.

"You were sick? Why didn't you tell me? I'd have come over."

"It was just a cold. I wasn't *that* sick."

They were walking home from the movie. They hadn't planned to. At first they debated about whether to go to Times Square and watch 1943 come in, but Gina said there'd probably just be a lot of drunken sailors, so they'd decided to go to Susan's and listen to Guy Lombardo play "Auld Lang Syne."

The New Year's Eve noisemakers were becoming more frequent. Somewhere a gun went off. Or maybe it was backfire.

Susan hummed the tune from *Casablanca*.

" 'Play it again, Sam,' " Gina said. "Didn't you just love that?"

"It was so sad when Ingrid and Humphrey parted. I don't usually cry in movies, but I did then."

"Does he love you?" Gina asked.

"Humphrey Bogart? Wish he did."

"Don't play dumb."

"He says he does."

"Does he know you're pregnant?"

"He's happy about it. He loves children. He says I don't have to worry about my job, that I can find someone responsible to care for the baby, and he'll help."

"He sounds terrific," Gina said. "You'd think it was his. How does your husband feel about the baby?"

"He doesn't know. I mailed him some Christmas cookies."

Gina laughed, then Susan laughed, too, somewhat reluctantly. "I'm afraid to tell him. He'll want me to go home."

"You'll have to tell him sooner or later."

Susan nodded and felt suddenly sad and ashamed of herself. She was treating Richard shabbily. She had loved him so much, so much, and now he was the enemy. She wondered where he was tonight, how he was celebrating his New Year's Eve. As they neared the Village, they saw more and more couples bundled up, cuddled up, laughing. She felt lonely, and glancing sideways at Gina, guessed that she must, too. She walked with her coat collar up, her hands dug into her pockets, looking dejected.

"Last summer Dan and I used to walk along this street together, but it was warm. Cold depresses me."

"Yes," Susan said, suspecting it wasn't so much the cold, but the loving couples that depressed her. "Let's grab a taxi, if we can find one."

Back at her apartment, Susan allowed herself a small glass of wine in honor of New Year's Eve. She didn't think one small glass would hurt the baby. She and Gina sat in the half-dark living room listening to the Times Square celebrants. "Eleven-thirty," Susan said. "Half an hour to go."

Gina sat sipping her wine, silent and withdrawn, eyes half-closed, long dark eyelashes, a pale perfect oval face. It seemed wrong for someone so beautiful to be alone on New Year's Eve, but, of course, she could have seen Dan. She said he'd called her every day since he was home from Yale on Christmas vacation. She always hung up, stubbornly refusing to speak to him. But if she didn't care for him, why did she look so sad, and why didn't she go out with someone else? She certainly had the chances. Or perhaps she was thinking of her brother Giuliano's death.

"Do you think it's possible to be in love with two men at the same time?" Susan asked, partly to distract Gina from unhappy thoughts and partly to get Gina's opinion. "They're both so different, Richard and Jean-Paul. Together they'd be perfect. Richard has a beautiful body, and Jean-Paul a beautiful soul. Richard is a top athlete, Jean-Paul a top brain. And he's a man. Richard's just a kid. He's older than I, but he seems years younger."

"Listen, if you love him, sleep with him. You can't get pregnant twice."

"You're not half as cynical as you sound," Susan said. "You're all bravado on the outside and butter on the inside."

"Don't kid yourself," Gina said, swiping a hand at a wayward tear.

"I could say the same thing to you," Susan said. "If you love Dan, why don't you sleep with him?"

"Oh, hell, I have."

"Then why don't you see him? Why make yourself miserable?"

"We're different religions. It would never work. I'm Catholic and he's Jewish."

"I thought you said you were an atheist."

"I am. So is he. But his parents aren't."

"You're not marrying his parents."

"You sound like him. I think he just wanted to marry me to spite them."

"That's crazy. He wanted to marry you because he loves you. And he obviously still does, or he wouldn't keep calling you. He'd have given up by now."

Gina looked hopeful.

"Listen, it's almost twelve. Do you know where he might be?"

"He's at his dumb friends' party, those so-called free spirits John and Tamara."

"Call him. Start the new year right. Anyway, you're not compromising yourself wishing him a Happy New Year."

"I don't hear you calling Jean-Paul and wishing him one."

"Okay, if you call Dan, I'll call Jean-Paul. But if his wife answers, I'll have to hang up."

"I can't call him," Gina said. "I forgot, I don't know John and Tamara's last name."

"Maybe he didn't go. Call his home."

"Okay, but if his father answers, I'm hanging up, he might recognize my voice."

It was Dan who answered. Susan could tell by the joy on Gina's face. Politely refraining from listening, she went to the kitchen and emptied the ashtray Gina had used. She was greeted with a kiss when she returned.

"He's coming over," Gina said.

"Oh, good, I'll get to meet him."

"No, to my place. Now, your turn to call."

Susan looked up Jean-Paul's phone number.

"Hallo," Jean-Paul answered sleepily.

"I have an important news bulletin. Happy New Year."

"Where are you? I hope you are not drinking."

"I'm home alone and cold sober." She would be alone when Gina left.

"I will be over to wish you *Bonne Année* in person," Jean-Paul said, sounding not at all sleepy anymore.

Down below, the noisemakers were going crazy in the street.

The man on the radio reported a huge crowd in Times Square.

It was 11:59, Thursday night, December 31, 1942.

Guy Lombardo struck up "Auld Lang Syne."

Gina and Susan clinked glasses.

"*Bonne Année*," Susan said.

"Happy 1943."

13. *Gina*

They had one week, the first week of the new year. Now that they were together, she wondered how she'd been able to bear his absence. She couldn't stand being parted from him for an hour. She called in at work and said she had the flu. He called his parents and said he wouldn't be home until late. He hated leaving. She almost had to push him out the door. That took willpower.

He said home was impossible with his mother's tears and his father's sighs. "First he made me feel like a goddamned draft dodger because all his friends' sons were in the Army. Now he puts on a sad face because I quit Yale and enlisted. I can't win. I signed up because it seemed so goddamned pointless reading *Lady Windermere's Fan* when there was a war on. And I thought the Army would help me to forget you."

She loved the reason if not the result. She kissed the freckles sprinkling his shoulder.

"After we finish basic training, we get a furlough," he said. "I'll come home and we'll get married. Mom's too upset about losing her little boy to the Army to spring marriage on her now."

"She won't like me. I'm not Jewish."

"She wouldn't if you were. You're stealing her darling son."

"Your father won't either."

"Dummy, he likes you. He was very upset when you quit. He didn't know it was because of me."

"He might like me as an employee, but not as a daughter-in-law."

"Let's not talk family. Let's make our time together count. We have a lot of lost time to make up for."

They made their time count. They went to plays and museums, ate in Village restaurants, and had snowball fights in Washington Square Park. But most of the time they spent in bed under the studio skylight. Snow-covered, it gave the impression of perpetual twilight, aided by her latest paintings in various shades of gray. They argued about art and life, avoiding the subjects of war and death.

"Basically, I like what you're doing," Dan said. "It's original. But it's elitist."

She sat up in bed. "Elitist? That's crazy."

"All that gray. The working class has enough gray in their lives."

"Oh, God."

"They want bright colors—oranges, reds, purples; the ocean, the mountains, the sun. And real people, not symbols."

"They've got Norman Rockwell, they don't need me."

"See, you're a snob."

"I'm true to my feelings."

"Nuts, you feel in primary colors. You're poppies and wild roses and orange blossoms."

"Orange blossoms. You say that because I'm from Sicily."

"Oh, Jesus. You're not from Sicily, your parents are."

"Same difference."

"That's the first time you've admitted it. You deny your Italian heritage. You should be proud of it. Jesus. Dante, Leonardo, Michelangelo, Cellini, Donatello, Donizetti, Puccini, and Verdi, and you won't go near a restaurant that serves veal scallopini."

"Jesus wasn't Italian."

"Oh, you know what I meant," he said, kissing her nose.

"I'd rather have pastrami. Just because I'm Italian, men think I've got hot pants or I'm some earth mother crazy to have a bunch of bambinos. And that includes Italian men. They're the worst."

"I don't want to hear about the men you go out with."

"Did I say I went out with them? I've never dated Italian men. They're pigs. And Italian women are no better, gossipy old mamas in black calling young girls whores just because they like to have fun."

"See, you think of Italians in clichés, the way you say people think of you."

The remark silenced her. Did she? "Do I?" she asked. Then, "Maybe I do."

"Don't start agreeing with me. It's more fun to argue." He leaned on an elbow and looked down at her. "Anyway, I go through the same thing. I'm one of the few Jews at Yale. Jews are clichés, too, to people. Let's forget all this mishigosh, let's make love." He circled her breast with a finger, gradually approaching her nipple. She felt as if she were one gigantic breast filling the room, the nipple nudging against the skylight.

He took off his glasses.

"Put something on," she whispered before he entered her.

"That spoils it. I'll withdraw in time."

Their lovemaking was interrupted by the ringing phone, but only temporarily. Gina took the phone off the hook.

Later, when Dan was poking around the refrigerator for something to eat (they were always hungry after making love), the phone rang again.

"Hi," Susan said. "I hope I'm not calling at an awkward time. I was just wondering if you and Dan would like to come over for grog and blintzes."

"Just a sec, I'll ask," Gina said, and called out to Dan. "Susan wants to know if we'd care to come over for grog and blintzes."

"Susan? Who's she? Is she Swedish or Jewish?"

"Neither. She's from the Midwest and likes to try different things."

"Yeah, okay, if you want to, but let's not stay long."

"What time do you want us?" Gina asked.

"Now," Susan said.

They were surprised by the dazzle of sun on snow when they went out, assuming the world was twilight like the studio. They slid on icy patches of the sidewalk, and Dan did what he said was a swan mating dance, taking both parts, male and female, hopping about, flapping his arms, cooing and whistling.

"Do swans coo and whistle?" she asked.

"If they don't, they ought to," he said, without interrupting his dance. He was the clumsiest swan and most adorable man she'd ever seen.

Two matrons looked on disapprovingly. "Drunk at this hour of the day," one said.

"He should be in the Army," the other said. "Carrying on like that while our boys are fighting and dying."

"He is in the Army," Gina yelled. "Mind your own business, you bitches."

"Hey, Gina, honey, calm down."

"They make me so mad. They don't know what they're talking about," she said, surprised to feel tears stinging her eyes.

"Aw, come on, forget it." He put an arm around her and kissed away her tears. But she couldn't forget that today was Wednesday and tomorrow their last day together. What were they doing wasting their time going to Susan's?

"Hey, look at these," Dan said, obviously trying to distract her. He was pointing to an odd assortment of items in a display window of a store called Ye Olde Village Curio Shop.

His ruse worked. Gina was entranced by a jade Buddha with an enigmatic Mona Lisa smile. "Isn't that wonderful?" she asked.

"Want it?"

"No, it would cost an arm and a leg."

"Only an arm," he said, pulling her into the shop.

He asked the clerk if he could see the Buddha. "It's the God of Things as They Ought to Be," the clerk said, handing it over the counter.

Dan placed the Buddah in her palm. It seemed to pulse with warmth. "Things ought to be as they are at this moment," she said. "Perfect."

"I'll buy that," Dan said, to her and the clerk.

Gina protested. Dan made her close her eyes while it was wrapped. She found an ebony-and-ivory abacus that he liked and made him close his eyes while the clerk wrapped his present, too.

They arrived late at Susan's. "Good thing I didn't start the blintzes," she said. Susan towered over Dan as well as the man in a pin-striped suit whom she introduced as Jean-Paul. "Jean-Paul's family is visiting up in Vermont and he's all alone in the city," she said. Jean-Paul didn't look too unhappy about it.

Jean-Paul made the grog and Susan the blintzes. They were practically a meal in themselves, with cottage-cheese filling, sour-cream topping, and accompanied by blueberries, pineapple chunks, and bacon.

"Hey, these are terrific," Dan said, "just like the kind Mother never used to make."

They stayed until midnight, despite their intention of leaving early. Jean-Paul held them all spellbound with stories of the French resistance.

"A fascinating guy," Dan said on their way back.

"Obviously more fascinating than I am. Now it's so late you can't come up."

"I won't go home. I'll call Mom and say I'm staying over with a friend."

"You'll wake her."

"She's probably awake anyway waiting up for her darling boy."

She was awake. Gina heard his voice change from protestation to placation. Finally he hung up. "Goddammit, you'd think I was ten years old," he said, sitting with his face buried in his hands.

"Dan, go home. Just come over tomorrow as soon as you can."

"Yeah, okay."

He arrived at noon. "I'm sorry. It seemed cruel to run off while she was crying, but I couldn't bear her tears. Let's try to be happy, forget it's my last day. What would you like to do?"

"What you'd like to do," she said. So they went to bed.

"Dance for me," he said later, asking almost shyly. "The way you danced at the party. Only naked."

She put "Malagueña" on the phonograph, and suddenly became self-conscious about her nakedness, although he lay on the bed naked too, except for his glasses. To hide her self-consciousness she clowned, pretended to be Carmen, and stuck one of the roses he'd brought her between her teeth, struck a pose with her hands wreathed over her head. Then she caught the mood of the music and began dancing, throwing herself into it as she did her painting. Her body was luminous in the twilight room, the rose the only spot of color. When the record came to an end, she collapsed onto the bed beside him.

"You make the rose so beautiful," he said, smiling, then took her into his arms. She removed his glasses. Without them he looked young, vulnerable. They made love again, not so much from passion as panic, clutching, clinging, and crying out.

Afterward they walked silent Village streets, the falling snow stilling their footsteps. Discarded Christmas trees lay forlornly next to garbage cans; here and there a single strand of silver icicle glinted in the streetlight. She remembered last summer and the late-night walks they'd taken to get relief from the heat. He must have remembered, too, for he said, "Let's go to our place." He meant, of course, the pier. They met no one on the way, except a drunken sailor sadly singing "The Beer Barrel Polka" to himself.

The pier lay like a white ice floe against the crinkled black water. Holding hands, they walked across slippery planks to the spot where they'd first made love in that summer storm. "The scene of the crime," Dan said. "God, what an animal I was. I just lost my head completely."

"Oh, Dan, come on, forgive yourself," she said, slipping her hand into his in his coat pocket. "Think how accomplished you've become since then."

"I'd have to improve," he said. "You know, after we broke up, I kept thinking the real reason you wouldn't see me again was because I was such a lousy lover."

Anchored nearby was a ship, cliff-high, dark, silent, and ominous. She wondered if someday the deck would be running with blood and echoing the screams of dying men. She shivered. He opened his coat and pulled her to him.

"I don't want you to go overseas."

"Hey, don't worry. With my eyesight, I'll get a safe desk job."

"Where's that place you're going to in Texas?"

"Amarillo. Some joker said Amarillo was where they had a girl behind every tree, but no trees."

"There better not be."

"It wouldn't matter. Other girls only remind me of you. I see a girl smile, and I think Gina. After we split up, everything I saw reminded me of you. A smile, the sun, the stars. It was always Gina Gina Gina. A big bore. A pain in the neck. I told myself the only way to forget you was to be with you." He sighed. "What hurts is the time we wasted apart."

It was cold, it was late, but she couldn't bring herself to mention either. When they went back, he'd have to leave.

"I think we'd better start back," he said softly. She nodded against his chest. They returned to her building in silence, footsteps lagging; the closer they got, the slower they went.

"I'd better not come up," he whispered when they got there. "If I did, I'd never come down."

"Come up, then."

He traced her lips with a finger, kissed her. His dark eyes shone brightly. The snow lay like a white cap on his dark curls. "Parting isn't sweet sorrow, it's sheer hell," he said.

"I'll see you to the subway."

At the subway entrance they embraced for one last time; then he turned and ran down the steps. She heard the train thundering in below and walked home seeing the double track of their footsteps in the snow.

Gina returned to work at Simon Brothers', glad she had a job to keep her mind off Dan. The models called the brothers Simple and Legree. She was so pale and listless that Simple Simon, the nice brother, said she should have stayed home until she recovered.

Her painting kept her from going into a deep depression. She painted furiously those first weeks after Dan left. But no matter how exhausted she was, when she fell into bed she snapped awake and lay there yearning to have Dan beside her, remembering the salty taste of his skin and the bristly hair at the back of his neck.

He wrote often. He was miserable in the Army. He said his sergeant was a sadist, his lieutenant a fascist, and his barracks mates a bunch of illiterates. He was either being restricted to the base or put on extra duty for insubordination.

Gina sympathized, since she also hated to be ordered around. She carried his letters with her. They made him seem closer. Often she reread the parts where he wrote how much he loved her. He said he got through rough times by the memory of her dancing naked with that silly rose in her teeth, and counted on the abacus the days until he saw her again. She kept the jade Buddha, the God of Things as They Ought to Be, by her bed.

Her letters to him were stilted. Although she could handle brush on canvas, she had trouble with pen on paper. She had to curb her tendency to use underlines, capital letters, and exclamation marks—what her English teacher had called crutches. (But I feel in italics, capital letters, and exclamation marks, she'd wanted to say.)

She looked at the jade Buddha and imagined herself and Dan married and living in California in a cheerful sunshine-filled cottage with a studio and a nursery. She couldn't decide whether they'd have a little Danielle, or a little Dan, so she settled for twins, both with dark eyes and tousled curls like their father's.

In one of life's ironies, her wish came true in a way she least wished. She discovered she was pregnant. Unlike Susan, Gina kept track of her periods, and two weeks after she was late, she had a rabbit test made that confirmed her suspicion. She immediately wrote Dan, not sure how he'd take the news. He'd wanted to get married, but had he wanted to be a father? So soon?

And when would he get home to marry her? The leave he was supposed to get after he finished basic training was canceled. They gave you a leave for a death in the family. How about a birth? If he couldn't get home, then she'd have to go to Texas to marry him.

Every night she rushed home to her mailbox, only to find bills or advertisements. Not since she'd written that she was pregnant had there been one letter from him.

She told herself there'd been a mail mix-up, or that he was in the hospital, or that his fascist lieutenant was punishing him for some act of insubordination by not giving him her letters. She told herself there was nothing coincidental about her writing him she was pregnant and his not answering.

After another two weeks passed, she decided to phone him. Her voice trembled when she put the call through. She listened as the telephone operator was referred from one area to another in her attempt to locate Private Daniel Freed. The referral voices were like a cross section of America—Yankee twangs, Southern drawls, broad New England A's. Finally someone knew who he was, if not where he could be found. "He ain't around jest now," a nasal voice told the operator. "I don't know where he's at. You kin try calling back later." The operator asked when. The voice at the other end said he jest wasn't sure. Gina told the operator to keep trying. Several hours later, the operator called Gina back to report unsuccess.

Gina tried again the next night. There was the same runaround from one area to the other. This time a clipped irate voice told the operator that Private Freed was no longer assigned to the base. He didn't know where he'd gone.

Gina saw that she'd been a fool ever to believe Dan would marry her. Any man serious about marriage would have introduced his intended to his mother. All he'd wanted was a fling before he went into the Army. But why had he bothered to mention marriage? She wasn't the one who'd brought up the subject. And to think one of the reasons she'd loved him was that she could trust him. What she couldn't forgive was his making her pay the price of his not wearing any protection simply because it made sex less fun. He was selfish, inconsiderate, and immature. She was better off without him. Lucky she found out before they were married.

But she still rushed home every night hoping to find a letter, and found only an empty mailbox.

It was the last week in February. She was nearly two months pregnant. She'd have to act fast to find an abortionist. Having a baby was out of the question. She couldn't afford one even if she wanted the child of a man who'd betrayed her. A bathing-suit model couldn't very well hide her pregnancy. She'd lose her job. Even if she got another job, she couldn't work and care for a baby. Even if she wanted a baby, she couldn't subject it to the kind of poverty she'd known. She remembered that one of the models, Jody, had mentioned a girlfriend of hers who'd gone to an abortionist in New Jersey. She called Jody aside.

"Listen, a girlfriend of mine is in trouble. She's pregnant and her boyfriend ran out on her. Who's that abortionist your friend went to?"

Jody gave her a knowing look. "I don't remember, but I'll ask her," she said.

The next day Jody handed her a phone number. "When you call, ask for Mrs. Murray. Say you heard she has a fur coat for sale. Ask for the price and when you can see it. They have to be very careful, you know. They can go to prison if they're caught."

"Is he safe?"

"My friend got through it okay."

Gina called during lunch hour, when the others were out. Mrs. Murray's voice was gruff and suspicious. She said the fur coat cost two hundred dollars and she could see it Friday night. She'd pick her up at the north end of the Newark train station at nine.

Two hundred dollars? Where would she get such a huge amount by Friday night? She had twenty dollars in the bank, and she got paid Friday, but her paycheck came to only thirty-five dollars. She'd have to borrow at least a hundred-sixty, since she'd need some money to live on. Her co-workers were always broke and in debt. Besides, she didn't want to borrow from them. They'd know for sure she was going to an abortionist after she'd asked Jody for the name of one. The only person she could think of who might have that much money was Susan, who besides her salary got an allotment from her husband. Gina was reluctant, though, to call and ask for such a big loan. She hadn't even seen Susan since the night she and Dan were over for blintzes. Lucky Susan, she didn't have to worry about getting pregnant by a lover when she was already pregnant by her husband. She had a dream apartment and a dream job. But maybe it wasn't all luck, maybe Susan was just smarter than most girls. Gina would have hated Susan if she didn't like her so much.

She called her that evening. Susan made it easy for her to ask, which was maybe what friendship was all about. "You sound so depressed," Susan said. "Is anything wrong?"

"Everything. Can you lend me a hundred and sixty dollars?"

There was a slight pause, then a rush of words to make up for the pause. "Yes, sure, when do you need it? I'll have to get it from the bank."

"Friday." And because she knew Susan wouldn't pry, she told her why she needed the money. "I'm going to an abortionist."

Silence at the other end. Then, "Gina, how did this happen?"

"The usual way," Gina said dryly.

"Oh, God. I'll get the money, but I want to talk to you first. Okay if I call you back?"

Gina judged from the question that she had company. Jean-Paul, no doubt. She said okay.

Susan phoned after midnight, apologizing for the lateness of the hour. "Are you sure this is what you want?" she asked.

"I don't have a choice." Gina told about Dan's betrayal. It was reassuring, if depressing, to hear that Susan was as surprised by his action—or nonaction—as she'd been. "But he loves you. I could tell by the way his eyes followed you everywhere you went."

"He's irresponsible. He got scared and ran out."

"You're jumping to conclusions. Have you called his parents?"

"Never. They don't even know about me. They'd think I was making this up to get my hands on their money or something. I mean, his father knew how I went out with married buyers when I worked there."

"Is the abortionist safe?"

"I don't know. My friend's friend lived through it."

"I'm going with you. And when it's over, you're coming back here with me."

"I wouldn't have asked."

"I know, that's why I'm telling you."

Gina was grateful for her company. They boarded the eight-twelve train. Although it arrived in Newark only about fifteen minutes later, she wanted to be there in time. There were a lot of soldiers whose smiles Gina refused to return, a mother with a whiny child, and a loudmouthed man in an iridescent raincoat. Tributaries of water ran down the windows. Outside, the reflection of train lights and seated passengers sped along with them as if it were another train racing alongside.

Gina chain-smoked and tried not to think of the horror stories she'd heard of abortions gone wrong. She saw her rain-streaked face in the window. It was as close as she'd come to tears, she vowed.

She'd deliberately dressed cheerfully in a plaid raincoat with matching hat. She'd also worn her good lizardskin shoes that the rain would probably ruin, but she'd worn them so the doctor might think she was rich and take better care of her. She hoped to God it was a doctor and not some veterinarian.

Susan had already given her the money. It was in her purse, along with the rabbit's foot Giuliano had given her for good luck months before he died. Poor sweet Giuliano, he should have kept the rabbit's foot instead of praying to St. Francis. But last night she'd prayed, too. She didn't believe in God, but she was taking no chances. Of course, Mary Donovan would have said she was praying for the wrong thing, since abortion was murder in God's eyes.

"Do you want to talk, or don't you feel like it?" Susan asked.

"Both."

Susan smiled. "At least you've kept your sense of humor. That's more than I'd be able to do."

"That doesn't mean a thing. You should see the funny letters Dan wrote while he was going through hell. Remind me to burn them."

"Do you hate him?"

"Not half as much as I'd like to. What makes me so mad is my own stupidity. I knew you couldn't trust men. I thought he was different."

"Maybe he couldn't take the Army and being a father, too. You said he valued his freedom."

"Yeah, well, so do I, and I'm the one who's stuck."

Susan put her hand over Gina's. The train was slowing; they were pulling into the station. When it stopped, they got off and were accompanied by two GI's who tried to strike up an acquaintance.

"Get lost," Gina said furiously. They got lost.

Susan and Gina walked to the north end of the platform. Susan looked at her watch. "We've got a half-hour's wait," she said.

Gina regretted arriving early. It was cold, their only protection a slanting roof that didn't keep out the gusts of rain. Susan was shivering in her navy-blue suit. It had started out one of those deceitfully sunshiny March days that had ended in rain. Gina worried that Susan might catch cold. She was noticeably pregnant in the tailored blue suit. What if she got pneumonia and something terrible happened to her baby? Gina half-smiled at the irony; here she was worrying about Susan's baby when she was about to murder hers. No, that was just propaganda she'd been taught in her childhood. What was in her womb now was just a sightless fish swimming around.

"I should have had more sense and worn a raincoat," Susan said. She looked scared, as if she were the one to undergo an abortion. She kept looking at her watch. Finally she said, "Ten minutes to go." Gina both dreaded and wished for Mrs. Murray's arrival. She wanted to put it off and wanted to get it over with.

Each time she saw car headlights, she braced herself, but nine o'clock came and passed with no sign of Mrs. Murray. Then, out of the darkness, a car pulled up into a parking place in front of the station. Gina clutched her purse, her heart began pounding. "I guess this is it," she said.

A woman got out of the car, her face concealed by the brim of her hat, her figure by a long shapeless coat. The woman strode toward them with a mannish, purposeful stride. "At least she looks efficient," Gina said, trying to comfort both herself and Susan, but she became apprehensive when the woman came up to them and looked them over with small sharp eyes. "You're too far gone," she said to Susan.

"It's not her, it's me. She's just a friend who came along for moral support."

"She's not coming with us," the woman said.

"I won't be in the way," Susan said.

"If she can't come, I won't go," Gina told the woman.

"Suit yourself," the woman said. She turned and headed toward the car.

"Wait, I'm coming," Gina called. She turned to Susan.

"Find a restaurant or someplace warm in the station. I'll be back soon."

"Gina, don't go. Please. I don't trust her."

"I have to trust her," Gina said. She ran and caught up with the woman, who took no notice until Gina got into the front seat beside her.

The woman put the car keys in the ignition. "Where's the money?"

"You want it now?"

The woman held out her hand. Gina placed the two hundred into the open palm, and the woman's fingers closed clawlike over the bills. After counting the money carefully, she folded it and tucked it into the inside jacket pocket of a suit she wore under her coat, then started the car.

They drove in silence, the windshield wiper sweeping back and forth, smearing the rain. The farther they drove, the more alarmed Gina became. They passed gray, diseased houses with weedy, junk-littered yards, an occasional rattletrap car parked in front. The woman drove on, then stopped finally before a house with slits of light showing beneath drawn blinds. A broken window was X'd over with brown paper.

Without saying a word, the woman got out. Gina followed her up rickety steps onto a porch with the rusty skeleton of a glider swing. The woman got out keys and unlocked the door. In a small shadowy foyer she took off her coat and hung it on a hook. Gina did the same. The woman walked ahead of her into a room lit at the far end by a floor lamp with an orange shade. A girl sat hunched in a chair in a corner, her face averted. All Gina could make out was brown hair and thin fingers twisting a handkerchief.

"Sit," the woman said to Gina as if commanding a dog. "Come," she said to the brown-haired girl in a similar command.

The girl kept her face turned when she passed Gina. She had the straight formless legs of a very young girl.

Out in the foyer, the woman exchanged her suit jacket for a large white canvas apron resembling a butcher's. On it was a rusty smear.

The woman pushed the girl through a door on the other side of the foyer. The girl had dropped her handkerchief when she'd left her chair. Gina retrieved it. It was knotted and damp, with the initials CL. Gina saw a cheap green coat hanging from a hook, which she thought must be the girl's and put the handkerchief into a pocket.

In the front room she kept moving from chair to chair, like Goldilocks. One chair had a broken spring, another teetered on weak legs, still another was covered with a scratchy horsehair blanket. Peeling wallpaper and cracked linoleum. With two hundred dollars an abortion, shouldn't the place be more decent? Maybe the doctor drank up the money. No, he might be a gambler. She tried not to think of the blood-colored smear on the apron.

"It won't be long, it won't be long, it won't be long," she chanted to herself. "It's always the waiting that's so awful."

Maybe the woman was the abortionist. But wouldn't she have an assistant?

There was no noise from the other side of the door. Nothing but a clock ticking away on the mantel. Nine-thirty-five. Only nine-thirty five? In an hour's time it might be over and she out of here. She became aware of a sickening smell of grease, of gasoline. The longer she waited, the more nervous she became. She wished Susan could have come along. But at least the woman knew Susan knew who she was, in case anything went wrong. But could Susan identify her? Her face had been half-hidden by that hat. Maybe that's why she'd worn it. "Don't think of such things," Gina told herself. "You've lived through worse. Other women go through this and survive."

Outside, a car splashed by, leaving a deeper silence. The clock ticked, the rain rattled the windows behind drawn blinds.

All of a sudden there was a scream. A horrible jagged scream, as if torn from a throat. The scream cut off in midair. Gina jumped up, ran to the door, and flung it open.

The girl lay on an ironing board, her head at the narrow end. Her eyes were rolling, her hair sweat-matted. The woman in the butcher's apron had a huge hand clamped over the girl's mouth. The doctor was bent over the lower part of the girl, his sleeves rolled up to his elbows. She saw the thinning black hair on the back of his head as he bent over the girl's spread legs with a sharp shiny instrument. Her feet were thrust through metal hangers twisted into makeshift stirrups.

The doctor turned a sweaty face toward her. "Get out."

"Is she hurt?" Gina said. "I heard her scream."

"What do you expect?" the woman said. "This isn't a picnic."

"Get her out of here," the doctor said.

Gina fled back into the foyer. She grabbed her raincoat and headed for the door. Then she remembered her hat and was just about to take it when she also remembered the money. She dug her fingers into the inner pocket of the woman's jacket and got the money, snatched her hat from the hook, and tiptoed to the door, quietly closing it behind her.

Her breath ragged, she ran down the wet windy streets away from the slummy houses toward a barely visible horizon of blurred lights. Finally she was able to find a cab. "Where to?" the driver asked. Gina still heard the girl's scream in her ears. But she didn't remember which house she'd run out of. "The train station."

14. *Ilse*

She arrived at the theater, umbrella dripping and shoes wet. As she squished down the hall to her dressing room, she saw Hans ahead standing in the doorway. He placed a hand on her sleeve and led her into his office. All this was done in silence. When she was about to ask what was wrong, he put a finger to his lips and pointed to the wall. At first she was puzzled. The wall was covered with posters of stills from past performances, and to prove his patriotism, Hans had also put up wartime posters advising civilians on behavior. One showed a giant ear, under it the words: "*Achtung! Feind Hört Mit!*" Attention! The enemy is listening!

Now she was too frightened to speak. Did he mean his office was wired, that somewhere someone with earphones was listening?

She watched as he walked to the window and lifted a blackout curtain, peering out into the twilight. Rain streamed down the glass. Although it was nearly spring, cold still penetrated the thick walls, but that wasn't why she shivered.

He let the curtain fall into place and turned on the radio. The sound was weak, and he hunched over it, playing with the knob, flicking the dial until he found a strong station with what she thought was a shrill female voice, then realized was the high-pitched strident voice of a man, enumerating Germany's recent military conquests.

When Hans spoke finally, he kept his voice lower than the man's on the radio. "I don't know," he said. "Maybe this is being melodramatic, but someone's leaking information. I guess I'd rather think they were listening in than that it was one of us informing." He paused. His professorial face, usually humorous and intelligent, was grim and drawn. "They got Claus. Late last night. Or early this morning. Picked him up at his house."

Claus and Fritz were the only contacts she knew by name. They brought refugees to the theater. Generally, Ilse found Hans's nervousness calming. She let him worry for both of them. But now she found it catching. "How did you find out?" she whispered.

"His kid biked over to my place this morning. That was stupid. He could have led the SS straight to me. He said he was careful and went a roundabout way and wasn't followed. A good kid, not a superpatriot like mine. He's a Hitler Jugend too, but while other kids report on their fathers, he reports *to* his."

"Maybe he's just more devious," Ilse said.

"God, don't say that. I thought of it and dismissed it. I'd hate to believe a kid could be that sneaky, but who knows, these days? Anyway, he'd have turned me in by now if that were true."

"Or they could be waiting for you to lead them to the rest of us."

"Yes, we'll have to sit tight. I've sent word to Fritz not to bring any more people here until things blow over. It's hard to know why Claus was taken in. Maybe his neighbor informed on the late-night comings and goings at his place."

Ilse felt fear and despair. Despair that the refugees would have to be rerouted, and there were so few routes. Fear that the Gestapo would pay her a late-night visit as they had Claus. Of course, that was a terror she lived with. She never went to the door if her Czech maid, Verni, wasn't home to answer. A senseless precaution. No flimsy door would keep out the Gestapo, and they wouldn't wait until you were home to take you in. The safest place for her was onstage. At least they wouldn't haul her off during a performance. Often she expected doom to descend with the last curtain.

After leaving Hans's office, she was more nervous than ever, and jumped in her dressing-room chair when a knock sounded. But it was only the stage manager announcing she was on in five minutes.

The night was uneventful. Or so she thought. She left the theater with Hans. It was still raining. She could see it splatter in the street beyond Willy's back, where he stood at the side door waiting for them to leave.

"Willy, our faithful watchdog," Hans whispered, making a face.

Hearing their footsteps, Willy turned. "Thought you two were spending the night," he grumbled.

"You didn't have to stick around," Hans said.

"It's my job."

His job to spy on them. "You're so dedicated, Willy," Ilse said sweetly. "You go above and beyond duty."

Calling out a friendly good night, she ran across the rainy street to Hans's car, but only to wait until Hans got there, since the door was locked.

Finally she was in, sitting on the passenger side, waiting while Hans wiped the fog from his glasses and watching Willy hurry toward the corner café. His long black leather coat glistened in the rain.

"When did he get that coat?" she asked. "I've never seen it before. Do you think it's a reward for a favor to the SS? And why does he go to that café, when he cracks that awful joke about their beer? You must have heard it. A customer sends the beer to a lab for tests and receives the diagnosis that his horse suffered from diabetes."

"That's not original with Willy. It's going around all Berlin these days."

Hans was having trouble getting the Minerva started. Finally the engine sputtered to life.

"Reach in back and get a rag so I can wipe off the windshield, will you?" he asked.

"Why didn't you wipe if off before you started the car?"

"An old handkerchief. On the backseat, I think."

There wasn't a handkerchief on the backseat, but there was a pile of rags on the floor. "My God, why are you saving these?" she asked, then suddenly let out a scream. The pile of rags rose up from the floor. A pair of feverish eyes in an ancient shrunken face looked at her. "The kid said you'd help," a thin voice said, and the apparition collapsed.

Hans was leaning over, looking down, too. Ilse trembled. "Is he dead?"

Hans signaled with his eyes for her to say nothing. He must think that creature had been sent to trap them. It seemed logical. How could anyone so near death manage to get into a locked car? Especially with Willy watching from across the street.

"Feel his pulse," Ilse said, reluctant to touch the gray, grimy flesh and find it already turning cold.

"He's alive," Hans announced after groping among the

rags, "but barely. No use taking him to a hospital. They've got too many air-raid casualties to bother with some bum. I'll put him under the marquee, where he can sleep out of the rain."

"Or die. He was sent to us to be taken care of."

"Or for someone to take care of us if we do. I'll see if I can find his ID."

Hans got a flashlight from the dashboard compartment. After rummaging through the rags again, he brought out a worn cheap wallet containing an ID. "Rudi Blessner, Munich, barber, age forty-one," he read. He played the flashlight on the shrunken face. "If that's Rudi Blessner, I'll eat my hat."

Ilse looked at the photograph of a dark-haired man with a low forehead and heavy jowl. The apparition had a few wisps of thin blond hair, high forehead, and scraggly blond-red beard. "And he looks more like eighty than forty," she said.

"Okay, let's dump him."

"No."

Hans looked at her.

"He came to us for help. How can we dump him?"

Hans gave her another look, refusing to say anything incriminating before this poor old ragbag who obviously was beyond hearing. He was breathing hard, small bubbles forming on his lips. His head lay sideways, as if his neck were broken. Under the grime and scraggly beard she detected a beautifully shaped head. Exhaustion and defeat were as deeply embedded as the grime. They couldn't throw this man on the street.

"I'm taking him up to the room," she said.

"Are you crazy? Even if he is a genuine refugee, it could be a trap, someone they expect to die and wouldn't have the fun of torturing, since he's so out of it. They might be watching now, waiting for us to go into the theater before they nab us, or waiting until we conveniently take him up to the room."

She looked at the shadowed doorways of the buildings lining the street, wondering who might be standing there screened by the rain.

"All right," she said. "Go on home, I'll take him up myself."

"You know damn well I wouldn't leave you. And you can't get him up there alone. You're placing us both in danger."

"I can get him there, he can't weigh much. If they suspected us, they'd have nabbed us by now. They don't wait for concrete evidence."

Hans sighed. "Stay here and watch. If someone comes, turn on the flashlight, and I'll just leave him in the hall. I'll say I felt sorry for the poor devil."

Hans got out and went to the other side of the car, where he picked up the old man. "It's like carrying a child. He can't weigh more than fifty pounds," he said.

"Hurry."

She watched as he carried the bundle across the street, set it down while he fumbled in his pockets for keys to unlock the theater, and dropped the keys. She shouldn't have told him to hurry; that had just made him more nervous. After retrieving the keys, he took out a handkerchief to wipe off his glasses, stuffed the handkerchief in his pocket, and tried the keys again. Oh, God, I can't stand this, she thought, and was about to run over and help when he finally got the door open. He picked up the bundle and went in, kicking the door shut behind him.

Ilse rolled down the window and strained her eyes and ears looking for someone to emerge from shadows, listening for footsteps, but all she heard was the pounding of the rain and her heart.

Then she saw them gliding around the corner on bicycles. Two Gestapo soldiers in rain capes and billed caps. Perfect timing. She was about to turn on the flashlight to signal Hans when she saw it was the regular patrol who made nightly rounds of the neighborhood. But were they sent to allay suspicion? Was it mere coincidence that they arrived at this moment?

Their black rain capes billowed out as they rode toward her. One dismounted and wheeled his bicycle to her side of the car.

"Terrible weather to be out in," she said.

"Late tonight, aren't you?"

"I'm waiting for Herr Lessing. He's still in the theater." She nearly added that he'd forgotten something, but excuses would only increase suspicion. The other Gestapo remained on the driver's side of the car. Both eyed her blankly, coldly. Were they going to stick around until Hans came out and take them both in, or would one of them go after Hans and catch him with the old man?

"I am so weary. How I long for bed," she said, sighing suggestively.

It worked. Their eyes implied they wouldn't at all mind a bed with her in it. But she didn't want them to get carried away with the thought. "I don't get a minute's rest," she added quickly. "Onstage every scene."

"Must be tiring."

"It is, but it's a good play. You ought to come see it. Would you like to? Give me your names and I'll leave tickets at the box office. You can pick them up there."

They looked at her, at each other, and gave their names. Ilse said she'd be sure to leave the tickets at the box office. They thanked her, called out "Heil Hitler!" and bicycled off. She turned and watched the caped figures disappear around the corner. A minute later Hans came out of the theater and crossed to the car. "What was that all about?"

"Routine checking. It cost two tickets to the play."

"How do you know it's routine?"

"They didn't pick us up, did they?"

"Not this time," he said, getting into the car. "We're taking a foolish risk for someone who may not live through the night." Grimly he tried coaxing the Minerva to life. She leaned over and kissed him. "Thank you," she said.

"You're not welcome," he said crossly, but after the car started up, he smiled over. "I never knew in a rash moment of passion when I promised I'd die for you that you'd put me to the test."

She moved over closer. "Did you promise that?"

"I must have," he said, placing his hand on her leg. She felt goose pimples on her thigh. Was it just Hans who excited her, or the presence of danger? "Let's have another rash moment of passion," she whispered.

"Okay, but no more rash promises," he told her rather sternly.

The car coughed and chugged down the street, sounding as if it might awaken the whole of Berlin. There was no other traffic, only the headlights spraying the darkness.

Hans parked across from her apartment building, and they took the lift up to her floor. Since the lift operator was now in war work, the lift had been converted into self-service.

She unlocked the apartment and they tiptoed to her bedroom in order not to awaken Verni. Ilse undressed quickly and helped Hans out of his clothes. As always, he kissed and exclaimed over her body as if he'd just discovered it. She loved his special attentions, but tonight was eager to get on with it, and pulled him on top of her. He scarcely had time to remove his glasses. Afterward she rolled over and was nearly asleep when she felt his breath on her ear. "Don't go to sleep," he said. "It makes me feel all you care for is my body." He spoke jokingly, but his voice was plaintive.

"I sleep better when you're with me. Stay the night."

"*Liebchen,* I can't. I don't want Hilde waking in the morning and finding her father away. She's insecure enough as it is, with her mother dead. Nicolas, I don't worry about. He's so self-sufficient. But Hilde's bright and sensitive. I don't know what the hell will happen to her if I'm caught, which is what worries me more than anything else."

"I hope you're not worrying about tonight. If it had been a trap, we'd have been taken in."

"Yes, but dammit, now we've got this old man on our hands. God knows why you wanted to risk your life to save that old bag of bones. Even if he lives, he'll be too sick to escape. What does he do, just hang around in that room forever? We don't even know if he's a Jew. Maybe he's some patriotic old bum who'll squeal on us the minute he's able to walk as far as the police station."

"But he knew about us from someone. He said Claus's son sent him."

Hans sighed. "Yes, and that worries me, too. Who's been talking? Someone's talking too much—deliberately or drunkenly, it doesn't matter. It amounts to the same thing."

Hans kissed her good night. But now that he was leaving, she was wide-awake. Without him she'd lie awake all night. When she heard the door close behind him, she became scared again, both by what he'd just said and by not having him here to worry for her.

She was still awake when daylight came. She got up, put on her robe, and went to the kitchen where Verni fixed her some ersatz coffee. She nodded toward an egg and roll and begged Ilse with her eyes to eat.

At first, when Ilse had heard that she could request domestic help from a conquered country, she'd held back. It was more like having a slave than a servant. Then she reasoned that she'd treat such help more decently than others, and applied.

Verni had arrived a month ago, a middle-aged woman with a harelip, silent and hostile. She was no longer silent or hostile, at least with Ilse. With Ilse's attempts to speak Czech and Verni's German they managed to communicate. Verni showed her a picture of her husband, a surprisingly handsome man who, she said, had died before the German invasion. She didn't say "thank God," but it showed on her face. She had children and grandchildren whom she worried about.

Verni thought Ilse's apartment was "just like a movie star's," an impression Ilse had wanted to give when she'd furnished it long ago with a white baby-grand piano and gold brocade chairs. Even though she'd sold off most things to pay off Private Gertig, and the remaining furniture was now chipped and scarred, to Verni's eyes the surroundings were luxurious.

Ilse felt relaxed in Verni's presence. Away from Hans's nagging doubts, and in the morning sunshine, she was convinced she was right in insisting they help the old man. Of course, he might have died during the night. But when she went to the theater, she learned from Frieda that he'd survived. Frieda had discovered him sleeping in the secret room, and plied Ilse with questions she couldn't answer.

"Poor old soul," Frieda said, although she must be close to the man's age, if not older, "he's exhausted. And he smelled awful. Ugh. I washed him and threw those filthy rags in the furnace. He slept right through his bath. I woke him up just long enough for some hot broth. He's been without food for so long he couldn't keep much else on his stomach. Come take a look. See if he doesn't look better."

Ilse entered the shoe closet with Frieda, who removed the riding boots hiding the paneling, pushed a middle slat opening the door, and went in. The room was so small there was scarcely space for the two of them. It held a chair, a washstand, and a cot, where the man lay sleeping. His face was gray.

"See, doesn't he look better?" Frieda whispered. "I shaved off that beard. Isn't that a dueling scar? Do you suppose he's aristocracy?"

"If he is, he's certainly come down in the world."

Frieda picked up the soup bowl she'd left behind, rattling the spoon. Whispering, "We'll let him sleep," she touched Ilse's elbow and they left the room, but not before Ilse had seen the man give them a sly look from half-open eyes. She was troubled as she remembered Hans's warning that he might be some patriotic old bum who'd turn them all in as soon as he was able to walk to the police station. But old bums didn't have dueling scars. Still, he could have drunk himself into his miserable state, and what would that have to do with his politics, anyway? She decided to keep an eye on him.

The next morning she went to the theater early, before Frieda arrived. She hurried to the small room, where the man lay sleeping, and sitting on a straight-backed chair a few feet away, stared at him.

Suddenly he jumped and cried out. A nightmare. It was terrible to see, the way his eyes rolled. Sounds of terror, as if he were being strangled. She was about to call out to comfort him when he fell back to sleep. An uneasy sleep, however, with tossing and turning. She made no noise. Perhaps the necessity of being alert even in sleep signaled to his unconscious that there was another presence, for his eyelashes fluttered open and slowly his blue eyes focused on her. "Have I died and gone to heaven?" he asked.

She smiled. "At least you're somewhere safe."

He looked as if he didn't believe this, as if nowhere was safe.

"Are you really Rudi Blessner?"

At first his face was blank. Just half-awake, he probably didn't remember that name. Then he said, "Yeah."

The sleep had taken years off his face, but he was far from forty-one, Rudi Blessner's age.

"Would you like some chocolate?" she asked. By now his stomach should be able to take something stronger than broth.

"Yeah."

She gave him a candy bar from her pocket. He wolfed it down, watching her as if she might snatch it away, and furtively hid a piece under the blanket.

"It's all right, eat it. I'll bring you more."

He didn't look too convinced, but he ate it, eyeing her. "You're pretty," he said. "Beautiful. You remind me of someone."

"Who?"

"I'm a wreck now, but you should have seen me when I was in my heydey, all the ladies fell for me. But I only loved one woman all my life."

He lapsed into silence. She touched his forehead. Hot. Feverish, in fact.

She heard sounds out in the wardrobe room. Frieda? She wondered how the refugees must feel, hearing those sounds in here and not knowing whether it was friend or enemy. The door opened. "What are you doing here so early?" Frieda demanded.

"Just stopped in for a chat," she said, which sounded ridiculous under the circumstances. She left. Before her dressing-room mirror she scrutinized herself. Admit you went up there not because you're worried you can't trust him but because you're attracted to him. But why would she be attracted to an old man? No, he wasn't all that old, maybe not a lot older than Hans. Who was it she reminded him of? This woman he'd loved all his life?

She gave Hans the slip that night. Left the theater early and hid in the doorway opposite until after Willy locked up and the Gestapo bicycled by. Then she ran back into the darkened theater, groped her way up three flights of stairs and through the wardrobe room into his. Only then did she switch on the light, a small table lamp on the washstand, whose reddish shade gave his face a healthier tinge. Yes, once he must have been very handsome. His eyes opened.

"I brought you some chocolate."

"Yeah? Thanks." Again he wolfed it down, but at least he didn't try hiding a piece under the blanket. "What time is it?"

"Early, a little after eight." He wouldn't know the hour, and he might think it strange if she were paying him a midnight visit.

"Where did you get your scar?" she asked.

"In a duel. An affair of honor," he said, drawing himself up. A pathetic attempt at refinement she found so comic she nearly laughed.

"What are you doing up here this hour of night?" he said. "It's a lot later than eight."

"How do you know?"

"Listen, when you've lived like me, you don't need a watch. You're wasting your time with questions, you won't learn anything." He turned his back to her, his face to the wall, and said nothing more for a half-hour or so while she remained in the straight-backed chair; then he turned and faced her again. "You still here?"

She nodded.

"The spies always send beautiful women out to learn secrets," he said. "What does it matter to you who I am? It could get you in trouble, too."

"How did you get in trouble?"

"Aw, I was dumb. A kid, see. I got mixed up with the wrong political party."

She said nothing.

"I've been on the run for years."

"How do you keep from getting caught?"

"I keep on the move, that's how. Trains, they're good. You don't get stopped so much, like on the street. And you see the Gestapo get on, you get off. Bombs. A big help. When the all-clear sounds, you go where they've hit hardest and find the nearest church. That's where people go after they've been bombed out. No one asks questions. No one expects you to have anything but the shirt on your back. The pews are always all grabbed up, but you can sleep in the churchyard. If it's warm and you get a bit of food, that's real luck." Then he said suddenly, "What's your name?"

She caught her breath. Would it mean anything to him? "Ilse. Ilse Lach."

"That's a pretty name. Suits you."

She was disappointed. But what had she expected? "That's my stage name. My real name is Lachermann."

Still no sign of recognition. But he leaned toward her now, looking at her with eyes the same color of blue that had given her that foolish hope. "I'll tell you something."

Her heart came to a standstill. "What?" she whispered.

"I'm not Rudi Blessner."

She knew that, of course, but she also knew it had cost him a lot to make that admission. At least he trusted her a little.

"Rudi Blessner, he was some poor bloke buried under rubble. I suppose you won't come to visit me anymore now that you know I've stooped to robbing bodies."

"That's silly, I know you had to do what you did to survive."

He was always waiting for her. With his uncanny sense of time, he knew when she should be there and was upset when she was late. Although she tried to keep her visits secret from Hans, he guessed after his offers to drive her home from the theater were turned down. He was furious. Jealous. "You'll get yourself in trouble, coming out of the theater hours later. You'll get us all in trouble. What do you see in that old scrap heap? He's vulgar and uneducated. He cracks cheap jokes. He's not a Jew, I'm sure of that."

But she wasn't so sure. Not after that joke he'd told her.

"Kohn," he'd said, "meets Goldstein, see? He tells him Davisohn is dead. Goldstein, he shrugs his shoulders. 'Well, if he got a chance to better himself,' he says."

"Where did you hear that?" she asked.

"I used to tell jokes for a living. Not like that one. That's for the dying."

It was night, the stillness of the theater immense. "You were in the theater, too?"

"Yeah. I ran a music hall. Did a vaudeville act myself.

Wasn't too bad. They didn't always throw rotten eggs," he said with a sly grin.

"What music hall? Where?" she asked, tipping forward on the straight-backed chair, nearly losing balance.

"What's it matter?" he said. "I've done a lot of things."

Fool. Her questions had made him back off, draw into himself. A wary look had come into his eyes. Then he said, "I lied. I wasn't in any music hall, but the coal mines."

Her heart gave a wild leap. By covering up, he'd revealed himself. "In Essen?" she asked. But his eyes were more wary than ever. She could get no more out of him.

Night after night she lay awake trying to piece things together. What did it matter if he had blue eyes? A lot of people had blue eyes. But eyes as blue as hers? And had worked in a music hall and the mines? And she reminded him of someone he'd loved. Aunt Greta? Her mother?

If only she hadn't had to burn those letters. There might have been a clue somewhere. No use asking him what his real name was. The high point in their relationship was when he'd admitted who he wasn't. Never would he say who he was. And that dueling scar. It puzzled her. Had she heard something about a dueling scar before, or just dreamed it?

It was Verni's remark that jogged her memory. Verni was going out to do the marketing. Do the marketing—that was a joke. She was going out to stand in line along with dozens of others waiting at groceries, butcher shops, and bakeries where if you got a loaf of bran bread you were in luck. As usual, Verni put on her hat with a veil, as if she were going out to dine instead of shop.

"Verni, why dress up just to stand in line?"

"I do not dress up. I wear this hat with a veil to hide my lip hair," she said in awkward German, meaning, of course, harelip. "My mother told me to think of it as a distinguishing mark, but it is not, it is a disfigurement."

Distinguishing mark? A light flickered on in Ilse's mind. It had been in his letter. Yes, the one about the stage scaffolding falling on him! He'd had to have stitches taken, he'd said. "It left a scar on my left cheek, but it looks very distinguished—like a dueling scar."

Her head was spinning, she felt dizzy. Was the scar on his left cheek? She was almost sure it was, but maybe she thought so because she so desperately wanted it to be. She must find out. Now. It was a little after twelve. Luckily today was a matinee day. She'd have an excuse for going in in the daytime. And it would make up, too, for last night, when she hadn't gone to his room. Hans had so frightened her with his warnings, she'd stayed away.

She arrived in the secret room breathing hard, but what she saw left her almost breathless. The scar was on his left cheek!

"You could at least have brought up some chocolates. I missed them," he grumbled. Then, "I lie. It was you I miss. I was afraid something might have happened to you last night. I couldn't sleep."

His face was blurred through her tears. She stood before him crying.

"You don't have to cry just because I scolded you a little. My God, you're a regular crybaby. Ah, well, don't feel bad about it. You're like her. Sometimes our happiest hours were when we were miserable, crying together."

"Her?"

"You know, I mentioned her."

"What was her name?"

"What's it matter? She's dead. All the best people are."

Ilse picked her words carefully. "I had an Aunt Greta who died. In Hamburg. She was an actress there at the Théâtre Jardin. Actually, it wasn't a theater but a music hall. And she wasn't an actress but a dancer. In a chorus line. And she wasn't my aunt, either. She was my mother."

A deep silence, as if the world stood still.

"And your father?" he asked softly.

She took a hesitant step forward. His hands reached out, then dropped, as if he were being presumptuous.

"*Vati?*" she said, and knelt by his cot.

Timidly he touched a hand to her hair. They smiled at each other in silence; then he said in a husky voice, "So there was a reason for me to go on. I wondered why. Dying would have been so easy."

"You're just what I hoped," she said.

"Oh," he said, looking at her with shiny eyes, "you're more than I'd ever hoped."

They were both crying and laughing at the same time. As he stroked her hair and looked into her face, she had a feeling that she'd never encountered before, not even with Hans. She felt that she was completely loved, that whatever she might do that he disapproved of, he would nevertheless love her. They were united.

"Your mother," he said softly, "she lived for her visits to

you. And when they were over, she was always so sad. She could see that your sisters—your cousins, I should say—were jealous, and she always wanted to take you more clothes and dolls and things, but she knew that would just increase their jealousy and make it worse for you.

"When she came back, she'd tell me all about you. How beautiful and bright and sweet you were. What good grades you got in school. What clever things you said. But she wouldn't tell me where you were staying. Even the married name of her sister. She was afraid I'd go there to see you. I wanted to. I longed to. She gave me a picture of you. When you were five years old. You were holding a little puppy and smiling. You had bangs, and one of your socks had slipped down into your shoes."

"Oh, *Vati*, you noticed *that*? I remember the picture. The puppy was Schneeball. I called him that because he was all white and round like a snowball. Oh, imagine your having that picture!"

"I kept it with me always. Until it got too dangerous to be a Jew, and I was afraid if that picture was found on me, the Gestapo bloodhounds would try to track you down, so I tore it up. It broke my heart, but I was glad for the first time that your mother had let your sister bring you up, so that you'd be safe."

"It broke my heart to burn your letters, too. I memorized them, though, before I burned them."

"My letters? What letters?"

"The letters to my mother just before I was born. That's how I recognized you, by what you called your dueling scar when the scaffolding fell on you."

She told him then of Private Gertig's blackmailing her, and how he'd been killed in the Polish invasion.

"A snake, a worm," he said. "Only your mother would have been kind to such a monster. She was kind to everyone."

"If only she knew we'd found each other. How happy she would be. Oh, *Vati*, were you there when she died?"

"No, my love, I had long since left for Essen. At her insistence. She was so worried about me. And about you, too. Of what might happen if it were ever found out that I was your father."

"But I'm proud that you're my father."

"Oh, and so was she, but she saw the danger. Even she, who saw only the good in people, couldn't close her eyes to what was happening. For her sake, for mine, and for yours, it must never be known that I'm your father. Tell no one. Not even those two kind people who visit me up here. Promise me that."

"I promise," she said. But now that she'd found her father, she couldn't leave him, and went to the secret room at every opportunity.

"Are you really the star here? The leading lady?" he asked.

"Oh," she said. It seemed immodest to say so.

"Yes, you are. You can always tell a star. Don't ask me how, but I've been in the business and I know. Anyway," he said with his sly grin, "like father, like daughter."

She never tired of hearing stories about the music hall, about him and her mother. She begged for details, and wanted to know what his other three children, her half-sisters and half-brother, were like.

"They were more like their mother than me. Practical-minded and concerned with other people's opinions of themselves. They went with their mother to Poland.

"She wanted to go. She said terrible things would happen here, but I couldn't see it. I told her it would blow over, that anti-Semitism had always been around. Anyway, what could I do in Poland? I'm German. I speak German. My wife, she was a Pole to begin with. Her brother was there, so off she went with the children. To Warsaw. I don't know what's happened to them. There's no address where they could write me, and when I wrote them, I could never be sure my letters reached there."

Shyly he stroked her hair. "My little Ilse. That's some kind of miracle we found each other, but please promise to tell no one I'm your father. And I must leave. The longer I stay, the more dangerous it is for you."

"No, don't. Stay, please, *Vati*. They've taken this man in—this Claus. And Hans said it wasn't safe to have anyone else for a while, that we must lie low. It would be even riskier for you to leave. Besides, I want you with me."

Hans was jealous. It hurt her to hurt him, but her father had told her to tell no one he was her father. Every night, Hans asked to take her home, and she refused. He was sure her father was her lover.

"I can't see what you see in that man," Hans said. "He's old enough to be your father. I'm getting him out of here. You're being reckless running up to that room all the time, putting us all in danger."

"There's only one thing I want before I go," her father said. "I want to see you onstage."

She knew that was dangerous, but she couldn't refuse him. Or herself. She wanted him to see her onstage.

She got a ticket for him in the fifth row. Not too far back, but not too near the front, where Hans looking out from backstage might spot him. Fortunately Frieda was out sick with the flu, and she could search in the wardrobe for a proper suit. She found a suit, old-fashioned, going back to the twenties, but since everyone wore old clothes, that didn't matter. She bought a special tie for him, however. A blue tie with tiny red figures. When she took the clothes to him, his face lit up. The next time she saw him, he was wearing them, preening before the mirror.

Now that he'd regained his health, their resemblance was so striking that she was amazed Hans hadn't noticed. Frieda might have if she'd been there.

The big risk was for him to get downstairs to the auditorium, but once there, he'd be lost in the crowd. He walked back and forth in the small room all day so he wouldn't be dizzy from lying on the cot. When the time came, she went up to the room and led him out through the wardrobe room and down the iron stairs. It made her nervous the way he kept looking around at everything, even though she understood that after so many weeks in one room looking at the same four walls, it was a treat to see something else.

When footsteps sounded in the hall, she turned to warn him, but he'd already melted into the shadows. It was one of the stagehands, who said hello and gave her a curious look for being up in this part of the theater, but he went on.

"*Vati,*" she called softly after the stagehand was out of hearing distance.

Her father stepped out of a narrow niche that she'd have sworn he wouldn't have fit into. He knew far more about how to disappear than she.

On the dressing-room floor, she directed him to the back stairs leading to the auditorium. This was as far as she could accompany him. But she quickly ran backstage and peeked through the curtain. A few minutes later she spotted him mingling with the audience, appearing completely at ease.

It was she who was uneasy. She wasn't sure whether there were more SS men and Gestapo in the audience than usual or whether she was aware of them because of the danger they presented. Not only that, there he was in the fifth row sitting with an SS officer on each side, as if he were their captive.

Hans came up from behind.

"What are you doing lurking out here?" he asked. "You'd think it was opening night and you were counting the crowd."

"I was looking for someone I didn't want to see," she said, a remark that he found sufficiently like her to accept. She took his hand. "Come along with me to the dressing room." She was afraid if he looked out he'd spot her father in the audience and be furious that she'd taken a new risk.

In the dressing room, she kept dropping and spilling things as she made up. "My God, you are nervous—you'd think it *was* opening night," Hans said, and in a way, it was just as exciting.

Although she was bored playing the part of Gisella, the country cousin, tonight with her father watching she played Gisella as if she were playing Ophelia, giving it her all. She glimpsed his beaming face in the audience and was more thrilled by his approval than she'd have been by the severest theater critic.

At curtain call the audience responded with cheers and foot stampings. And there in the fifth row, clapping harder than anyone else, was her father, showing pride and delight. She threw kisses, aiming one directly at him. Both of the SS men at his side thought the kiss was meant for them.

After the final curtain, she rushed back to her dressing room to take off her makeup and put on her street clothes and hurry up to the secret room to join her father. At first she was scarcely aware of the commotion in the hall. Then, a minute or so later, there was a sharp rap at the door. She barely had time to slip into her dressing gown before the SS barged into her room.

She hoped the cold cream on her face hid her fear. "What is going on, please?" she said, pretending indignation. "Don't you see I'm dressing?"

They didn't bother to answer. There were a half-dozen of them, and they went over her room inch by inch, pulling aside the carpet and inspecting the floor, tapping the walls. Blood pounded in her ears. She tried to console herself with the fact that they couldn't have found her father or they wouldn't be inspecting her room so minutely. But they knew there was a room, or they wouldn't be searching. She heard similar noises coming from the adjoining rooms, so that she knew those were being searched, too. Questions whirred in her brain. Had her father gotten back to his room? What had brought the SS here tonight? Who notified them? Only she and Hans and Frieda knew, and Frieda was out sick. Perhaps Claus had broken down under torture and confessed.

Finally the SS officer in charge gave a slight bow. "I regret the interruption, Fräulein," he said, and they left. Not the theater, but the dressing rooms. She could hear the bootsteps out in the hall. It sounded like an army.

Quickly she tied the tasseled belt of her dressing gown and went out. She was in time to see them going up the stairway, the dim lights casting broad-shouldered shadows on the wall as they stomped up. Soon she heard the trample of feet overhead in the prop room, and knew it wouldn't be long until they climbed up that short flight of iron stairs to the wardrobe room.

What if her father had forgotten to lock the door to the wardrobe room? Or, worse yet, not put the riding boots back in place as he closed the door to the secret room? She assured herself that her father was very careful about such things. But his mind might have been on the play tonight instead of on what he was doing.

Others had joined her in the hall: Hans; his assistant, Helmut Bruer; the whole cast of *Country Cousin*; the stagehands; and Willy.

"What happened?" they asked each other. "Why are they here?" "Are they searching for someone?" No one dared to ask the soldier who stood at the foot of the stairs blocking the way with a rifle.

And then Ilse heard it. The rattle of iron steps as they went up to the wardrobe room. She glanced at Hans. He looked as impassive as one of the SS men. Would he have reported her father out of sheer jealousy, intending to get revenge on the man he thought was her lover? He might have casually mentioned to Willy that he'd heard some strange noises upstairs. Willy would take it from there. Hans's conscience would be clear; he hadn't actually squealed, and his remark to Willy would put him above suspicion. No, Hans wouldn't do such a thing. No matter how jealous, he wouldn't incriminate her and Frieda. But he was upset because he thought she no longer loved him. And Frieda was out with the flu. Had he warned Frieda to stay away?

Suddenly an SS officer came down the stairs and demanded the key to the locked room above.

Hans stepped forward. "I'm very sorry, but that's the wardrobe room, and the wardrobe mistress who keeps the key is out sick," he said.

Ilse could have kissed him. She was deeply ashamed of suspecting him earlier. But Hans was putting himself in jeopardy. Willy knew Hans had a key. Did she imagine that flicker of light in Willy's eyes?

Of course, such things as a lack of keys didn't bother the SS. A minute after the officer went back upstairs, there was a loud rush of feet and the sound of crashing wood as the door gave way.

Ilse stood cemented to the floor. In a minute they'd break down the shoe-closet door, too. And after that? She pictured her father, frail in his blue suit, being yanked from the room and shoved down the stairs in a swarm of soldiers. The end for both of them. Her father wouldn't talk, but that didn't matter. Obviously someone had. Certainly her frequent trips to the wardrobe room had been noticed and would be mentioned.

Suddenly Hans was beside her. "Leave," he whispered. She knew he was thinking the same thing. But she couldn't leave without knowing if they'd found her father. Besides, her departure would arouse suspicion.

"At least get dressed," he pleaded. She squeezed his hand.

Dear Hans worried about the impropriety of her going out into the street in her dressing gown. Surely even the SS would give her time to put her clothes on.

After an eternity, the SS came back down the stairs. Her heart outpounded their boots, and the sound of their steps was even louder than when they'd gone up. The stairway shook under the impact. She strained to see without appearing to look, dreading what might be seen. Was her father with them, hidden by those brute shoulders? They were not in the big hurry they'd been in going up. They swaggered arrogantly, but it must have been to disguise defeat. They had nothing to show for their trouble. Her father was safe. She tried to hide her relief. Willy's small eyes in his beery face were darting about, but they kept homing back to Hans.

15. *Gina*

The night they came back from Newark, Susan insisted that Gina stay at her place. It was torture to lie still in bed so that Susan could sleep, when she wanted to fling herself about in her anguish. If I'd only gone through with it, it would be over now, she told herself, and hated her cowardice in running away.

In the morning, Susan tried tempting her to eat a big breakfast, serving bacon and eggs and buttermilk biscuits. Gina was tempted by the smell of bacon but wouldn't let herself eat. If she deprived the fetus of nourishment, it wouldn't develop so fast.

"It's not too late," she told Susan over coffee. "I can still ask around and find someone."

"You don't want to go through another night like that."

"If I'd gone through with it, the whole thing would be over."

"Maybe for you, too," Susan said. "Consider yourself lucky."

"That poor girl, I wonder how she is. I'd have called the cops, but when I thought of it, I was too far away and couldn't remember the house." Susan nodded. Gina realized she was being repetitious; she'd already said that several times. "There has to be a safe abortionist somewhere. Other women go through abortions and survive."

"Gina, there are worse things than not being married and having a baby."

"Yeah, you can say that, you're married," Gina said. Then, "I'm sorry, you've really been a good friend. It's just that things seem so damned hopeless. Oh, god damn Dan, how could he do this to me? I'll never go near another man again. Oh, hell, I'm sorry to be such a crybaby."

Susan put a hand over hers. "It's okay, I know how you feel."

But Susan didn't, she couldn't. Gina left early to be alone with her misery. It was a short walk from Susan's place on Thirteenth Street to hers on MacDougal. The rain had stopped sometime during the night, but it was a gray, blustery March morning.

She entered her apartment building and stopped off to pick up her mail. Suddenly her heart leaped. Inside the mailbox were letters. She couldn't tell how many. Her hands shook as she unlocked the box and took them out. V-mail envelopes.

Clutching the letters in a damp hand, she hurried through the foyer door and nearly fell over a mop bucket in the hallway.

"Hey, you're tracking up my clean floor," the super yelled.

She scarcely heard. She ran up the stairs to her apartment, telling herself on the way not to be a fool and get her hopes up. He's writing to tell you he knows the kid isn't his.

Heart pounding, hands trembling, she sorted the letters according to postmark dates, although she wanted to rip open the first one she came to. There were four, each dated a few days apart. The first was postmarked February 23. Almost three weeks ago. Just long enough for her letter telling him of her pregnancy to reach him. She tore open the envelope. The writing was crammed on the page, the paper so thin and ink so blotchy it was hard to read.

> Gina, my love,
>
> I've been going crazy ever since I got your letter telling me the news. What drove me really nuts was, I didn't get your letter until after we'd been restricted to base before shipping out. We weren't allowed to write or make phone calls. I'm writing this on a troop ship. God knows when you'll get it. I hate like hell to think of what you're going through. If only I'd insisted on our getting married before I left.
>
> You must have thought I'd deserted you. When my goddamned sergeant told me with a fat smile on his fat face that some girl had been calling me from New York, I could have shot him and then myself. He's Regular Army and the war is his oyster. The trouble is, he should be on the other side.
>
> Darling, I hope this letter doesn't arrive too late, that you haven't done anything drastic like going to someone. Please, please, don't. Something terrible might happen to you, and anyway, I want that baby with all my heart. I know I've made stupid remarks about being trapped with a wife and kids, but that

was when I was young and immature. It's the thought of you two that's kept me going.

After I finish this letter, I'm writing my folks and telling them about you and our baby so you'll have their support. I'm also making out my allotment checks and GI insurance to you (if I can). I love you, I've always loved you, I will always love you. I don't have to tell you to be brave—you're the bravest kid I know. Please write. Often. Tell me every move our baby makes, the first stir, that first kick. It will be my way of being there.

Love forever,
Dan

She saw the wet splotches making the ink run before she realized she was crying. She read the other letters through tear-blurred eyes. He begged her to write, wondered why she hadn't. He wrote mostly of her and the baby. He said when he got out of the Army he was going to write a novel exposing the Army instead of the garment industry.

After rereading the letters several times, she called Susan to tell her the good news. "I'm so ashamed of myself for thinking he'd run out on me. I should have known better."

"God," Susan said, "just think if you'd gone through with that abortion."

"I'd rather not."

She'd no sooner hung up than her phone rang. "Gina?" A man's voice, sounding familiar. "This is Dan's father. We just got the news. Honey, it's the same to his mother and me as if you two kids were married. You've got our one-hundred-percent support. We both want to see you as soon as we can."

Gina promised to go over for dinner the next day. After he gave her the address, she wrote Dan telling him how much she loved and missed him, telling him everything except about the abortionist. She wrote a happy letter, not wanting to worry him. Her heart contracted when she wrote his APO address on the envelope. Where was he going? Maybe he'd already reached his destination. God, keep him safe for me and our baby, she prayed, wishing there were a God to hear.

Despite Mr. Freed's friendly phone call, Gina was nervous about meeting prospective in-laws when already pregnant and without Dan along for moral support. She dressed carefully. She didn't want to look too pretty or showy. The trouble was, all her clothes were bright-colored and on the flashy side, except for one or two equally inappropriate sexy black cocktail dresses. She found a gray suit in the back of her closet and put it on, adding a green Robin Hood hat for a bit of color. She looked as if she were going for a job interview.

She took an IRT subway train to 116th Street and walked downhill toward the river. The Freeds lived on Riverside Drive. The building was a big gray stone mausoleum with gargoyles and grillwork.

She entered a vast marble lobby, her footsteps echoing on the freshly waxed floor as she walked to the elevator. The only furniture was a long table holding a vase of lilacs reflected in the mirror above. Gina tilted her hat in the mirror and tried a smile before the elevator arrived. The operator took her to the twelfth—and top—floor.

The minute she rang the doorbell, the door was opened by Dan's father, as if he'd been waiting behind it. He greeted her warmly, pumping her hand, and introduced her to Dan's mother, who looked more like Dan's older sister. She was trim and pretty, with curly brown hair and brown eyes, and wore a bright-flowered showy dress of the kind Gina had avoided.

"We were just bowled over by the news," she said, her eyes lighting momentarily and speculatively on Gina's flat stomach. She looked as if she either didn't believe Gina was pregnant, or if she was, that her son was not responsible.

Mr. Freed behaved with a nervous hospitality, simultaneously urging Gina to sit down and make herself at home and to admire the living-room view. Impossible to do both at the same time, since the furniture faced away from the window. Gina went to look at the view. Down below was Riverside Park, and across the river, the Palisades. It was a view similar to that she and Dan had seen outside the Cloisters, except on the opposite side of the George Washington Bridge. Funny, how things happened so fast. Back then, she'd never dreamed she'd be here in Dan's home with his parents, pregnant with his child.

"If you lean out a little farther, you can get a really wonderful view of the bridge," Mrs. Freed said. Gina saw enough of it without leaning out any farther. The temptation to push her might be too much for Dan's mother, who must be disappointed in her son's choice. She came from a Lower East Side slum, not a respectable middle-class family. And she was Catholic, not Jewish. Of course, she wasn't religious, but Mrs. Freed didn't know that. Italian meant Catholic. Had Mr. Freed mentioned to his wife how Gina had gone out with married buyers at work?

"What would you like to drink, Gina?" Mr. Freed asked. "Scotch, bourbon, gin, rum, or rye?"

She said Scotch. She said it more to make him feel at ease than because she wanted one. She'd have preferred soda or fruit juice, but he was so anxious to please.

When Mr. Freed asked Mrs. Freed what she'd like, she said she was having apple juice and would get it herself. She returned a few minutes later with her apple juice and a platter of deviled eggs, followed by a maid carrying a tray of cheese and crackers. The maid wore a frilly apron over a black dress like a maid in a cartoon of the *New Yorker* magazine.

The living room was large and luxurious, in cream and cranberry. Gina had a feeling it had been done by an interior decorator, since everything was so perfectly matched: cranberry sofa with four chairs, two cranberry, two cream; cream-colored walls; cranberry wall-to-wall carpeting; cranberry drapes with cream tiebacks. Silver candlesticks with cranberry candles on the top of the baby-grand piano. (Why not one cranberry candle and one cream? she mused). She couldn't imagine Dan amid such perfection. Mr. Freed looked un-at-home in his home, wearing a suit with a carefully knotted tie. At work he generally never wore a jacket, and his tie was either loose, crooked, or both.

Mrs. Freed daintily sipped her apple juice and urged Gina to try the hors d'oeuvres on the coffee table. Although the coffee table was scarcely a foot away, Gina couldn't reach it without getting up. She'd sunk too deep into the cranberry chair, only her toes touching the floor. She felt like a midget.

"Well," Mr. Freed said, smiling, "you two kids really pulled a fast one. I didn't even know you were seeing each other."

Gina nodded. "We didn't want anyone to know at work."

"How long *did* you see each other?" Mrs. Freed asked. "You couldn't have known each other for very long."

"Long enough," Gina said defensively, then regretted it. That sounded like long enough to get pregnant, and how long did that take? "All last summer," she amended. "Then we had a big fight." The Freeds looked interested, but Gina hurried on. "I don't remember what about, something dumb," she said, not wanting to mention it was about her dancing publicly in her underwear.

"So then you made up," Mr. Freed said helpfully, accounting for his son's part in her pregnancy, which his wife appeared to doubt.

Gina nodded again. "So then we made up."

"May I ask when?" Mrs. Freed asked.

"New Year's. He kept calling when he was home for Christmas, I mean Hanukkah," Gina corrected, realizing too late she should have said for the holidays." No one said someone was home for Hanukkah. It pointed up her consciousness of religious differences. "Anyway, he kept calling, but I wouldn't see him. He said if I didn't, he'd join the Army. I thought he was kidding, so I said go ahead, that's your business. Then New Year's Eve I called him and he came over and we saw each other every day before he left."

Mrs. Freed looked angry and triumphant. "I told you there was some girl behind all this," she said to Mr. Freed. "Didn't I tell you? Didn't I say it was some girl?"

"Now, Francine . . . now, honey," Mr. Freed said.

"I am not just some girl," Gina said.

"Now, Gina . . . now, honey," Mr. Freed said.

"And I told him he'd be sorry if he enlisted in the Army. Didn't I tell him? I told him to go back and finish his schooling. And now look, there he is on a troop ship going to be killed or crippled for life. Naturally, he wouldn't listen to me. After all, why should he, I'm only his mother. And now, look. Look at this mess he's got himself into," Mrs. Freed said. Her face caved in, and she started to cry.

"It's obvious who you mean by 'mess,' " Gina said.

Mrs. Freed paid no attention. She just went on crying.

"Now, Francine . . . now, honey. Now, Gina . . . now, honey," Mr. Freed said.

Gina felt sorry for him, caught between warring camps, but she didn't feel the least bit sorry for that old bitch. She arose from the chair with as much dignity as she could muster, quietly set her glass on the coffee table, and very politely thanked Mr. Freed for the drink. "I'd better be going," she said.

"Gina, honey, you can't go. You're staying for dinner," he said.

In answer, she headed for the door.

"Gina . . ." Mr. Freed said, trying to stop her. But he shouldn't have, for between sobs Mrs. Freed called out, "She doesn't give one damn about dinner or Dan or anything. How do we know that baby is his? How do we know she's even having a baby?"

"You don't," Gina called from the doorway. "And you never will, because you'll never get a chance to see it."

She didn't bother with the elevator, but ran down twelve flights of steps and out into the street.

Mr. Freed called that night to apologize. "I'm sorry, honey," he said. "Believe me, so is Dan's mother. She didn't mean what she said. You have to understand, sweetheart, how upset she is."

"I understand only too clearly," Gina said, and hung up.

Mr. Freed kept calling. He said she was just like a daughter to him. He said he worried about her alone and pregnant. She couldn't work much longer, could she? Come live with them. Their home was her home. Dan loved her, that was enough for him.

Gina said she was doing perfectly fine by herself, thank you.

The visit to the Freeds was a joyful occasion compared to her visit home. First she telephoned to make sure her father was out; then she went over. She thought it best to tell her family she was pregnant so they wouldn't suddenly see her with a big stomach. They'd have to find out sooner or later. The minute she stepped through the doorway, she was depressed. The place looked as if it hadn't been cleaned since her last visit. The same dusty religious pictures, the broken-down furniture strewn with dirty socks and underwear, the smells of grease and garlic. She suddenly remembered the cranberry-and-cream perfection of Dan's house.

Her older brother, Vince, and her two kid sisters were home, her other two brothers out. Her mother wore a faded flowered housedress. Her graying black hair was in a loose knot with strands of hair escaping at the sides. "Mama, can I speak to you in private?" Gina asked.

Immediately her mother looked distressed. Any news was bad news. "Now what?" she said, and went out to the kitchen, Gina following.

"Now, Mama," Gina said when they were alone, "I don't want you to get excited, but I think you should know, I'm pregnant."

Her mother let out a wail that brought Vince and her sisters running. "Mama, what's wrong?" Vince asked.

"Oh, my God . . . oh, my God," Mama said, "what did I do to deserve this?" She started wailing again. The others looked at her.

"I'm having a baby," Gina said.

Her little sisters appeared shocked and scared. Vince raved. "Who's the father? I'll kill the son-a-bitch he don't marry you," Vince said. Once, Vince had been a nice-looking kid.

Now he looked like what he was—a small-time hood working for a big-time gangster. His wavy hair was brilliantined, his eyes shifty. He kept a cigarette, lit or unlit, in his mouth at all times. He wore a striped zoot suit.

Gina wished she hadn't said she was pregnant. Even though she felt only contempt for Vince and hatred for her father, she pitied her mother and worried about her sisters.

"Just gimme his name and lemme talk to him. He don't marry you, he'll be floating faceup in the East River," Vince promised. She'd have laughed at that in a movie, but in real life it made her shudder. He was acting a part, but he was also what he acted. She didn't let him know she was scared. "You'd have to go to war to find him," she said. "That's not your way. Your way is no one has a gun but you."

"Maybe he'll be killed," her kid sister Angela said. Gina knew the remark was meant to placate Vince, but she found it hard to forgive, all the same.

"Listen, I love him and I'm having the baby, and who he is is between him and me. Everyone else can go to hell," she said.

"Whore," a voice called. Her father stood in the doorway. "Get out of here, whore. And stay out. You bring shame to your family. Set a bad example for your sisters."

Gina turned to face him. "You say that after what you tried? To use me to pay off Don Guidetti? It was you who wanted to make a whore out of me, and you know what that makes you."

"Liar," he said. "Whore," he repeated. He limped forward, his face tight as a fist, his fist ready to hit her. He would have if she hadn't ducked. But it wasn't her father she was afraid of. It was Vince. She got out fast. At least her sisters knew now what she'd been trying to warn them of.

For weeks afterward she expected Vince to exact some sort of strange justice, either to contrive to cause a miscarriage or to choke the father's name from her. She even made up a phony name in case he caught her. Franco Russo. A nice Italian boy. She checked the phone book to make sure there was no such person, just in case Vince tried to murder him. She was wary when she went out, and careful whom she opened the door to. But there was no sign of Vince, and soon she relaxed.

At work, the mean Simon brother, whom they'd nicknamed Legree, told Gina she was getting fat and better diet if she wanted to go on modeling swimsuits. She admitted she was pregnant. He was surprisingly sympathetic and said she could stay on and do office work. In her off hours, Gina spent her time painting and writing long letters to Dan. Sometimes on sunny Saturdays she went to Washington Square Park with Susan. Susan's baby was due in July, Gina's in September.

Susan looked lovely and serene knitting away on the park bench with leaf shadows freckling her rosy face and full-blown body. Actually, she was nervous and jumpy and had taken up knitting not just in the spirit of approaching motherhood but to keep from smoking. She paid so little attention to her knitting, however, that her child would have to be born a three-armed freak to wear the finished sweater.

Gina enjoyed sitting and chatting with Susan while watching small children at play in a nearby sandbox. "Just think, this time next year our kids will be playing there, too," she said to Susan. She felt a deep contentment carrying Dan's child. It brought him closer. Not everyone was as sympathetic as Mr. Simon about her being pregnant and unmarried, though. She received cool looks from her neighbors, which she ignored, and walked about in proud defiance.

In a way, Susan had more problems than she. It made Gina glad to be rid of Dan's family and hers. "I don't know what to do," Susan said. "I either get pathetic letters from Richard pleading with me to go home to Ohio, or else angry ones ordering me to. Then my father writes and begs me to come back. Then my brother, Eddy, writes and tells me what a rotten thing I'm doing and how it's my fault if Richard is killed. He's coming here when he gets leave soon. I just know what that's going to be like. But that's not all. Jean-Paul wants me to marry him after the baby is born."

"What about his wife?" Gina asked.

"Good question. He says he'll get a divorce if I do. That's crazy. I can't divorce Richard when he's risking his life on bombing missions. I told him if he isn't happy with Natalie he can get a divorce, but not on my account. He says that's my way of shirking responsibility. He says he loves her but can't live without me. Oh, God, you don't know how lucky you are not having people trying to run your life for you."

"I was thinking that a minute ago," Gina confessed.

"Sometimes I think, to hell with everybody. The baby is who is important. And my job. I'm not leaving that until the very last minute."

She didn't. In fact, she went into labor in her office around six in the evening when she was working late. Luckily Jean-Paul was working late, too. He called Gina the next morning and told her about it. "It's a *jeune fille*," he said as proudly as if he were the father.

When Gina arrived at the hospital during visiting hours, Jean-Paul was there, too, beaming happily. The nurse didn't seem to be sure whether Jean-Paul was the baby's father or Susan's. Jean-Paul appeared to be far happier than Susan, who eyed the docile infant in her arms apprehensively. "Poor little thing," she said.

"Why do you say 'poor little thing'?" Jean-Paul asked indignantly.

"Because I'll make a rotten mother, the way I'm a rotten wife."

"That is nonsense. You are a rotten no one. Please to not worry, I will make a good mother," he said with a smile.

Gina suspected he would, at that. She was struck by the contrast between his high position on the newspaper and his sentimentality.

"What are you calling her?" Gina asked.

"Laura," Susan said. "I thought of naming her after you, but I don't want her to feel she has to be a copy of anyone else—even me."

Gina had just returned from the hospital and was unlocking the door when she heard the phone ringing. She rushed to answer it. "Gina, this is Dan's mother," a voice said, and then began crying. Gina listened, not knowing quite what to say. "I'm sorry." Mrs. Freed said, "I can't help it. We just received word about Dan. He was killed in action." She went on talking, but everything in Gina came to a stop. She listened, or rather kept the phone to her ear until finally Mrs. Freed hung up; then she hung up, too. Somewhere outside, a bird sang. Gina wanted to strangle it.

Gina had two comforts: the baby who grew in her womb and the hate that grew in her heart. She nourished both. She saw no one, not even Susan. She ignored the Freeds' pleas when they called. Once she lay perfectly still in bed listening to Mrs. Freed's voice begging her to be let in while she hammered at the door.

Often at twilight Gina went over the last days she and Dan had spent together, picturing the snow on the skylight and their lovemaking in slow motion. She felt his breath on her neck, tasted the salty sweat on his shoulder. She thought, too, of Giuliano. There was the same sweetness and love of life in both of them, and because of this, they were dead. If you were gentle and life-loving, you were destroyed. She'd learned that a long time ago when her father had tried to hand her over to Don Guidetti. Her mistake was in forgetting.

She was returning from the grocery when she saw the letter in the mailbox. A V-mail letter. Dan's. She nearly fainted from happiness. Alive! The Army had messed up, saying he was dead. Just as Dan said they always did. Only, this time she blessed them. It was a miracle. All the time she'd been mourning his death, he was alive.

Gina fumbled with the mailbox key, finally got the letter out, and stared at it through tears. It was then she noticed the postmark. July 21, 1943. Weeks ago. Before she'd got that call from his mother. Her joy vanished. The letter had been written before he was killed.

She walked heavily up the stairs, hanging on to the banister, her legs leaden, the baby in her belly weighing a ton. Inside her apartment she collapsed in a chair by the window, letting the letter lie on her swollen lap. Maybe she should tear it up. What good was a letter from the dead?

Later, she wasn't sure when, but just before the outside light became too dim to read by, she opened the letter and looked at the words without comprehension, as if they were written in a foreign language. Then, slowly, she read:

> Gina, darling,
>
> How are you, my love? And our kid? Listen, this sounds crazy, but I've got a trip planned for us. We're coming back here after the war's over. I want you to meet the people who saved my life. Sicilians yet. You know, your relatives you've always hated? Okay, maybe not your relatives, but they're mine. Their name is Tedesco. There's irony there—I know you know that means "German" in Italian. If it weren't for them, I wouldn't be alive now writing this.
>
> I thought I was done for, hiding out behind some rocks on some hill, surrounded by Germans and dead GI's. Then this little kid, a boy of about eight, came up, saw me, and wandered off. I thought he thought I was dead. Except people—especially kids—steal anything when you're dead, and this one just walked away.
>
> That night they came and got me, carried me to their place. I was only half-conscious. I didn't know what the hell was happening. It was a big family—husband, wife, kids, uncles, aunts, cousins,

grandma, grandpa (I don't think they all lived there, just visited). They fed me, nursed me, hid me at great risk to themselves. Later, when I was well enough, I showed them your picture, told them my wife was Sicilian, too. It wasn't a big lie. After all, you will be someday. They just assumed you were my wife anyway, and my Italian wasn't so good I could have set them straight.

Darling, I've changed, in case you haven't noticed. I've grown up, looked death in the face. When you do that, you don't whine anymore about how lousy people are or tough life is. Life is a gift. There are those who love and cherish, and those who hate and destroy. It's better to love, even if you look like a fool. Or are one. Even if you lose, you win. Tell the kid that, okay? I'm going on patrol tonight. Maybe my luck won't hold, but I was lucky enough to learn this. *Ciao.*

Love forever,
Dan

Gina pressed the letter against her womb as if to engrave it there. Then she got up and went to the phone. "Mrs. Freed," she said, "this is Gina." And she began to cry.

16. *Ilse*

The alarm shrilled. Ilse groped for the clock on her night table and stilled the noise before it awakened Verni. Sleep-groggy, she lay in darkness wondering why she'd set the alarm for this ungodly hour. As soon as she remembered, she jumped from bed and hurriedly dressed, throwing on her black winter coat, although it was late spring. Black to match the night. Black to match her grief. She would have only minutes to say good-bye to her father.

She'd wanted to see him after last night's performance, but Hans had said that was impossible. He was right. She could no longer wait across the street for Willy to lock up and leave. Not after she discovered that Willy, after locking up, waited too. She'd seen him one night cross the street and hide in a dark doorway only a few feet from where she was hiding. It would have been funny, if it hadn't been so grim. She waited for him to leave, while he waited for her to arrive. Of course, he didn't know it was her he waited for. Lucky that she'd seen him and that he'd chosen another doorway. It had been a good hour and a half before she'd worked up courage to leave. When he was busy lighting a cigarette, head bent, fingers cupping a flame, she'd slipped away, nearly having heart failure when she'd accidentally kicked a stone that noisily rolled across the pavement.

After she'd told Hans about Willy, Hans had taken up a post where he could watch Willy watching the theater. Sometimes, Hans said, Willy crouched on the doorstep and fell asleep on the job—Hans could hear his snores—and he usually left before dawn. It was the time to get Rudi Blessner out of the theater, Hans said. They couldn't wait for the SS to come back and discover him. Someone had talked, that was clear. What wasn't clear was who or how much.

"I've made arrangements for his next stop," Hans said. "If Willy dozes off or leaves early, we'll go tomorrow morning. If not, it'll have to be delayed, but we can't put it off much longer."

They spoke in low voices in her dressing room, Hans nervously picking up and putting down objects on her mirrored tray, not aware of what he was doing.

"I'll take him," Ilse said.

Hans set a box of powder down so hard that some swooshed out. "No, I am. Don't look so suspicious. Frieda will be along. You can trust me. I'm aware you two are lovers. I don't know what you see in the man, but then, I never knew what you saw in me. I think, though, you've deluded yourself, as I deluded myself with Eva, confused sympathy for love. And guilt. Mine was personal. When Eva fell apart, I blamed myself. Yours is general. You see what Germany has done to the Jews, and you want to atone for your country's sins by loving this pathetic man. But you don't even know if he is a Jew. Your affection is misplaced. He's a vul—"

"Don't you dare criticize him."

"Sorry. Maybe it's jealousy, but I don't see how a beautiful, talented, intelligent girl like you—"

"Hans, will you just shut up for one minute and listen? He is not my lover. He is my father."

Hans shut up. Behind horn-rims, his eyes widened with incredulity, then shone with joy. Joy because she was a Jew?

No, of course not. Because Rudi Blessner wasn't her lover. She told him about the blackmail, the letters from Max Kramer, the "dueling" scar that made her realize Rudi Blessner was her father. Not in that order. She backtracked, amended, stopped for words or ran them together while Hans interjected "My God" with a dozen different intonations. "So you see," she said finally, "finding him was my dream come true."

Hans embraced her. "Ilse, *Liebchen*, if you'd only trusted me and told me all this before. How much grief you'd have saved me. But I'm thinking about myself—it's you we have to worry about. You see, I was right about saying I'd take him, even though I didn't know. You couldn't possibly. What if you got caught? They'd immediately assume he's a Jew and find out you are, too."

"How? No one knows but you two. My father would never tell."

"You're forgetting your family. Lach-Lachermann. It would be a simple matter for the SS to track down your parents and ask questions."

"My so-called parents," she corrected. "They'd never breathe a word. The shame of having harbored a little Jew. You don't know them. Or my sisters. But they probably aren't even aware of who I am."

"My dear, darling Ilse, please listen. It wouldn't take the SS long to get your parents to talk. They'd merely hint to your father he'd lose his bakery. They'd threaten torture. But, they'd say, all will be well if you admit the truth. They'd promise silence, that no action would be taken if the truth is told. Believe me, the truth would be told. You're taking no more chances."

"I'm at least going to see my father to say good-bye."

That Hans could not talk her out of.

As she crept down the back streets of the city, Ilse wondered why she'd never thought of the threat of her family before. Not until Hans mentioned it. After all these years! Was it because she'd pushed them so far back in her mind they'd ceased to exist? Of course, they mightn't have been aware of the fact that Greta's illegitimate child had a Jewish father. But as Hans pointed out, if she got caught with him, they'd tell who her real mother was.

Either her eyes were becoming accustomed to the dark or else it was lighter now, the roofs of the buildings—what roofs remained after the bombings—emerging in the night. Hurry, she must hurry. She had so little time to be with her father.

Had scarcely seen him since the night the SS had made their search. And during those short periods there were no longer smiles and jubilation. Her father was uneasy, urging her to go, although she knew he wanted her with him. He was right to worry. All the same, she chattered about that dream time when the war would be over and he'd live with her and Hans and, who knows, maybe grandchildren. His eyes brightened. Like her, he was an optimist.

After seeing her and Hans together, he'd caught on how they felt about each other, although from habit, neither she nor Hans ever displayed any special signs of affection around others. Her father admired Hans, and Hans, now that he knew the man he'd worried about wasn't a lover, found remarkable qualities in her father.

Ilse was just a few blocks from the theater when she heard the shouts. She couldn't make out the words, but the harsh intonation frightened her. A second earlier she'd been perspiring in her winter coat; now her whole body was icy. Her ears picked up more sounds as she hurried forward—motors running, car doors slamming. And suddenly, shattering the night, a barrage of gunfire. She stopped as if she'd been shot, a cry frozen in her throat.

Slowly, carefully, she made her way forward, clinging to the sides of buildings as much for support as for cover.

When she went around the corner, she saw the theater's facade lit up by the headlights of military vehicles. A group of soldiers stood in a circle, faces shadowed by visored caps. They were looking down at the pavement. Ilse inched closer, although she felt a chill of presentiment that made her want to run away. And then she saw, between the black boots, a body sprawled in blood. A boot shot out and kicked at it. "Get rid of this."

The circle broke up. Two soldiers, one each taking an arm, dragged the body in the blue suit along the street, then hurled it into the back of a truck.

Ilse felt a hatred so intense that it blurred her vision. And also pride. It had taken so many of them to kill him off—big, healthy men armed with rifles and machine guns pursuing one small, sickly, unarmed, courageous man. But how had it happened that they'd found him? And where was Hans? It was time for him to arrive. What if he walked into their waiting arms?

Then she became aware of the near-silence. All of the military vehicles had left except an official car and the truck with her father's body. And now the car was pulling away. As it passed, she caught sight of a glint of glasses in the backseat between two visored caps. Recognized that professorial profile. Hans!

Life no longer mattered. She watched as the truck started up, and wanted to run out and throw herself in front of its wheels, to be run over or shot down. But what if neither happened, if she were grabbed and taken in like Hans?

The truck rumbled off. Now the silence settled in as complete as her despair. She stood in the doorway, uncertain of what to do or where to go. Then slowly a shadow separated itself from shadows. At first Ilse didn't recognize the bent, creeping figure so different from the upright, brisk-stepping Frieda she knew. Ilse waited until Frieda neared the doorway, then softly called her name. Frieda turned. When she saw Ilse, she threw her arms around her, her tears dampening Ilse's cheeks. "Oh, my God," Frieda whispered. "Did you see?"

"I . . . Not . . . What?" Ilse said, having trouble with words.

"It was very strange, very peculiar," Frieda said, still whispering. "I got a call a few hours ago. From Hans, or so I thought. 'Come to the theater,' he said. 'We're leaving earlier than planned.' I said I'd be there right away. But something bothered me. It didn't sound quite like Hans. Well, I thought, it's just a bad connection. Then my cat got out just as I was leaving. It took me about five or ten minutes to find her and lock her up. Thank God.

"Just as I got near the theater, I heard some low voices, saw a cigarette hidden in a hand, and all those cars and jeeps. My God, I thought, I'm surrounded. So I very quietly tiptoed back a couple of buildings and hid. None too soon. A minute later the theater door swung open, and there, caught in the light of a flashlight, was Hans, blinking, glasses crooked, all messed up, hustled along between two soldiers. Right behind him was poor Rudi, escorted by what looked like a whole army. I don't know how he managed to break away, but he did. Of course, he didn't have a chance. Someone yelled, and all hell broke loose. Suddenly, headlights everywhere, soldiers running from all directions, firing, wonder they didn't kill each other. Too bad they didn't." Frieda was crying again. "You saw what they did to him. And now they've got Hans. You didn't get a call?"

"I don't know, I left early."

"Find out," Frieda said. "Your Czech, call her, she'd know."

"What does it matter? I'll find out when I go home." What did anything matter?

"No, call now. There's a phone booth on the corner. Maybe it works. Go see, call, and come tell me. I'll stay here. You shouldn't be seen with me. It's dangerous. Maybe they don't know about you."

Ilse went to the phone booth. Miraculously, the phone worked. She called her number, half-expecting an SS man to answer. Frieda was right to insist she call. This way, she'd know and not go back. But it was Verni whose sleepy voice she heard. Ilse asked if she'd received a call. Verni said she hadn't.

Ilse found Frieda waiting. "No one called."

"Go home, then, you'll be all right. So will Hans. Don't worry."

Poor deluded Frieda. Even Hans admitted that he'd be unable to withstand torture. He wouldn't be able to hold out long. But perhaps he'd claim to be the only person in on the escape route, protecting them. Or would he be so terrified, he'd mention everyone? Ilse didn't particularly care about herself, as long as she could manage, like her father, to get herself killed instantly. She had no reason now to live. But Frieda, despite her age, enjoyed life. "What are you going to do? They'll be looking for you. If that person impersonating Hans called, that means they know."

A sly look appeared on Frieda's tear-ravaged face. "Don't you worry about me. You just go home, and if the SS asks questions, you know nothing. Now, I have to go, it's getting late."

"Where to?"

"That would be telling," Frieda said. She kissed Ilse goodbye, then patted her cheek. This time Frieda was once again walking briskly and soldier-straight.

It was dawn by the time Ilse reached her apartment. Verni was still sleeping. Ilse went to her room and lay down in her clothes, knowing sleep was impossible. She should be packing and running, but she was overcome by apathy. Now that Frieda had got a presumably safe hiding place, Ilse even wished that Hans would confess so that he wouldn't be subjected to torture. She lay in bed trying to think of some quick, painless way to kill herself.

When she heard the pounding on the door, she opened her eyes, less surprised that they'd come to get her than that she'd slept. But it was Verni rapping at the door saying it was time to get up and go to the theater.

"But what time is it?" Ilse asked out in the kitchen. "It can't be noon yet."

"You received a call to report to the theater at eleven. I did not want to wake you."

"Who called?" she asked, suspecting the same kind of trap as that set for Frieda. Perhaps everyone at the theater was going to be taken in.

Verni had written it down. "Herr Bruer."

"Oh, Helmut," Ilse said with relief. "The assistant director. That fool. Now that Hans is out of the way, he's going to bully everybody."

She was right: Helmut was swaggering and bullying. But he hadn't called them in, the SS had.

Ilse was last to arrive, and joined the others waiting outside Hans's office, where one by one people were being taken in for questioning.

"What's going on?" Ilse asked her co-star, Gunther Wald. Gunther didn't reply until Helmut had gone to the far end of the line checking off names. "I'm not sure. Hans is suspected of something, however. He was taken in last night."

"For helping Jews escape," said Erica Blount, who was the mother in *Country Cousin*. "But it wasn't him. I was here when Helmut got the phone call and overheard him talking to that SS man in Hans's office. It was Frieda. She admitted everything, then turned on the gas. A neighbor smelled it and found her, but too late. She left a note confessing everything. Silly old woman, no better than a Jew herself."

Ilse bit her lip to keep from saying anything, turned her head to hide tears. Brave, wonderful Frieda. She'd done it to save Hans. To save her.

"I don't see why we can't wait in our dressing rooms," Gunther Wald said, his handsome face petulant.

"Orders are to remain here," Helmut Bruer said. "And to remain silent."

"My God, I hope when Hans comes back he puts that stupid nincompoop in his place," Gunther said. "Remember what an ass-licker he used to be? Now listen to him."

"Don't count too much on Hans coming back," Erica Blount said darkly. Ilse wondered if Erica, who'd had some run-ins with Hans lately, had caught on to something and reported him out of spite. Or was it Helmut, who saw a way of becoming director? Or Gunther Wald, protesting too much? She knew from now on she'd suspect them all.

One of the stagehands came out of Hans's office looking

confused. It was the same stagehand she'd met in the hall the night she was taking her father to see her performance.

"May as well go in and get this over with," said Gunther.

"No, you wait," Helmut said. "You next," he told Ilse.

Why her? She'd been the last to arrive. Because of her position in the theater or because she was under suspicion? She tried to collect her wits before going in. She must say nothing to make things worse for Hans. Frieda had killed herself to save him; the least she could do was to convince the SS of his innocence.

She opened the door and went in. A blond SS officer squinted at her through a monocle, then stood up from behind Hans's desk. After an exchange of "Heil Hitlers," he extended his hand. "Fräulein Lach? I am Captain Rohr. So delighted to meet you. I've seen *Country Cousin* three times. All because of you."

"Oh, how wonderful. I like to think it brings cheer to our brave men at the front so they go back and fight with renewed determination after seeing it."

"And after seeing you, to fight for pure Aryan womanhood," he said.

Was he being ironic? The blackout curtains were pulled back, and the full glare of the sun was in her face so that it was difficult to see him except for the glinting monocle. He ceremoniously poured her a cup of coffee from a silver pot on a hot plate that would ruin Hans's desk. Ilse took a sip. Real coffee. So long since she'd had any. After lighting a cigarette in a gold holder, Captain Rohr leaned back in Hans's chair. "I suppose you do not know what this is all about?"

The fact that he wasn't using the usual SS scare tactics put her even more on guard. The best thing to do was openly admit what he knew she knew. "I heard Herr Lessing was picked up and is under suspicion of some kind."

"It is not suspicion. It is fact. He was hiding Jews here in this theater and sneaking them out under everyone's nose."

"Hans? But he despised Jews. He often told me so."

"You should not be so foolish as to believe everything you are told."

"Oh, but I . . . Hans wouldn't lie. I'd have been able to tell. I know him."

Captain Rohr's smile circled his cigarette holder. "Yes, I am aware that you know him quite well," he said, stressing the "know" to imply its biblical sense.

She went along. "Of course, we never really discussed politics. There was the theater and . . . well, other things."

"Including his wife?"

How did he mean that? Including the fact that his wife's murder had triggered his actions? Or merely to imply a married man was trifling with her affections? Safer for her to assume the latter. "He didn't talk much about her except to say she was quite mad and in a mental institution. That's why we could never marry."

Captain Rohr gave her a pitying look. "His wife is dead. She's been dead for years."

Not for years, for a year, but this she pretended not to know, playing the part of a woman wronged. She put down her coffee cup. "Dead? But why is it he never told me?" Was she carrying this too far? Everyone in the theater knew she was dead. But Captain Rohr flicked cigarette ashes onto the floor as if it were an ashtray, while curbing a smile. Obviously he was enjoying too much being the bearer of ill tidings to wonder. For a long moment he was silent. Was he waiting for her to blurt out information now that she'd discovered Hans's deceit? What could she say that was harmless yet indicate she'd fallen into Captain Rohr's trap. "And all this while I believed him. Why, do you know, he had the nerve to suggest I visit a *Lebensbun* to be impregnated by a soldier of superior stock?"

"Was that such a bad suggestion?" Captain Rohr asked.

Ilse knew she'd gained a point for Hans, never mind at her expense—she could take care of that. "Fine for an ordinary peasant girl, but I am neither ordinary nor a peasant."

Captain Rohr nodded. "And could therefore help our Fatherland by producing infinitely superior stock. You should be glad that Herr Lessing did not suggest marriage, otherwise you might have become the mother of a little Jew. There is reason to believe he is of that inferior race."

"Hans a Jew? Impossible. I'd have known. I can smell Jews. They have a particularly rank odor." It was a particularly ridiculous theory that Ursula propounded.

"How very interesting that you say that. I know someone who is of the same opinion. But perhaps Herr Lessing cleverly hid his scent with a strong cologne. Then again, there is a remote possibility that he's not a Jew, although it is rumored that the man he was hiding was a Jew relative of his. Do not worry, dear Fräulein. We will learn the truth. Of course, since you were innocent of his origins, you would not be punished for keeping his company. It would, however, benefit you and us if you reported anything you might remember that would help our investigation."

"I can't think of anything at the moment, but then, I didn't suspect anything. From now on I'll keep my eyes and ears open. Only, I'm sure Herr Lessing isn't . . ." She swept her arms to indicate she'd prefer not even to use that hateful word. ". . . what they say."

Captain Rohr smiled skeptically. "That we shall soon see."

God, that Hans would be punished because of her. Certainly he looked the popular conception of Jew, while she and her father fit the popular conception of Aryan. Hans would smile at this paradox as he smiled at all life's ironies.

Captain Rohr had risen to indicate she was dismissed. She promised to pass on any helpful information she might think of.

"It wasn't so bad after all," she told Gunther Wald, who appeared to be a nervous wreck from waiting.

"I'm glad to hear that," he said. "I was beginning to wonder if they were going to haul you in, you were there so long."

The rest of the day, Ilse kept a cheerful smile painted on her face like a toy whose battery had died. Helmut Bruer made himself obnoxious before the night's performance, insisting on changes he considered more effective. After the performance he strolled into Ilse's dressing room.

"You might have knocked," she said.

His blond hair was so heavily pomaded that it stood up like porcupine quills, reminding her of Private Gertig. He was staring at her. Ilse, discovering her robe had slipped to uncover a shoulder, quickly covered it.

"Too bad about Hans," he said with a smile that showed he far from felt it was. "Who would have thought . . . ?" He let the sentence trail off, as he had a habit of doing.

"Nothing's been proved."

"They caught him with a Jew."

"Maybe it was a setup job. Maybe he didn't know who the man was. After all, with Frieda's confession . . ." Ilse, shut up, she told herself. It doesn't matter what this idiot thinks, and you might let something slip.

"Oh, you heard about that?" he said, eyeing her suspiciously.

"Hasn't everyone?" she asked, shrugging.

"Old fool," Helmut said. "She was always so crazy about Hans, she'd do anything to save his neck. As would some others." He was standing behind her chair, looking at their reflection in the dressing-table mirror, smiling at what he saw.

"I've got a new idea. A play I've always wanted to do. *A Soldier's Dream*. Have you heard of it?"

"It's scarely new. It was playing when I came to Berlin nearly ten years ago."

"A good play. A smash hit."

"A terrible play. Hans and I left after the first act."

"Naturally, he wouldn't like it. It was patriotic. He never fooled me as easily as he did some people. I've suspected something fishy for a long time," he said. He slipped his hand under her robe onto her bare shoulder.

"Hands off, please."

His hand remained. "I'm running things now," he said, running his hand over her shoulder to prove it.

She jumped up from her chair, spilling a bottle of perfume in her hurry to get away from him. "You couldn't run a flea circus. Stay away from me if you don't want to be fired."

His eyes darkened. "Who's firing me? Your lover? He's not coming back."

"How do you know?" she asked, sickened by his words and the pervasive smell of perfume.

"Because I was put in charge by order of the head of the state theater himself. Dr. Goebbels. Do as I say, or you might be the one who's fired."

"Too late, I'm leaving. As of now. Get out of here so I can get dressed."

"Better think twice. You'll soon be back here begging for your old job back. No one's going to hire you after they hear about Hans."

His teeth showed in a mirthless smile before he left.

She told herself he was lying. That Dr. Goebbels wouldn't have appointed him director. That Hans would be back. That even if he weren't, she could still walk into any theater in Berlin and get a job. But she knew how gossip made the rounds in the theatrical world, and that of course everyone knew Hans was her lover, just as they'd soon learn, as Helmut Bruer said, that he'd been taken in.

She hurried out of the theater. She'd have liked to go up to the secret room to see if she could find some memento of her father, but it would be too risky now. Willy wasn't at the door. Maybe he'd decided he didn't have to keep watch, since Hans and Frieda had gone.

She came across the Minerva several blocks away. It was on a side street where Hans must have parked it last night before going to the theater. Looking at it, she felt a sudden ache, remembering the happy times she'd spent with Hans.

She carried a spare set of keys, since Hans was always losing his, and decided she'd take charge of the car until Hans returned. If he returned.

She had just unlocked the door and was about to get in when headlights bore down on her. An engine purred softly. It was the von Frisches's blue Mercedes. The back door swung open. "Get in," Ursula said in a whispered command. Ilse hesitated. "Quickly, I have news of Hans."

Ilse jumped in, and the car moved on. Ursula flung her head back and laughed. "I thought that would get you in here," she said.

"I can always get out."

"Oh, no, you can't, we're going too fast."

Ursula's small black eyes peered at her from a beaky face. "Actually, I didn't lie. Freddie's found out some things from his SS friends."

"What?" Ilse said, her heart speeding as fast as the car. "Is Hans all right?"

"He's waiting back at the house. He'll tell you."

"Hans?"

"Oh, my, what hope in that word. No, Freddie, of course."

She wondered if it were a trick on Ursula's part to get her to her place. But Freddie, after all, might have found out something. The car went swiftly and silently down the streets. Ursula put a hand over Ilse's. "Poor pet, how you must miss your Hans."

Ilse shook Ursula's hand off. Ursula merely laughed. My God, I've become prey to everyone without Hans, Ilse thought. First Helmut, now Ursula, who next?

They were on the outskirts of Berlin before Ursula spoke again. "Who was that Jew Hans was hiding?"

"He wasn't hiding anyone. It was Frieda. She wrote a note of confession, then turned on the gas."

"Oh, that. It's obvious she did it to save Hans. They even caught him with the Jew. He was hiding him up in a little room behind the wardrobe room."

Where had Ursula learned that?

"Who was he?"

"Don't ask me, you're not the SS."

"You speak as if the SS were the enemy," Ursula said.

Ilse sighed to imply boredom. "Everyone's been asking me questions today. I'm sick and tired of being cross-examined."

"Poor pet," Ursula said, and put a hand on Ilse's leg. Ilse removed the hand. Ursula placed her hand farther up on her thigh, and again Isle removed it. It was like fending off a schoolboy.

Now they were in the country of castles, of trees, hills, and winding lanes. The von Frisches's castle looked like a black cutout against the moon-silvered lake.

As soon as the driver stopped, Ursula opened the door, and grabbing Ilse's wrist, pulled her up the walk and through the front door, as if she were taking her prisoner. Inside, the impression was intensified by the gloom and dungeon dampness. No one was around. Probably Fritz, the old butler, had retired for the night. Ursula's face, eerily white in the shadowy room, had a sly gloating expression that made Ilse even more wary. "Where's Freddie?" she asked.

"In the nursery. Come along, we'll go up and see him."

"Nursery?" Ilse asked, wondering if she'd heard correctly.

"Oh, you know Freddie, he's just an overgrown child."

Ursula lit a candle. "It is so much trouble turning lights on and off with the blackout, candles are simpler," she explained.

Ilse followed Ursula's black-caped figure up the stairs and down halls lined with portraits of dark-eyed, small-eyed ancestors, who looked like birds of prey, suggested perhaps by the batlike shadows the candlelight threw on the ceiling or sent winging along ahead of them. The route was complicated, the halls as many as in a dream. "I'd need a blueprint to get out of here," Ilse said. Ursula gave a laugh that chilled her. Perhaps she was deliberately confusing the route so that Ilse couldn't find her way out.

At the end of a long, narrow corridor Ursula opened a door and stood back for Ilse to enter. The candlelight suddenly paled in a glare of lights. Freddie, wearing a frayed silk dressing gown, was down on his knees running a toy electric train. A wonderful train complete in every detail, with a bell on the engine, passenger cars, open gondola cars carrying tiny glittery pieces of coal, and a caboose. The track wound through a replica of the Rhine Valley, past toy villages complete with churches and gas stations, and toy farms with toy cows, pigs, and sheep grazing in fields, and an occasional windmill. Toy boats and barges sailed on a blue-painted Rhine.

Freddie pushed a button, and from a watchtower a figure leaned out and waved a red flag, while a crossing gate of red-and-white-striped boards appeared on each side of the passing train. Then he pushed another button and stopped everything. He turned shining eyes up to Ilse, batted long lashes. "Isn't it wonderful?" he asked. "I got it for my tenth birthday and have kept it in perfect condition ever since." He stood up and dusted off his dressing gown. "Would you like a drink, my love?"

She would like to find out about Hans, but obviously a drink came first. She nodded. Freddie limped over to a cupboard painted with circus scenes.

"This is the first nursery I've seen equipped with a bar," she said.

"Isn't it cozy? I had it fixed up. Of course, dear Ursula thinks I'm hopelessly juvenile, playing with trains and all, but it's a nice recreation after the rigors of work." He tittered nervously.

Ilse suddenly noticed that dear Ursula had slipped away. She was glad of that. Finding out about Hans would be easier without her around.

"Do you like cherry brandy?" Freddie asked. "That's all we had left in the cellar." Ilse said fine, and he poured a deep red liquid, nearly the same color as his dressing gown, into three lead-crystal glasses. Three? That meant Ursula was coming back. "About Hans," she said.

Freddie didn't answer immediately, but fussed with the glasses, while occasionally glancing nervously toward the door. "I'll take you to see him," he whispered as he handed her a glass. "But don't breathe a word to sister. We'll leave as soon as she passes out. Look," he said, squeezing drops from a rubber-tipped bottle into a glass. "I'll give this to her. It won't kill her, unfortunately, but she'll sleep until noon." He gave her a shy, enchanting smile. Ilse smiled back. She'd never dreamed that Freddie hated his twin sister so much, but why not? She was eminently loathsome, and poor Freddie had to live with her.

Ilse looked for a place to sit down and settled on a daybed. She sat on edge and kept her eye on the door. How soon would Ursula be back? "Drink up, pet," Freddie said in a tone very similar to Ursula's. Ilse took a sip. The brandy was sickeningly sweet. "Where is Hans?" she asked.

Freddie took some keys from his dressing-gown pocket and dangled them in the air. "Here!"

"Where's here?"

He pocketed the keys. "In the home of a mutual friend," he said just before Ursula came in.

A new and different Ursula. Her long thick hair was severely pulled back into a schoolmarm's bun. In fact, wearing a white starched shirt and black skirt, she looked exactly like an old-fashioned schoolteacher, or perhaps tutor. To complete the picture, she carried a birch switch, greenish-white and flexible, looking exactly like what Ilse was so frequently whipped with when she was a child.

She wasn't sure what Ursula intended to do with that switch, but she was glad Freddie had put the knockout drops in her drink so she wouldn't have to find out. She held her breath when Ursula took a sip from her glass and made a face. "This tastes very peculiar," she said.

"Perhaps it's just age," Freddie said. "One of our few remaining bottles. No doubt it's turned slightly rancid."

"It isn't rancid, it's too sweet. Don't you think so, pet?" Ursula asked her.

"Rather," Ilse said. "But then, I thought you had a sweet tooth."

"For desserts, not brandies," Ursula said, but nevertheless continued to drink from the glass.

"This room is horribly stuffy," Freddie said. In fact, Ilse had found it chilly. But Freddie unselfconsciously proceeded to take off his dressing gown, revealing, however, not underwear but a pair of short black pants, knee socks, white shirt, and bow tie. How strange. Ursula looked like a schoolteacher and Freddie a schoolboy.

"Don't you find our outfits fetching?" Ursula asked.

"Very," Ilse said, suddenly too weary to try to figure this out. She'd slept only a few hours this morning after that nightmare night followed by a nightmare day. It's too much trouble to keep awake; I'll be asleep before Ursula passes out, she thought. But she must stay awake to get to Hans. Thank God, he'd gotten away from the SS. But she couldn't understand what Freddie had meant by a mutual friend. What mutual friend would Freddie and Hans have? She yawned and shook her head. Her eyes kept closing on her. Freddie was acting strangely in that silly schoolboy outfit, hopping up and down while the toy train careened crazily around the track.

Ursula scolded him. "You're going to wreck that train, you bad boy. And it's long past your bedtime. If you don't go, you'll get a good lashing." She cracked the birch switch in the air as a warning.

Freddie pouted. "I am not going to bed. You can't make me, can she?" he said, giving Ilse a pleading look. "Don't let her send me to bed. I'm old enough I don't have to go."

My God, Ilse thought, what is this? But she was too weary to wonder long. She fell back on the daybed. Her eyelids were swollen, heavy. Perhaps she was asleep and dreaming that Ursula was whipping Freddie across his bare legs, that Freddie was running to her, Ilse, kneeling and locking her knees in his grasp, crying out, "Make her stop, make her stop."

Ursula, brandishing the birch, told Ilse to mind her own business or she'd get a good lashing, too, and gave her a sample flick across an ankle. The pain was like the thrust of a knife. Freddie was wailing, Ursula whipping, calling out, "Stupid child, crybaby, quiet or you'll get something worse . . . And you," Ursula said to Ilse. "You're as bad as he is."

More flicks of the birch across her stockinged legs. They bit into her flesh, stinging her into wakefulness.

There was something terribly wrong that she couldn't figure out with her numbed brain. Ursula had drunk the brandy with the knockout drops, but it was she who was blacking out. Consciousness came and went in wave after sickening wave. Ursula's laugh vibrated like a thin high wire as she slashed the birch across Ilse's arms, face, breasts, and buttocks, while Ilse dragged herself away from the knife-point flicks like a weary workhorse staggering under a mountainous burden, wanting just to sleep, to sleep. Blinded from tears and pain, she groped her way toward the door until her knees buckled.

Ursula's long bony fingers emerged from a shirt cuff, pulling her roughly by one arm, while Freddie pulled her by the other, dragging her across the floor and hurling her onto the daybed. There were only two, but they swarmed over her like a mob tearing at her clothes, Freddie bleating baby cries, Ursula's laughter as piercing as a dentist's drill. A low, faint humming in Ilse's ears. She would, she hoped, pass out. But the humming was not, after all, in her mind, for the other two had heard and grown still.

The humming grew louder. A car coming from somewhere, roaring up and stopping below.

"It's Captain Rohr," Freddie said. "He's come to collect her."

"That's not fair. He said we could have her for the night."

Ilse half-opened her eyes to see Freddie and Ursula peeking out from behind the blackout curtain.

"It's him, all right. And he's brought his friends. Maybe they've come to join us. Such fun."

"And leave me out," Ursula said. "No, they don't. Go down and tell them we couldn't find her. Listen to that infernal racket they're making. They'll break the door down."

"Drunk, I suppose. I'll run down and let them in."

"You will not let them in. After they get through with her, there won't be anything left for me. We've barely begun."

"There has to be something left. So they can make him talk. He swears she's not a Jew."

Down below, they pounded at the door. Up here, they bickered. Ilse drifted off, returned to their voices.

"He'll talk when he sees she's about to croak, and it won't make any difference."

"We'll both go down and get rid of them. They can have her tomorrow. We'll say we found her later."

"They won't believe us."

"Who cares? Hurry, before they crash through the door."

"Should we tie her up?"

"No, just lock her in. She's out. You overdid the dose, fool. That always spoils the fun."

Heels clicking across the room, behind a dragging limp.

"Put on your dressing gown, you can't go down like that, idiot."

A few minutes later the door clicked shut.

As soon as they'd gone, she pushed herself up on her elbows. From behind the curtains she looked out through tree branches, but she could see nothing. She yearned to fall back onto the bed, to sleep, but forced herself to dress. Her fingers were thick and clumsy. Her mind wrapped in muslin. Think how to get out! Through the window onto the tree branch? It wouldn't hold her, maybe. That didn't matter. Worse would be to get caught alive. If they saw her, they'd shoot. Her father knew that.

She pushed at the window. It wouldn't budge. Weak, and oh, so sleepy. She lay back on the bed, closed her eyes; sleep crept up. No, she must stay awake, must move, must get away. Forcing her eyes open again, she looked around for something to break the glass with. The brandy bottle? It was clear across the room. She shoved herself off the bed, moving slowly, slowly, as if underwater. Reached it, finally. Her fingers closed on its neck. She made the long trip back.

Feebly she hit the bottle against the window glass, cracking it only. She sank back again. Down below, noises. They were coming for her. Again she hit the bottle against the window. A shattering of glass. They'd hear. Come running. And she hadn't made a big enough hole. She hit again. Chill air blew in, awakening her. She reached out for the tree limb, held on for life, straddling it she pulled herself forward. It bent low under her weight. Swayed. Finally she made it to the fork of the tree, sagged against the branches. But she couldn't stay.

They were at the nursery door. Embracing the trunk like a lover, she slid down, feeling the scrape of the harsh bark.

She dropped to the ground, stumbled, got to her feet, and ran. Above her she heard their voices at the broken window. The moon was bright. She crept, zigzagging from shadow to shadow.

They would be down in a minute looking for her. She made a run for the lake, where there were trees to hide her. Each step brought pain where the switch had lashed her body, as if it were happening again. She almost wished for her earlier stupor, when she had felt nothing.

She reached the lake just as she heard their voices outside the castle, the flashlight beams bouncing about in the darkness. Although from a distance the trees had looked thick, up close she saw they would offer no cover. The shouts sounded nearer, the flashlight beams appeared more numerous. She spied a rowboat pushed up onshore. It was old, with missing boards, and might sink, but there were oars in the locks. Lucky she'd learned to row on the Rhine as a child. She jumped into the boat and pushed off with an oar out into the moon-silvered water. When the oar no longer touched bottom, she sat down and rowed with all her might out toward the middle of the lake. The oars creaked loudly in the rusty hinges. Certainly they'd hear, even if they didn't spot her immediately, but it wouldn't take long to find her in the moonlight. If she could just get out of bullet range. Her arms ached with her effort to row; the boat was filling with water.

They had gathered on the shore. Flashlight beams like fireflies darted among the trees. Suddenly she saw a bullet skipping through the water, and then the shots were winging all around her. She threw herself down into the bottom of the boat, hoping they might think they'd hit her. She lay cramped between the middle and back seats, knees to chin in a fetal position, half-submerged in water, hearing the shouts and the zinging of bullets. How long, she wondered, before the boat sank?

She lay for what seemed hours, feverish and freezing from the icy water, her sliced body aching from each tiny wound, her muscles twitching from inaction, waiting, waiting, long after the gunfire had ceased, before she even so much as dared to raise her head and look around. There were no flashlight beams, but perhaps they'd deliberately turned off the flashlights and were keeping to the tree shadows, waiting for her to show herself. Or they'd gone somewhere for a boat to come after her. One of the neighbors must have a boat of some kind, maybe a motorboat that would reach her in minutes. They wouldn't give up. Even if they thought she was dead, they'd want to make sure.

She'd have to take her chances and row to shore, then make a run for it. She began rowing. The rusty oars screeched in the silence. With each screech she expected to hear an answering shot. The boat was fast filling with water, making the rowing even more difficult. If she could only reach shore before it went down.

She almost did. Just before it sank, she got out and waded in. She'd have collapsed on the bank if the bone-penetrating cold hadn't kept her awake. But her wet, clinging clothes slowed her down. In an effort to keep going, she bit her lips until they bled.

She kept off the road, and thought several times that she'd lost her way, but by noon the next day she reached the outskirts of Berlin. She didn't go any farther for fear someone might see her. She'd attract immediate attention with her ripped clothes and bruised flesh. It was beginning to rain, but that didn't really matter, since her clothes were still damp. She found a bombed-out building and crept behind a wall under a shred of roof. There she slept until dark.

Her father's stories of how he'd survived helped her to stay alive in the weeks that followed. She would wait for an air raid and go to the neighborhood where the bombs hit hardest. Then she'd seek out a church, and in the confusion of the aftermath of the bombing, be treated as others made homeless. She scavenged for bits and pieces to trade for crusts of bread or a rotten potato. One night she found a woman's foot sticking up from a pile of rubble. Using a broken piece of pipe, she dug through the rubble and found a hand clutching a purse. In the purse was an identification card. She went forth as Helga Kuntz, forty-three, housewife, as her father had gone as Rudi Blessner, barber. She looked an easy forty-three. She even, as her father would, made a joke about her past: Ilse Lach had drowned at the bottom of a lake. At least, that's what she hoped they believed.

She never went near her apartment or the theater. She wandered from one bombed-out building to another until she found a suitable two rooms in the back of a building that appeared totally demolished from the front. The only other inhabitants were a slightly mad old man and some rats.

17. Diane

The first thing Uncle Clayton did was to try to get the marriage annulled. He claimed that Michael had used undue influence when she was in a state of shock at the hospital. His strong points were that Michael had illegally entered the hospital and the suddenness of the marriage, implying that Michael was a fortune hunter.

Michael was half-amused and half-annoyed. He told Diane he wouldn't touch her money with a ten-foot pole. Diane had no money to touch. On Michael's advice she countered by suing her uncle for mishandling her inheritance. She hired a lawyer from an Atlanta legal firm, Edwin Derwent of Heard, Derwent, Masters, and McKee. According to Colonel Forsythe, he was a crack lawyer who wouldn't be intimidated in his investigation, as a local lawyer might be. Colonel Forsythe was a friend of Michael's. Michael was now in charge of the officers' club instead of the motor pool. Through the auspices of the officers' club, Michael regularly got liquor at discount rates for Colonel Forsythe, a party-giving man.

"Isn't that illegal?" Diane asked.

Michael smiled. "Would a provost marshal do anything illegal?"

"Michael, I think you're a cynic."

"No, just a realist."

Diane had hired Edwin Derwent on a percentage basis, since Michael's pay wouldn't have covered his fee. She spent a long afternoon in Atlanta discussing her situation in his office. He'd said the important thing was to find out what he could quietly, so her uncle wouldn't become suspicious and cover up his tracks. "Although he's probably doing just that right now," Mr. Derwent added, "since he knows you're due your inheritance, now that you're married."

He looked at her shrewdly, as if that might have been why she'd eloped, then asked if her friend Miss Wilkinson could be trusted. She'd told him about Cindy's saying that Mr. Wendall, one of her uncle's legal assistants, had told Cindy's father about her uncle siphoning off the money.

Mr. Derwent said if Cindy could be trusted to keep silent,

he'd like to talk with her. She might have some important details to add. Diane wasn't sure Cindy could be trusted. She'd seemed so enchanted by Uncle Clayton at the hospital that she could have shifted allegiances, and, in fact, might even be trying to get Uncle Clayton to marry her.

Diane hadn't seen Cindy in the nearly three weeks since she'd come back from what Michael referred to as their honeymoon, although Diane thought of honeymoons in terms of Niagara Falls or Bermuda, not Charleston, South Carolina. Of course, with the war on, Bermuda would have been out of the question anyway. Diane phoned Cindy and invited her over for a Saturday afternoon, picking a time when Michael would be home. It might be awkward being alone with her.

Cindy arrived all smiles, exclamations, and congratulations. "You certainly fooled us," she said. "Your uncle was fit to be tied."

"Have you seen him recently?" Diane asked cautiously.

"No, but I've heard. He called me on the phone and ranted and raved about how Marybelle and I'd been in on things all along and how deceitful we all were and were going to pay for it. The more I denied knowing anything, the more convinced he was I did. He wasn't so nasty to Marybelle, since he knew what he said would be reported to Grandpa," Cindy said, meaning Judge Pierce.

It sounded enough like Uncle Clayton to be the truth. She asked Cindy if she'd speak to her attorney, Mr. Derwent. Cindy was happy to. She was spending a boring summer waiting to go to Vassar that fall. She was also willing to accompany Diane to Colquitt Hall to collect Diane's possessions. Diane wasn't so much concerned about her clothes as getting her doll collection and her tropical fish. She hadn't worried about feeding the fish, since Delia could be trusted to do that.

"We'll go Monday afternoon around three," Diane said. "By that time Chester's apt to have drunk himself into a stupor and Uncle Clayton will still be at work."

It was a great relief to have Cindy along when she turned into the oak-lined lane. Cindy's sunny nature helped dispel the gloom of long shadows and dripping moss.

She parked the white convertible in front and ran up the steps to hug Delia, who'd come out to greet her. "I'm just going up to my room to collect a few things," she told Delia.

"He done told me not to go near your room," Delia said.

Diane was alarmed. "You mean no one's been feeding my fish?"

"If he don't, no one does. He keep that door locked."

Diane said to Cindy, "Wait here, I'll be right back."

She went into her uncle's library. The smell of tobacco and cologne was so strong that she felt an irrational fear, as if her uncle might be lurking in the shadows. She lifted off the heavy oil portrait of her grandmother that covered the wall safe and set it on the floor. With shaky fingers she worked the safe combination. She hoped she remembered the numbers correctly after watching her uncle open the safe back in those days when he'd plied her with brandy and dangled the heirloom jewelry under her nose. After she'd started to show hesitancy about letting him in her bed.

By trying different number sequences, she finally got the safe open. It was almost four-thirty. She worried that her uncle might come home early, especially if Chester, who'd no doubt seen them drive up, gave him a call at his office. In the safe she found folders, the jewelry box, and keys to the house. She grabbed the keys, ran out, and called to Cindy to follow as she dashed up the stairs. Behind Cindy's light steps came Delia's more ponderous ones.

When she opened the door and looked in, she put her hands to her throat in shock. Dolls lay strewn about, faces smashed, bodies broken. It looked like a mass murder. The closet door stood open, revealing clothes savagely ripped. She breathed in a strong smell of ammonia that became stronger as she approached the aquarium, where she found the fish floating, bellies up, goggle-eyed.

Behind her Cindy let out a gasp, and Delia murmured, "Sweet Jesus!"

"At least they didn't starve to death," Diane said.

"When he got your telegram, he just flew into a rage," Delia said.

"He's crazy," Cindy said. "No sane person would do this."

"I told you, but you didn't believe me. In the hospital, you just thought he was the sweetest thing on earth."

"I did no such thing," Cindy said hotly. "I was just pretending to for your benefit. I never once believed you were in that hospital because you got thrown by a horse."

"She done got thrown," Delia said. "I saw her lying there with my own eyes."

Diane didn't want to upset Delia, who, after all, had to work here. She could tell Cindy about it later. "I'll just take a few things," she said, getting her suitcase.

"Why, what you going to take? He done ruined everything," Delia said.

"There are a few things I want," Diane said. She scooped up a ripped dress and a pale green nightgown with cigarette burns and stuffed them into the suitcase. She might need evidence of what lengths her uncle would go to. Then she said, "Come on, let's go." Delia and Cindy left willingly enough. She locked the door and ran down the stairs ahead of them into the library, where she got the folders and the jewelry box. After putting the keys back, she slammed the safe door and rehung the painting of her grandmother.

"Chester around?" she asked Delia out in the hall.

"Oh, he gone on his monthly toot," Delia said.

Diane wished she'd asked earlier; she wouldn't have had to worry about his interfering. She hugged Delia. "Don't mention I was here," she said. Delia promised not to. With Chester away, and with luck, Uncle Clayton might not notice what was missing for a while, giving Mr. Derwent time to act.

In the car, Diane waved good-bye to Delia, took a last unremorseful look at Colquitt Hall, and skidded on gravel as she turned into the lane, worrying not about speeding but encountering her uncle on the way home in his Lincoln.

"I'm sure glad I never have to go back there again."

Cindy gave a rueful laugh. "To think I used to be so green-eyed about your living there. So jealous generally. Here I was an upstart, or my parents were, and you felt so secure about everything—background, ancestors, money, and a big ol' mansion to call home. It would've helped to know how miserable you were, I'm sorry to say."

"And I was jealous of you. No, envious. You had parents. And you could have friends over and were the most popular girl at school."

"I guess I don't mean jealous either. I guess it was more admiration. I mean, even losing your parents in that tragic way just made you all the more glamorous. And you're so beautiful." Cindy smiled over at her, eyes crinkling in a friendly, carefree smile, but there was something else in her eyes, too. Was she remembering that time in bed together? "How do you like being married?" she asked.

"Oh, I love it," Diane said quickly. "Michael's so sweet."

"You deserve someone decent after what you've been through." Cindy paused. "You didn't say how you ended up in the hospital."

Diane told her how Uncle Clayton had maneuvered her into riding a killer horse. By the time she'd finished, they'd reached the guardhouse at Fort Benning. Diane flashed her pass and drove to the married officers' quarters on the field, parking in front of a neat red brick house, identical to blocks of other small neat red brick houses. Diane gloried in this sameness. It made her feel like any other normal officer's wife. Ever since her parents' death, she'd felt left out, different from others, and had always regarded families enviously. She'd been deprived of both sets of grandparents, then her parents. There had been only Uncle Clayton, and after that weekend in Atlanta, she'd felt not just different, but set apart from normal human beings.

She jumped out of her convertible and waved gaily to Sally Berger and another officer's wife, who were coming out of Sally's house, unaware that she wasn't at all considered an average, normal officer's wife by those who were. For one thing, there was the white convertible; for another, the astronomical amounts spent for food and clothes. Michael never suggested that this might be otherwise, humoring her in whatever she did. He wasn't getting richer by marrying a rich wife, but poorer.

In the house, Diane got two Dr Peppers, one for Cindy, who was also fond of them. She opened the suitcase and set aside the folders. They all seemed to be in code with numbers and initials. Perhaps they contained records of what had been hers, since transferred to him. She'd have to check later. They might prove helpful to Mr. Derwent. She took the jewelry box to the sofa, where Cindy sat leafing through the *New Yorker*, looking at the cartoons.

"Now I'll see what's really in here," Diane said.

"My God," Cindy said as Diane opened the box, "it looks like buried treasure."

Diane sifted through pearl necklaces, diamond clips and earrings, bracelets of precious and semiprecious stones.

Cindy picked up a sapphire ring encrusted in seed pearls. "Oh, isn't this beautiful?"

"Try it on for size."

Cindy slipped it on. "Perfect fit."

"It's yours."

"Diane, you're crazy, this must be worth a heck of a lot."

"It was worth more having you along this afternoon."

Cindy leaned over and kissed her cheek. "We're engaged," she said. Then: "Oh, Diane," she murmured, "you're so darling. So sweet and generous," and planted another kiss on Diane's lips.

Diane wouldn't let herself return the kiss, but she couldn't bring herself to break away from Cindy's embrace. Behind her she heard a small click. She turned to see Michael standing just inside the screen door, dry cleaning draped over one arm. He looked at her, at Cindy.

Diane jumped up. "Oh, Michael, home at last!" She threw her arms around him. "We went out to the house, and it was a terrible shock," she said, wanting to distract from what might have been a shock to him if he'd actually seen.

She and Cindy both chattered away, telling him about the smashed dolls, slashed clothes, and destroyed fish. He listened, turning his head from one to the other as if watching a tennis match.

She got him a Scotch and soda and sat on the arm of his chair. He'd dropped the dry cleaning over the chair back, and still hadn't spoken. The room became quiet. Unusual for Michael to be so silent; he was usually talkative. "I guess I'd better go," Cindy said, rising. "It's almost suppertime."

Ordinarily Diane would have invited her to stay.

"Thanks for everything," Cindy said to Diane at the door.

"Thank *you*," Diane said.

She stood behind the screen door, watching as Cindy climbed into her yellow DeSoto and drove off.

"What was that all about?" Michael asked.

Diane remained standing at the door, her back turned to him. "Oh, I got some of the family jewels out home and gave her a ring. It was touching how grateful she was, considering the ring wasn't worth all that much."

"Very touching."

Diane turned and went to get the dry cleaning from the back of the chair. He reached up and pulled her down on his lap. "Honey," he said, "I don't know how to say this, and maybe I'm wrong to be suspicious, but you're such an innocent kid. Just kind of watch out for Cindy, okay? That was more than just gratitude she displayed."

Diane said nothing, always feeling guilty when people told her she was innocent.

"There are some women, you know, who only like women. Oh, hell, never mind, maybe she's just friendly. You Southern women, I love you but don't understand you." He gave her a squeeze and set her on her feet. "I'll put this away," he said, taking the dry cleaning. "I don't want my wife to be a drudge."

She prepared a dinner of Michael's favorite food—steak and french fries—with onion rings as an extra. The onion rings tasted funny. It wasn't until she saw Michael furtively removing burned skins that she realized she should have peeled the onions.

The telephone rang during dessert. Diane answered and heard nothing but breathing. Then: "I could have you put behind bars for theft," Uncle Clayton said. "However, I won't take any action if you return what you stole and call that Atlanta bloodhound off my trail. If you don't, you'll regret it." He hung up.

Diane put down the phone with a shaky hand. When she told Michael of her uncle's threat, he laughed. "He's running scared, don't let it worry you."

Michael was so good, so strong and protective. It never occurred to either of them that her uncle had meant Michael when he spoke of regret.

Diane didn't see Cindy before she left for Vassar. They said good-bye over the phone. She was glad, so glad that Cindy was leaving. She wanted to lead a normal life. If only she had a baby, everything would be perfect. But Michael didn't see it that way. "We're enough for each other," he said. "At least you are for me. Plenty of time to have a family. Besides, we can't afford a baby."

Diane tried to be the perfect wife. She insisted on preparing Michael's breakfast, setting the alarm a half-hour before he got up so that she had time to shower, brush her teeth, comb her hair, and put on a pretty robe. She squeezed oranges, scrambled eggs, fried bacon and baked biscuits. Since she'd never so much as boiled water in her life, she ran into problems that a shelf full of cookbooks couldn't solve. Once when she'd invited Sally Berger and her husband to dinner, the coffee mousse she'd served for dessert had been so bitter and grainy that neither of the Bergers had touched it after the first spoonful, although Michael gallantly finished his. "I don't know what went wrong," Diane said afterward. She showed Michael the recipe. He pointed out that the coffee called for in the mousse should have been in liquid form, not coffee grains.

Cleaning house was another problem. It didn't occur to her that refrigerators had to be defrosted or ovens cleaned. She hired a cleaning woman and followed her around to see how things were done. This made the cleaning woman nervous and irritable. She thought Diane was following her around to see that she did things correctly.

Diane enjoyed going to the commissary with Sally Berger or some other friend in the officers' quarters and loading the supermarket cart with groceries. She always bought more than she and Michael could possibly eat, and the pantry overflowed, food spoiling or rotting. Her big regret was not having a child to push about in the supermarket cart along with the groceries. She loved babies, their delicacy and perfection, their smell of orange juice and talcum powder and pee. Whenever she visited someone with a baby, it always ended up in her arms or on her lap. If Michael were along, she held the baby in a becoming mother-and-child pose so that he might be tempted into fatherhood.

Michael resisted temptation. He spoiled her, he doted on her, he deferred to her wishes except when it came to having a baby. She suspected he didn't want her figure "marred" by pregnancy. He loved showing her off, having her with him at the Officers' club. He taught her intricate dance steps so that they were almost as good as a professional dance team. While onlookers watched admiringly, she and Michael performed, she blond in something white or green and floating, he dark in a custom-tailored uniform. Everyone said they were the perfect couple.

In the movies he paid more attention to her than to the people on the screen; he held her hand, occasionally raising it under the cover of darkness to kiss her fingertips. At such moments she thrilled to his touch, moved closer. What she didn't like was his putting a hand on her thigh or draping an arm around her shoulder, letting his hand fall on her breast. It embarrassed her; she was afraid someone might notice. But what worried her was where it would lead. To bed. The minute the movie was over, she began complaining of a headache. The headache was real. She always got one when she knew sex was in the offing. Hoping to deflect Michael from his amorous mood, she undressed for bed in the bathroom, aware that her nakedness further excited him. She used delaying tactics, brushing her hair, cold-creaming her face, cutting her toenails. But there he was wide-awake and waiting, eyeing her with lust as she crossed the room, even though she'd purposely put on a plain, unsexy white cotton nightgown.

When she got into bed, he reached for her. "Please don't," she said. "I have an awful headache."

"Take some aspirin."

"I did, but it didn't do any good."

He didn't insist. He sighed, kissed her cheek, and turned away. But she could feel his tenseness and resentment. At least with Uncle Clayton I could lock the door, she thought, and was immediately ashamed. Michael was kind and loving. He tried. Oh, how he tried.

She ran across the sex manuals hidden under his underwear in the bottom drawer: *How to Satisfy Your Partner, The Art of Sex, Successful Sex, Sexual Techniques,* and *What Every Husband Should Know.* He spent hours fondling and caressing her, when all she wanted was to get pregnant and get it over with.

She told him that using a rubber spoiled her enjoyment, hoping he wouldn't use one so she could have a baby. It didn't work; he just switched from Trojans to another brand. She went to a doctor and got a diaphragm, told him she was using one, but didn't always put it in.

And suddenly she was pregnant. And rich.

She kept the news of her pregnancy from Michael, afraid of his reaction. He thought she was happy because of all the money she was coming into. A long list arrived from Mr. Derwent, detailing what was hers. She was staggered by the holdings in peanuts, pecans, paper products, lumber, chemicals, and soft drinks. She also got Colquitt Hall. All she had to do was sign. She let her uncle live at Colquitt, stipulating that upon his death, it would be turned over to her. She toyed with the idea of throwing him out, but she was too happy about her pregnancy to bother with revenge. She didn't press charges as Mr. Derwent suggested. She didn't want a breath of scandal on the baby-to-be. She even let Uncle Clayton continue running things, subject to receiving a monthly report on the earnings. After all, he'd been doing a good job.

She showed the list to Michael. "Jesus, it looks like you own all Georgia," he said.

She smiled. "You didn't know you'd married an heiress."

"I knew you had money coming to you. I didn't know you'd be a millionairess."

"Now we can afford a baby," she said teasingly, watching his reaction.

"For Christ's sake, we can afford a whole goddamn orphanage."

"I don't want an orphanage, just a baby of my own."

"Diane, honey, please, we've discussed all this."

"That was before I was pregnant."

"You didn't use that thing, did you?"

She looked away. "Well, I tried, but it's so complicated to put in just right, so I, uh . . ."

"Aw, com'ere," he said, and cupped her face in his hands. "Don't apologize. If I'd known you'd wanted a baby all that much, we'd have had one sooner. If it makes you happy, it makes me happy."

And in a few days he was nearly as delighted with the idea of having a child as she. "I want a little girl exactly like you," he said.

He treated her as if she were made of porcelain, insisted on having someone in to cook and clean, and wouldn't allow her to lift anything heavier than a newspaper. He refrained from sex, afraid it might harm the baby. It was she who insisted on sex. She checked with her doctor, who said it wouldn't hurt anyone. Maybe it was just gratitude she felt toward Michael, or maybe it was that he made love to her so tenderly that she'd come to enjoy it.

Everything was so perfect.

And then he came home one evening with the news that he was to be shipped out. "I can't understand it. I don't know why I got overseas orders when no one else did. And I want to be here while you're going through all this, dammit. It's not as if you had a mother or someone to look after you. I can't bear to think of your being so alone."

She stroked his hair and kissed the frown between his eyes. "I want you with me, too," she said, surprised at how much she did. "Maybe you won't be sent overseas, but to some other Army base, where we can still be together."

"That's the hell of it. They're overseas orders. And I'm the only guy in my company who's being sent. Guess I should have given one of my party-giving buddies a bigger discount on liquor," he said with a bitter smile. "Only, I don't know who. Or why I was the one who was singled out."

They had a few weeks together, and then he was gone.

She was amazed that such a small house could suddenly be so huge and cavernous. She longed to have him next to her in bed, missed their lovemaking. Sometimes she forgot and set an extra place for him at supper, and then she would cry. When she remembered she'd married him to escape her uncle, she found it hard to believe. It seemed that she'd fallen in love with him at first sight, as he said he'd fallen for her. Maybe she had. Maybe she was just slower to realize it.

The thought of the baby kept her from being depressed. She read numerous books on child care and fixed up the extra room as a nursery. That was just before she received notice that she could no longer live on base, now that Michael was no longer assigned there. To leave the house was to be doubly bereft. It contained all their memories, and she wanted to stay among her friends.

"Why don't you get a job on the base?" Sally Berger said. "That way, you can keep busy and not feel so lonely, and you can live here in the civilian quarters, so we can still visit each other."

"But what about the baby? Maybe I won't get a job if they know I'm pregnant."

"You don't have to say."

Diane applied for a job at Personnel. Since she didn't know typing or shorthand, she was given a general test and assigned to the finance department.

"I guess they figure you must know all about money, since you're so rich," Sally said.

In the finance department she was put to work in Payroll, where she was promoted in two months to assistant payroll clerk. She was, ironically, good at figures. Captain Delmore, her immediate superior, spent more time on his golf game and left her in charge. A newspaper reporter and a photographer showed up one morning for an interview with her. The reporter said he'd cleared it with the proper authorities, and that all he wanted was a little human-interest story. She carefully explained the procedure, but he was more interested in what she did off the job than on. "I don't do anything much, now that my husband's away," she said. She couldn't tell him that she was again fixing up the spare room for a nursery, since no one knew she was pregnant. The photographer took several pictures. "Show more leg," he said. Diane laughingly refused.

The story and her picture were published in a local paper under the heading "HEIRESS IN SERVICE TO HER COUNTRY." Much was made of her being heir to the Colquitt millions while living humbly as a GI bride on an Army base and seeing to it that GI's got their paychecks. It somehow sounded as if their pay came from her own pocket. The story was picked up by several other newspapers, one in Atlanta. She was variously described as a Fort Benning Belle and a Georgia Peach.

A copy of the story along with her picture was sent to her anonymously. Written across the picture was "Fools' names and fools' faces, always seen in public places." The handwriting was unmistakably Uncle Clayton's.

A copy of the story with her picture was also sent from Cindy, along with a note: "I guess this puts you on par with Gloria. It was in one of the less intellectual papers in New York City, the sort a Vassar girl shouldn't be caught dead reading."

It took Diane a while to figure out Cindy meant Gloria Vanderbilt, who was often in the news as a GI's bride. There had even been mention of her scrubbing floors.

If she hadn't missed Michael so much, Diane would have been perfectly content. She enjoyed her work, and her pregnancy lent a golden glow to the grayest day. She was disappointed when Captain Delmore suggested that it was improper for her to work when her pregnancy began to show.

Michael wrote cheerful letters, disguising his concern. "Take your vitamin pills, drink plenty of milk, get plenty of rest and exercise, and wear low heels," he advised. She followed his advice.

Duncan Colquitt Deal was born on July 16. He was an exact duplicate of his father, brown eyes and black hair. Looking down into the small white satin coffin, Diane could not understand how such a perfectly formed baby could be defective. She hadn't even had a chance to hold him in her arms. He had died the night of his birth of a respiratory ailment.

18. Susan

"Susan Lund, New York *Courier*, here to see Lieutenant Colonel Weigand, Public Relations," she said to hurry things along. The security officer—blond crew cut, pressed tans—was someone new at the Pentagon security desk. The old one would have waved her through without any fuss. The new one examined her press card carefully, pretending not to hear, or to notice her anxiety. He took his own good time consulting the appointment list. "Lund?" he said.

"Lund," she said.

"Susan?" he said.

"Susan," she confirmed.

"New York *Courier*?" he said.

She'd have liked to bat him over the head with her notebook.

"That's Lieutenant Colonel Weigand, news briefing, room 4017, fifteen hundred hours."

"Yes, and it's three o'clock now," she said, irritated. She'd had one hell of a day. First, Mrs. Overhauser, who took care of Laura, had arrived late this morning. Mrs. Overhauser was never late. Next, Susan had had to run to the *Courier* office to bone up on background material for the briefing. It was classified top secret and had to be read under the eyes of Jean-Paul's secretary. Then Jean-Paul had come in while she was reading. He sent his secretary out on a spurious errand and resumed their argument where they'd left off last night.

"Can't you see I'm busy?" she asked. She felt guilty later at the airport, where there'd been a delay because of engine trouble. Jean-Paul deserved better than such an abrupt answer, but she was sick of the subject. It seemed futile to discuss it again. She wouldn't divorce Richard while he was flying dangerous missions. She wouldn't be the cause of a breakup in a marriage that had been perfectly fine until she came along. Jean-Paul's sons, six and ten—or was it seven and eleven?—were at an age when they needed their father. And they adored him. His wife was a sweet, pretty woman who took pride in home and family. It was cruel to destroy happy domesticity. Natalie DuPres lavished care on her home. Susan had immediately seen that at the parties she'd attended there. Jean-Paul's wife had told her how she'd searched department and specialty stores for just that kind of material to cover that particular chair. They had little in common except Jean-Paul, but Natalie didn't know that.

The security officer had finally finished filling out her pass.

"Take the elevator to the fourth floor and—"

She snatched the pass from his hand. "I've been there before."

She managed to jump on the elevator just before the door closed, and got off on the fourth floor, walking fast down the hall, hearing her heels click. Once the Pentagon had intimidated her with its top military brass and labyrinthine halls. Now she was used to it. Since Jean-Paul hated flying and the train took too long to get to Washington on short notice, he sent her in his place. Not that she minded. She loved it all, including the flying. What she didn't love was the paternal or playful treatment she got from Pentagon officials. Being young and female had its advantages and disadvantages. Sometimes an official would say more than he should to impress her. Other times her questions were brushed aside as something a silly young girl would ask, no matter how pertinent the questions. There were few women in the Pentagon—Wacs or civilians—above the level of secretary.

Susan could hear Colonel Weigand's stentorian tones long before she reached room 4017, even though the door was closed. At the prospect of being late, her cheeks grew hot as she turned the doorknob. She tried to make herself inconspicuous as she walked to a nearby seat. It was like being late in Jean-Paul's class all over again. Colonel Weigand gave her a disapproving glance but continued talking. He snapped down a map of Europe over a blackboard and with a wooden pointer indicated a pink area in France, toward the top. Dunkirk? "If the French hadn't gone to pieces and run," he said, "and stuck it out like the British, France would be free today." Jean-Paul said that wasn't true, that the French wouldn't have panicked if communications had been better and they'd known they weren't alone, but maybe he was being patriotic.

"Any questions?" Colonel Weigand asked finally.

The questions were on methods of strategy. No one asked the big question of where the Allied invasion would take place. Not that they'd get an answer. Susan raised her hand. Colonel Weigand pretended not to notice. She kept her hand up until he did. "Could you give us an idea of where the Allies will make their big offensive move in France?"

"What makes you think it will be France?"

"Won't it?" she countered.

"Even if I knew, you wouldn't expect me to spill the beans to the press now, would you?" Titters from the audience. "The element will be surprise." He spoke with painful patience, as if she were a child. The other journalists, all men, avoided looking at her. Of course, she hadn't expected him to tell her, but she thought his answer might give a clue.

She'd been right, however, about where the Allied invasion would take place. It was in France, not North Africa as so many had thought. But she hadn't dreamed that it would take place the very next day, on June 6, 1944, or that someone dear to her would be killed.

After the news briefing, Susan visited several Pentagon officials with whom she was on good terms and got some nuggets of information, especially from Colonel Goodman, with whom she had lunch. She didn't take notes during these informal visits, aware they'd inhibit. She listened carefully, filed facts in her mind, knowing that what was said was highly colored by who said it. There were those who underplayed the importance of an event and those who exaggerated.

She had dinner that night with Major Mercer, formerly Captain Mercer, still in Washington, D.C., after two years. She saw him frequently on her visits here, and he slept on his couch—which she now considered hers—on his visits to New York. The fact that Major Mercer stayed overnight shocked

Mrs. Overhauser, who didn't know the major preferred men. Susan couldn't blame her for wondering about her morals. Here she was married to a pilot, entertaining the major at what Mrs. Overhauser must imagine were lovers' rendezvous, while having similar rendezvous at the apartment with her boss.

Susan met Nelson Mercer in a small French restaurant where few military officials went, which was why he'd chosen it. He said he got enough of the military during the day. There were candlelight, checked tablecloths, and posters of the Seine and Eiffel Tower. Nelson looked his usual neat self, with blond clipped mustache and pressed olive-drab tunic. His face, however, was haggard even in the candlelight.

"Hard day at the office?" she said. He worked for the OSI—Office of Secret Information—and couldn't talk about his job, since it was of a highly secretive nature.

But he did tonight. He paid scant attention to the bouillabaisse or wine, although he didn't say what was bothering him until he had his after-dinner coffee and brandy. "I'm going to stick my neck out," he said, meditatively swirling his brandy about in the glass.

"I can keep a secret."

"This is a secret that shouldn't be kept. That's why I'm sticking my neck out. There's this man in Egypt. He claims he's had a talk with Eichmann and that Eichmann's offered a swap—ten thousand trucks for a million Hungarian Jews who will otherwise end up in the ovens."

Nelson Mercer picked up his brandy, pinpointed her with pale blue eyes, as if she could take it from there. She was too stunned to answer. People said the death camps either didn't exist or were highly exaggerated. War propaganda. Like nuns getting raped and their tongues cut out. Jean-Paul insisted that the death camps all too horribly existed, but he'd been politely informed by the managing editor to tone things down, that he was sounding hysterical.

"Well?" Nelson Mercer said.

"My God, what do you mean, 'Well?' Give him the trucks. Or at least promise them to him. Stall. Eichmann wouldn't have made a deal like that if Germany weren't losing."

"Dearest Susan, you'd never get far in the military, you're much too logical. That's my reaction, too, but unfortunately, we're not running the war. The British have turned down the offer, and so has Roosevelt. My superior—in name only—Colonel Holland, says this guy is just another Zionist crackpot. He says why would Eichmann talk to a Jew? It's all being hushed up. That's why I'm sticking my neck out."

"Is there anyone in Washington who knows this man?"

"Roosevelt sent some special envoy to Egypt to talk to him."

Susan drank her brandy as if it were water. "Could I talk to the envoy who talked to him?"

"Why do you think I'm telling you this? You journalists, all you write about is Rosie the Riveter or Four Jills in a Jeep or interviews with Mamie saying she runs the house and lets Ike run the war. I'll see if I can get his name and put you in touch."

"Okay, call me tomorrow at the hotel."

But she checked out of the hotel in the morning. Jean-Paul called her at six A.M. telling her to come back immediately. The Allies had landed in Normandy. Her first worry was Richard. Was he part of the invasion?

When she got a chance the next day, she told Jean-Paul about the man in Egypt and asked if she could return to Washington to talk to the envoy who'd talked to him. Jean-Paul said to call Nelson. Susan called. Major Mercer was out of town on a work assignment, his secretary said.

"Where can I get in touch with him?"

"I'm sorry, but his destination cannot be disclosed."

"When will he be back?"

"I'm sorry, but that cannot be disclosed either."

"Keep calling," Jean-Paul said.

But she always received the same answer. She wondered if Colonel Holland had deliberately sent him to an out-of-the-way place. For weeks after that, Susan led a topsy-turvy life. She and Jean-Paul scarcely saw one another. While he slept, she ran the office; while she slept, he was there. She kept an eye on all the incoming tapes giving Axis losses, Allied gains. It wasn't until the end of June that the events she wrote of hit home.

She reached her apartment close to ten-thirty that night. The radio was playing when she walked in. Mrs. Overhauser, pillows propped under her head, lay on the living room couch reading *A Tree Grows in Brooklyn*, a cup of cold tea on the coffee table, her shoes underneath.

"Late again. I'm sorry," Susan said.

"That's okay, honey, I knew you'd be home sooner or later, and I don't have far to go."

Mrs. Overhauser lived two floors below. She was a widow, mother of four, and grandmother of many, her children scattered all over the country, so that she scarcely got to see them. With her hennaed hair, plucked eyebrows, thick mascara, and too-tight dresses, she looked more like a gun moll than a grandmother, but she was completely trustworthy, always available, and invariably pleasant. Also, she loved Laura. But then, who didn't?

"We had more fun than a barrel of monkeys today," Mrs. Overhauser said as she fastened her dress at the back of her neck and simultaneously slipped her feet into her high heels. "Went to the park and chased squirrels and dogs. I took Adam along, he's such a sweet little boy, and he and Laura get on so well."

Adam was Adam Sabatini, Gina's son, two months younger than Laura. Whenever Susan and Gina had a free afternoon, they, too, went to the park with the children, but generally she was tied up at work and Gina at her studio. "Any calls?" Susan asked.

"You got a long-distance call from Ohio."

"Oh, God, something must have happened. Daddy never calls unless it's bad news."

"It was some woman. Just a second, I'll get the number the operator left to call back."

A woman? Who? Some nurse at the hospital where her father lay sick and dying? Should she call at this hour of the night? But someone was always on duty at a hospital. "I'll call now."

Mrs. Overhauser lingered while Susan gave the operator the number. After nearly a dozen rings a woman answered, sounding sleepy. Probably a nurse napping on the job. "This is Susan Lund, I'm calling for information about my father, Edward Varner," she said, trying to keep her voice steady.

"Susan, honey, is that you? This is Martha Cooper."

Martha Cooper? The only Cooper she knew was the cook in the school cafeteria. A widow. Was her first name Martha?

"Your father's asleep now. I think it's better not to wake him. It's been so terrible for him."

Susan's heart stopped. Richard! He'd been killed. They'd tried to notify her, and when they couldn't, notified her father. No, that was absurd; it was his parents they'd notify in that case. "Terrible? What happened?"

"I'm afraid it's bad news, honey." Susan's palms were damp. "Your brother, Eddy. He's missing in action. In the Normandy invasion. Your poor father just heard this morning."

Eddy? She'd thought he was in Guadalcanal. Martha Cooper talked on, but Susan's ability to understand had stopped at the words "missing in action."

She heard a voice—hers—say that she'd try to get the first flight out to Vandalia tomorrow, and sat with the phone in her hand hearing a click somewhere before she remembered to hang up.

"Missing in action" meant "dead." She pictured Eddy, tall and lanky, in his green-and-white basketball uniform, standing on tiptoe, practically handing the ball through the hoop. Only, that wasn't the kind of action meant. She pictured him as she'd last seen him, in his Marine uniform carrying a duffel bag and boarding the train at Penn Station, turning to call, "So long, squirt."

He'd come to New York to talk her into going back to Ohio. She'd tried to avoid the subject. She'd taken him to plays and a ballet, when all he'd wanted to see was the Empire State Building and the Statue of Liberty. Why hadn't she let him see what he wanted to?

"Bad news?" Mrs. Overhauser asked.

Susan had forgotten she was still here. "My brother, Eddy, missing in action."

Mrs. Overhauser put an arm around her. "Why, he might be all right, honey, 'missing' just means he can't be found."

"I'm flying home tomorrow. Probably have to use my press card to get on a plane. Daddy will need me."

"Of course he will. Do you want me to keep Laura?"

"No, she'll be a big comfort to all of us."

She called Jean-Paul from the airport and told him about Eddy. "Do you think I can be spared for a week?" He said she could, but during a time like this, it was sometimes better to keep busy.

She couldn't use her press card, after all, with Laura along, but she was given a seat when she told the ticket clerk her reason for going home. People trying to get on flights gave her dirty looks as she went past them, and those on the plane gave her dirty looks when she boarded with Laura. She supposed they were worried about being a captive audience to a screaming child. But Laura was her usual sunny self. The worst thing she did was tear apart a *Life* magazine and shower pieces on her fellow passengers.

As usual, everyone remarked on Laura's good nature. True. Laura was always in high spirits. Where did she get that from? Certainly not her, and although Richard was outwardly genial, he was inwardly gloomy. Nothing bothered Laura, who paid little attention to Susan's departure in the morning but was quite delighted to see her at night. "You're too good to be true," Susan told her. Laura reached up and patted her cheek.

Susan was surprised to see her father waiting on the other side of the airport fence. She'd expected to take a taxi home. Although his face was drawn in grief, he'd put on weight and looked healthier than she'd ever seen him. "Why, there she is!" her father said. He didn't mean her, but Laura, whom he took into his arms and hugged. Laura laughed and hugged him back. "She's just like you," her father said.

"Daddy, you know I was never that good-natured."

"You were the sweetest-natured child I've ever seen," he said. "I often wonder what happened."

He insisted on carrying both Laura and the suitcase. They walked from the air terminal to the car, the same old Plymouth. Susan held Laura on her lap while her father drove. He went so slowly that her foot itched to step on the accelerator.

"What else did the telegram say?" she asked.

"Just that. 'Missing in action.' "

" 'Missing in action' could just mean he hasn't been found," Susan said, quoting Mrs. Overhauser. She knew better, but he didn't.

"No, now, don't delude yourself."

She was surprised to hear him say that. He'd always spoken of her mother as if she'd been in the next room long after she'd died.

"Your brother didn't want to sit the war out. He told me that the last time he was home on leave. They'd offered him a safe desk job, but he wouldn't settle for that. Not Eddy."

Then "Eddy . . ." she echoed, and they both became silent, as if his name were said in prayer.

They passed fields of young corn and wheat just turning gold, farms with run-down houses and well-kept barns. The metal wheel of a distant tractor glinted in the sun.

"I'm proud of that boy. Always was. Remember what a good basketball player he was? Both him and Richard. Stillcreek wouldn't have taken the tournament without them. Won it three years running while they were on the team."

"Remember when he played the trumpet in the Salvation Army Band? Every single Friday night on a street corner," she said.

"Yes, well, he's a good, religious boy." (Susan didn't remind him that he'd used the wrong tense.) "God will look out for him." (But God hadn't looked out for him, she thought.) "You don't find any atheists in the fox-holes," he said. ("No, they're all in the officers' club," she didn't say, remembering that joke she'd heard.)

"Your brother never gave me a minute's worry," her father said, rewriting history. "Of course, I'm not saying he was perfect, but he never caused me grief."

She knew that despite his genuine sorrow over Eddy, he couldn't pass up the opportunity to point out her failings, first running away, then refusing to return. But it wasn't all my fault, she wanted to say; you caused me grief by trying to keep me here. You don't own a child. And silently she promised Laura that she would never hold on to her.

"Well, what've you been up to there in New York?" her father asked. They were on the road to the covered bridge, near home.

"I've been busy at the *Courier*. Or flying to Washington to see some general or other at the Pentagon," she said, promoting the colonels to impress her father.

He wasn't impressed; he was more concerned about Laura. "And who takes care of that little girl while you're running around?"

"Oh, a very nice woman, Mrs.—"

"You mean you leave that child with some stranger? At a time when she needs her mother most?"

Laura saved the day. She leaned over and butted her head against his. Susan hoped it was in reproof. "Why, hello there," he said. Laura said "Hi" and began talking in Laura language. Maybe she was telling him off. Maybe her father thought so, too. "Jabber, jabber, jabber," he said, but he said it kindly.

Just as they drove onto the covered bridge, her father mentioned Mrs. Cooper. "Martha's a fine woman. She comes over to cook and clean."

Susan wondered why he'd left this out of his letters.

They turned off the bridge onto the gravel road leading to the farm, where the trees looked greener, the sky bluer, the house whiter. The house also looked smaller. Perhaps that was perspective; when she was little, it was bound to have looked bigger. "Did you paint the house?"

"No, but I intend to one of these days."

Perhaps that was perspective, too. It didn't look as gray as she remembered, because her feelings had made it that color. She noticed a parade of wooden ducks going down the hill as they were going up. The ducklings wore little hand-knit capes in pink and lavender, while the mother duck, heading the group, wore yellow. "Who put those tacky ducks out there in those tacky capes?" she asked.

"Now, that was Martha, she knitted those capes herself. You're always so critical."

Whimpy hurried to greet her when she got out of the car. He hurried, but he didn't move fast. His poor old legs were stiff. "Da," Laura called reaching for him.

"Da," her grandfather said, misinterpreting. "Yes, honey, one of these days your daddy will be back." He turned to Susan. "You'll have to take that child to see Richard's parents."

She knew that and wasn't looking forward to it.

She paused in the kitchen doorway. There was a brand-new stove, refrigerator, and linoleum. "You wrote you had a bathroom put in, but you didn't mention this."

"Well, I couldn't expect Martha to cook on that old stove."

Or walk on that old linoleum. "How often does she come over?"

Her father blushed under his weathered face. "Oh, a couple of times a week," he said. She bet it was more often than that. And why had he written pretending to be so sick and neglected, when he was perfectly healthy and looked after by Martha Cooper? To get her home, of course. That wasn't fair. Laura was wet, she weary. "I think it's time Laura had her nap," she said, and hurried upstairs before she gave vent to her feelings. After all, she'd come home to comfort, not to quarrel.

Laura went to sleep right after Susan changed her. Susan went to the window and looked down the sloping hills to the willows and the summer-green river, remembering when she and Eddy had gone out in the rowboat in the fall to toss corn to migrating ducks that stopped over on the river before flying on south. Probably feeding the ducks was Eddy's idea. He'd always been considerate, never bullied her the way big brothers were supposed to, had in fact protected her. The worst he'd called her was "squirt." It was only when they'd grown up that he said things to hurt her feelings. After she'd gone to New York.

She tiptoed out of her room across the hall to his. Never had his room looked so neat. The trumpet was in its case on top of the dresser. An Ohio State pennant hung over the bed. Eddy had spent only a year and a half there. He'd majored in phys ed, wanted to be a coach. Right after Pearl Harbor, he'd quit school and enlisted.

She fingered the small items on a tray on top of the dresser: cufflinks, a pocket comb with some missing teeth, pennies, a scout knife, a toy Scottie dog on a keychain that still held the key to his green coupé, which had finally ended up in the junkyard. The Scottie, of course, was for the Stillcreek Scotties.

She opened the closet door and looked at his good dark suit, the sport jacket with suede elbow pads still retaining the shape of his arms. She held a sleeve to her cheek. What had it been like, that last day of his life? She'd read about it, even written about it, but what had it *really* been like? Planes screaming overhead, platforms dropping from LST's as you ran off into a hell of gunfire so loud you couldn't think straight, on to a foreign beach you'd scarcely heard about, to fall there, your blood darkening the sand. Or was it sand? Was the beach pebbly the way Jean-Paul said the Riviera was? Oh, hell, what did it matter where you dropped when you were dead? But somehow it did. And he'd never gotten to see his niece, or she to see her uncle.

Susan's glance fell on a flowered sleeve toward the back of the closet. She pushed aside a suit and saw a dress. Also, a polka-dot housecoat and plaid robe. There were more dresses with rickrack trim and little girlish puff sleeves. Martha Cooper's, of course. She crossed the room to the bed, pulled back the white candlewick bedspread, but found only a mattress. No sheets. No, Martha didn't sleep here. Obviously Martha slept in her father's bedroom. She probably kept her clothes in his closet until she knew Susan was coming home, and then had put them in here, thinking it was a place Susan wasn't likely to look. Dumb of her not to have guessed. She'd merely supposed that night Martha answered the phone that she was staying late to comfort her grieving father. Not that it mattered what he did; he was of age. But at *his* age? Then she laughed at herself. You're jealous—admit it. She admitted it, but defended herself. She wouldn't half-mind, if only Martha didn't have such awful taste and put pastel knit capes on wooden ducks.

Susan took Laura over to see her grandparents. Her father went along. Mr. and Mrs. Lund looked as if they'd posed for the Grant Wood painting of *American Gothic*. Mrs. Lund even wore steel-rimmed glasses. All that was missing was the pitchfork. Susan was torn between regret at not letting

Laura's grandparents see Laura sooner and a desire never to let them see her again.

"Poor little tyke," Mrs. Lund kept saying, patting Laura consolingly, although there was nothing to console Laura for. She bubbled and gurgled and was obviously not a deprived child.

"She's got the Lund nose," Mr. Lund said. "Hasn't she, Mother? And a smile just like Richard's."

"She's got the Varner ears. We've all got good-sized ears," Susan's father said proudly, as if big ears were a sign of beauty.

"Poor little tyke," Mrs. Lund said again. "So thin."

"I can tell you one thing," Susan's father said. "That child isn't undernourished. She eats like a horse." There was an edge to his voice, usually Southern-soft. Susan could have kissed him. Laura acted out her feelings for her. "Papa," she said, reaching out her arms to him. Susan's father beamed. He couldn't know, of course, that Laura called all men Papa. So that Laura wouldn't confuse her real father with Jean-Paul, who was around so often, Susan frequently pointed to Richard's picture, said "Daddy," and told Laura that Jean-Paul was "Jean-Paul." Laura had picked up on "Paul," saying it "Papa," and using it thereafter for all men. Jean-Paul was equally deceived and delighted. "You see, she already thinks of me as her father. She even uses a French accent. Papa," he said, encouraging Laura.

"I can't tell you how glad we are you're back for good," Mrs. Lund told her. "Now we'll get to see our little Laura."

Susan knew they knew she wasn't home for good. She kept her voice neutral. "I have to return to my job at the end of the week," she said. Jean-Paul would probably let her stay longer, but she was bound to explode and say things she'd regret if she did.

Mr. and Mrs. Lund's expressions became even grimmer. Mrs. Lund clutched Laura to her breast as if to never let her go.

"Susan has responsibilities," her father said. "Do you know this young lady flies to Washington, D.C., to report on goings-on at the Pentagon?"

And she'd thought he hadn't listened.

"Who takes care of that child while you're away?" Mr. Lund said, asking what her father had asked her, but now it was her father who gave the answer, saying that Susan had a dependable woman looking after Laura, a mother and grandmother.

"I'll stay until Monday," Susan said, extending her time in gratitude to her father. She promised to let Laura spend an afternoon with the Lunds, telling herself that Laura was too young to be corrupted.

"Daddy," Susan said when they were back in the car, "do you know I love you?" She leaned over and kissed him.

"I've never doubted that," he said, patting her hand, "but you can be a difficult young woman."

"How about coming to New York and living with Laura and me?"

"Oh, goodness gracious no, honey. Big cities and I don't get along." He cleared his throat. "Besides, there's Martha."

"Is it serious?"

"I'm too old for anything serious."

"That's silly. She's a lovely person," said Susan, who scarcely remembered her. "And she takes good care of you. I've never seen you looking so healthy."

Her father sighed. "I wanted you and Eddy to have the farm when I go. It's your roots. Now it will be yours and Laura's."

"But you'll be around for a long time. Anyway, Martha doesn't have any children." Susan refrained from pointing out that she wouldn't be likely to either, since she was in her late forties.

"Well, marrying would certainly please Martha."

Poor Martha, who must be ashamed of what she'd consider living in sin.

Susan met Martha before she left. Martha was Mother Earth. Plump and nourishing. She understood Susan's father's grief over his son's death and was warmly sympathetic, but didn't encourage his depressed moods. It was the first time Susan realized that tact and good taste were not necessarily synonymous.

Susan got a letter from her father two months later, announcing his marriage to Martha. A few weeks after that she received another letter in an unfamiliar handwriting, a letter from one of the men in Eddy's outfit who'd written her father about Eddy. Martha had copied the letter and sent a note saying, "I know this will make you proud of your brother." The letter told how Eddy had risked his life for the men in his division, and ended with: "Your son died a hero's death."

She showed the letter to Jean-Paul. After reading it, he stroked her hair and said nothing. He always knew when not to say anything.

"You know, I thought heroes were fools who didn't care about life or realize death was permanent, but Eddy wasn't like that. He was very bright and loved life and knew all about death. When you grow up on a farm, you learn about life and death."

"I imagine he was impetuous, like you," Jean-Paul said.

"Oh, I'd never be so impetuous as to risk my life."

"No?"

"No, and neither would Eddy. The thing is . . . I know this sounds corny . . . but Eddy was . . . well, decent, honorable, and noble." She choked on "noble" and smiled through tears. "God, that sounds sophomoric."

"We need a few noble men to make up for the monsters."

"I'm going to write about Eddy. I'm going to start off with this letter, misspellings and all, and just tell about him and send it to the *Times*. They have a wider readership."

She wrote about Eddy. Although she'd intended to show warts and all, she didn't mention his cheating on the Every Pupil Test or the time he was arrested for drunken driving. She did mention the stink bomb he'd set off in the seventh grade. When the piece was published, she sent a copy to her father, who wrote back that it was a fine tribute to her brother. He wished, though, that she hadn't mentioned the stink bomb.

Jean-Paul said now since the Allied invasion the war wouldn't last much longer. "At least in Europe. I cannot see it going beyond a few months. Your husband, he will be back, and then you can get a divorce, and I, too. We will live happily ever after, as they say in storybooks," he said, delicately removing Laura's sticky fingers from his Countess Mara tie.

"Your wife and sons won't live happily ever after.

"My sons can visit when they like. You do not mind? Natalie is happy with the house. I am just part of the furnishings."

"That's not fair. I've seen how she looks at you."

"In public. In private, those looks are not so adoring. With you, it is the opposite. In public you either ignore me or disagree; but in private occasionally you will bestow upon me an adoring look."

"I have to ignore you."

"You do not, however, have to disagree."

"Yes, I do. If I disagree, does that make me disagreeable?"

"You are agreeable even when disagreeable," he said, pleased with his proficiency in English.

After they put Laura to bed, they went to bed. It wasn't late, only eight-thirty, but Jean-Paul had to leave at ten, and they both enjoyed leisurely lovemaking.

Saturday afternoon, Susan and Gina took Laura and Adam to Washington Square Park. It was a lovely fall afternoon, amber-aired and spicy as cider. The children wore sweaters, and Adam a bright red tam that bobbed as he bobbed. "He's as fast as greased lightning," Gina said. "With that tam, I can keep track of him more easily."

Adam was incredibly beautiful, with his mother's long curly lashes and huge black eyes that Gina insisted were actually dark brown and more like Dan's than hers. It didn't seem fair that Adam, a boy, should be the beautiful one, while Laura was rather plain, with her longish Lund nose, although she had lovely white-blond hair Susan kept in a Dutch-boy bob. Boys didn't need looks; girls did. Or did they? Gina said it was always a wrestling match when she went out with men. Men never saw beyond her breasts. Susan, although this side of pretty, had an inkling of what Gina meant. She had good-looking legs. (Jean-Paul said she was the only woman he knew who looked like she was wearing high heels when barefoot.) Yet, Susan thought, despite our complaints that men don't notice our minds but our bodies, we display what attracts them. She happily wore the knee-length skirts in fashion these days, while Gina wore low-cut blouses or tight sweaters. Gina also wore long gypsyish skirts or slacks to conceal thick calves, while Susan avoided tight sweaters that emphasized her flat chest.

"He's really wonderful," Gina was saying now, "a genius."

"Who?" asked Susan, pleased that Gina was finally interested in a man. Since Dan's death over a year ago, she hadn't even looked at one.

"Hans Hoffman, I told you. My teacher. I'm crazy about him."

"Is he attractive?"

"What's that got to do with it? I don't fall for my teachers like you."

Touché, Susan said to herself. Then: "*Touché,*" she said aloud.

"I don't mean that. I was only cross because you weren't listening. He's very selective about who he teaches. I'm flattered he accepted me. The funny thing is, I thought I was original in my abstractions, but it's something in the air. A lot of painters are doing the same thing. Hans says that happens." Her eyes followed Adam, as they so frequently did. "I think he'll be a writer, like his father," she said. "I let him paint on the studio wall while I work, but he keeps making loops and squiggles like words."

They were sitting on what they considered their bench, under a shade tree near a sandpile where Adam and Laura companionably threw sand at each other.

"Someone's going to be crying in a minute," Gina said.

"Actually, they get along beautifully. Wouldn't it be great if they grew up and fell in love with each other?"

"Ssh. If they hear, they'll do the exact opposite."

Susan laughed. "You mean rebel the way we did?"

"Only we had reason to."

"But if they rebel, they'll be conservative. Maybe we should send them to Sunday school before it's too late."

"Maybe I should move in with Dan's parents, as they keep begging me to. Then he'll have something to rebel against—like Dan. In a way, they're very nice. They love Adam and they're always showering me with money and Adam with presents. Their one big worry is I'll marry and deprive them of Adam. They don't have to worry about that."

"I do."

"What do you mean?"

"I mean, you may as well dress in black and go in mourning permanently, like those old Italian women you're forever knocking."

"I don't knock them anymore, I understand. I've got Adam and my painting—that's enough for me. I've gone out with a few men. They just don't measure up to Dan. The more I go out with them, the more I miss him."

"Admittedly, there's not much choice at the moment. But the war won't last much longer, and then things will be different."

"Not much. The best men were killed." Gina's eyes were bright with tears. Susan didn't argue. She thought of Eddy, and felt a great guilt, not at his death, but of what that death had done. It wasn't just the best men who'd been killed, were being killed. It was the best men and women and children. While she'd been mourning Eddy's death, she hadn't followed up on that story Nelson Mercer had told her about Eichmann's offer to swap the lives of millions of people for thousands of trucks. True, she'd tried to reach Nelson, but she hadn't tried hard enough, and he was no longer in Washington, where he could have tracked down the man who'd spoken to the man in Egypt; he was now stationed in Alaska. She wondered if that were America's equivalent to Siberia, if he'd been sent there purposely because he'd been creating too much of a stir.

III

1946–1947

19. *Ilse*

The snow fell slowly, silently. It fell into bomb craters, piled up on twisted girders and the skeletons of buildings. It made Berlin beautiful again. If only it could cover the people with their skeletal frames and bitter faces, Ilse thought. She shivered. The coat she wore was thin as a dress. Damp snow soaked through the cardboard lining her shoes. It was a long walk to the New York Bar. Claus said it wasn't really a bar but a nightclub run by a black-marketeering American major.

Ilse got one of her coughing fits and had to stop until it was over. She was a fool to try out for a job she didn't have a chance to get. All she'd get was pneumonia. On the other hand, it was so frigid in her unheated rooms, where the windows leaked icy air, she might as well be outside as inside. She passed a bakery and was tempted to go in and stand in its warmth, but the smell of baked bread might be more than she could bear. Also, she might get thrown out. It was obvious she didn't have a mark to her name.

Ahead of her an old woman, bundled in rags and carrying a basket, moved slowly, kicking aside snow and occasionally bending to pick up a twig, which she put in her basket. When Ilse drew near, she saw that the woman wore unmatching men's shoes, cracked and several sizes too big. Two American GI's, warmly clad in heavy overcoats, were besieged by little boys begging for cigarettes and chocolates. The children's faces were too old, their eyes too wise. One wore a Hitler Jugend cap with the insignia removed. Ilse remembered Hans's son, who'd been so proud of belonging to the Hitler Youth, and wondered what had happened to him. Once she'd taken the risk of visiting Hans's married sister, knowing that she would be caring for his children after the SS had taken him in. She couldn't have helped, but she'd thought she might hear something of Hans. His sister hadn't let her set foot in the house. She stood blocking the door. Yes, the children were all right. No, she'd heard nothing of Hans, why should she? She eyed Ilse coldly. "We never had anything to do with each other." Yes, that was true. But fear shone in her eyes. Guilt by blood relation.

It wasn't until she'd run into Claus a few days ago that she'd heard of what happened to Hans. A gust of snow blew into her face, stinging her eyes. She welcomed the false tears it brought. She couldn't cry over Hans. She couldn't cry anymore. It had all happened three years ago. Hans was dead. Her duty was to survive. It wasn't that she wanted to live, but survival was a kind of victory. And habit. She didn't know how to die.

Claus hadn't recognized her. Little wonder. She didn't recognize herself these days. Sometimes she forgot, and looked into the mirror expecting to see dimples and big blue eyes, and saw instead a gaunt-faced woman with heavy-lidded eyes, dark-circled, as if bruised. Luckily the flesh laid open by Ursula's birch on her face had healed, so that the only remaining scars were on her back. She'd met Claus when she was out foraging for food in the Unter den Linden section, where there were no more lindens. "Claus?" she'd said, and he'd given her a blank look, so that she had to say who she was. "Ilse, the Berlin Theater, remember?" Back then they'd met for only a few moments under tension, when he was delivering refugees, but it had been as important to remember every feature at such moments as it had been to forget afterward if apprehended.

Claus had treated her to coffee and pastry. The nearest thing she had to a meal in weeks. At first, they hadn't mentioned the past, as if it were still dangerous to do so. They approached the subject gradually, circuitously, Claus finally getting around to the night he'd been taken in by the SS. "The irony was," he said, "that it wasn't for harboring refugees. They didn't know about that, thank God. I was picked up for listening to foreign broadcasts on the shortwave. First they beat me insensible, then kept me in prison, saying I was a threat to the security of the state. While I was in prison, I became friends with this guy who was in because he'd had a feud with his neighbor and out of spite the neighbor reported him for making anti-Hitler remarks. Later, when he learned I could be trusted, he admitted he'd made them, but never in the presence of his drunken neighbor. He was released for lack of evidence, but taken in again—when Hans was there.

"In the beginning I didn't know it was Hans he was talking about. He just told me about this man who in his words was 'a true hero,' a short dumpy little guy in glasses who underwent every torture the SS could dish out and still didn't talk. He told me some of the things they did to him. I won't tell you."

"Don't, please."

"He ended up taking his own life, my prison buddy said. They kept this light on in his cell day and night, and somehow he got that light bulb. I don't know how—the ceiling was fairly high and Hans was short—but he managed to get to it, break the glass, and slash his wrists."

Hans, brave, wonderful Hans, who'd flinched over a cut finger, had slashed his wrists. She wouldn't let herself dwell on what had brought him to that. And she'd loved him too late, longed for him after his absence while half-ignoring him during his presence, just as those times she'd turned over and slept when he was there beside her in bed, only to wake and miss him after he'd gone. And now that he was gone, she was no longer capable of love. Her love was for the dead—Hans and her father.

Claus had said he was a bartender, and asked what she was doing.

"Surviving. Looking for a job when I'm not looking for food, but I'm an actress, I don't know how to do anything else, and who'd want to see a wreck like me onstage?"

"All you have to do is fatten up a bit," Claus said, and as if to help this along, ordered her another pastry. "Can you sing? The guy who runs this bar where I work is looking for a singer. Come on in and give it a try. I'll put in a word for you. Give me a few days, he's a hard guy to see."

Ilse didn't mention she couldn't carry a tune. She'd had various singing teachers who'd all thrown up their hands in despair.

"I know it's a comedown from being a theater star to singing in a bar, but we've all come down."

"Some of us to end up beneath the ground."

"That was the honorable thing. Sometimes I feel like a traitor for being alive."

"Do you mind working for an American?" she asked him.

"I'm just glad to get a job. Most Americans, they're like children, but then, hell, these *are* kids, just young boys sent over here to keep order, weren't even in the war. This major, though, he's different, he's seen action, and he's a tough son of a bitch, and he hates Germans. Hates everyone, I think. All he's out for is money. His name is Deal. Major Deal. They make a joke of it, his friends. Call him Big Deal. That's a play on words in English."

"If he hates Germans, how'd you get your job?"

"I was lucky. Someone told him I was a political prisoner, or he'd never have hired me. Hell, who can blame him for hating us, the way we all complain, as if we didn't bring it on ourselves. We complain about being hungry, losing our homes, and suffering, and don't consider ourselves responsible for it all. It's history. Over. Do you notice no one mentions Hitler anymore?"

Ilse couldn't answer. She had another coughing fit. Claus waited it out, then gave her the address of the New York Bar, along with some money. He told her to buy food and cough medicine. Instead, she'd bought soap and cosmetics so that she might look presentable.

She was in the American sector now, feeling like an alien in her own city among these well-dressed GI's wives with their hair freshly waved, who hurried their children along as if to protect them from the sight of her and the few other Germans in the vicinity.

And then, like ghostly apparitions in the blur of snow, she saw them—Freddie and Ursula. She wanted simultaneously to confront them to show that she'd survived and to hide in order to deprive them of the joy in seeing what she'd come to. She didn't have to hide. They didn't recognize her, walked right by. Ursula gave her an incurious glance, as one of the GI's wives might, as if she, Ursula, were also a conqueror and Ilse only another starving, ragged German. Freddie, limping at Ursula's side, paid her no attention whatsoever. They looked completely untouched by the war. Freddie's clothes were somewhat shabby, but he still managed to look dapper, and although Ursula's mink was ratty, what other German woman had a mink coat these days?

Ilse felt a mounting rage, watched as Ursula entered a smart dress shop patronized by American officers' wives, and Freddie got into the backseat of the blue Mercedes parked at the curb, where Horst still sat at the wheel. She wanted to scream out to the Americans, "Here are your criminals," but she'd either be ignored or called crazy. And what exactly could the von Frisches be accused of? Ostensibly, they'd done nothing more than entertain the SS. Freddie had been smart enough to shoot himself in the foot and stay out of the war. He'd worked for Dr. Goebbels in Propaganda, but that wasn't considered a war crime.

Ilse's steps became even slower, her coughing fits more frequent. How much farther to the New York Bar? She'd turn back, if she didn't have so far to go. At least at the bar she'd be out of the cold. And then she saw it at the end of a honky-tonk street of run-down burlesque houses and flashing neon signs that colored the snow. Although it was only early afternoon, drunken soldiers were already weaving through snowdrifts and wading through slush, circled by the ever-present little boys, who danced to keep warm, and begged for cigarettes and chocolates. Some older German civilians huddled in doorways and pounced on cigarette butts the soldiers tossed into the street, but usually the little boys got there first.

Before entering the bar, Ilse reached into her coat pocket and brought out a nearly toothless comb to slide through her damp hair. She brushed snow from her shoulders and walked in to a blast of warmth and staticy radio music. The bar, where Claus worked, was lit, but the rest of the room was in darkness. Chairs stood upside down on tables while a man swabbed the floor. German. Maybe if she couldn't get a job singing, she could get one cleaning.

Some GI's sitting at the bar who had looked her way when she came in turned back to talk to each other. Even in this bad light she was considered unworthy of notice. Old at twenty-six. Just as well she had no interest in men since they had no interest in her. Claus nodded to indicate he'd seen her, but went on to serve a GI a drink before coming to the end of the bar where she stood.

"He's still in his office on business," Claus said. "He'll be out in a while. I told him about you. Take off your coat so he can see what a good figure you've got." She took it off. He looked at her for a minute. "Better put it on," he told her. "It's chilly in here."

Of course. She was just a bag of bones. He'd even said a few days ago she should fatten up. You didn't fatten up on bread crusts and rotten potatoes. "Here," Claus said, and set a shot of whiskey on the bar before her. Poor Claus. He was sweating. No doubt he regretted mentioning this job. He had his own livelihood to think of. What if this major fired him for wasting his important time on a skinny old hag who would repel, not attract customers. There were thousands of out-of-work Germans who'd love to have Claus's job. She'd have left if it hadn't been for the warmth.

A GI banged his glass on the counter. "Hey, Kraut, gimme another one." He looked over at Ilse and smiled a loose drunken smile. "Hey, Fräulein. *Sprechensie Deutsch? Ich sprechensie Deutsch*, too."

Ilse smiled. He looked her over and said something to the GI seated at his side. They laughed rudely. She was glad her English was so poor.

Now the bar felt overheated rather than just warm. Her

nose started to run. She sniffled and seized a wadded napkin on the counter and blew her nose furtively. She waited. And waited. Once Claus came down to her end. "Have patience, he is conducting some business deal. He is always conducting something or other."

Finally a door opened and two men came out, one a German civilian, the other an American officer. The officer wore a major's insignia and a frown. The light in his eyes was like a polished reflection on a hard surface. He wasn't at all like the baby-faced GI's at the bar. No doubt this was the man who could prevent her slow starvation, and no doubt she'd starve. He wouldn't let sympathy get in his way.

The German civilian held out a hand to shake the major's in leavetaking. Ilse hadn't seen a German so well dressed since before the war. He wore a broad-brimmed hat, imported overcoat, and carried a pair of smart gloves. The major gazed at the proffered hand with such smiling contempt that the hand went limp, and the well-dressed civilian hurried out, walking abnormally straight to disguise his humiliation.

The major sauntered over to the bar. Although his uniform was beautifully tailored, the exactness of fit was a waste, since he wore it so sloppily. He was jacketless, his shirttail hung out, and his tie was loose. "Gimme a bourbon," he said to Claus. A bourbon? What was that? Claus knew. He hustled a drink up in a hurry and handed it deferentially to the major, then nodded her way and murmured a few words.

Ilse smiled uncertainly. The major smiled back at her with the same smiling contempt he'd shown the well-dressed German. "You the girl looking for a job?"

She could figure out his English, but her English and her energy weren't up to more than a nod.

"Well, what're you waiting for? Sing something, sister."

Words would not come. She moved her lips, but no sound came out. She looked helplessly at Claus and at the piano, which, of course, she couldn't play. It was suddenly very quiet. Claus had switched off the radio. They waited. The drunken, baby-faced GI's and the major with the nasty smile. She'd planned to sing some suggestive songs. The major might not understand German, but he'd get the idea from her gestures. Suggestive gestures would, however, be wasted with her coat on. She took it off. The GI's laughed before she'd even opened her mouth. She ignored their laughs, found some words, finally, and began to sing. She wiggled bony hips and shook a scrawny chest. The soldiers laughed all the louder. Claus, who understood the words, looked disgusted.

"Give her a shot," the major ordered. Claus set a shot glass down in front of her. She downed the whiskey and went into a coughing fit.

The soldiers roared and hit each other on the back.

"Maybe I should do a comedy routine," she said to Claus when the coughing spasm was over.

"Sing something in American," the major commanded.

"I do not know American," she said in her best English.

"What language were you just talking?" the major said, then yelled, "Hey, Eddy, com'ere." A few minutes later, a short sleepy-looking *Schwartze* came sauntering up. It looked as if he were imitating the major in his walk and sloppiness of dress. But he had kinder eyes. He didn't smile, either, as if she were something funny. Maybe that was because of the unlit cigar clamped between his teeth.

The major nodded at the piano. Eddy sat down and played a few bars of an American tune, the cigar still clenched between his teeth.

"Sing her something," the major said.

Eddy fiddled with the keys, put the cigar on the edge of the piano, and began to sing after playing a few introductory notes. It was something about night and day. His voice throbbed with the words. He stopped singing after one line and played the music over. She caught on and repeated his words. She didn't actually sing, since she couldn't carry a tune. She talked what he sang, her voice hoarse from her cold, from whiskey and despair, and when she forgot the words, he repeated them, or sometimes she just hummed.

The soldiers swiveled around on their bar stools to listen. She caught the throb in the black man's voice and made it her own.

When she finished, there was a deep silence; then the soldiers were calling out requests. She sang something called "White Christmas," and "Black Magic" and "Blues in the Night." Were all American songs about color? she wondered. She sang on and on, Eddy feeding her the lines. She knew that she had them all in the palm of her hand, the way she'd known it when she'd been onstage, from the hush as they listened. The song Eddy sang now did not have color in it, it was about a fight for love and glory. Love? There was no love. Glory? No more of that, either. She would have sung until her voice gave out, but her legs gave out first. She sank to the floor.

When she came to, they were pouring whiskey down her throat.

"Stop that, you idiots," the major was saying. "Want to choke her to death? She needs food, not whiskey."

Before she was aware of it, he'd pulled her to her feet, thrown her coat over her shoulders, and was guiding her out the door and into a gaudy red convertible. He got in on the other side and drove off at breakneck speed, the car careening dangerously on the icy streets. "Where's a good Kraut restaurant?" he yelled.

She pointed to the first restaurant she saw, and a few minutes later an obsequious waiter was bowing low and presenting them with menus, the large scrawly handwriting perhaps meant to hide the fact that there were few dishes to choose from.

"What do you want to eat?" the major demanded. She shook her head, the handwriting on the menu jumbled before her eyes.

"Bring her something good," the major shouted to the waiter, as if English were understood if yelled loud enough.

"Gut?"

"That's right, *gut*."

The waiter appeared with a steaming platter of meat and vegetables. She looked at them rapturously, her nose quivering at the smells, and ate as the major commanded.

Out on the street, she threw up. On his shoes. "Jesus," he said. He kicked his shoes in the snow, hustled her back into the car, and asked where she lived. She directed him as best she could in German-mixed English, wondering if she wouldn't get the job, now that she'd thrown up on his shoes.

He cursed angrily as he drove down the slippery streets, as if the slipperiness, too, were her fault. She didn't mind. It was like riding through heaven, with the snow coming at them in the reflected headlights and the wonderful warmth of the heater. What worried her was whether she got the job or not, but drowsiness won out over worry. She'd have gone to sleep if he hadn't kept yelling over, demanding directions.

"Here," she said finally.

He stopped the car and looked around. "Here? You don't live here. No one lives here."

Of course, that's why she'd picked the place, because it looked uninhabitable. On one side of the street the buildings had been completely demolished; on the other side, where her building stood, if it could be called a building and said to be standing, was a deep crater filled with snow that glittered in the light of a three-quarter moon. From the front, her building was just roofless walls.

"How in hell can I see you to your door when there isn't any goddamned door?" he demanded, still angry.

"That is not necessary, I go," she said, and was about to jump from the car when she remembered the job. Should she ask him?

But he was already out of the car and pulling her door open, so that she nearly fell on her face. He followed her up the steps and through the space where a door had once been, into a pitch-black hall where there was the sound of scurrying feet. "What the hell's that?" he asked, pausing.

"Rats."

He took her arm in the darkness, and she became rigid. "That's okay, honey, I'm not going to hurt you, I just want to be able to get to where we're going."

They walked side by side to the back of the building. She gave her door a hard kick. "Jesus, don't do that, the whole place will cave in," he said. But she had to give the door several more kicks before it gave way. Inside she reached for the candle and matches she kept on a table by the door. She lit the candle and held it up, seeing his horrified expression as he looked around.

She gave a bitter laugh "It is not all that bad, and it is rent-free."

"Yeah? Well, it depresses hell out of me," he said, and fled through the doorway.

Ilse took off her coat, then her dress, which she hung up carefully since it was the only dress she owned, put her coat back on again, and after blowing out the candle, lay down on the lumpy cot huddled under a piece of rug she'd found on a foraging trip. Wind rattled the windows, where icy air leaked in. She thought with yearning of the steaming platter of food. If only she'd been able to keep the food on her stomach. Her throat was sore. That's all she got for her singing. What had she expected? Nothing ever came of anything, or if something did, it was worse than nothing. She closed her eyes to induce sleep, and wished that she could weep.

Minutes later there was a pounding at the door. "Hey," a voice called. "Is this the right goddamned door?"

She groped for the candle, wondering why he'd come back. Certainly not to rape her. He could do better than a skinny bag of bones. After she got the candle lit, she opened the door. "Here," he said, and flung a blanket at her. It had "U.S. Prop." stamped in a corner, was an ugly green, scratchy, and marvelously warm.

"Thank you."

"Yeah, that's okay." He reached into his pocket and took out a thick billfold from which he extracted a wad of bills. These he put in her palm and closed her fingers over. "That's your week's wages in advance. Buy yourself some decent food and an indecent dress and come in tomorrow night at eight, *verstenzi*?"

She nodded.

She bought herself some food and a high-necked black dress with spangles and a slit up the thigh. The high neck covered her scrawniness, and the slit showed off her leg. Despite her thinness, her legs still looked good.

After a week the crowds had doubled at the New York Bar, and in a few weeks tripled. As Ilse's popularity grew, Major Deal cut down her appearances to fifteen minutes at hourly intervals. At closing time he always drove her home.

"That is nice of you but not necessary," she said the first night he made the offer.

"It is not nice of me, I'm just protecting my property. It's dangerous for you to be out this hour of night with so many drunken GI's around."

She was reminded of the nights Hans had insisted on driving her home from the theater, but there were enormous differences. Hans had driven his old car cautiously; Michael Deal drove his new convertible recklessly. Hans and she had chatted all the way home; mostly she and Michael Deal were silent. Hans and she frequently made love in her dressing room or at her place; Michael Deal kept his distance, which was fine with her.

Between her singing appearances she either sat at a back table with Eddy and Michael Deal or went to his office, where she curled up in a large leather chair and read or slept.

Some nights after the bar closed, she'd sit in the chair and watch him count the night's take, which he put in a metal lockbox. He handled the bills with a respect he did not show people. After the money was put into the lockbox he'd make a note of the amount in a small black book, which he placed in his jacket pocket over his heart. Then he would put the lockbox into an iron safe. Once he caught her watching. "Money," he said, patting the metal box, "that's what makes the world go round, not sex."

She shrugged.

"You don't care for money?"

She shrugged again.

"How about sex?"

"Is that an invitation, or do you seek my opinion?" she asked in her careful English. "I am not interested in either."

On the rides home, he became increasingly talkative. She didn't half understand what he said, but perhaps that was why he talked. Often he spoke of what he intended to do when he got back to what he called "the States."

"I'll open a big fancy bar in New York. Not like this dive. It'll have class. Leopardskin upholstery and a white piano."

"That is class?"

He looked over at her. "Isn't it?"

"No," she said, and paused in an effort to translate from German to English. "Class is . . . subtlety. It is suggesting, not shouting."

"Yeah, guess you're right. Like you. You've got class. Of course, I don't believe in that class crap. You wouldn't believe it, but I had a real classy wife. Have. We're still married. First thing I do when I get back is get a divorce."

He stopped the car before her building. Although he was now silent, she sensed he had more to say, and she waited politely. There was a full moon hiding out behind a cloud, silvering its edges. The complete stillness and the ruins around them gave an illusion of their being the only two living people in a dead city. But we're dead, too, she thought. Dead people in a dead city.

He dug into a pocket and pulled out his billfold. "Take a look," he said, thrusting a picture into her hand and flicking on his cigarette lighter for her to see. She looked at a young girl, slim and blond in white, squint-smiling into the sun. "She is very beautiful."

"Yeah. That's our wedding picture. I'm not in it because I was taking the picture. But I never was in the picture. Only, I didn't know it. Yeah, she's very beautiful, very rich, very everything, including pathetic."

"Pathetic?"

"Sad."

"Why is she sad? Because you are away?"

He laughed. "That's when she's happiest."

"I do not understand. My English is not so good."

"You understand. I'm the one who doesn't understand."

She handed the snapshot back. He looked at it. "I don't know why the hell I'm keeping this," he said, tore it into pieces, and dropped them in the street when he got out. She was irritated. Always she jumped from the car, called good night, and went in. Now she supposed she'd be stuck with him and his sad memories all night. She'd have to hear all about this beautiful girl-wife who'd mistreated him.

She was right. He sat on the cot, his cap thrust forward over his forehead, talking while she made tea. After the tea was made she had to stand, since the only place to sit was the cot. As little as she cared to hear the intimate details of his life, that was at least preferable to the possibility of their becoming intimate.

"It's not that I blame her," he was saying. "I was like some dumb dog sitting on his hind legs and begging to be kicked. I'd have kicked me, too." He put the teacup on a knee. "You've got two of these. You have visitors?"

"I never have visitors."

"Then why two? Just in case?"

"I found two."

"You never talk about yourself."

She shrugged.

"You either shrug or say no."

"What else is there? Tell me about your wife."

"Oh, hell, you don't want to hear my sob story, do you?"

"No."

He laughed. "I guess that's why I'm telling you."

The candlelight fingered his face, two points reflected in the polished surface of his eyes. How long did he intend to stay? Many women would want him to, she thought dispassionately. He has a firm strong body, he is good-looking. He has that look women fall for, a suggestion of having been hurt. Women go for that. They like to think they can cure hurt. Sometimes he left the bar with a woman. It was never for more than an hour, and never the same woman.

"How long have you lived here?" he asked.

"Oh, years. I was lucky to find it. When I came here, there was an old man who lived across the hall. He was mad, but a nice kind of mad. He had been the hall porter here. What you call a janitor. He died. These cups were his."

"Why don't you move now that you can afford to?"

She shrugged. "It is getting warmer. In the morning the sun shines in. I do not pay rent."

"I think you like money as much as I do," he said with a grin.

"I like better to be alone."

"Like Greta Garbo, 'I vant to be alone.' You don't like men?"

She shrugged.

"Women?"

She laughed.

"Don't laugh, that's not so unusual. My wife did. She had a girlfriend, a lover. I didn't catch on. She married me because she wanted to get away from home. It was cramping her style. But I cramped her style, too. So she arranged with some hotshot general in Washington, D.C., to get me sent overseas. I didn't catch on. I thought it was damn funny that I was being shipped out when no one else in my company was. I found out why finally when I ran into this buddy of mine in North Africa. He told me what no one told me back at the base because they didn't want to make waves.

"That sort of thing didn't seem so important with guys dying all around. Then the secrets came out. He told me that this General DeWitt—a family friend of my wife's—he'd had special orders cut in Washington to get me sent over."

"Maybe it wasn't her fault. Maybe her family did it."

"No, she didn't have any family but an uncle. She just wanted to get rid of me, so that's how she did it. And wrote me the most loving letters. She was pregnant when I left. I felt bad about that, you know, leaving her all alone with no one to look out for her. Hell, what a dummy I was. She'd wanted to have a baby—that was one thing I could do for her her girlfriend couldn't. So she fixed it that she got pregnant before I left. Only, it didn't work out. The baby died."

"Didn't that make you sad?"

"Sad? Hell no! That kid wasn't real to me. By the time I got this pitiful letter telling me the baby had died, my buddy had told me how I happened to get shipped overseas. I didn't have much sympathy for her then. In fact, I did my damnedest to get killed, took all kinds of crazy risks. I should've been killed a dozen times over, but I came out without a scratch. That's what happens when you don't give a damn. When you do, that's when you get it."

"More tea?" she asked.

"You know what I like about you, Ilse? You don't have any feelings and you don't pretend to have any. You're like me, don't give a good goddamn for anything or anyone."

"Oh, but you care about money."

"You must have cared about something in your life. Someone? Claus said you were an actress. Did you like that?"

"I loved it, but I did not at all like the plays I was in."

"So why not go to another theater and do the plays you wanted to?"

"I loved the director."

"Yeah?" He looked as if he couldn't believe she could love anyone.

"And anyway, during the war we could only do certain plays. Most lousy."

"Lousy. Your English is improving."

"He hated those plays as much as I."

"Him? The director? What happened to him?"

"He committed suicide."

"Because of the lousy plays?"

The candlelight was paling in the dawn. "It is daylight," she said. "You must be sleepy."

"I don't sleep. I'm sorry I made that dirty crack. Why did he commit suicide?"

"He was afraid he could no longer withstand torture and might reveal things to the SS."

Michael Deal got to his feet, tilted his cap jauntily, and gave her a smile to match. "Okay, kid, so long. I can't compete with a hero. See you tonight."

"You may stay if you like, but don't expect too much." Meaning, of course, love. He caught her meaning. "Yeah, that's okay, don't expect too much from me, either."

She pinched out the candle flame, since it was now daylight.

On the cot they turned toward each other, reassured that it was lust and not love.

After that morning, he always accompanied her to bed when he drove her home. Like Hans, he admired the long line of her back. But her back was flawed now. He touched the scars with his fingertips. "How'd you get these?"

"Oh, those are my souvenirs from the night I made my escape, when they discovered I was a Jew."

He kissed each scar as if he foolishly believed a kiss might heal. After he made love to her, she fell asleep. When she awoke, he was frowning down at her. "Why do you always frown?" she asked.

"I frown when I'm happy."

"Like others smile?"

"Yeah," he said. "Listen, I have an idea. This is a hell of a lot of bother, driving you home every goddamn night. What do you say we move in together? Don't tell me you like it here, I know you don't. And you'll be alone, I promise that. I'll get us a house in the American sector. They won't come near either of us there."

"You mean because I am a German and you associate with me?"

"Yeah. I might have to call you my wife."

"Oh, that. What does that matter? As long as it is not true in fact."

20. Susan and Diane

The plane, a converted Army transport, lumbered down the runway. Susan was surprised it managed a liftoff. "Is this the way we won the war?" she wondered.

It was called Operation Family. Susan thought it an ill-chosen name. It sounded as if they were going to the hospital instead of to join husbands and fathers in occupied Germany. Around her, children fretted, squealed in delight, or screamed in fright. Laura, almost three, took it in stride. She'd flown several times before, an old veteran.

"I'm so happy, I could get out and walk. Who needs a plane?" the woman across the aisle from Diane said. "I can't wait to see my Jack. It's been years," she marveled.

Diane envied the woman. She felt not happiness but apprehension, pulled a thread loose in her new beige suit. She'd spent months dieting and a week shopping in New York for the right clothes. Yesterday she'd had a facial, shampoo and set, manicure, pedicure, and massage. And sent a cablegram to Michael that she was coming over. At the last minute. On purpose. If she'd sent it earlier, he'd have sent one back telling her not to come. But what if he wasn't at the airport to meet her? Each time she'd written suggesting she join him in Berlin, he'd written back telling her he'd be home soon and to stay put. Never had he written so often. In fact, before then she'd scarcely heard from him after Duncan's death, when she was under sedation. His letter had been short, cryptic, and cruel. "So you got what you wanted," he'd said. Had he meant she'd wanted their baby to die? He'd known how much she longed for one. She'd had to take heavier sedation, pleading with Dr. Gurney to give her something to get her through that horrible time. She still barely managed to get through her days. Her makeup kit contained more pills than cosmetics.

"Mommy, will Daddy be at the airport?" the little girl to her left asked.

"Oh, yes, he'll be there with bells on, don't worry.

Mommy didn't sound so happy about it, Diane thought. She looked over the child's flaxen hair, cut like a Dutch boy's, to the mother, who sat by the window. She was surprised to see the mother was so young, near her age, when she sounded so sure of herself, so completely in control. Unlike the other women on the plane, she appeared unexcited. Or perhaps she was apprehensive, too. Diane felt a certain kinship and a great deal of admiration for her. She was wearing just the right thing for flying, a dark suit that didn't muss, a bright scarf for flair. Her dark blond hair fell over one eye in Veronica Lake style curtaining a face with less-than-perfect features. She wasn't pretty, but striking. She did have beautiful legs.

I bet she knows exactly what she wants, and gets it, Diane thought enviously. All I know is what I don't want, but that doesn't prevent its happening. I not only can't do anything, I can't *not* do anything. No, she shouldn't think like that, Dr. Gurney said. He said she was too hard on herself, to let up a little. She'd been seeing him ever since she lost the baby. He was listed in the phone book under nervous disorders, but most people knew that was a euphemism for "crazy," and she kept her visits secret.

Uncle Clayton had always said she'd end up in a nuthouse. Maybe he was right. A pity he wouldn't be able to enjoy it. He'd died of a stroke on the golf course. ("He keeled over from a stroke making a stroke," she'd said to Dr. Gurney, laughing and laughing. Dr. Gurney had nodded, looking at her with benign blue eyes. She hadn't been such a fool as to tell him what happened that weekend in Atlanta.)

The little girl was peering into her face. "Hi," she said.

"Hello," Diane said.

"My name's Laura, what's yours?"

"Diane," she said, trying not to mind the child's damp sticky fingers on her jacket sleeve, but she did want to look good when she met Michael.

"Let go of the lady," Laura's mother said. "Here, have a cracker." She held out a box of animal crackers. Laura plunged a hand in, scattering crackers around until she came up with what she wanted. "Would you like a giraffe?" she asked Diane.

"Yes, thank you very much," Diane said, smiling, and felt an old familiar ache. Children liked her. Why hadn't she been allowed to have her baby? She'd have made such a good mother.

"When she gives anyone a giraffe, that means they're something special," Laura's mother said.

"I'm honored," Diane said, and as the child leaned over on her arm, Diane nearly cried with pleasure and pain.

"I guess you're going to meet your husband, too, after all these years," the woman said.

Diane nodded.

"I confess I don't know what to expect," the woman said, making Diane feel better immediately. If such a capable person didn't, who did?

"To be perfectly honest, I'm scared to death," Diane said. "I just sent my husband a cablegram yesterday saying I was coming. I don't know what kind of reception I'll get. I don't even know if he'll be at the airport."

"If he isn't, you can always call him," the woman said, making it all sound so easy and in the realm of possibility that Diane relaxed. "I'm Diane Deal."

"I'm Susan Lund. You've already met Laura."

"I'm going to see my daddy for the first time," Laura said.

"So she doesn't know what to expect either," Diane said.

"Yes," Susan said, and put an arm around Laura. "We're all in the same boat—or should I say Boeing?"

"She'll take it in her stride, just like her mother," Diane said, liking them both immediately.

"Oh, I'm sure *she* will," Susan Lund said, implying she wasn't all that sure about herself. She was, however, full of information, telling Diane that there would be a commissary and a PX, and that they'd be assigned to government-requisitioned houses in the American sector. Diane was thrilled. She and Michael could start over again. It would be just like Fort Benning, where they'd spent their happiest days. "We'll be in a place called Konigsgarten," Susan Lund continued. "My husband writes that they're two-story houses with trees and cinder paths."

"Oh, that sounds so perfect. It'll be wonderful living close to a friend. I hope you don't mind my putting you in the friend category on such short acquaintance."

Susan said she felt highly complimented. She did. But also slightly baffled. She'd never met anyone so lacking in confidence, with so little reason to be. Diane Deal was young, beautiful, and slim, with delicate features and eyes as clear green and lovely as Laura's. She was obviously rich, looking as if she could have bought her own plane to fly over. Money was there in the faint lilt of expensive perfume, old Southern money, judging from her accent and the sapphire ring set in antique silver. She wore a Dior suit, or what looked like a suit by some famous designer, with that subtle detailing and cut. A soldier's dream of a wife, with her dainty silk blouse and blond beauty. Susan suddenly felt tacky and unfeminine in her dark tailored suit and slightly run-down heels she'd worn for comfort. She should have dressed like Diane to greet Richard.

"I hate to impose, but would you stay with me until I find my husband?" Diane Deal asked.

Susan promised she would, while warning herself to watch out or she'd have this woman on her hands for as long as they were in Berlin. She was definitely the clinging-vine type. Once a clinging vine got a grip on you, it could be a stranglehold. Steer clear of her, you've got your own problems, she told herself.

Diane, overjoyed to have a good listener, chattered all the way across the Atlantic, boring little details about where she'd gotten her facial, clothes, and hair done while in New York, a completely different New York from the one Susan knew. Laura had wisely dozed off. She'd chosen, however, Diane's lap to doze off in. "I'll take her," Susan said. "She's getting to be quite a heavyweight."

"No, no, I love holding her, she's so adorable," Diane said, and looked at Laura so yearningly that Susan forgave her everything and tried to listen. She was ordinarily a good listener and found this no trouble even with bores, but her mind was occupied with how she'd break the news to Richard that she was getting a divorce and marrying Jean-Paul. Of course, she wouldn't mention Jean-Paul immediately. It seemed so cruel to give Richard a glimpse of his child and then snatch her away. And did she want to marry Jean-Paul? She loved him and she didn't. She'd stupidly promised a long time ago to marry him when the war ended, both to put an end to his nagging and because it sometimes seemed the war would go on forever. And she could no longer use the excuse of breaking up his marriage. His wife had apparently been seeing someone, too, all the time Susan had felt so guilty about being with Jean-Paul. She'd already asked Jean-Paul for a divorce.

What she'd love, Susan thought, was to have everything as it was—with the war over. To go on working for the *Courier* and spending days off with Laura and nights off with Jean-Paul, to visit Gina at her studio and take their children to the park. She must write Gina. What a painful time it was for her now, with all the husbands and lovers returning, while the man she loved was dead. In Italy. And Eddy dead in Normandy. And millions of murdered Jews in death camps. Susan looked down at her sleeping daughter, fingers curled, thumb in mouth. What if some maniac swooped up her fragile child and smashed her brains against the wall? Unthinkable. But it had happened to women whose children were as dear to them as Laura to her.

Again she was haunted by the story Nelson Mercer had told her, and by her inaction. Ridiculous to think you could have saved anyone, she told herself; you're not that powerful. But she could have tried harder, could have maybe interviewed Roosevelt's special envoy sent to Egypt. Written it up. But would anyone have believed it? Even now, with the evidence in, people were having trouble absorbing the truth.

And in a few short hours she would be in the country where it all began. She felt a mounting excitement and guilt. She wasn't excited about seeing Richard, but about seeing Berlin. She wanted to view the destruction firsthand, to talk to the Germans and find out how it happened.

The truth was, she loved to travel.

Laura slept away on Diane Deal's lap. Diane Deal slept, too. Susan couldn't sleep. Or so she thought. The next thing she knew, she was awakened by the commotion around her.

Looking down, she saw pewter lakes and deep green forests. Soon the plane was circling over Templehof Airport. There was a sudden hush as if everyone on the plane held their breath in fear and anticipation, not at the thought of landing but what happened once they had. Then the plane was rolling across the ground, and around her was an outburst of talk and hysteria-tinged laughter.

Diane's lap felt empty after she'd handed Laura back to her mother. Her throat constricted, blood rang in her ears. Please, God, she begged, let him be here. Let him be happy to see me. She took Susan Lund's hand.

Of course, he'll be here, but will I recognize him? Susan asked herself. Laura held one hand, Diane Deal the other. It was as if she had two children. Poor Diane. Poor thing. I hope to hell her husband is here. For her sake and mine. What if he isn't and she keeps hanging on? But I promised to stay with her until she found him, didn't I? What's Richard going to think of all this? He'll be annoyed, I bet.

Around her, names were called. Men and women rushed into each other's arms, children were lifted up, looked at, and hugged. Susan saw Richard craning his neck. He didn't look at all like the lean and embittered soldier she'd expected.

Maybe she'd seen too many war movies. Lean, yes, but otherwise fit and smiling. At her! At Laura! She ran to him, happy at how happy she was to see him.

"Richard . . . oh, Richard!"

He kissed her, swung Laura up in his arms.

"Are you Daddy?" Laura asked .

"That's me," Richard said, nuzzling her. "I don't have to ask who you are. I knew the minute I saw you."

Laura was enchanted with her father. She patted his cheek. "Daddy! Daddy! Daddy!" she crooned.

When Richard put Laura down to pick up the suitcases, Laura cried.

Susan had to take the suitcases so he could carry Laura. She was totally ignored. So this is the gratitude I get from my child. I'm the one who saw she got her vitamins and that her shoes fit and worried about fevers, and she has eyes only for him. Silly. Laura could love whom she pleased. Susan, after all, had the privilege of loving Laura.

Richard put his cap on Laura's head. She was almost lost in it. "Hey, you two, let's go home," he said. He turned to Susan. "I wish it were home. Ohio instead of here. I hate this place."

Diane listened to the happy voices around her, watched embracing husbands and wives with envious tears. He wasn't here. She might have known. But give him time. Maybe he was delayed. He might not have received the cablegram yet.

Susan Lund's handsome husband was smiling down at her. Susan introduced them. "Diane didn't decide to come over until the last minute," Susan explained. "Her husband may not even know she's here."

"Of course, he might be here and not able to find me in this mob," Diane said. But the mob was already thinning out.

"I'll have him paged," Susan's husband said. "What's his name?"

"Major Michael Deal."

Susan's husband disappeared, and a few minutes later she heard a loudspeaker requesting that Major Michael Deal report to Gate 7.

They remained at the gate for a good half-hour—or a bad half-hour, considering the agony Diane underwent; then Richard told her to come along with them, and they'd call her husband from their place.

Diane was grateful she'd found such wonderful friends. She sat in the backseat of an Army car with the luggage.

They passed blocks of rubble, bomb craters, skeletons of buildings.

"They say this was a beautiful city," Richard Lund said. "Hard to tell. About the only thing still standing is the Brandenburg Gate. Here's Unter den Linden. I hear they're going to plant some trees here soon."

"Daddy, Daddy, Daddy," Laura crooned.

"You're my girl," he said, hugging her with his free arm.

"You two," Susan said, "don't mind me."

"Hey, you jealous?" Richard Lund asked. He let go of his daughter and affectionately mussed his wife's hair. Diane could have cried, they made her feel so lonely.

About a half-hour later they came to a sign saying "KONIGSGARTEN" with an arrow pointing to block on block of houses under shade trees. Along the curb were garbage cans marked "U.S. Property."

"This is our so-called home," Richard Lund said, "our home away from home."

He stopped before a house identical to the others. It was like Fort Benning, Diane thought. Soon she and Michael would be living here. They'd start another baby. It wasn't too late. The war, Dr. Gurney had said, was a wonderful time for romance and a terrible time for marriage. But the war was over, and she and Michael could pick up where they'd left off.

Richard Lund carried his daughter and a suitcase into a house already furnished.

"Did you do this, or did it come this way?" Susan asked.

"It came this way, more or less," he said. "Mostly more. I got rid of some stuff, it was too dark and depressing."

"I'm glad," Susan said, kissing him, then remembered it was tactless to show her happiness before poor unhappy Diane. She turned to Diane, who wore a fixed smile. "Why don't you try calling your husband where he works? He might still be there."

"I don't know where he works."

Susan tried to hide her amazement.

"Do you know his unit?" Richard asked. "You can call there, and they'll tell you where to reach him."

"I've never spoken on a German phone before."

"Don't worry, the phone system here is handled by Army personnel or German civilians who speak English."

Diane nervously put the call through. While she waited on the phone, Susan made some tea and brought her a cup. Diane was thanking her for the tea when a woman's voice announced, "Special Services."

"Is this Major Deal's office?"

"He's out at the moment," the woman said.

"Do you know where I can reach him? This is urgent."

"Well, you might try calling him at home. If he's not there, his wife might be able to tell you where to find him."

"But I'm his wife," Diane said.

21. Diane

Diane was in the Lunds' bathroom washing her tear-streaked face when the doorbell rang. A moment later there was a rap on the bathroom door and Susan calling, "He's here!"

She was seized by panic and astonishment. How could Michael get here so soon? It was scarcely ten minutes since, at Susan's suggestion, she'd called his office again and left the Lunds' address and phone number for him to get in touch with her. Her hands shook as she rifled through her makeup kit for the yellow pills Dr. Gurney had prescribed for their calming effect. She swallowed four. Two never worked anymore. She applied lipstick and combed her hair and asked that person in the mirror what she was so scared of. She was beautiful; that wasn't mere vanity—everyone said so. The man out there was her husband, with the nice frown-smile, who looked at her as if she were the only woman in the world. He'd promised he'd love her forever.

When she went out, she found Susan questioning Michael. "Don't you remember," she was saying, "that train going to New York. In the diner? And those two rich old ladies?"

"I'll be damned," he said, smiling. Then he became aware of Diane's presence, and there was a long silence. He smiled at her, but there wasn't the warmth in it even that he'd had for Susan. He was looking at her with the merciless eyes of a hardened criminal. This wasn't the Michael she knew. He looked mean and tough and years older. Had the war done this to him? "Michael . . . ?" she said tentatively, as if he actually were a stranger.

"How've you been, babe?" he asked, and kissed her on the cheek.

Even the Lunds looked incredulous. He turned toward them. "Thanks for your trouble," he said, picked up the various pieces of her luggage, and nodded her way. "Let's get going, it's not going to be easy finding you a hotel room."

Outside a showy red convertible glinted in the light of a weak sun. He dumped the luggage in the backseat and let her open her door.

"Would you put the top up, please?" she asked. "It'll blow my hair. I had it done special." She didn't add "for you." He should know that.

"Yeah, okay," he said, and pushed a button. The top descended over them like a dark cloud. After fastening some clasps and before starting up, he looked over. "So, why did you come over, when I asked you not to?"

She bit her lip and looked down at her gloved hands. "I thought when we saw each other . . . things might be different."

"Now you know," he said, started the car, and sped off.

Now she knew what? How much he hated her? But why? She looked out at the gray city blurred by her tears. A city of ruins and rubble. Signs in a strange language and strange people on strange streets, but no more strange than this man she'd married, the only familiar thing about him that billed cap set rakishly on his head. He'd always said he'd never make a good soldier, that he wasn't one for Army rules and regulations. He didn't abide by any rules.

He looked over. "Don't cry, goddammit. Tears aren't going to do you any good." But his voice had softened.

"You didn't get my cablegram?"

"Nope. The Army always screws up."

"At your office that woman said to call your wife. What did that mean?"

"That means they screw up there, too. She's German, she doesn't understand English so well."

"Michael?"

"Yeah?"

"It wasn't my fault the baby died."

"Jesus, who said it was?"

"That letter you sent after I wrote you, saying, 'So you got what you wanted.' That was cruel. Isn't that why you hate me, because our baby died?"

"Oh, my God, that was bad timing. I wasn't referring to the baby, I was referring to what I found out over here.

Yeah, I knew you felt bad about it, wanted a kid. It was the one thing your lover couldn't give you. So when you got pregnant and I'd done my duty, you got rid of me. Had me shipped out. So here you are back again. You want me to give you another kid?"

Lover? Shipped out? Maybe she wasn't the crazy, confused one, maybe it was he. "I don't know what you're talking about."

He slammed on the brakes. "Here's the hotel. I'll get you a room so you can rest up before flying back."

She put her hand on his sleeve. "Michael, what do you mean, I got rid of you?"

"Hands off," he said. She took her hand away. "Listen, don't try to lie your way out of it. I ran into my old outfit in North Africa. And found out there what I couldn't back at Fort Benning. You had that hotshot general at the Pentagon cut special orders to send me overseas. General DeWitt. A friend of your family's.

"I went off my head when my buddy told me. Hell, I got some of my boys together that night and we wiped out every goddamned Kraut sniper within a ten-mile radius. That's how I made major and got a lot of hardware. Medals to you. But I didn't want anything but to die. Then you write saying the baby died. That baby wasn't real. What was real were my buddies dying all around me in Africa. And when I wrote that, it wasn't about the baby's dying but about your getting rid of me."

"Michael, I didn't know anything about it. Believe me, please. General DeWitt was Uncle Clayton's friend, not mine. Uncle Clayton must have done that behind my back. Remember when he said I'd regret it if I didn't call off my lawyer?"

"Oh, yeah, sure. Easy to blame him now that he's dead."

"He might be dead, but he's still managing to ruin my life. Go ahead, leave. If you believe that, you'd believe anything. I don't know about any lover. I don't know about anything. Anything. Don't get me any hotel room, I'll get my own."

She jumped from the car, crying, careening into passersby, and ran into the hotel past a doorman who looked for a minute as if he might block her way.

Michael came in after her. People were staring. He put his hands on her shoulder and in a soft whisper said, "Wait here a minute, honey, I'll get your luggage and check us in."

Honey. Us. She could wait for him forever.

After Michael registered, the bellboy—who was a man in his fifties—took them up to a room. It was chilly and depressing, with dark claw-footed furniture and a worn carpet. But there was a double bed.

"Shabby but clean, as they say," Michael said. "Sorry, I couldn't come up with anything better, but this is short notice, and the best hotels have been taken over by Occupation."

He was looking at her in that old Michael way. "You're so beautiful. I'd forgotten."

"I don't feel so beautiful at the moment."

"Yeah, you must be tired. I shouldn't have thrown all that at you the first thing. But I couldn't keep it in."

"I'm glad you didn't. I couldn't bear your believing I'd had you sent out. I love you so much, Michael, so much." She put her arms around him and held him to her. "How could you think I'd do such a thing?"

"I guess when I figured out what was going on between you and your pal Cindy, I was ready to believe anything. At first I thought it was her, then I thought it was just kid stuff . . ."

"It was, Michael, it was. Cindy was so sweet to me. And she's very affectionate." Michael was watching her; she was getting mixed up. "I mean, you know, Southern girls are like that, we kiss each other and things, and it doesn't mean anything. We're very . . . demonstrative."

"Yeah? I wish you'd been a little more demonstrative with me."

"Michael, wait a minute," she said, and kissed him. "Just stay here and keep your eyes closed until I say open, all right? Here," she said, and tilted his cap over his eyes. "I'll only be a minute." She took the overnight bag containing her nightgown and practically ran into the bathroom. There was a bath but no shower. Anyway, she didn't have time for a real bath. She washed under her arms and between her legs. The water was tepid. The chill bathroom helped to hurry her. She slipped on her nightgown, a pale green one with eggshell-colored lace straps and bodice. Her nipples peeked through the lace like pink buds, and the curved outline of her body showed through the diaphanous silk. After dabbing perfume between her breasts and thighs, she tiptoed back out to the bedroom. Michael still sat in the chair, but he didn't so much sit as slump. The cap pulled down over his eyes gave him a look of dejection.

She tilted his cap back. "Open," she said, and whirled around in front of him.

"Hey, are we going dancing?"

"In bed," she said.

He stood up, put his hands lightly on her shoulders, and kissed each cheek. "You're tired, honey, get some sleep. I have to go back to the office and catch up on some work."

"Work! It's dark out. You don't work at night."

"There's an important report I've got to get out tonight."

"If it's so important, why weren't you working on it this afternoon?"

"Because I had other things to attend to. Now, don't nag, you've just got here. Tell you what, I'll order your supper sent up. Then you can have a good sleep, and by that time, I'll be back." He was backing away from her as he talked, as if she were a crazy person and he was trying to get out of harm's reach, as if he were afraid of her. By the time he finished saying what he had to say, he opened the door and disappeared.

In his hurry to leave, he'd left his cigarette lighter behind. It was gold-plated, very handsome, with the initials M.D. Dr. Deal. She sat flicking it on and off, thinking: I could set fire to this nightgown and burn up; then he'd be sorry. No, that was too terrible. I could take pills. How many? But she really didn't want to die, and what if he didn't come back in time? It wasn't work he was hurrying off to, but some woman. Maybe the one who'd answered the phone in his office. She could even have torn up that cablegram and made up that business about staying with his wife to deliberately cause trouble. Some German woman. He'd said she was German, hadn't he? Some Kraut trying to come between them, break them up. She wouldn't succeed. Michael had loved her once, he'd love her again.

A knock sounded; she jumped up and ran to the door. Back so soon? In her excitement she had trouble with the door handle. "Just a minute," she called. A man said something in German. "Who is it?" she asked, frightened. "Is food," the voice said. Food. Michael had said he'd have supper sent up. She put on her robe and opened the door to a thin, aged man in a red jacket. He was carrying a tray, which he set on the table, then bowed and smiled. "Is all right?" he asked. She nodded. "If you would anything else like, please to call," he said, and bowed his way out.

On the plate was a gray slab of meat, sauerkraut, and potatoes. She wouldn't have to worry about wrecking her diet here. She left the food untouched and took two more yellow pills, then rang for the waiter to collect the tray so she could sleep until Michael came back. She worried that the waiter would be upset that she hadn't touched the food, but she needn't have. She saw his eyes linger hungrily on the plate and knew the food wouldn't be wasted.

The minute he left, she got into bed, or rather sank into it, pulling a thick quilted comforter up to her chin. She closed her eyes, waiting for sleep. But the strain of the day and the strangeness of her surroundings kept her awake despite the pills and her weariness. Outside, heavy steps trod the halls, and voices spoke in a heavy, coarse language. Finally she submerged into something that was more like a thick soup than sleep, but kept jerking awake at sudden sounds: an abrupt laugh, a clink of keys, footsteps that she hoped might be Michael's.

A hand reached toward her in the darkness, a beautiful hand with tapered fingers and manicured nails. She recognized the fact that it was a man's hand because of the oval shape of the nails and the clear polish. A finger curved into a C, beckoning her onward. She floated too close, and the hand clamped around her wrist, pulling her down and down. He was smiling up at her from the coffin, and then laughing that awful mocking laugh of his. Her body became damp with sweat and fear. She screamed noiselessly and struggled up out of blankets into wakefulness. Gray dawn pressed against the curtains. She saw her suitcase beside the claw-footed armoire, and heard strange sounds down below in the street. He still hadn't come back. Where was he? Why had he left her alone on her first night here in enemy country? What if he never came back?

He came back about an hour later. She kept her eyes closed, feigning sleep, hearing him tiptoe across the room to the bathroom and hearing running water as he washed off the smell of that other woman. She'd be damned if she'd let him in her after he'd been in someone else.

But he settled down on the far side of the bed and stayed there. Slowly she realized what he'd done. He'd gone to some whore out of consideration for her. She'd aroused him to the point of no return, and realizing how tired she was, he'd sought out a prostitute. Poor, darling Michael. It wouldn't happen again. She rolled over and put her arms around his naked waist. But he didn't respond. He was either asleep or pretending to be.

A few hours later she got up, bathed, brushed her hair and her teeth, and returned to bed, waiting for him to wake up and discover her. But the longer he slept and the brighter the room became, the less she wanted to make love. Maybe after coffee and a good breakfast, or better yet, tonight, after dinner by candlelight. But men didn't care about romantic settings. Uncle Clayton, after that weekend of courtship in Atlanta, hadn't the patience for champagne, candlelight, or soft music. Men wanted it when they wanted it. It wasn't Michael's fault. The best thing to do was get it over and done with; then she could forget about sex and have a good time.

She pressed against him. When he shifted away, she shifted, too, easing a leg between his legs. She liked feeling his smooth back and buttocks against her. If only it could be just this, this snuggling. But he was awake now, turning toward her. At first he was hesitant, his hands slowly caressing her while she wondered if she should mention moving to a better hotel. There must be a better place than this, she thought as his hands stroked her thighs. His breath was now hot on her face, and she had her thoughts interrupted as he climbed on top of her and pushed in. She faked enjoyment, uttered little screams of ecstasy, stared up at his face blind with passion. She gave a deep sigh of relief when it was over. There were worse things.

He smoothed her hair back from her forehead, smiled. "Poor Diane, I'm sorry."

"Sorry?"

"You deserve an E for effort, at least. You don't have to sacrifice yourself for me."

The more she protested enjoyment, the less he believed. God almighty, she thought, not only do I have to do it, but I have to convince him how much I love doing it. It's not fair.

"It won't work," he said. "It's too late. I don't know, maybe you aren't lying about having me shipped out. But the damage has been done, it's still hopeless, it's too late."

"It's not too late. I haven't had a chance. You've hated me all these years for something I didn't do. Now you hate me from habit."

"I don't hate you, I don't hate you," he murmured, and his voice had that same soft furry quality as when he'd loved her.

"You loved me once. You'll love me again," she said confidently.

"It's not that easy. Anyway, you won't like it over here, there's nothing but poverty and hunger. No bright lights or fancy stores or restaurants, I'll be at work, you'll be bored."

"We could live out at Konigsgarten. It would be just like being back at Fort Benning, and I'd have Susan Lund for company."

"We can't get in there. All the places are taken."

"Well, we could live somewhere else until someone is sent back home and moves out."

"The waiting list is a mile long."

"You mean you've looked into it?"

"I mean all waiting lists are long over here."

"I'm not going home. I'm staying with you. Even if you won't have anything to do with me. There's nothing for me back there. Home is where you are."

"Suit yourself," he said coldly.

She turned away so he wouldn't see her tears, then thought: No, tears are my only weapon, and turned only just far enough away so he'd think she was hiding them.

He stroked her hair. "Diane, I'm sorry, but it's better if you went back."

Again she refused; again she pleaded for a house out in Konigsgarten.

"I told you Konigsgarten was out," he said, then sighed. "Okay, I'll look around and see if I can find something decent."

She'd won the battle if not the war.

What he found was more than decent. It was beautiful. Almost as beautiful as Colquitt Hall. And she hated it almost as much. Seated beside her in the red convertible, Michael pointed to it proudly. "The Army requisitioned it from some top Nazi who's presently in prison. I had to pull strings to get it from some colonel who wanted it for his family."

She wished he'd let the colonel have it, and wondered if it were her fate to live in luxury and misery. All she wanted was a nice little two-story house in Konigsgarten, Michael, and eventually a baby. But she couldn't even broach the subject of a baby to Michael. He'd think she wanted him around for baby-making purposes only. And he imagined he was keeping her in the style she was accustomed to and preferred.

The house was in fairy-tale country, with lakes and dark green fir trees. Its terraced hills overlooked a castle. Although their place wasn't a castle, it might as well have been. It had been "modernized" with plate-glass-window walls in the living room on the first floor. On the second floor a balcony ran the length of the master bedroom. The house came with the Nazi's furnishings (he'd get it all back when he'd served his prison term) and a battery of servants, who might or might not have been his. There was a cook, gardener, houseman, two maids, and a woman who came once a week just to polish the brass. Diane was uneasy around them and made herself scarce. They stole food, liquor, and cigarettes. In fact, snitched more than any colored servants she'd ever heard of. Yet they called themselves the master race and considered themselves superior. She knew they stole from need and hostility, but wasn't that why the colored servants had stolen, too? Wasn't that what anyone would do? She asked Michael. He said people stole not only from need but also from greed. She'd forgotten his cynicism.

His war experiences had only justified his beliefs. If he didn't love her, she comforted herself with the thought that he loved no one. And he appeared happy in his hate. He wore his hat at a jaunty angle, smiled contemptuously, and walked with a spring in his step. He laughed when she said she felt sorry for the Germans.

"After what they did to the Jews?" he said.

"But they didn't know what was happening."

"Crap."

It was one of their few conversational exchanges. He slept until nearly noon and didn't return until nearly dawn. When she commented on the odd hours of his work, he said Special Services meant seeing that the troops were entertained, and those were the entertainment hours.

Diane called Susan and invited her over, but like her, Susan's husband had the car all day and she couldn't get away. The only other form of transportation was the tram lines, and they didn't run out as far as where Diane lived. Occasionally Susan would get her husband to drop her off in the morning, and she and Laura would spend the day. Diane loved having Laura there, too, and Susan thought the fresh air and country good for her.

Talking to Susan was like having a session with Dr. Gurney. She didn't know how it came about, but soon she was telling Susan all the sorrows in her life—except, of course, the secret sorrows of Uncle Clayton and Cindy. The only difference was that Susan couldn't prescribe pills. Diane was worried about this. Although she'd brought a big supply along, it was fast dwindling. She imposed a daily ration, but the fewer pills she took, the deeper her depressions became.

She wandered about the house, trying to keep out of the way of the servants. She tried to understand Michael. Sometimes she thought he deliberately avoided her so that she'd go back home.

She was not going back. Not until he did. She tried to find out what he wanted to do after he got out of the Army. "You don't have to worry about money, you can have fun," she told him.

"Making money is fun. I'm not going to be kept by a rich wife."

"Michael, you don't have to get so mad, it was only a suggestion."

"I don't need your suggestions. Or your money."

She almost wished he were a fortune hunter. The trouble was the war and Germany. The war had hardened him. Germany depressed him as much as her. Back home they'd be happy.

The high point in her life these days was when she received reports from her various holdings. She went over the reports carefully, seated at her desk by the window wall overlooking the terraced hills and the castle below with the silvery lake. She sipped coffee, unaware when it became cool, and with a calculator Michael had given her, checked expenditures, profits and losses, looking for inaccuracies. She kept tabs on everything. Since it was known that she did so, she wasn't cheated. Or not cheated as much as she might have been, she amended. Once, she'd added up the yearly profits and was gratified to see that she was a multimillionaire. That wasn't counting the paper profits. But what good was the money doing her, just lying there and accumulating?

She was at her desk the day she saw the woman coming up the winding road toward the house. It was a chill spring morning with gusts of wind dispersing wisps of fog. In the distance the lake was a dull silver between the greenish-black forest. The woman, tall and thin, wore a black hooded cape that billowed in the wind. Diane was fascinated but a little frightened by the sudden appearance of this witchlike woman in this fairy-tale countryside. She glimpsed a face, startlingly white, under the hood, before the woman disappeared along the path leading to the side of the house where the main entrance was.

A minute later Diane heard the reverberating gong at the door. She wanted to run and answer it to find out who the mysterious woman was, but forced herself to sit and wait. She couldn't usurp the houseman's duty.

The houseman, in a striped jacket and dark trousers, appeared in the doorway to announce that a Fräulein von Someone was here to see her. Before Diane could get the name straight, the woman swept into the room. She might have been one of the conquered people, but she acted as if she were the victor and Diane the conquered. "I have come to speak to Frau Major Deal," she said arrogantly. "Is not your mother here?"

Diane said, "Huh?" then laughed. The woman apparently thought she was the daughter of the house. "I'm Mrs. Deal."

"Oh? I did not expect to see someone in saddlebacks and bobby socks," the woman said with an air of disapproval.

Saddlebacks? She must mean saddle shoes. Maybe that was British for them. Her accent was.

"I have come on behalf of Colonel von Sachen. There is a particular painting that he claims he cannot live without. He asked would you be so kind as to let him have it. It belongs, after all, to him."

"Are prisoners allowed to hang paintings on their cell walls?"

"He is no longer lodged in prison. He has served his term. By all rights he should be permitted to return here, but no . . ." The woman glared at Diane. "So, he is at present living in inferior quarters and wishes his painting."

"If he wants it, he can have it, but he can come and get it himself."

"He is too embarrassed to ask. I am doing so as a favor."

"I'm sorry, I didn't hear who you were." Diane knew she was just stalling; there was no standing up to this woman.

"I am Fräulein Ursula von Frisch. I live down there," she said, pointing to the castle with the lake. "It is where the von Frisches have lived for centuries."

Diane could hear Michael saying "Bully for them." But she could only be polite. "What is this painting like?"

"It is a still life of a dead rabbit on a table with blood. A knife also with blood, if I remember correctly."

"Oh, yes, that gory one. I took it down and put it in a closet. He can have it."

"Thank you," the woman said. "It is Major Deal, your husband, who drives that red automobile, is it not?"

Diane nodded.

"We see him pass by frequently, but you are not with him. You do not go out often. Is it not lonely?"

Diane nodded again. "I wish we lived closer to Berlin. At least near the tram lines."

"Oh, but that is too sad. If at any time you would wish to go anywhere, you must let us know. We go to Berlin often. Or Horst, our driver, can take you."

Diane was touched by her generosity. To offer a complete stranger the use of her driver and car when that stranger was the enemy, an American, was a kindness she wouldn't have expected from this arrogant woman.

After Ursula von Frisch's visit, Diane wasn't so lonely. Ursula invited her to the castle, which despite its dampness and gloom was nevertheless a castle with ancestral portraits, marble fireplaces, and numerous rooms she'd love to explore. And Michael was wrong about there no longer being any fine shops or restaurants in Berlin. Ursula knew of them and took Diane there. In turn, Diane took Ursula to the PX and commissary, where Ursula chose exotic cans (which Ursula called tins) of quail eggs and vichyssoise and pâté with truffles, while lamenting that there was no caviar. Friedrich von Frisch usually accompanied them. At first Diane thought he was Ursula's husband, not twin brother, as she later learned. He was by far the more attractive of the two. Ursula called him Freddie. He had long curly lashes and a touch of silver at his sideburns. His limp was more of an enhancement than a handicap. Ursula said he'd acquired the limp in the early days of battle and after that had nothing to do with the war. Even so, he loved the toy soldiers displayed in the children's section of the PX, and Diane had bought him a Rebel Army complete with horses and cannons that he was delighted with.

She kept her friendship with the von Frisches a secret from Michael, sure he'd object to her consorting with the enemy. But wasn't he consorting with his German secretary at his office? Fraternizing, they called it. Anyway, the von Frisches weren't really the enemy. They'd been against the war from the start and always despised the Nazis. "It was only the lower classes who were for Hitler," Ursula said.

Diane didn't like being so dependent on the von Frisches for transportation and asked if there were any cars available, even something secondhand, if necessary.

"Oh, you can buy anything, if you have the money," Ursula said. "If you are interested, I know of a charming little sports car. You will adore it. There is a belt that fits over its hood, just so. It looks like a British Mackintosh and drives like a dream. But I warn you, it is very, very expensive."

Diane said price was unimportant.

"You Americans, you are all so rich," Freddie said.

"Ah, but I think our little Diane, she is richer yet. Is that not so?" Ursula said, patting her hand affectionately.

So that Diane wouldn't have to go to any extra bother, Ursula drove the car to her house. Diane fell in love with it immediately. Actually, the car was quite cheap. She paid Ursula in dollars, which the buyer preferred, and half-expected

Michael to object to her buying a car without consulting him, but he didn't mind at all. In fact, he admired the car, too. "How much did you pay for it?" When she told him, he whistled. "You really got taken for a ride. Well, it's your money, kid. Enjoy it."

Ursula also took her to the smartest dress shops. She knew all about Paris fashions and was very particular about fit. "Yes, the dress looks lovely on you," Ursula said, "but then, you look lovely in anything."

Diane stood before the three-way mirror in a dressing room, eyeing herself in a white crepe dress with cape.

"Here, you see," Ursula said, removing the cape. "It does not drape right over the bust. You will have to have it taken in, *comme ça*." Her hands lightly touched Diane's shoulders and came to rest on her breasts. Diane, looking at their reflections, full face and in profile, had a sudden uncanny sensation that the person standing behind her was a tall, dark, and attractive man.

22. Susan

Susan was upstairs dressing when she heard the car drive up. In stocking feet she padded to the window and looked down to see a smart foreign sports car with belted hood swing into the driveway. A woman in white wearing dark glasses and a straw cartwheel hat got out. She looked like a movie star traveling incognito. Susan recognized the car before she recognized its owner. Diane had described the car on the phone.

Susan hurried down the stairs, reaching the door just as the doorbell sounded.

"I came early to help," Diane said, "but maybe I'm too early," she added, looking at Susan's stocking feet.

"It's your party, you can be as early as you like. There's nothing to do, though. Frau Munger took care of the sandwiches and things before she left."

Susan was giving an informal afternoon party for Diane to meet other Army wives now that she had her car and could get around.

"Excuse me, I'll just be a minute," Susan said, and started

back up the stairs to put on the finishing touches. Diane followed. Susan fervently hoped Diane would make friends at the party. She felt sorry for Diane, but it was disconcerting the way Diane shadowed her whenever they were together. When Diane had more friends, she'd have less cause to hang on to her.

But apparently Diane had made some friends. She was speaking enthusiastically about a couple called the von Frisches. "They're neighbors. They live in that castle down below. You know, by the lake. And they have such wonderful old-world charm."

"Are they German?"

"Oh, yes, but not Nazis, if that's what you mean. They're from an old aristocratic family and were against the war from the start. She's really a godsend. She knows just where to find the best beauty shops and dress shops and dressmakers. She chose this dress," Diane said, pivoting around on a high heel for Susan's benefit. "How do you like it?"

"Very nice," Susan said, "but then, you look good in anything."

"Ursula said the same thing, but she was a bit more complimentary about it. Of course, Americans don't appreciate the quality and workmanship that goes into European clothes."

The dress was somehow both too old and too young for Diane. Certainly it was far too dressy for an informal party. Susan wondered what the other women would think when they arrived in their simple cotton dresses and sensible heels. She was glad when Diane took off her hat and dark glasses.

She needn't have worried, the other wives were clearly admiring—of Diane and of her car, which they noticed when they came in. Diane had the kind of beauty that wasn't competitive, since no one could compete.

Susan passed about tea sandwiches, poured tea and coffee, and felt pleased with herself. Diane would make new friends. She wouldn't have her on her conscience, feeling that she was negligent when Diane phoned to remind her she hadn't called. Also, she wouldn't have to worry about those von Frisches in that castle with all that old-world charm. She hadn't liked what she'd heard, but her dislike might be only because they were German.

Soon her guests were playing the game they frequently played whenever they got together, the "What-I'm-going-to-do-when-I-get-back-home" game.

"I'm taking my kids to the corner drugstore and we're going to fill up on hot-fudge sundaes until we burst," Betty Flowers said.

"You can get sundaes at the PX."

"Oh, but they're not the same thing at all."

"I'm going to have a kitchen with all the latest modern conveniences," Patsy Murphy said.

"And a bathroom where the plumbing works," Glenna Millhauser added.

"Me, I'm just going to get down on my hands and knees and kiss American soil," Ruth Lederman said.

"Michael—he's my husband—and I are going to take a year off and travel all over America," Diane said. "We'll go see the Grand Canyon and Hollywood and Old Faithful and Niagara Falls. It'll be a kind of second honeymoon," she added, blushing, "since the first was such a dud."

The other wives looked at her with sympathy, envy, and wonder. Sympathy for the dud honeymoon, envy that her husband could take a year off to travel while theirs had to find jobs, and wonder that anyone who wore foreign clothes and drove a foreign car was so eager to see America. Susan wondered, too. She wondered if Michael had actually agreed to this tour of America or if it were merely a dream of Diane's.

Glenna Millhauser said she was going to turn the radio dial from station to station just to hear nothing but good old English spoken instead of either stilted English or German grunts.

"Be glad you only have to hear German on the radio," Betty Flowers said. "Pity poor us. We live next door to a German, and there's nothing we can do about it, because she's married to an American officer."

"You mean that showoffy major?" Glenna Millhauser asked. "My husband says he's a black marketer."

"Does he drive a big fancy red convertible?" Ruth Lederman asked.

"That's the one," Betty Flowers confirmed. "You can't miss him."

Diane looked from one face to the other. "Red convertible?" she asked.

Susan saw disaster coming, but didn't know how to avert it.

"What's his name?" Diane asked in a near-whisper.

"I don't know, Major Someone. That's why we have to be nice—my husband is just a lowly lieutenant."

"Oh, I need more hot water for the tea," Susan said. "Diane, would you do me a favor and get some?"

But her ruse didn't work, perhaps Diane didn't even hear the question. "Is his name Major Deal?" she asked.

"Oh, you know him," Betty Flowers said.

Diane's face was as white as the crumpled napkin she let fall onto the coffee table. She was out the door like a shot. Susan ran after her, but by the time she got outside, it was only to see the sports car skid around the gravel circle and speed off.

"Did I say something wrong?" Betty Flowers asked. Susan could hardly blame her for not remembering Diane's last name during introductions. She blamed herself.

"But my intentions were good," she told Richard when he came home.

"The road to hell is paved with good intentions."

Susan kept calling Diane's house, but only got the German maid.

"Maybe I should call the police and tell them to be on the lookout. Her car's easy enough to spot. The awful thing is, you know, her parents were killed in a car crash. I'm afraid she might unconsciously try to kill herself the same way in her hysterical state. I don't know what to do."

"There's nothing you can do," Richard said.

"I could call her husband."

"Stay out of it," Richard advised. "What you should do is mind your own business. If you spent more time on your house and child, this would never have happened."

"That's not fair. Laura has her playmates. She doesn't want me hovering over her. And why bother with the house when Frau Munger does such a good job for next to nothing? You know I hate housework."

It was not a new argument. It was just a new opportunity for Richard to repeat her shortcomings. Worse yet, he was right. She was bored. She meddled and gossiped with the other wives. She'd love to see more of Berlin, but since Richard had the car, that was impossible. The most she saw of the city was driving to and from the post exchange or commissary with some lucky wife who had a car for the day. No one ever wanted to go sightseeing. They hated Germany and pretended they were home. She missed America, too. Or rather New York. She missed her job, Gina, and Jean-Paul.

In that order. Poor Jean-Paul. She'd treated him shabbily. Written him just once as soon as she'd arrived to tell him it was all over. That she still loved Richard. She'd tried to be kind, but anything said under such circumstances was cruel. It was seeing Richard after such a long time and wanting to love him that had given her the illusion she did. She didn't love him, either.

Now she sat at her dressing table in her slip, with her back turned to him, stalling. She kept hoping he'd fall asleep before she got into bed. She cold-creamed her face and brushed her hair, glancing from time to time at his reflection. He lay on his side, blond-crew-cut head profiled on the pillow. By the tense way he lay, she knew he was awake. Why couldn't she love him? She had once. He hadn't changed. That was the whole trouble. She had.

"Aren't you ever coming to bed?" he asked.

"In a minute." She realized stalling was pointless. She got her diaphragm from the dressing-table drawer and started toward the bathroom.

"Why do you always have to put that damn thing in? It's so calculating. Anyway, we should have another kid."

"Why? You're always complaining about what a lousy mother I am to Laura."

"I didn't say you were a lousy mother. I said you should spend more time with her."

She sighed. "You're away all day. How do you know how much time I spend? I see that she's fed, clothed, cuddled, and read to. I can't monopolize all her time. She prefers Timmy Anderson to me. And I don't want to be one of those awful possessive mothers who won't let their children live their own lives. That's no kind of life for her—or me."

"I know it's not much of a life for you here," he said, completely missing the point. "Things will return to normal when we get back to Ohio."

"I don't want to go back to Ohio."

"You don't know what you want until I tell you," he said, smiling. "Come on to bed, honey, forget about that thing."

But she didn't. And he made love to her the way he always did these days. Routinely. She guessed that he'd probably been faithful all these years. She almost wished he hadn't. Maybe if he'd slept with more women he'd have learned more about lovemaking. When they'd first married, she'd tried to be innovative, but now she lacked interest. She sensed that he preferred it this way, anyway. Frequent and fast. Over, in, and out, like the Air Corps calling code.

In the morning she phoned Diane again and was told by a German-speaking someone she was sleeping. Susan left her name for Diane to call back. She was relieved to hear Diane was safe at home at least.

The postman brought a fat letter from Gina. Delighted to hear from her, and further delighted that the letter was long, she got some tea, sat at the kitchen table, and hurriedly opened the envelope.

Dear Susan,

It's three in the morning, so don't expect me to make much sense. I'm too excited to sleep. Just finished what I think is my best work. Wonderful feeling when you know you've done something good.

Guess what?!!! I've just been invited to show some stuff in a London gallery. One of the best. Isn't that terrific? I think dear darling Hans had something to do with it. I'm still studying with him, although he says there's not much more he can teach me. But I can't give him up.

Finally, people are beginning to understand abstract expressionism. No more blank looks and "how-interestings." I hope all this talk about painting isn't boring you. Hans says all geniuses are monomaniacal. And I'm not going to be humble and protest I'm no genius. At the moment I feel like one. Of course, tomorrow I'll look at what I did and think it's all wrong. Then on to something else, and I'll think that's all wrong, and like what I did earlier or else hate everything. Remember at the New School when we used to have our discussions on art and life? That seems centuries ago.

You don't say much about what you're doing. What is it like in Berlin? If you stay in Europe long enough, maybe we can get together. Wouldn't it be fun to meet in some sidewalk café in Paris?!!! I'm taking the grand tour this fall. The London show is in September. After that I'm going to Sicily, with stopovers in between. Or maybe I'll go to Italy first, then England. Everything's up in the air just now.

Adam is—what?—Adam. A little devil, a delight, and very, very determined—just like his father. I'm trying not to hang on to him, to let him make his own mistakes. He has to try his own wings, as I did, as we all should, as his father never had a chance to.

Naturally, I'm taking him with me when I go to Europe. Much to his grandparents' consternation. I mean Dan's parents, not mine. Papa died, did I tell you? I'm not sorry. Now I can go home and show Adam to my family. The reason I'm going to Sicily is to thank that family who befriended Dan. I want Adam to become acquainted with his Sicilian heritage, too. Although I have a sneaky feeling Dan's parents think Jewish is enough. But Dan would understand. In fact, in his last letter to me he said we'd all go to Sicily to meet this family when the war was over.

Glad to hear all goes well with you and Richard. Poor Jean-Paul! He drops in at the studio sometimes while I'm painting, and we talk about you. But don't hate yourself, he's taking it very philosophically, says he half-expected you not to come back after you left. He's being very helpful with advice in planning my grand tour, where to go, what to see, what to eat, what to wear—the climate and such. Mostly he talks about Paris. Think if you could fly there from Berlin and we could go to the Louvre and everywhere!

I love your letters. Do write and tell me what you're doing. Adam misses his pal Laura.

Forgot to say I've met this really terrific guy!!! He paints, too. A sort of Greek Chagall. He wants to get married, but I'm happy with things as they are.

Write! Write! Write!

Your New York correspondent,
Gina

Just reading Gina's letter cheered her. Susan wished Diane had one particle of Gina's resilience. Here, Diane had been born rich and beautiful into old Southern aristocracy, while Gina had been born poor and beautiful with Sicilian ancestry, but Gina was the survivor. It did a lot to make her believe in democracy. Of course, Diane's parents' death had occurred at a crucial time in her life, and it had been a particularly horrible death, but almost at that same crucial time in Gina's life, her father was willing to palm her off on a perverted old man to pay off a debt. And all that time I was sitting under a willow tree bemoaning the fact that nothing ever happened to me. Little did I know how lucky I was. And aren't I being unfair to Diane? There's something she's hiding, she hinted at several times, something to do with her uncle. And if I ask questions, she clams up, saying, "If you knew, you'd never be my friend again."

Which is no compliment to me; I'm not a fair-weather friend. I tried to tell her that, but she wasn't convinced.

By noon, Diane hadn't returned her call. Susan phoned again, and the maid or whoever called Diane to the phone. It was a long time before Diane got there, and when she did, she sounded as if she were still half-asleep.

"I'm sorry if I woke you up," Susan said. "I can call back later. Or you can."

Diane insisted she was awake.

"I kept calling you last night, but you were out."

"I was out, all right," Diane said with a giggle. "I was flying off into the wild blue yonder."

"You mean drinking? Driving? What?"

"I mean sniffing. They gave me some of this wonderful white powder. One sniff, and you're in heaven. It's a hell of a lot better than Dr. Gurney's little red pills."

"I hope you're not talking about cocaine," Susan said.

"Oh, don't get all preachy and moral. Just because something makes you happy doesn't mean it's wrong. I refuse to be preached to," Diane said. And hung up.

Susan called back immediately. "Diane, please, I'm not going to be preachy, I'm just concerned. Promise you'll stay away from those two."

"Who on earth are you talking about?"

"You know who, that couple in the castle with their old-world charm. Is that their charm, cocaine?"

"How did you know who it was? Anyway, they're real friends. They're *happy* to see me. And they know who that German whore is Michael's living with, too. Ilse Lach. A Jewess. She kept it a secret during the war that she was one."

"It's not the sort of thing you'd shout in the street then."

"See? You're on her side. Michael's left me for her, and you're defending her. I gave him an ultimatum. Ursula said to. I told him this morning, either it's that Jewess or me, and he chose her. He left me." Suddenly Diane was sobbing in Susan's ear. "He left me," she repeated. "And he's staying with her in Konigsgarten, where *I* wanted to stay."

"Diane, I'm sorry."

"It doesn't matter," Diane said. All the defiance had gone out of her voice; it sounded small and hopeless.

"Maybe he'll get tired of her and come back," Susan said.

"Oh, no, he loves her. He's crazy about her."

"Maybe if I talked to her, she'd see she was hurting you and let him go."

"*Her*? Ha. She's got a good thing. What all the German girls want. A GI with money." There was a pause. "All right, talk to her. Tell her I've got money. I'll pay her to leave Michael. Whatever she asks."

"Diane, I'm not so sure that will work."

"You promised to talk to her."

She hadn't promised, she'd offered, but she didn't mention this. Diane was in a bad way. Now was not the time to quibble.

"Yes, okay, I'll see what I can do."

"Call me back as soon as you've seen her. I'll be waiting."

The minute Susan hung up, she knew she shouldn't meddle. What would Richard say? And how would she have reacted if some stranger had offered her money to return Jean-Paul to his wife? But she wasn't Ilse Lach, and Diane was counting on her. As Susan got ready to pay Ilse Lach a visit, she tried to imagine what she was like. No doubt a slatternly woman wearing stale makeup, a sleazy kimono, and oozing sex.

Laura was playing with Timmy at the Anderson house a few doors down. Susan stopped by to ask Gladys Anderson if she minded keeping Laura until she got back. "Mind?" Gladys said. "Not at all. She can stay forever, she's so sweet."

Walking the few blocks to the Flowers house, which she knew Michael and his *Fräulein* lived next to, Susan wondered if she didn't appreciate her child as much as she should. She loved Laura, but she didn't have Richard's patience with her, and Laura clearly preferred her father to her mother.

Since Susan didn't know whether Ilse Lach lived to the left or right of the Flowerses' she chose the closest, on the right. At first she thought she'd selected the wrong house, for a middle-aged gray-haired woman with a harelip answered the door.

"May I speak to Fräulein Lach?" Susan asked in her best German.

The woman eyed her suspiciously, muttered something, and went away, leaving Susan standing on the doorstep. A few minutes later a younger woman appeared, although she could hardly be called young. She eyed Susan not only warily but wearily, her eyes heavy-lidded, as if she'd stayed up every night of her life. She was blond and bony and wore no makeup. Her hair was drawn back from her face into a French knot, and she wore a simple shirt and skirt. Susan thought of fresh-faced, lovely Diane and wondered how Michael Deal could prefer this haggard woman to her.

"Yes?" the woman said.

Susan hoped that "yes" wasn't the extent of her English. "I . . . I'd like to speak to you about something. Someone. A friend."

"A friend? Who is that?" the woman said guardedly. Probably husband snatchers didn't have many women friends; then Susan remembered that once she'd have fit that category, too.

"A friend of mine. I'm Susan Lund."

The woman looked as if she might leave her on the doorstep.

"You *are* Ilse Lach, aren't you?"

"I am Ilse Kramer. Once I was Ilse Lach." Then, finally, she said, "Come in."

Susan followed her into a living room with a piano, books, and a white sofa. It was charming and cheerful, with bright prints and comfortable easy chairs.

"Sit down, please," Ilse Lach Kramer said.

"This is the most cheerful place I've been in since I came here."

"Thank you. I do not like big fat furniture with claw feet. So gloomy. I grew up in gloom. When I was little, I say to myself, Ilse, if you ever get away, you will never live so gloomy again."

"You wanted to leave home, too, when you were little?"

"Oh, yes. My family, as gloomy as the furniture. The only time they enjoy themselves is once a year at the wine festival. Then they—everyone—gets drunk. Even the dogs. It is a small town with small people where I come from. I do not mean in size, you understand?"

Susan understood. She was also beginning to understand why Diane's husband might prefer this woman with her charm and humor to poor sad clinging Diane. She wondered, too, that she hadn't noticed that the woman was beautiful. Or perhaps it was her voice that made her beautiful, husky, with a lilt. But those eyes, too, so blue, so haunting. "I grew up on a farm in Ohio and felt the same way you felt here in Germany," she said. "Ohio is in the Midwest."

"Oh, yes, I know. Michael is from Pennsylvania. That is next door to Ohio, is it not?"

Susan nodded. "No one ever had a good time where I came from either, and we didn't even have a wine festival. I used to sit under a willow tree by the river and dream of leaving."

"Oh, and I would sit on the bank of the Rhine and dream of leaving. To Hamburg. That was where my aunt lived. An actress. Excuse me, she was not an actress, she was not my aunt. That is, what you say, another story."

Susan would have loved to ask about that story, but the gray-haired woman came in with coffee and pastries on a tray. Susan was glad for food, since she'd neglected to eat lunch. The woman with the harelip no longer eyed Susan suspiciously. Ilse said a few words to her, and she withdrew.

"That wasn't German," Susan said.

"No, Czech. During the war, they—we—brought people here from conquered countries. Verni, she comes to me from Czechoslovakia. After the war, she goes home to her family, but does not stay. Half are no longer living, and those living have changed. She says I am her family, so she comes back to me and stays."

"I thought she'd send me away when I came to the door. She doesn't like Americans?"

"Oh, she is—what do you call it—a measurement of my feelings. Thermometer?"

"Barometer."

"Yes, thank you—barometer. She is unfriendly to everyone until she sees I like them."

Susan smiled her thanks at the implied compliment. She already knew she couldn't offer this woman money to leave Michael, sensed the woman wouldn't leave him for any reason. She lived with him because she loved him, and no argument could prevail against love.

"Your aunt, this actress who wasn't an actress, or even your aunt. Did you run away to see her in Hamburg?"

"Oh, no, I got an offer to act in Berlin, so there I went. My aunt would come to visit us when I was little. Those were the only times I was happy. She was my mother, but I did not know that. She worked in a music hall. I was illegal."

"Illegitimate?"

"Yes, thank you, I was an illegitimate."

"You didn't know who your father was?"

"Oh, yes, I found him, my father. Or he found me. Or we found each other. And then they killed him. He was a Jew. They shot him and tortured the director of the theater, but he never talked. He did not say I was a Jew or that we were hiding people."

"Hiding people? Where?"

"You did not come to visit me about that."

"But tell me, please."

"You would not believe. I do not believe, but it happened. Why did you come to visit me? Who is this, your friend?"

Susan braced herself. "Michael's wife."

"Ah, you think I am a bad woman. I steal her husband. You come say give him back, no? I am sorry, I do not give him back. Even if I did, he would not go."

"Yes, I've already guessed that. I don't think you're a bad woman—whatever that means. If you are, then I am, too. Or was. I had an affair with a married man. I can't ask you to do what I didn't." Poor Diane, she wasn't helping her at all.

"And what happened?"

"I didn't so much love as admire him. It ended after I came here and joined my husband. No, it ended long before that, but I didn't know it. He was my . . ." She was about to say "boss," but guessed Ilse might not know the word. ". . . employer. We worked on a newspaper. I'm a journalist. What you mentioned about hiding people, I'd like to write about that and send it in."

"You would not believe."

"A lot of things happened that people are finding hard to believe."

Ilse nodded. "Okay, I tell you. About Hans, my director. A hero. He does not look it. He is short and wears thick glasses. Or act it. He cries when he cuts a finger. But he does not talk under torture. He kills himself. Slashes his wrists with a broken lightbulb. And there is my father. He almost made it. He hid out all during the terrible times when all the Jews were rounded up and sent to the death camps. He is not, what you say, an educated man, but he is kind and clever and loving of life. And there is also Frieda. She, too, commits suicide, to save Hans."

"And there is you."

"Oh, yes, me, I am there, too."

Susan didn't notice the time pass. She was only half-aware of the Czech woman coming in with more coffee and pastries and the shadows that darkened the room, as if the room were a theater darkened to those times Ilse told her about.

She hurried guiltily homeward. Richard was furious. He'd already collected Laura from the Andersons' and demanded to know where she'd been. By the time she'd calmed him down and put Laura to bed, it was nearly nine. She dreaded calling Diane. What would she say to her? Like her husband, she'd fallen under Ilse Lach's spell?

She needn't have worried about what to say. Diane was out. This worried Susan even more. Did that mean she was visiting those two "friends" at the castle?

Susan couldn't sleep. The events Ilse told her of kept circling in her mind. Finally she got up and went into the spare room, where she kept her typewriter. She closed the door and began writing. She wrote until gray seeped into the room and turned to blue. Finally, exhausted, she leaned back in her chair and remembered Gina's words: "Just finished what I think is my best work. Wonderful feeling when you know you've done something good."

23. Diane

Diane fled from her humiliation at Susan's party, the speedometer needle climbing and wavering as she took the curves of the winding road on two wheels. When she reached her home, she cut off the motor, jumped out, and ran into the house yelling, "Michael! Michael! Michael!" Screaming his name, she went from room to room, although by now she realized he wasn't there. No doubt she'd have found him just a few blocks from the Lunds' in Konigsgarten, with his mistress. But in the near-madness of her misery, she kept calling him as if his name would conjure him up.

The little sounds that the servants made as they went about their chores had suddenly ceased. They were listening, she knew—the cook, the maids, the houseman—smiling to themselves or at each other over her crazy behavior. Suddenly, unable to bear the silence or the idea of encountering one of the servants after making such a spectacle of herself, she ran back out of the house, flung herself behind the wheel, and careened around curves to the von Frisches'.

It was twilight. The castle looked deserted, but then, it usually did. There was someone home, since the Mercedes was parked in the courtyard.

Behind the castle, between the dark firs, the lake was still and as dull as unpolished silver.

Fritz let her in. He was a sour-breathed old man in a threadbare black suit with a yellowish shirt. He looked at her with disapproval. She realized she must be a mess, with mascara tracking her tears and her uncombed hair.

"I will tell Fräulein von Frisch you are here," he said, and led her to a room with dusty maroon draperies, carved high-backed chairs, and two couches, one of worn velvet, the other frayed silk. Before he left, Fritz turned on a tasseled floor lamp leaving a pale island of light in the gray twilight.

A few minutes later, Ursula appeared. "Why, pet, what's wrong?"

Diane could only shake her head. Too humiliating to tell Ursula that her husband was living with a German woman and calling her his wife. Ursula seemed to understand her reluctance to speak. She took Diane into her arms, and Diane sobbed against a shoulder. Although bony, it was comforting.

Her sobbing had barely subsided when Fritz appeared to announce dinner. Ursula insisted she stay and eat with them, saying she'd feel much better afterward. It was generous of Ursula to invite her, since the portions on the dinner plates were so meager. It looked incongruous, the rich, old oak dining room with the Gobelin tapestry on the wall, the silverware, candlelight, and Freddie and Ursula seated formally at each end of a long table, and the tiny amount of food. Just as well Diane couldn't eat. She was amazed at how poor the von Frisches must be, and chided herself for not helping out with more money. She'd made "loans" before, for the servants' salaries and repairs of the castle and the Mercedes. Loans, of course, being the polite term, since they had no money to repay her.

The only advice of her uncle's that she'd heeded was not to buy friendship with money. But the von Frisches were different. They cared for her, not her money, and would accept it only in dire need. Being once rich themselves, they must find their poverty doubly humiliating. She did wonder if they managed their money poorly, however, for the loans she'd made were of significant amounts.

After they finished eating, Ursula led the way back to the room with the maroon draperies. Freddie poured three glasses of brandy and limped across the room to hand one to her where she sat on the frayed silk couch.

"Now, tell us what happened to make you so unhappy," he said. "Whoever it is, I shall kill the beast, if you like."

"My husband."

After some coaxing on Freddie and Ursula's part she told about what had happened at Susan's party. "It was so humiliating for me. He'd said we couldn't get in Konigsgarten because there weren't any vacancies. He told me it was a dump, I wouldn't want to live there, anyway. And all the while he was living there with someone."

Ursula took her into her arms: Freddie gave her more brandy.

"It is Ilse," Ursula said. "I know it is she." She turned to Freddie. "Remember I told you I encountered that actress at her theater and she said Ilse was alive? But you, dear brother, preferred not to believe this. You preferred to believe she was at the bottom of the lake."

Diane was bewildered. "You thought she'd drowned?"

"It was rumored she had committed suicide rather than to admit to the shame of being found out a Jew."

"She may be alive, as you say, dear sister, but there are any number of German women living with American servicemen these days. Just because you are so obsessed with Ilse Lach does not mean it is she who lives with Diane's husband."

"Ah, but you see!" Ursula said triumphantly. "This Erica Blount, this actress, told me that she was living in a place called Konigsgarten."

"How can it be that she lives with an American in American quarters, when that is illegal?" Freddie asked.

"Oh, probably he just said she was me. I don't suppose they interview the wives."

"But if this were known, they would both be in trouble."

"Not him, not Michael. He always knows who to bribe. At Fort Benning he was constantly doing favors for the right people and getting away with murder."

"You did not say he was a Jew," Freddie said.

"He isn't."

"Are you sure?" Ursula asked. "He sounds very much like one. Like her. She is very clever, very deceitful. We had befriended her, Freddie and I, lending her money that she, of course, did not repay. And we invited her here to parties to meet the best people of high military rank, even though we suspected then that she was of inferior origin. You must tell your husband to give up this woman or you will leave him."

"But what if he leaves me instead?" Diane asked. She put down the brandy glass, disliking it nearly as much as champagne, since it, too, was something Uncle Clayton foisted on her.

"He will not leave you, with your riches," Freddie said. "Allow me to get you some more brandy."

"No, thank you."

"Brandy is not what she needs," Ursula said. "She is not suffering from frostbite, but from heartbreak. Give her something that lessens her pain."

"I have some red pills that are supposed to cheer me up, but I'm almost out of them. Besides, they don't do much good."

"Oh, we have something far more effective, do we not, brother dear?"

"You mean this?" Freddie said, indicating the long-stemmed pipe he was smoking.

"No, no, I do not mean that. I mean something of a more immediate effect," Ursula said. She gave Diane's check an affectionate tweak. "I have just the thing for you. I shall get it myself."

She left the room and returned a few minutes later with a small cut-glass jar resembling a perfume bottle and a tiny silver spoon. She removed the stopper from the jar, dipped the spoon in, and gently tapped it on the rim so that nothing in the spoon was wasted. In the spoon was a white powder looking somewhat like pulverized aspirin. Perhaps Germans took it in this form for headaches.

"Is it for headaches?" she asked.

Ursula smiled mysteriously. "Oh, it is for everything. Take a small sniff. You will feel wonderful. Glorious. Here, like this," Ursula said, demonstrating by delicately sniffing the powder. Then, dipping the spoon into the jar again, she tapped it on the side and handed it to Diane. "Sniff gently, please."

Diane sniffed gently and was lifted to glory on angel wings. Around her spread a golden haze, within her a deep serenity. She felt like a child in a swing sailing up, up into the sky, but the swing did not return to earth, it kept on going, sailing her out into a golden beyond. She looked down at Freddie reclining on the velvet couch in a brocade smoking jacket while, appropriately, smoking. He offered her his pipe, but Ursula indignantly said that opium and cocaine didn't mix. Opium? Cocaine? Opium was smoked in pipes, she knew that. The magic powder, then, must be cocaine.

There were times during her heavenly flight that she was vaguely aware of being enfolded in Ursula's winged sleeves, tenderly caressed by sister and brother. Their caresses were gentle and comforting, and she didn't protest. Besides, Ursula might get mad and take the magic powder away.

Once, from a great distance, she heard the sound of a passing car. She knew it must be Michael returning home, since the road was so seldom used. "I have to go, there's Michael," she said.

"Stay," Ursula urged, and offered her more of the magic powder.

She stayed until nearly dawn. She extricated herself from Freddie and Ursula, who slept curled around her, and left the house, wading through ragged bits of mist to her car.

Michael was asleep when she went into the bedroom. She undressed and got into bed. She was feeling too good to spoil things with a fight about some German whore.

When she awoke, the sun was bright, so bright it hurt her eyes. It glared through the French windows, casting a shadow of the curlicued balcony on the floor. She closed her eyes and drifted off to sleep, hearing water running in the bathroom. Sometime later she was reawakened by the sound of bare feet slapping across the parquet floor, occasionally muffled by an Oriental throw rug. The closet door creaked, and she opened her eyes to see Michael standing by the closet, his back turned, pulling on his trousers. He must have felt her eyes on him, for he turned. "Where were you last night?"

She laughed at his question. "You're out every night, and I'm not allowed to ask where you are, but I'm out once, and you ask me?"

"All right, I retract the question."

"Anyway, I know where you are. With your German mistress."

He zipped up his trousers. His expression, too, became tight, zipped-up. After a minute he said, "Where'd you hear about her?"

"At a party Susan gave for me. Some party. Everyone else but me knew about her."

He crossed the room to the bed, touched a hand to her shoulder. "Diane, I'm sorry."

"Don't. Don't pretend. I know you find me repulsive."

"It's you who find me repulsive. You can't bear to have me touch you."

"Not after you've touched that whore."

"Don't say stupid things about someone you know nothing about."

"Oh, I know all about her. Boy, she's really pulled the wool over your eyes. She fooled the von Frisches, too. They didn't find out until later that she was a thief, whore, and Jewess."

"You've been here too long," he said, his voice icy.

"You're adopting the Nazi mentality. Who in hell are the von Frisches?"

"Our neighbors. Naturally, you're never here long enough to become acquainted."

"They don't sound like anyone I'd want to become acquainted with. I want you to steer clear of that German scum."

"You live with *her* and you call *them* scum?"

"Be careful what you say about her."

He stood there fully dressed, cap in hand, looking down at her in bed.

"Where are you going? Are you off to see her already? If you go to see her again, it's all over between us."

"There hasn't been anything between us for a long time."

"I mean it, Michael. Take your choice. It's her or me."

He put on his cap and started toward the door.

"Michael? Did you hear?"

"I heard."

"I could make trouble, you know. For both of you. Do you think I'm too dumb not to guess that you sneaked her in using my name?"

"I think you're too smart to try to make trouble. It won't do you any good," he said, closed the door behind him, and left.

She lay there crying into the pillow, softly calling his name.

After a while she got up and took her remaining red pills. She took six, but they didn't have any effect. She wished she had some of that lovely white powder to lessen her pain.

She felt better after talking to Susan on the phone, and waited around the house all day for Susan to call back to tell her whether or not Ilse Lach had accepted her offer. What she couldn't understand was why it was taking so long, but maybe Michael was there and Susan had to wait until he left.

She went over that night to visit the von Frisches and was disappointed that the jar containing the white powder wasn't brought out. Ursula said it was very, very expensive, and they couldn't afford any more. Diane offered to pay.

Susan didn't call until the next morning. She was very apologetic. "I didn't make the offer because I knew she'd be terribly offended," Susan said.

Diane suspected that Ilse Lach had won over not only Michael but also Susan.

Only the von Frisches saw Ilse Lach in her true colors. Only the von Frisches were her friends.

After a while she tired of Susan's phone calls warning her of the von Frisches and the dangers of cocaine. Sometimes she pretended to be out when Susan called, but most of the time she didn't have to pretend, since she was so often at the von Frisches'.

Michael didn't call, didn't come back, not even for his clothes. His uniforms hung in the closet, his razor and shaving cream remained in the medicine cabinet. Funny, although he'd scarcely been around, she was still keenly aware of his absence.

The castle was chilly even in summer, with a dampness more pervasive than at Colquitt Hall. But Freddie and Ursula's warmth more than made up for the chill. And, of course, there was the magic powder. Susan was wrong to worry about taking it. Ursula said it wasn't in the least habit-forming.

Diane treated the castle as home, exploring the many rooms when Freddie and Ursula weren't around to entertain her. A lot of the rooms looked as if they hadn't been lived in in years. Ursula and Freddie used only the first floor, one or two rooms on the second, and the nursery, which they appeared to be especially fond of, perhaps because of happy childhood memories. Only these rooms were cleaned, or what passed for cleaning. They were cared for by Fritz and his equally ancient wife, who also did the cooking. Generally the cleaning wasn't much more than a stirring up of dust. Uncle Clayton would have fired Fritz and his wife on the spot, but Ursula and Freddie were kindhearted and loyal and said they couldn't bring themselves to dismiss the old couple, who'd been at the castle for ages.

Diane tried Freddie's opium and found that opium and cocaine did mix. At least it worked for her. She didn't know where the von Frisches got their supplies. She did know that on Thursday nights Freddie disappeared for a few hours and returned looking content. Diane didn't at all mind paying. It was the least she could do, since she also benefited. Ursula and Freddie no longer objected to her paying for things. There was something childlike in their acceptance of this. She found it touching and flattering that these two elegant, charming people depended on her. They were, in fact, childlike in many ways. Especially Freddie, with his passion for the toy department at the PX and for his toy train up in the nursery, where he and Ursula spent so many happy hours.

Sometimes, though, she thought they carried their nursery games too far, Freddie with his tantrums and Ursula with her whip. Diane didn't at all like it when Ursula told her to whip Freddie, too. She didn't like it, but she'd rather whip him than have Ursula whip her for not doing as she was told, or worse yet, being deprived of her magic powder that she required more and more of, especially before their "nursery nights."

She was sometimes frightened of Ursula, whose tongue flickered like a snake's when she became angry. Once she'd mistakenly confessed to Freddie that she didn't like these games. Freddie had pouted and tattled to Ursula.

"No one is keeping you here," Ursula had said scornfully, "or forcing you to play our games."

For a panicky minute Dianc was afraid Ursula might order her out of the house. They were her only friends, she needed them, and more than them she needed that white powder.

Sometimes she awakened in the canopied bed feeling sick and frightened, all tangled up in so many arms and legs as if she were in the tentacles of an octopus. Lying there beside her, Freddie no longer looked elegant as in his smoking jacket, but ugly, bony, and white, while Ursula's black heavy hair lay in coils that seemed to writhe as Medusa-like snakes.

Ursula would awaken and sense immediately how she felt. Sometimes she would be cruel and tell her to go; other times she would caress her. "It is all right, pet, what you need is some hairs of the dog," she'd say. Diane didn't correct her, knowing how Ursula hated to bc corrected, and not wanting to irritate her when she was about to hand her the tiny spoon with the white powder. If only she could get the cocaine herself, but that was hopeless. She had no idea where Freddie got it and knew that while it would be shared with her if she paid, never would it be bought for her alone. And she was as dependent on their opinion as the cocaine.

"You are well rid of such a stupid husband who does not appreciate your beauty," Ursula said. "You are far more beautiful than that Jewess."

Freddie nodded in agreement. "Your kind of beauty is appreciated only by the discriminating."

"Our friends will adore her, will they not, Freddie?"

"Oh, yes, they will be captivated."

"Where are your friends?"

Ursula's face darkened. "They have left Germany or are imprisoned or impoverished. I am so sick of this depressing poverty. Of seeing nothing but ruins. Sometimes I think I should leave. It is so terrible to see our proud country on her knees to barbarians. What do you think, Freddie? We could sell perhaps the Gobelin tapestry? It would pay for our travels."

Diane's hands began to shake. If they deserted her, she'd have no one. "Where would you go?"

Ursula shrugged. "Away. To some warm sunny country. Italy perhaps."

"Or Greece," Freddie said. "Such splendid young boys."

"But what would I do if you went?"

"Come with us, of course."

"We would not leave you behind, my pet."

"Go home, Diane. For God's sake, go home," Michael said.

He had come to get his things, finally. She'd called at his office to say she was moving out, and if he wanted them, he'd better pick them up. She'd been at the von Frisches' when he arrived, but he stayed until she got back.

She laughed. "Why? I'll have a wonderful time. I'll go to Greece, Italy, everywhere."

"With those German scum?"

"With my good friends. Why not with my friends?"

"Because they'll destroy you. Have you taken a look in the mirror lately? You're all skin and bones. Your eyes don't focus. Don't kid me you're not on drugs. I know the signs. You could have searched all Germany and not come up with a worse pair than those two."

"Oh, but I didn't have to search, did I? You moved me in right next to them."

For a long moment he was silent, looking at her. He nodded. "I wouldn't have if I'd known, believe me. Ilse knows those two. She told me—"

"Any enemies of hers are friends of mine. She took you away from me. You leave me alone, and when I find friends, you tell me they're no good. Who is any goddamn good, Michael? You deserted me. Everyone deserts me. They lock me up and throw away the key. Don't stand there looking sorry for me. I don't need your sympathy. *Bro-ther*, if you knew, if you only knew. I'm not the innocent you think. You talk about how bad the von Frisches are, they're not half as bad as me. I killed my parents and my baby and I seduced my uncle and my best girlfriend. What you see here is just the tip of the iceberg, you don't know how evil I am."

She wasn't sure whether she'd said it or thought it, or maybe just said some of it or none of it. He came toward her, holding out his arms, but she knew if he caught her he'd clamp on handcuffs and haul her off to a funny farm. She dodged him and ran out and jumped into her car and drove over to her friends.

Sometimes she had this dream. A silly dream that made her laugh at herself. She saw this small, neat house of red brick and climbing roses warmed by sunlight. In the doorway stood a woman with an infant feeding at her breast. She stood there watching as a car drove up and a man got out. He went up the sidewalk and into the house, where he embraced the woman and infant and said how he'd had a hard day at work and was so glad to be back home. And they told each other about what they'd done that day, and the man took the baby while she went to the kitchen and prepared his favorite dishes, and the radio played, and . . .

24. *Susan*

"I hope I do not get you back too late," Ilse said, swinging the small Opel into the driveway.

"It was worth it," Susan said. But she felt qualms at the sight of the tall slim man in suntans walking slowly along the cinder path hand in hand with the tall child in sweater and corduroy pants. They ignited pride and guilt, pride that the husband and child were hers, guilt that she was late.

It was nearly six o'clock, and Richard ate supper early, still on Ohio farm time. While she'd cruised around the autumnal German countryside enjoying herself, husband and child awaited her return. Actually, she hadn't been enjoying herself all that much. It was business. A sad business. Ilse had said that Claus Zwinger, the barman at the New York Bar, would make a good story. He had. But it was another horror story. They'd gone to see him on his day off, to a village on the Rhine where he lived with his wife and three children. "How could all those terrible things have happened in a country that looks so serene and beautiful?" she asked.

"Yes, I have myself often wondered that," Ilse said. "Hans said you expect the Rhine to run red with blood and the trees to shed tears."

"Is that from a poem?"

"No, but Hans was a poet in his own way. Such a gentle

man. Michael, too, but he is ashamed of it and hides it, you know? He is going back soon. He speaks of taking me, but many GI's say that to German girls before leaving, and then they forget, once they have left."

"You can go back on the stage here. You're wasting your talent singing in a nightclub."

"No, I do not want to. The memories, too sad. I would love to act on your Broadway, but my English leaves still much to be desired, even though I take now private lessons. In fact, I think it was better before the lessons."

"You have just enough of an accent to be charming. And you don't have to worry about syntax when you read from a script." She'd like to discuss Ilse's acting career in more detail, but Richard was looking impatiently in their direction. "I have to go now. Thanks for taking me to Herr Zwinger."

"You are welcome. I am looking forward to read what you write."

"You'll be the first to see. I'll get started on it tonight, while it's still fresh in my mind."

The moment she got out of the car, Laura ran up and threw her arms around her legs. "Mommy, Mommy, I'm hungry."

"There were plenty of leftovers in the refrigerator," she said to Richard over Laura's head. "You didn't have to wait for me."

"I wouldn't have if I'd known you'd be gone for so long."

He unclasped Laura's hold on her legs and hoisted the child to his shoulders. All three went inside. Richard and Laura sat expectantly at the table while she threw supper together.

"We'll have to hurry," Richard said after they'd finished eating. "You'd better take a bath, you look a mess."

"What's the occasion?"

"The Flowerses' party. You've forgotten?"

"Are Michael and Ilse invited?"

"I don't know. I doubt it."

"That's rude, having a party and not inviting their next-door neighbors. I'm not going if they weren't invited. Everyone invites next-door neighbors here."

"Oh, for God's sake, Susan, it's an office party. Mike Flowers works in my office. My boss will be there. We have to be."

Damn. She'd planned to write Claus Zwinger's story tonight. The deadline for her next piece was only three days off. She longed to go up and work in what she called her office—the spare room she'd equipped with desk and filing cabinet after receiving the breathtaking news that her column was to be syndicated.

"I have a deadline to meet. You go, and I'll stay with Laura."

"Frau Kuntz is sitting with Laura," he said.

Frau Kuntz was always in demand as a sitter, since she had a way with children, but the Lunds received top priority because Richard had a way with Frau Kuntz. Everyone loved Richard; why didn't she?

"I'd just as soon not go."

"You have to. My boss wants to meet you."

"Why?"

"I don't know. He said he'd like to."

Susan knew. He wanted a happy, hard-working staff, and husbands couldn't concentrate on work if they had domestic problems. He wanted to meet her and cheer her on to cheer Richard up. "I don't want to go," she said stubbornly. "Those parties are always a bore. The men talk about sports and the women about BM's."

"What's a BM?"

"Lucky you, you haven't heard. Bowel movements. How often baby shits in its potty."

"You never used to be so foul-mouthed and sarcastic. You've changed," Richard said for what must be the hundred-thousandth time.

"I wish *you* had," she said for the first time. "How anyone could go on dangerous flying missions and see his buddies blown to bits and still emerge the same sweet innocent innocuous person, I don't know."

"Is that more of your sarcasm?"

She didn't answer.

"I'm not the simpleton you like to think, Susan. I've always believed in fair play and family, and the hell I went through just confirmed those beliefs."

She was ashamed. She went over and kissed him. "I'm sorry."

"You should be," he said, playfully swatting her on the behind. "Now, go take a bath."

They set off for the Flowerses' in tranquil twilight. There was just a touch of chill in the air. Richard had changed from his suntans to his olive-drab tunic in honor of fall. Susan wore her favorite navy suit with a white silk blouse to change its severity to a party occasion. Or so she hoped. She didn't care for fuss and frills or sexy things except in nightgowns, and then she went wild buying all the lacy, clingy, sexy little numbers that appealed.

Despite the fact that the Flowerses lived near most of their guests, everyone drove the few blocks but the Lunds. Susan and Richard walked over, holding hands. Whenever a car approached, they dropped hands, as if caught doing something indecent.

The party was under way when they arrived. They were greeted with smiles and handed drinks by their host, Mike Flowers. The conversation wasn't quite what Susan had predicted. The women were concerned with the kind of schooling their school-age children would get from the Army. The men were concerned with mustering out. Susan stood on the fringe of the women's circle, sipping a Scotch. An Army captain stood on the fringe of the men's circle sipping a Scotch. He was of stocky build, and his crew cut was growing out, so that his hair seemed to stand on end.

He noticed her at the same time she noticed him. They drifted toward each other. "All these parties are the same," she said, feeling she could be frank with this man.

"I'm not a party man," he said, "politically or otherwise."

"What are you, then?'

"An adventurer," he said with a slight smile.

"What fun. I'd like to be one, too, but then, a woman would be called an adventuress, which doesn't carry the same connotation."

"Maybe in the nineteenth century, but we're in the twentieth."

"Sometimes I wonder."

He smiled at her. "I'm Martin Kessler."

Martin Kessler must be Captain Kessler, Richard's boss. "I'm Susan Lund." Instead of saying "Your husband works for me," he said, "I admire your writing."

"You've read it?" She couldn't believe Richard would show it around; he was embarrassed by her columns, as if they were something she wrote to support the family.

"In my hometown paper, the Clairmont *Daily Call.* It was strange to read about Berlin there, and stranger still to find it was someone in Berlin writing it, and that that someone was Lieutenant Lund's wife. At first I thought the name Lund was just a coincidence, so I checked it out with Richard. He didn't mention it?"

She shook her head.

"What are you going to do for material after you leave?"

"I hope that won't be for a while," she said, knowing that

Richard would happily throttle her if he heard. He was dying to get back, and Captain Kessler could speed things up.

"You like being here in Germany?"

"I like traveling and seeing things."

"Here, too. When I get my discharge, I'm going home just long enough to say hello to my folks and then flying to Palestine."

"Palestine? Why Palestine?"

"I told you, I'm an adventurer."

"What are you going to do there?"

"What I was trained to do. Fight. I was at Auschwitz when the prisoners were liberated. I'll never forget it. I feel it's my duty to fight for Palestine. You might say it's guilt, pure and simple. We let it happen. We can't let anything more happen. Or I can't. Palestine is little enough recompense for millions of Jews."

Susan nodded, remembering with pain her failure to follow up on Nelson Mercer's information. "You'll be fighting England, an ally," she said.

"They violated the Balfour Declaration."

She was about to ask what that was when Captain Grubbs, who was standing by listening, asked about the Arabs. "It's their homeland. You can't take their own country from them."

"We took America from the Indians," Captain Kessler said. "Anyway, if you knew your history, you'd know that Palestine belonged to the Jews long before the Arabs."

"It belongs to the Arabs now," Captain Grubbs said stubbornly.

The conversation was growing heated. Captain Grubbs's face was red. Captain Kessler, however, remained calm. Although others entered the circle, they didn't enter the discussion. After all, Captain Grubbs might argue with Captain Kessler, they were of equal rank, but Captain Kessler's staff couldn't very well argue with him, although it was clear from their expressions that they were on Captain Grubbs's side.

Richard came up and took Susan's arm. "Time to go," he said. He had a determined look on his face. She didn't argue, but resented his dragging her away just when the party was getting interesting.

"You did it again," Richard said as soon as they'd left the Flowerses' house.

"Oh, God, what did I do this time?"

"I've told you not to stir up trouble or push into men's

conversations and give your opinion on things. You don't see other women interfering."

"I didn't push into anyone's conversation. It was Captain Grubbs who butted in. Martin Kessler and I were having a discussion."

"It's *Captain* Kessler. He's my boss. I hope you didn't call him Martin to his face."

"That's how he introduced himself. He also said he liked my columns. He didn't even know I was your wife until he asked you. You didn't mention that."

"I forgot. Anyway, you're impossible to live with for weeks if you're paid the slightest compliment."

"You're impossible to live with period."

Richard strode angrily ahead. It was going to be another of those tight-lipped nights.

She became intrigued with Palestine. Naturally, she could find little information on it in Germany. She thought of asking Captain Kessler, but Richard would object. She wrote Jean-Paul, asking him to send information, especially on the Balfour Declaration. Jean-Paul promptly sent a large envelope containing newspaper and magazine articles and a list of books on the subject. This was accompanied by a long, detailed letter that she'd just begun reading in her "office" when she heard someone moving around downstairs. It was early afternoon, Laura was taking her nap, and Richard was at work. Or so she'd thought.

"Anyone home?" he called from below, then came galumphing up the stairs.

"Guess what?" he asked, all smiles, like a sunny weather forecast.

"You got a promotion."

"Better than that. I got my orders to go home. It won't be long until I'm discharged. I've got a lot more than the necessary eighty-five points, so that means I'll probably be a civilian in a matter of weeks. Back we go to Ohio."

Ohio. She'd become an Ohio farmwife. A blanket of gloom descended. How could she write syndicated columns about cows and chickens?

Richard was still standing in the doorway, still smiling.

"You and Laura can leave as soon as you've packed. I'll be flown back to the States in Air Force transport and process out in New York. In a week or two I'll join you in God's country."

He was looking at her expectantly, as if she should drop

everything and pack immediately. "Yes," she said, "okay," and went back to Jean-Paul's letter.

"Why can't you be happy when I'm happy?" he asked.

"Because what makes you happy makes me sad, I suppose."

"Because you're selfish. I've been away from home for four years. This is a moment I've dreamed of."

She put on a smile. "I'm happy you're happy."

"Oh, shit," he said, and turned away from the door. It was the first time she'd heard him say anything stronger than "damn."

She returned to Jean-Paul's letter. He said he still cared for her and missed Laura, but he wasn't going to try to pressure her into marriage again. He realized now that it had been a mistake to do so. He asked why she'd taken such a sudden interest in Palestine. "I hope you're not thinking of going there," he wrote. "It's dangerous. If you go anywhere, come back to New York to me."

For a moment she considered stopping off and seeing Jean-Paul before returning to Ohio. Jean-Paul would love to see Laura. But it would be a mistake to get his hopes up. Although he might say he wouldn't pressure her into marriage, he might try when he saw her. She didn't love him. She didn't love Richard. She didn't want to go back to Ohio. She looked over the material Jean-Paul had sent, and began to read.

That evening when Richard was in a good mood after eating a special supper she'd prepared of steak, mashed potatoes, and tapioca pudding—his favorite foods—she took a deep breath and broached the subject.

"Since you won't get home for a few weeks or so, I think I'll take a little side trip to Palestine."

He was reading *Stars and Stripes*. "No, you're not," he said in that soft voice that permitted no further argument. "You're going straight home."

"I just want to see what's happening there," she said, trying to keep her voice as low as his, but her heart was hitting so hard in her chest he'd hear that instead of her words. "It would make a good column. A lot of good columns."

At first she thought he wasn't going to answer. Finally he spoke in the same low, slow voice. "There's a war going on there. You're not taking our child where there's any danger."

"I won't take her where there's any actual fighting. We'll just stay near enough to see what's happening."

"You will not take her anywhere but home."

He didn't use contractions when he was deadly serious. She answered in kind. "I *am* going to Palestine."

"You are not."

"Maybe I won't take Laura, though. You might be right about that. I'll leave her with Frau Munger, or Frau Kuntz if I can get her."

"You are leaving her with no one," he said, then forgot contractions. "She's your child, and you're staying with her. Susan, look at me." She looked. His face was pale and grim. "We're not just talking about Laura. We're talking about our marriage."

"I'm talking about what I want to do."

"You do what you want to, kid, but you're not going to wreck my child's life."

"She's not just yours."

"She is if you don't come back to Ohio."

"I'll come back."

"Oh, yes, sure, you'll come back. Maybe ten years from now. After you get bored with Palestine, you'll hear of someplace else where there's a war going on, and take off for there."

It sounded, Susan thought, rather appealing.

"You'll come back when our daughter is grown and doesn't need you."

"She doesn't need me all that much now."

"All children need their mothers."

"Nuts, she'd rather be with you than me."

"And that's exactly how it will be if you go to Palestine. Sometimes I think you're an unnatural mother. You don't love Laura."

"I do love her. That's a nasty thing to say."

"That's how it looks. How many other women would leave their child and fly off to a pint-size country, all desert, that some crazy Zionists want to steal from some Arabs, just to write some half-baked opinions and see their names in a byline?"

"Your bad syntax is surpassed only by your misinformation."

"To hell with my syntax, we're talking about your morals. You seduced me. You ran away from home pretending it was me you wanted to see, when it was New York. You wouldn't go back when I shipped out, even though everyone begged you to. You want to work for that French guy when I ordered you not to. God knows what went on between you two when I wasn't around. When I was risking my life for what I believed in, you were doing just what you always do, what you want to. Not anymore you're not. I'm willing to forget and forgive, but from now on you're toeing the line."

Susan arranged for Laura to fly back with Timmy Anderson and his mother. The Andersons lived in Dayton and would go to the Vandalia airport, where Laura's grandfather and new grandmother would pick her up. Laura would stay with them until Richard got back. Richard didn't yet know about the arrangements.

The night before they were scheduled to leave, Susan sat on the bed beside Laura, reading once again "The Little Engine That Could."

After she finished the story, she closed the book and stroked Laura's Dutch blond hair. "Honey," she said, "do you remember when Daddy was fighting the war and there was just you and me?"

Laura nodded.

"Now Mommy's going to a war for a while, too."

"Are you going to fight, Mommy?"

"No, I'll be writing about the war."

The battle would be when she got back. It wasn't fair. If it were Richard who went, he wouldn't be blamed for abandoning his child or threatened with having to give her up. "You'll be with Daddy for a while, is that okay?"

Laura pulled at the loose ear of her teddy bear, a slight frown appearing on her usually sunny face. Susan wondered what she'd do if Laura said it wasn't okay. But wasn't leaving as important as staying? If she stayed, the bickering between her and Richard would become more and more bitter. If she left, she was showing Laura that women accomplished things.

She took Laura's hand. "Mommies aren't just people who pick up after people, they can do other things, too."

"Why can't we go with you?" Laura asked.

"Daddy's had enough of war. He wants to go home and grow things and take care of animals—cows, pigs, and horses. You'll like them. Mommy had some calves when she was little. And you'll have trees to climb and hills to run up and down and grass to turn somersaults on."

Selling Laura on what fun she'd have, she almost sold herself. She thought of the willows and the river, the Ohio blue sky and the fields of golden wheat and green corn. There had been beauty besides the loneliness. And by being so much alone, she'd learned to look into herself. By being with animals, she'd learned about life and death. The worst it had done was make her restless, and was that so bad? Also, although Laura might prefer her father to her mother, it was she whom Laura resembled most. She was independent and spirited. It was important when she grew up that she knew she didn't have to fit the niche of housewife, schoolteacher, or secretary.

Susan bent and kissed her daughter. "I love you very much," she said. Laura smiled and patted her cheek as if in benediction.

Susan sat on the bed long after her daughter had gone to sleep, partly because she wanted to be with her as long as she could, and partly because she dreaded to go out and break the news to Richard.

25. *Ilse*

"You are behaving in a very suspicious manner," Ilse said.

"Who, me? Suspicious?" Michael set his visored cap back on his head in a most unmilitary way and gave her a smart military salute and a grin.

She suspected the reason he was so happy was that he'd received his orders to return home. She'd known, of course, that this would happen eventually. She just hadn't expected him to act like any other GI in Germany, not caring what happened to his *Fräulein* now that he was leaving. But what did she expect? Even if he weren't married, there was the marriage ban. Marriage papers could be applied for, but took forever to process. No scenes, she told herself. No tears. Accept it.

"What do you plan to do when you return?"

He gave her a quick look. "I told you, I'm opening a supper club. Classy. Soft lights, snotty waiters. Big menus with prices to match. All in French, of course. And a little piano music supplied by Eddy, if I can talk him into it."

"There will be no singer in your classy club?" she asked, avoiding his eyes. If she had a job, she might be able to become an American citizen.

"Not unless I can find someone who belts out a song like you. But there's only one Ilse."

"You should be leaving," she said coldly. "It is late."

It was late. Even for him. Four o'clock in the afternoon.

Ordinarily he slept until noon and went to his office at three, where he worked for two hours until five, when he went on to the New York Bar. He claimed his office staff ran the office better without him. The reason for his lateness made her even more bitter. They'd spent longer than usual in bed making love, the lovemaking even better than usual. He had been particularly tender. Perhaps it was a private way of saying good-bye to her.

He was now standing in the doorway looking at her somewhat uncertainly, as if there were something he wanted to say. Obviously trying to decide if he should tell her he'd gotten his orders.

"Is there something you have to tell me?" she asked, bracing herself.

"Later."

"You had better leave," she said, unable to stand that foolish grin anymore. "It is snowing, the roads will be slippery." Why warn him? Why not let him go out and drive like a madman and kill himself?

"Yeah, okay," he said. "And, listen, wear something fancy tonight. We're celebrating."

"Celebrating?" Drinking toasts to his leaving her?

"Don't remember, do you? A year ago today a shivering, starving kid came to the place and sang songs that made strong men weep. Afterward we went out and you ate and then you threw up, and then we went to that bombed-out building and made love."

"You are wrong on all but one count. I did throw up. We did not make love until much later. It was not a year ago today. This is December. It was in February when I first sang at your bar."

"I take poetic license," he said, kissed her, and touched a finger to the tip of her nose, as he often did. "Such a stickler for details. Otherwise, you're an okay kid," he said. He opened the door and left.

She watched him walk to the car with that special walk, as if he had springs built into his shoes. When you had no conscience, it was easy to be carefree. A few weeks back in America and he'd have forgotten all about her. So what? Perhaps she'd fooled herself into thinking she was in love with him. He was not, after all, her kind of person. Not at all like Hans. He knew nothing about the theater. Unlike Hans, he had supreme confidence in his ability. He joked and swaggered. For all his cynicism, he was hopelessly sentimental. No, he was not like Hans. He was like her father. That was the whole trouble. And as she'd believed that she hadn't loved Hans when she was with him, but loved him unbearably after he'd left, she knew that it would be the same with Michael

Well, so what? She'd gotten through worse.

Out in the kitchen Verni sang some sad Czech song. Ilse stood at the window watching the movers carrying crates from the Flowerses' house to the moving van, their galoshes sinking into the deepening snow. Every day someone left. Soon Konigsgarten would be inhabited by German families, among whom she'd feel almost as out-of-place as among the Americans. What would she do with the rest of her life? Things had been better when they were worse, back before she'd met Michael, while she was starving and without hope and cared for no one but the dead. Now Michael had reawakened love and hope, only to leave her with nothing when he left.

She disregarded Michael's suggestion to wear something fancy for the celebration. For her there was nothing to celebrate. She wore what had practically become a uniform—a simple black dress with a V neck, which no doubt showed up her haggardness under the spotlight.

She left late for the bar, wondering if she should go at all. But perhaps she wouldn't even get there. The snow fell thickly, the wind threatened to blow her little Opel off the road. She was fond of the car. Michael had generously given it to her last fall. She should have refused it. She saw now that the gift would ease his conscience. She didn't even have the consolation that Michael was dutifully returning to his wife, giving up love for responsibility. His wife had left, or was leaving, with those twin monsters Ursula and Freddie. She felt guilty about that, as if she'd delivered that beautiful young girl-wife into the von Frisches' hands. If she'd left Michael, would he have gone back to her? He said not. He said he felt only pity for her. But, Ilse thought, perhaps he told me that to keep me with him. She wondered at the pattern of her life. Was it the same for others? Each time, she had fallen in love with a married man whose wife was mentally ill. Although Michael's wife wasn't, he said, so much crazy as incapable of dealing with reality.

The drive from Konigsgarten to the New York Bar usually took no more than twenty minutes. Tonight it was taking nearly an hour. As she drew near, she looked for a parking space among cars and jeeps already white-blanketed by snow. She found a place finally, and as she fought her way through wind toward the bar, thought that Michael was right in a way: although it wasn't actually the anniversary of their meeting, tonight was very much like that night, but the stinging snow wasn't what caused the tears in her eyes as it had then. The tears were real. She, who thought she could never cry again, was crying. She didn't so much hate Michael for being so lovable, as herself for loving him.

She tugged at the door and went in. Despite the rotten weather, the bar was crowded with GI's and their *Fräuleins*, the air a smoky blue.

Michael sat at his usual back table with Eddy. There was also a GI. A private. She'd always liked Michael's choosing his Army friends as he pleased, caring more for friendship than rank. This private, however, rivaled Michael for carelessness in dress. Michael's uniforms were at least carefully tailored. His looked two sizes too big; his shirt was rumpled and open at the neck, tie crooked, and his hair long and shaggy. He had a pudgy face and thick glasses, looking like a scholarly drunk, although before him on the table was an improbable glass of milk.

As soon as Eddy saw her, he headed for the piano, balanced his cigar on the edge, and began to ripple the keys impatiently. She took her own good time, however. Removed her coat, ran her fingers through her hair, and sauntered to the piano as if she'd just happened into the bar. Of course, that was part of the act; the customers knew it, and there was an immediate silence.

The spotlight came on, and standing in its stark light, knowing she must look wrinkled and haggard, she felt tense and nervous, as if this were her first performance.

"What'll it be?" Eddy asked, punctuating his question with the piano keys.

She decided that if Michael wanted to commemorate the occasion she'd go along with his game and choose the song she'd first sung that afternoon nearly a year ago. " 'You Must Remember This,' " she said.

"You mean 'As Time Goes By'?"

"Yes, that one."

Eddy took off on the tune and sang the first line. He didn't need to, but this was part of the act now, too. She sang almost in a whisper, the ache in her throat getting in the way, her voice nearly as hoarse as the cigar-smoking, whiskey-drinking Eddy's. Michael, who had been conversing with the private, stopped talking and looked her way, that frown-smile on his face that soon she would no longer see.

Don't cry, you fool, she told herself. Remember you've

given up crying. She got through the line about a fight for love and glory but couldn't suppress the tears from then on. They lingered on the edge of her lashes. She'd have liked to run away after she finished the song. If she must cry, she wanted to cry at least in privacy, but they were calling requests from the audience, and she sang on . . . or talked on . . . or cried. The milk-drinking GI at Michael's table requested "Lili Marlene." She didn't wait for Eddy to feed her the lines; this time she sang first in German while Eddy translated into English. Under other circumstances the applause would have been gratifying.

"No more," she whispered to Eddy. "I cannot sing any more."

And she could not stay here any longer, either. She picked up her coat and started toward the door. The protests arose all around her. "Ilse, stay. Ilse, hey, where you going? Ilse, don't leave us."

Michael came up and caught her hand. "Where do you think you're going, kid?" he asked.

"Home. I am not feeling so well."

She hated the deceptively tender look he gave her. "Okay, I'll drive you, but first just come back and meet my friend."

Why did she have to meet his friend? She didn't want to meet anybody. She passed by well-wishers, who reached out to grab her hand or just touch her, letting Michael lead her to the table where the milk-drinking GI sat. He got to his feet. "This is Private Gelman," Michael said.

"Private First Class Gelman. Don't bust me again."

They all sat down. "Private First Class Gelman is the newest member of our staff and has the honor of being busted more times than anyone else in the United States Army."

"Busted but not broken," Gelman said. He took a sip of milk and smiled at Ilse. He was not only the sloppiest GI she'd seen but also the oldest. He'd have been old even for a colonel.

"You are in Special Services with Michael, then?" she asked politely.

"Yeah, I call it the SS."

"The SS isn't the sort of thing Ilse jokes about," Michael said.

"Yeah, right, I'm sorry." He paused. "When I heard Marlene Dietrich sing 'Lili Marlene,' I thought it was written for her. I was wrong. It was written for you."

"Don't forget Eddy," Michael said, and they all laughed,

including Eddy, and even Ilse, who would very much like to hate Michael but found that no easier than not loving him.

She turned her attention to Gelman, who had also heard Lotte Lehmann sing. He was very knowledgeable about German cabaret and German theater. It was fun to talk shop again.

"You were with the Berlin Theater?" he asked.

She nodded. "Years ago. It no longer stands. Demolished in an air raid."

"Too bad," he said. "I'd like to have seen that secret room. Michael showed me a clipping of that column written about you and the others who hid refugees," he said in answer to her questioning look. "It's a fantastic story."

"Yes, it seems unreal."

He cleared his throat. "About this musical. I don't want you to think just because it's a musical it's lightweight. It's to be a combination of cabaret and theater. Good sharp satire."

Ilse nodded politely. Musical? What musical? Had she missed something in their conversation? "What is it about?"

"A German girl who has a boyfriend in the Russian, English, and American sectors. She gets her nights mixed up, and they all arrive at once. Then she's accused of being a spy by all three countries. I'll play you some of the score after the place closes. I've left it in Michael's office. Just a minute, I'll get it so you can take a look at it."

She watched as he set down his milk glass, pushed back his chair, and waddled and wove past tables.

"He is too old and too fat to be in the Army," she said, more to herself than to Michael.

"Yeah, well, never underestimate short, fat guys who wear glasses."

"Michael, what is this all about, this musical?"

"You'll see."

He had a sly grin on his face. Did he think he'd fix things up so she'd have a man and a part in a musical and not miss him when he left? "I know you are going home. You do not deceive me," she told him. "You are under no obligation to find a replacement. I did very well for myself before you, and I will do so after."

Eddy was listening. Drinking whiskey and smoking that infernal cigar. She liked scenes only onstage, and she didn't want to make one in front of Eddy, but she wanted to get things straight so she could leave. The cigar smoke was making her sick. Eddy's eyes looked wise, hooded under his lids. He was smiling; so was Michael.

"Honey, Ilse, will you please goddammit listen?" Michael said. "I guess I should have told you, I almost did, but I didn't want to make you nervous. That little fat guy Gelman is a big Broadway producer."

"Oh?" she said.

"Oh," Michael said, echoing her. "That's right. Think I'd go home without you? I've been going crazy trying to find a way to take you with me. And then Gelman was sent to my office. An answer from heaven. When I read his personnel records and saw he was a director, I knew I'd found the way."

"I do not understand."

"He's getting out of the Army soon, too. And when he gets back, he's putting on this musical. And you're going to be in it."

"What if he does not think I'm right for the part?"

"You're perfect for the part," Michael said confidently. He leaned over and kissed her. Eddy smiled behind his cigar. The smoke no longer bothered her.

"Here's the score," Gelman said, coming up to their table. "We'll run through it after the place closes. That is, if you're not too tired."

"We'll close early," Michael said. "I'll just say a word to Claus and he'll stop serving drinks, that'll get them out."

After the last customer left, the door was locked. Claus hung up his apron but stuck around when he saw her and Gelman head for the piano. Eddy and Michael remained at the back table. Ilse was becoming nervous and wished Claus would give her a shot of whiskey as he had when she'd first tried out here. The lights were dim in the room, and the snow piled up at the windows intensified the sudden silence.

Gelman set the score on the piano and peered at it through his glasses, leaning forward. He played a few chords. Ilse leaned forward too, over the piano, as if in conversation. He read aloud her lines, feeding them to her as Eddy did. She repeated them. After a few minutes he stopped and looked up.

"Your English is too good," he said. "Think you could make your accent a little bit more so?"

She sighed. "And after all those English lessons?"

She made her accent a little more so. She sang about love for her GI, how he'd take her to America and she'd eat banana splits and drink Coca-Cola and live in a cottage small by a waterfall and everything would come up roses.

Seated at the back table, Michael raised his glass to her.

She sang on. Life in America would not, of course, be anything like that. But she would be with Michael and on Broadway, and it would be good.

26. Gina and Diane

Gina sat under a striped umbrella in a sidewalk café on the Via Veneto, sipping espresso and writing postcards. Across from her, Adam alternately played with his toy goat cart and spooned up his *gelato*. It was eleven in the morning, too early for the arrival of the rich, the famous, and the fashionable who frequented the cafés on the Via Veneto, but not too early for the little boys who flocked to the cafés begging for cigarettes and lire. The waiters chased them away, but they only momentarily scattered, then regrouped to beg when the waiters' backs were turned.

Clouds like white sailboats scooted across a sky bluer than the postcards she wrote on. *Bella Italia.* So much beauty, but so much poverty.

"Is there anything you'd like to say to Grandma and Grampa Freed?" she asked Adam.

He thoughtfully pressed the spoon down on his ice cream, which he preferred mushy. Long dark eyelashes fringed his cheeks. Then he smiled up at her. "*Ciao,*" he said.

She remembered with a pang a letter written a long time ago when his father had signed off with the same word. She turned to the postcard. "Adam says *Ciao,*" she wrote. "That means hello in Italian." She didn't mention that it also meant good-bye.

After signing "Love, Gina," she picked up another postcard, one she'd bought in Sicily to send to her family. What to say? Now that her father had died, she had no one to hate. Now that Vince was safely in Sing Sing, she had nothing to fear for her little sisters. By the time he got out, they'd be too old to attract Don Guidetti's interest. She'd like to tell them to be proud of their heritage and not ashamed as she'd been, but that didn't seem the sort of message to put on a postcard. She'd like to write about her visit to the Tedescos, but that would take up too much space. She'd tell them when she got home.

They were a wonderful family, the Tedescos. A mob, all warm and loving. She'd bought them only small inexpensive gifts—she couldn't afford much else—and had insisted on paying for her and Adam's board. They'd treated her like visiting royalty. They remembered Dan clearly. They adored Adam. It was the old grandfather who had carved the goat cart for him.

She wrote her family that they'd been in Sicily, were now in Rome, and later would leave for London to see her show. Adam says *"Ciao,"* she added.

She was just about to write Susan when her attention was diverted by a couple descending on an adjoining table. Or rather the woman descended on the table, appropriating it as if it were hers by right, as if, in fact, the whole café and even all Rome were hers. The man trailed slightly behind, slightly limping. He looked like an aged boy, dark hair combed in bangs over his forehead to hide a receding hairline. The woman wore heavy makeup of the kind popular a decade ago in the thirties: crimson lipstick, clown spots of rouge on white bony cheeks, penciled-in eyebrows. They had mean mouths and small bright eyes and looked seedy and sinister.

"Come along, pet," the woman called in German-accented English, and Gina noticed the sleepwalking girl for the first time. She was far younger than they, but not so young as to be their daughter. Also, she didn't look at all like them. She had a pale, fragile beauty and a stunned face. Her eyes stared as dumbly as doll's eyes, as if the pupils were painted on. Then, just as Gina was thinking this, the eyes lit up. The girl was looking at Adam. People often said what a beautiful child he was, far too much for his own good, but in the girl's eyes was a look of loving and longing.

"Sit here," the woman told the girl. "You will have a better view of the passersby." The woman indicated a chair that the man held out for the girl, who obediently sat down, her back to Adam. Gina was sure she'd have much rather watched him than the street.

When the waiter appeared, there was much changing of orders between the man and woman, who couldn't decide whether to have cappuccino, espresso, Viennese coffee, something to eat, or nothing to eat. It was almost as if they were testing the waiter's patience. If Gina had been the waiter, she'd have told them both to go jump in the Tiber and walked away. But, of course, he couldn't afford to. No doubt he had a big family dependent on his small earnings.

The girl didn't appear to care what she had, if anything.

The man ordered American coffee for her. She lit a cigarette with trembling hands, the long sleeves of her dress nearly catching fire. Why long sleeves on such a warm day? It was a summery chiffon dress, but still . . . Gina remembered when she'd worn long sleeves to hide the bruises from her father's beatings. But, of course, this couldn't be for a similar reason. Or could it?

After the couple had finally decided what they wanted and the waiter left, the flock of small begging boys swooped down. *"Cigarette? Lire? Cioccolati? Prego! Prego!"* they pleaded with outstretched hands.

The girl was about to reach into her purse, when the woman scolded her. "I have told you. If you give them money, we shall have no peace. Let them starve, little thieves."

The girl hesitated. The boys, seeing this, increased their pleas, concentrating on her. Although Gina didn't believe in encouraging children to become beggars, she knew how desperately hungry they were and was relieved to see the girl defy the woman by dipping into her purse and holding out a handful of lire. For a minute it looked as if the man and woman might grab the money themselves. The woman's face showed scorn; the man's mouth became petulant. "I'm sorry," the girl said in a low voice, "but I couldn't bear it."

Gina wondered why the girl had to apologize to those greedy vultures, why she couldn't spend her own money as she wished. The woman ordered the waiter to chase the children away after her attempts failed. The man opened a newspaper. *Il Mondo.*

"Why do you buy an Italian paper when you cannot read one word of Italian, my sweet?" the woman asked.

"They did not have a German newspaper, and my Italian is very good, thank you," the man said peevishly.

The woman laughed derisively. The girl ignored them. Behind the painted pupils, her eyes were terrifyingly empty.

"Now, here, you see, I find something," the man said. "On Palestine. They fight there. The English and the Arabs and the Chosen People."

"The Chosen People are not who I would choose," the woman said.

"Perhaps I read wrongly. It says that they have suffered enough."

"Oh, that! What do you expect from Italians? They are children. Even though they fought on our side, they refuse to hand over their Jews," the woman said with a crimson-mouthed sneer.

"But this. It is not written by an Italian. Some Swede, I think. Is not that strange? A female Swede. A certain Susan Lund."

"Susan Lund?" the girl asked from a distance, but Gina scarcely noticed in her surprise at hearing Susan's name. "Excuse me," she said, making a grab for the paper. "I can read Italian, I'll read it for you."

"We are not in the least interested in hearing," the woman said.

"If you would be so kind as to return my paper," the man said.

"But I'm interested in hearing," the girl said. "She's a friend of mine."

Gina smiled at her. "Mine, too," she said, and turned to the column. "It's called 'Notes from the Underground' and begins, 'I write this while hiding out with the Haganah, the underground military group in Palestine who are now literally underground, fighting from a cave. This column will be transmitted on a faultily working radio. It will be sent in code. All information and reports are sent in code. I am not free to say where I am or even where this will be sent.

" 'Before going back to what has happened in the past two weeks after the Haganah blew up eight bridges, I will go back thirty years to 1917. At that time Foreign Secretary Arthur Balfour wrote the following to Lord Rothschild as representative of the Zionists: *"His Majesty's Government view with favor the establishment in Palestine of a national home for the Jewish people, and will use their best endeavours to facilitate the achievement of this object."*

" 'Now, back to the last two weeks. After the bridges were blown up, the British declared a curfew. Armed men patrol the sidewalks, and armored cars patrol the streets. Shots are fired to warn people to stay indoors. Settlements are surrounded by cordons, and searches made for hidden arms. The British have confiscated mortars and machine guns, the pitifully few arms this country has to protect itself.' "

"They should have shot them down with those machine guns," the woman said. No one had to ask whom she meant by "they."

Gina answered by ignoring her and translating on. " 'The British have sent hundreds of young men to concentration camps. Concentration camps? Six million Jews slaughtered in Auschwitz, Buchenwald, Treblinka, and elsewhere, and still there are concentration camps?' "

"Six million, an exaggeration," the man said.

"They were political dissenters and criminals," the woman said. "I have heard enough."

But the girl was listening. Gina read on for her, for her son, for his father, for the murdered and the survivors. She read in a loud clear voice, reading first in Italian so that the Italians might know, and translating into English so the tourists would hear.

" 'There are those who ask about the Arabs and their rights. They forget that Palestine belonged to the Israelites before the seventh century, when the Arabs took it away. It is doubtful that anyone asked back then, "How about the Israelites and their rights?"

" 'I am here in this underground hideout among a small band of brave and desperate men who fight for their right to exist. I am here with those who underwent torture and escaped slaughter, who have come to the Promised Land only to find their promises once again broken. The British are acting immorally and illegally. To those who wring their hands over the Holocaust and ask, "How could it have happened? We'd have stopped it if we knew," I say: "This is happening to the survivors of that Holocaust, and what are you doing to stop it now?' "

"Such nonsense," the woman said. "She calls herself a Swede? It is clear what she is."

Gina smiled sweetly. "It was your brother who called her a Swede. Actually, she's an American from the Midwest."

"Oh, isn't it a coincidence that you know her, too?" the girl said. "We were friends in Berlin."

"We were friends in New York."

"I think the next remark will be, 'Is it not a small world?' " the woman said sarcastically.

"Is it not a small world?" Gina asked the girl, winking; then: "Susan and I made a pact a long time ago to meet in a sidewalk café in Paris. It would be fun if you came along and surprised her."

"Perhaps she will be blown to bits in her underground hideout," the woman said hopefully.

"It will be impossible for you to go," the man said to the girl. "We are not going to Paris. We are going to Morocco. You will adore Morocco. There you will get excellent medication."

Gina, knowing Morocco was famous for its contraband drugs, knew what kind of medication he meant and why the girl looked so dazed.

"We must leave if we are going to see the Sistine Chapel,"

the woman said crossly. She and the man immediately got to their feet, ready to whisk off the girl.

"Oh, what luck. You're going to the Sistine Chapel? So are we," Gina said. She'd already been to the Sistine Chapel twice, but she didn't want to leave the girl at the mercy of these fascists. Once, a long time ago, Georgette, the dance-hall girl, had rescued her. Now it was her turn to come to the rescue.

The girl looked happy enough to have her and Adam along. She invited them to share a cab. "I'm Diane Deal, and these are my friends Fräulein and Herr von Frisch."

Gina introduced herself and Adam.

"Perhaps sightseeing will be too strenuous for a child," Fräulein von Frisch said, ignoring the introductions.

"Oh, our hotel's near the Vatican. If he gets tired, it'll be easy enough to go back there," Gina said.

"It will be too crowded, five people in a taxicab," said Herr von Frisch.

Gina agreed. She suggested that Diane take a taxi with her and Adam so they could discuss their friend Susan. Adam, who had apparently fallen in love with Diane, was being most cooperative by clinging to her hand. Gina spied a taxi and her chance. She signaled the driver, pulled Adam into the cab, while he in turn pulled in Diane, still hanging on to her hand.

"See you at the Sistine Chapel," Gina called out gaily to the von Frisches, who glared at her.

In the taxi, Gina turned to Diane. "I know, let's go to the Borghese Gardens instead. It's such a perfect day, a shame to waste that sun."

"Oh, I couldn't. My friends would be furious."

And withhold your medication and punish you, Gina added silently. She sighed. "Okay, I was thinking mostly of Adam. He'd have more fun there. You know, space to run around."

"Oh, I . . ." Diane said, hesitated. Adam gave her a look that would melt a statue. "Oh, I . . . Well," she said, "okay."

Gina leaned forward and told the driver to take them to the Borghese Gardens before Diane could change her mind.

Outside, the sun laddered down on a church as in a religious painting. She'd like to catch that on canvas. For a moment she regretted being an abstract expressionist. But she could catch the feeling. Her fingers fairly itched to get back to holding a brush again. In the meantime, there was her show to see in London, and Susan to meet in Paris. If Susan got to Paris. If she weren't, as Fräulein von Frisch so hopefully put it, blown to bits in that underground hideout. But Susan was under a lucky star. The Haganah would be safe with her. It was Diane Deal she had to worry about. Maybe she wouldn't be successful in her rescue mission, but it was worth a try.

ABOUT THE AUTHOR

Eleanor Hyde is *Cosmopolitan* magazine's most published fiction writer. Her stories have appeared in other national magazines as well as in literary quarterlies, many reprinted in a variety of European countries. She lives and works in New York City.